Art of the Chase

TRACY BROGAN

OLIVERHEBERBOOKS

For Joan.
May your heaven be filled with romance novels.

praise for tracy brogan

"Heart, humor, and characters you'll love. Tracy Brogan is the next great voice in contemporary romance."

New York Times bestselling author Kristen Higgins

"Brogan shows a real knack for creating believable yet quirky characters, providing surprising emotional twists along the way."

Booklist

"With trademark humor and lovely, poignant touches, Brogan's books are charming, witty, and fun."

USA Today bestselling author Kimberly Kincaid

"Brogan successfully blends a sassy heroine and humor with deep emotional issues and a traditional romance. The well-developed characters and sweet story with just a touch of heat will please readers looking for a creative take on romance."

Publishers Weekly

HIGHLAND SURRENDER features plenty of action, romance, and sex with well-drawn individuals – a strong yet young heroine and a delectable hero who don't act out of character. The story imparts a nice feeling of "you are there" with a well presented look at the turbulent life of the 16th century Scotland."

RT Book reviews

"Treachery and political intrigue provide a well-textured backdrop for a poignant romance in which a young girl, well out of her depth, struggles to reconcile what she *thinks* she knows with what her *heart* tells her. HIGHLAND SURRENDER is a classic sweep-me-away tale of romance!"

New York Times bestselling author Connie Brockway

one

C harles David Bostwick was a grown man. A serious man blessed with an innate intellect – thanks to his superior parentage – and a brilliant head for business – thanks in no small measure to his very fine, very expensive, East Coast education. The highest echelons of Chicago society considered him to be both charmingly handsome and exceedingly capable – even while acknowledging that by all accounts *he* also found himself to be both handsome and capable. Yet no one could deny that Charles Bostwick was a man of lofty ambitions and inevitable success. Indeed. The man had finesse. He had panache. He had *plans*.

Yet nowhere in the breadth or depth of his wildest dreams could Charles Bostwick have foreseen how his finely tuned plans could be so unceremoniously waylaid by two long-bodied, stubby legged dogs – although calling them *dogs* put an even further strain on his imagination – and he himself was the very picture of ridiculousness walking them down Main Street of Trillium Bay clutching their delicate leashes – leashes made of ribbon, no less! Pink, grosgrain ribbon tied in petite bows around the neck of each wee mutt.

It was an utter humiliation to be strolling in public with two such unappealing creatures, not to mention doing so during a torrential downpour that left rain streaming from the brim of his bowler hat. An umbrella would be a fine thing just now, but he'd left the Imperial Hotel in such haste he hadn't bothered to check the sky and now it was too late. He looked the fool with every aspect of the situation injurious to his pride. Especially since he *should be* working right now. He should be at his desk – in his office – in *Chicago*! But no. He was here, all but marooned on this tiny resort island off the coast of northern Michigan.

And all because of just fourteen damnable minutes.

Fourteen minutes, a mere 840 seconds that had forever relegated him to being *the second son*. He could have been the first born, but thanks to fate or destiny or midwifery malpractice, Alexander had come first. Alex, his twin brother in looks if not in temperament, had come forth into this world at 4:08 p.m. with a smile and a coo *(or so the story went)* while he himself had loitered in the womb for nearly another quarter of an hour and arrived on his own schedule at 4:22 p.m. with a scowl and a squall. It was *the longest quarter of an hour* of his mother's entire existence *(according to her)*, and he'd spent much of his life trying to make that up to her – and to catch up, if only figuratively, with his *older* brother. Throughout childhood, such was his fervor to be first whenever possible, his family had all but abandoned calling him Charles and instead, called him Chase.

Intellectually, he knew none of this should trouble him anymore. He'd proven himself his brother's equal – if not superior – in virtually every way, and in truth was far more like their father than Alex was. But of late, the old sibling rivalry had been gnawing at him again – because it was Alex who had recently become engaged. And because it was Alex's future son who would one day carry the family moniker of Alexander James Bostwick – *the Third*. And because, if Chase were being brutally honest with himself, he was upset because it was his brother who was engaged to none other than Isabella Carnegie.

She was a distant cousin to *those* Carnegies, but it wasn't her wealth or societal connections that made her so appealing a bride. No, it was something much simpler. Isabella Carnegie was a true beauty with thick blonde tresses and cornflower blue eyes that appeared innocent one moment and sultry the next, causing every single young man who looked upon her to dream of marriage – and causing every settled husband to dream of being single.

And – in yet another wicked twist of happenstance – Chase had missed out on the opportunity of her by mere moments. Because he'd been *working*. Delayed by a business matter, he'd arrived late to the Kimball's annual St. Valentine's Day dinner party and Alex had met Isabella first.

Had Chase himself arrived on time and captured her in conversation first, he felt certain he could have wooed and won her, and did, in fact, try. He'd paid her a call the very next afternoon and had sent a robust arrangement of yellow jasmine in honor of her elegance and grace only to discover that Alex had already been to visit (*in the morning!*) and had been so very bold as to arrive with pink Camellias (*in hand!*) to indicate his longing. Alex may as well have shown up with an engagement ring and a preacher for all his lack of subtlety. When, a mere three weeks later, Alex confided that he and Isabella had come to an understanding, all Chase could do was shake his brother's hand and congratulate him for finding such a lovely, well-tempered bride.

That had been nearly four months ago and the whole incident had left Chase with a bruised heart. Or perhaps it was his ego? He wasn't entirely sure. Regardless, it put him off the idea of matrimony for now. He had plenty of time to find a wife. He was only twenty-five and right now work was his passion, his true mistress – not that he was ever in want for female companionship. Aside from the bevy of eager debutantes vying for his attention – and his proposal – he had a recurring appointment with a lovely young widow whose company he enjoyed very much. The casual (*and very discreet*) arrangement suited them both and neither wished to take it beyond the bedroom.

And, of course, there were the lonely wives of *other* men who occasionally sought him out – not that a gentleman would ever kiss and tell – but other than his infatuation for Isabella Carnegie, he'd yet to feel the pull to find a wife of his own.

For Chase, work was not a replacement – it was his preference, especially since he knew his father relied on him, so much more so than he relied upon Alex because, quite simply, Chase worked harder. His business instincts had proven to be both bold and lucrative while Alex was prone to error and more of a *let's try this and see what happens* kind of operative.

So, it was an unexpected blow to Chase's pride when A.J. Bostwick, Sr. consigned *him* to the role of chaperone to *Mrs.* A.J. Bostwick while she summered at the Imperial Hotel on Wenniway Island along with the youngest Bostwick offspring, Chase's sister, Daisy. The assignment wasn't quite the same humiliation as walking these dogs but three months of involuntary captivity catering to his wearisome mother and boisterous little sister made this island more purgatory than paradise. The whole arrangement left Chase feeling... diminished. Banished. Punished somehow although his father had assured him it was no such thing.

"I need Alex in Chicago, son, so I'm relying on you. I know I can trust you to handle things on the island and, quite frankly, your mother needs looking after," A.J. had said with a hearty slap on the shoulder and the offer of a fine cigar.

While Chase wasn't prone to questioning his father's judgment, on this matter, he felt entirely certain A.J. was mistaken. Constance Bostwick did not need anyone looking after her. His mother was as rugged as a badger, running the family with steely resolve from a velvet settee. Prison wardens displayed a warmer countenance than she, but a recent bout of influenza had left her with a lingering cough, and it was decided a few months away from the soot and stink of downtown Chicago might restore her health to its typical vigor. Thus, plans were made to visit Trillium Bay and Chase was consigned to play nursemaid.

Lately though he'd begun to suspect his mother's cough was more a clever ploy than a real health concern since she'd informed him that very morning of her desire to have a summer cottage constructed on the island. She'd tried to play off the idea as a spontaneous thing, a whimsical notion or a passing thought, but Chase knew nothing his mother ever did was spontaneous. She was as calculating as a politician. She'd probably never even had the flu at all. She'd probably decided months ago that she needed a way to lure them here for a season to give her time to plot and plan.

"Well, it's not Newport, of course, but it is closer to Chicago so I suppose one must make do," she'd said to him just an hour prior. "Tomorrow you must hire a carriage and we'll tour all the available properties. I've heard the Pullmans are building here, as well as the O'Douls and the Cahills, and I know for a fact that Breezy VonMeisterburger has her eye on a spot near the west bluff. We must see it posthaste, before her husband has a chance to make an offer."

"Isn't Breezy VonMeisterburger your dearest friend?" he'd asked, more as a reminder to his mother rather than an actual query.

She'd gazed back at him with a well-practiced air of guilelessness that might have been convincing had he not known her so well.

"She's my *closest* friend, not my dearest. There's a difference. But either way, as my friend, it would be selfish of her to claim the most coveted location before we've even had a chance to see it."

Chase knew there was no point in arguing with logic such as that, and not much point in arguing with her moments later when she'd told him to walk her precious little dogs either, which is how he now found himself trudging along in the rain behind two soggy, long-haired dachshunds and feeling rather sorry for himself. He wasn't prone to self-pity, but his wool suit was wet and beginning to itch, the dogs seemed disinclined to do their business, his brother was engaged to the most beautiful girl Chase had ever seen, and it would be weeks – months, actually – before he could return to Chicago and get on with *his life*. He was already bored with this island, and they'd only been there for four days. Four days!

Never was a man more ill-suited for relaxation than Chase Bostwick.

He knew he was the exception rather than the rule. Thanks to fast, sleek steamships and miles upon miles of new railroad lines simplifying travel, Trillium Bay was fast-becoming a holiday mecca for wealthy, city-weary patrons, but Chase wasn't weary of the city. He loved the hustle and bustle of Chicago, the crush of people moving with purpose toward their destination, the ever-present cacophony of voices and hoofbeats and construction, the pungent aromas sweetened by robust breezes off the lake, and above all else – quite literally – the brand-new buildings so miraculously tall they were called *skyscrapers*.

Yes, he loved his city. He didn't *need* a vacation, and he didn't *want* a vacation with its string of lazy days providing him with nothing to do but sail and play lawn tennis and wonder if his brother had yet to slide a hand up under Isabella Carnegie's skirts. An improper curiosity to have about one's soon-to-be sister-in-law to be sure. He did realize that and admonished himself for the thought, but that was precisely why he needed to be working. He needed a distraction. Any kind of distraction.

Crossing the street, his foot sank into a puddle in the middle of the muddy road, and he didn't even bother to flinch or lament the ruination of his shoe or worry that anyone noticed. The whole day was turning into one big metaphorical puddle anyway, and the only saving grace of this pelting rain was that all the other poor souls out on the street right now were keeping their heads lowered, their vision shielded by black umbrellas.

Perhaps that's why she didn't see him, and why he didn't see her.

Or perhaps it was because one little dog in his charge tried to avoid the next puddle by dashing ahead while the other little dog dove into it nose-first and their leashes got tangled and intertwined as they bolted hither and yon, and the rain was drip, drip, dripping from the brim of his hat and blowing right into his eyes. Perhaps it was because thunder rumbled ominously overhead just as a flash of lightning brightened everything with the brilliance of the sun, blinding him for the length of a blink, or perhaps it was due to the sudden surge of people disembarking from the ferry and streaming into the street en masse like a flock of honking geese.

Whatever the cause, she didn't see him, and he didn't see her. Until it was too late. Suddenly, there she was, colliding with him, getting her feet twisted up in the pink ribbon leashes with the dogs barking and leaping against her dark blue skirts. She swayed intimately against him for the space of a heartbeat, and somehow the bulk of whatever she carried in her arms was knocked free and crashed with a squelchy thud upon the soaked ground and pieces flew every which way. It happened so fast, yet Chase's mind was quick to register this as an unfortunate mishap while not quite a catastrophe.

"Oh, my goodness! You nincompoop!" she cried out, shoving at his chest which naturally caused his arms to move, which only served to tighten the noose of the leashes now wound around her calves. She teetered precariously against him once more and her face twisted with a look of surprised dismay before she fell backwards onto the road – and into the mud.

Now it was a catastrophe.

"Oh!" she exclaimed again, fists clenching against her legs as she sat on the ground, rain pelting her. "Look what you've done!"

He wasn't sure if she was talking to him or the dogs – because he felt quite certain that she was the real culprit behind this blunder. Nonetheless, he was involved *and* holding on to the leashes from which the woman, a mere slip of a girl, really, was now trying to extricate her dainty ankles.

"I'm dreadfully sorry, miss," he said magnanimously, offering his hand to help the clumsy girl up. Surely the first order of business was to get her off her bustle and back onto her feet.

She spared him only the flicker of a glance, long enough for him to be certain she had dark eyes and wasn't very old. Eighteen? Twenty perhaps? It was hard to ascertain due to the scowl and the rain and her rather unfashionable hat.

She ignored his hand and instead rolled to her knees and began gathering up the items she'd dropped, seemingly indifferent to the mud – a rather unladylike reaction, in his opinion. Almost shocking. There seemed to be a wooden box in pieces around her, the base in one spot and the top in another, and around that lots of silver tubes and little pots that, as the rain hit, splashed with colors.

It was a painter's box, he realized as he tightened the ribbon leashes around his fists trying to regain control of the dogs while bending to help her retrieve her items, but the hounds were eager to make friends, and this just served to incite them more.

"Oh!" she gasped again as one licked her face.

"Flossie, stop!" he commanded although the dog paid no heed. "Heel."

Flossie did not heel, and Chase resorted to scooping up the soggy mutts, one under each arm which rendered him useless in helping her. The dogs squirmed for their freedom, and he tightened his grip, wondering if perhaps he would be justified in squeezing them until they fainted. He wouldn't, of course. He actually liked dogs. Just not *these* dogs.

"I am sorry," he said again, meaning it sincerely because regardless of the cause of the accident *(It was her. She was the cause.)* here was a damsel in true distress and he was failing quite miserably in coming to her aid. It made him feel uncharacteristically inept. *Damn these dogs.*

Suddenly they were surrounded by people, each reaching out a hand to help the girl, some retrieving the items or pieces of the box, and one burly young man in a denim trousers and cotton shirt so well-worn that Chase could barely tell it had once been plaid lifted her about the waist and set her on her feet, not seeming to realize the abuse of his familiarity, but the girl gave him a tremulous yet grateful smile.

Well... damn again. Chase would have helped her up if not for the dogs and he vowed silently to never walk them again. They could pee on the rugs at the hotel for all he cared.

A few others handed the young woman items, and she tucked them into the box. Everything was soiled and the continued rain blended the random paints together until they too were the color of mud as it splashed on her dress and her gloves. Thunder rumbled once more followed seconds later by a lightning flash and the good Samaritans scattered, leaving just Chase, the girl, and the denim-clad man.

"Best to get under cover, Miss," Chase heard the man say while handing her the final piece of the lid. "If you bring that box to the hardware store, Davey will fix it up for you. I can take you there now, if you'd like. I'd be happy to."

She set the wooden pieces on top, holding her bundle together with both hands, and shook her dark, damp, ill-hatted head.

"Thank you, but no. I'm in a rush to get to the Imperial Hotel. They were expecting me two days ago. Can you tell me which way it is?"

"I'll see you to the Imperial," Chase said, stepping forward, determined to reestablish himself as someone useful. He was a *Bostwick*, after all. "I'll secure us a carriage and deliver you safely to the front door."

The girl looked at him warily, anger flaring in those dark eyes, as if *he* were the sole cause of this unfortunate event yet he was still fairly certain it was *she* who'd plowed into *him*. It was she who'd shoved him in the chest causing herself to tumble to the ground. Not that a gentleman would ever say as much.

"It's the very least I can do," he added. "It seems I owe you a painter's box as well." He nodded at the cargo she held tightly to chest. Whatever his role in the matter (w*alking down the street,* *minding his own business*), he'd fix this. And since the box appeared decades old, she'd come out all the better on the other side. A new artist's box would be far superior to that dinged up antique she clutched. Perhaps she'd even consider the whole mishap an unexpected blessing.

"There's no replacing this painter's box," the young woman said, her quiet voice cracking slightly with emotion. "It was my father's. But I'll accept a carriage if it'll get me out of the rain and to the hotel."

two

This was an inauspicious start to the new life Emerson Joan McKenna hoped to create for herself – although, all things considered, not that shocking. Nothing had gone well for her in quite some time, and this latest unpleasantry would simply have to be dealt with in the same manner in which she'd dealt with nearly everything else of late – with grit and denial.

Over the past several months, her life had shifted seismically from comfortably predictable to thoroughly precarious, and only recently had she concluded that flailing in an abyss of "why me?" got her nowhere. Looking back was a trap of torment, a doorway leading to nothing but melancholy and regret so now, all she could do was look forward and hope and pray her circumstances would improve, although hope was a fickle friend on whom she could not rely. She wasn't exactly on good terms with prayer, either.

She kept tossing requests upward, hoping the good Lord might overlook her past misdeeds, but lately it seemed His responses were more mercurial than ever. Even for God. While He'd graciously seen fit to prevent her steamship from sinking to the bottom of Lake Michigan on its journey from Chicago to

Wenniway Island, He *had* sent the storm in the first place – a storm so severe it pitched that ship to and fro until every passenger onboard was either green with illness or white with fear. Or somehow both.

In addition to causing fright and seasickness, the foul weather delayed her arrival to the island by two full days, which made her late to the start of her recently acquired position of artist in residence at the Imperial Hotel. While her new employer would likely forgive her tardiness *(she could hardly be held responsible for bad weather, after all),* she knew – unequivocally – that there were other things about her person of which the management might be less tolerant, so it was essential – imperative, even – that she make an excellent first impression, but arriving wet and bedraggled in a soiled dress with her hair in knots was not the stuff of good impressions!

Oh, but good gracious! How on earth was she to clean herself up? Her skirts were so stained with mud that even this hearty rain could not wash it all away. The wind had torn all but the most secure pins from her hair, and her shoes were heavy with muck. Cleaning them to a respectable appearance would take a stiff brush and more time than she had. She needed lodging to change into one of her few other gowns, gowns that were still in a trunk on the steamship, but she couldn't check into her hotel room without announcing her arrival in this current state of deshabille. A conundrum, indeed.

But those aspects of this situation were trifles compared to the distress she felt over the demolition of her father's art box. It was her greatest treasure, the only tangible thing of him she had left. The only thing that hadn't been stolen – along with her heart – and now both were irreparably damaged – and all because she'd been, once more, distracted by a handsome face.

Heaven, help her. Had she learned nothing from her past? Didn't she know that men were naught but the source of trial and strife? Wasn't this latest blunder more verifiable proof? She had places to be and work to do yet one glimpse of a tall, attractive man with droplets of water clinging to his sculpted, clean-shaven face was all it took to blind her *(yes, completely blind her)* to the dachshunds at his feet and the next thing she knew, she'd stepped right into a tangled web of leashes and paws and a chest so solid it was like slamming into a brick building. She'd bounced off that man's torso, dropped her art box, and landed right on her bum in the mud, ruining her second-best dress.

She was the nincompoop. This was her fault for not watching where she stepped – although she'd never admit it. Besides, the man should have had better control over those furry little monsters. Honestly, how difficult was it to wrangle a couple of miniscule lap dogs? At present, they remained tucked under each of his thick arms, but the dogs continued to wriggle like fish on hooks and their apparent eagerness to be free coupled with his expression of intense consternation made a comical picture indeed. She could not have drawn a caricature more absurd, but she was not in the mood for comedy. Especially since she wasn't certain if his palpably growing frustration was because of her, or the dogs. She *had* shoved him rather firmly in the sternum, but in truth, her wrists probably hurt more than his ribs.

And surely neither were more bruised than her dignity.

Nonetheless, she'd just agreed to climb into a carriage with this fortress of a man and his dainty little dogs for a ride that was sure to be awkward. She would never have agreed to it if not for her dress getting wetter – and heavier – by the moment and her desperate desire to get off the street. She had no idea how far the walk to the Imperial Hotel would be, and she most certainly could not afford a carriage for herself. Though she was loathe to admit it, quite frankly, she couldn't refuse the charity.

Ah, charity. What a detestable word. What a labyrinth of emotion it evoked because, as she now understood, help offered *freely* was often anything but charitable. There was always a price. Always a catch. Always strings attached, and if she wasn't careful, she'd end up owing this man more than she was prepared to pay. Perhaps she *should* walk to the hotel after all, no matter the distance. But thunder crashed, and lightning flashed, and Jo decided this was a risk she needed to take.

With some scrambling and assistance from the helpful worker in the plaid shirt, Jo found herself sitting across from the impeccably dressed man in a well-appointed carriage with the two wet, pink-leashed she-devils now resting quietly on the floor. She held the remnants of her art box on her lap and used the back of one gloved hand to brush the raindrops from her cheeks. Lord above, she must be a sight. And there *he* was, damp as she yet somehow looking far less worse for wear, his stiff collar not suffering for the rain, and the brown of his suit hardly showing any moisture at all.

She couldn't deny her companion was ruggedly handsome, with eyes the shade of Antwerp blue and chestnut brown hair that showed a bit of curl around the brim of his hat. An almost imperceptible bump on the bridge of his nose kept him from being too pretty, and she wondered if it was the result of a break during some kind of acrimonious scuffle or a rigorous game of rugby, or perhaps even American football. He looked the sporting, collegiate type. Muscular, self-assured – despite the dainty dogs – and yes, dangerously handsome.

No wonder she'd stepped right into his path, and yet she knew *(oh, she knew)* that this was the type of man to be avoided at all cost. Oliver had been broad with muscles and gloriously attractive too and look what that had gotten her.

The man cleared his throat a moment into the ride.

"Circumstances being what they are," he said formally. "Perhaps you'll allow me to introduce myself. I'm Chase Bostwick of Chicago. I'm staying at the Imperial Hotel, along with my mother and my sister. Please accept my apologies for that mishap in the street. Those are my mother's dogs," he added with a jut of square chin toward them, as if to apologize – again. His voice had a smooth timbre to it, rich and cultured, and she wondered if her sudden shiver was due to the chill of the air or the warmth of his tone.

Or the fact that she knew who he was, by name if not appearance. Egad, everyone in Chicago knew who the Bostwicks were. A.J. Bostwick, Sr., the family patriarch, was a self-made millionaire who, although not a Knickerbocker by birth, had married into high society and established his place among the Rockefellers and the Guggenheims. His sons – of which this was apparently one – had followed him into the family business and were earning their own reputations as men to be reckoned with. A sudden flush of embarrassment stole over her for she was certainly the first person in this man's life to shove him in the middle of a street, or to hurl slurs at his head.

An inauspicious beginning for her indeed.

"I accept your apology, Mr. Bostwick," she answered with a calmness she did not remotely feel, adding after a pause, "I'm sorry, as well. I should have been paying closer attention, but the rain impaired my vision." (*The rain and his damnable face.*)

"Yes, it's quite a deluge," he said. "And neither one of us with an umbrella it seems."

She wondered if he thought perhaps she should have one? A proper lady would've known – somehow – that rain was imminent. Then again, so would a gentleman, and he was definitely that, yet he had no umbrella either. She'd not mention it. She'd already insulted him once today. That seemed enough.

"Might I be so bold as to ask your name?" he asked after her hesitation. "As I mentioned, I would like to replace your art kit. I'll have it shipped to the hotel." He glanced at the splintered remnants in her lap, and she instinctively pulled them closer.

She paused again. It would mean nothing to him to purchase a new one. Lord knew he had the money, but that wasn't the point.

"I can't possibly accept a gift from you, Mr. Bostwick. We're not properly acquainted. I don't know you." She only knew *of* him. And she also knew what *gifts* from men led to.

"It's not a gift. It's a replacement for something that has

broken. If you won't accept it from me, I'll have my mother send it. Very proper."

He smiled at her, a charming, comfortable smile, and she knew, had this happened to her a year ago, she'd have responded in kind and trusted him implicitly because he had a sincere way about him. And dimples and tiny creases at the corners of his eyes. Everything about his easy, relaxed demeanor said, "I'm a decent person," and she'd never heard otherwise about any member of his family.

In fact, his father had made so sizable a donation to the Chicago Public Library after the great fire that A.J.'s portrait now hung in one of the reading rooms. She'd gazed at that painting so often it was a wonder she didn't recognize his son on sight, although truth be told, Jo had been more interested in the brushstrokes and artistic techniques, rather than the picture itself.

"It's not necessary, Mr. Bostwick. I appreciate your generosity, but I simply cannot accept."

Yes, a year ago she would have believed his sincerity and accepted his offer without hesitation, but now it was that very *appearance* of decency that made her wary. And a year ago, the art kit would not have meant as much to her.

Mr. Bostwick looked disappointed but nodded. "Of course. I understand. If you should change your mind, you need only send a note to Mrs. Constance Bostwick at the hotel, and she'll handle the rest."

"Thank you," she said, then turned her gaze to the window so he might not realize how badly she wanted to say yes.

They rode in silence for a few moments with nothing but the staccato rhythm of the rain tapping against the carriage roof in much the same rapid tempo as Jo's heart. She was nervous. Not because she thought herself in any personal danger, but a girl such as she, in her present dire circumstances, riding in a carriage with a man such as him, well, it made a person nervous.

One of the tiny dogs snuffled, repositioned, then settled back down with a woofy sigh. Jo continued to stare out the window, trying to regain her equilibrium while also trying to get a better look at the island that was to be her home for the next few months. She could see various buildings along the main thoroughfare. O'Doul's General Store. Callaghan's Leather Shop. Persimmon's Candy Emporium. She could see a military fort off in the distance, high on a hill as they passed a white-steepled church, a stable, and a hotel called The Island House that was so vast she could not imagine one more impressive. She'd been assured by her new employer, however, that the Imperial Hotel was the largest and most grand hotel on all of Wenniway Island, and that its guests expected only the finest in accommodations, food, and entertainment.

She was to be a part of that entertainment, hired to teach drawing and painting classes to eager debutantes and bored society matrons.

Well... sort of.

She had sort of been hired for that. There were a few technicalities to work out but pressed between her corset and chemise was a signed contract offering the job to Emerson J. McKenna. And she was Emerson J. McKenna, so the job was legally hers. She'd tucked the contract there for safekeeping during her travels and hoped the ink hadn't run due to the rain. As if a smeared signature was the real problem. Uncertainty stirred in her veins, but she ignored it. Another method of coping.

"Is your name to remain a mystery then?" Mr. Bostwick asked pleasantly a moment later. "I find myself quite full of questions but if you'd rather not converse, I won't disturb you."

She tore her gaze from the scenery and looked back at him. It was no hardship, truly. In fact, she'd very much like to draw him, his face all interesting angles and planes, but talking to him was another matter entirely. Conversations in general, especially those full of questions, were not likely to go in her favor, but she could hardly refuse for fear of appearing rude, and perhaps she could even turn this to her advantage.

She smiled back, but not too brightly. It wouldn't do to appear too eager to make his acquaintance.

"Of course, you're not disturbing me, Mr. Bostwick. Please forgive me for being distracted by the landscape. I'm Emerson J. McKenna... *uh...Talbot*," she answered, suddenly not sure what to say after that. She was still getting used to the addition of Talbot. All things considered, it made her cringe to even say it, but that was, in fact, her name.

Like Mr. Bostwick, she was also *of Chicago* but not the parts he and *his people* traveled in. And, unlike him, she didn't actually *have people*. In fact, for most of her life it had been just her and her father in a cozy, modest house with lots of windows that let in abundant light and doors that were always open to visitors.

Until Oliver had come along.

Then for a while it had been the three of them. Until it wasn't.

Now it was just her. Because her father had died last year. A shock she was still growing accustomed to.

And Oliver?

Well, Oliver Talbot was her husband.

Sort of. There were some technicalities to work out there, too, and that was another shock she was still growing accustomed to. But, for her purposes on this island, she was married, so she squared her shoulders, extended a bold hand to Mr. Bostwick, and repeated herself, emphasizing the prefix.

"*Mrs.* Emerson Joan McKenna Talbot. I'm a portraitist and the new artist in residence at the Imperial Hotel."

If he was surprised by her position, he didn't show it, and if he was disappointed by her marital status, he didn't show that either and she reminded herself to be glad. That was the whole point, after all. To present herself to the Trillium Bay community as a seasoned artist and a devoted wife so they'd more readily accept her. No one would have allowed a single girl to travel alone all the way from Chicago to Trillium Bay, and they certainly wouldn't have hired a painter's *apprentice* to teach art classes at the Imperial Hotel, but she knew she was talented and an excellent teacher. She was entirely qualified, and being a married woman gave her gravitas. It gave her substance and morality and protection. Ironically, in this case, marriage gave her the freedom to do what she wanted to do.

And – legally – she was married. To Mr. Oliver Talbot.

It wasn't her fault he'd vanished in the wind just days after her father's funeral, leaving her with nothing to live on except the mercy of others and her own wits.

That part of her story she had no intention of sharing.

"It's a pleasure to officially meet you, Mrs. Talbot," Mr. Bostwick said smoothly. "And a portraitist, you say? How interesting. I confess I've no artistic talents whatsoever although my sister is modestly gifted. She's tried to educate me on the merits of the Impressionist movement but I'm a sorry student. So, is this your first summer on Trillium Bay, then? Or have you been here before?"

She bit back a smile because this was actually her first visit anywhere outside of Illinois, but she didn't want to admit that and sound provincial.

"Yes, this is my first trip to Trillium Bay although I've travelled quite a bit." That was vague enough to keep her out of trouble.

"Have you? What's your favorite destination?"

Drat. "Oh, I don't think I could choose just one place. Let's say... anywhere in Paris. What's your favorite destination?" Maybe she should let him do the talking.

"Truly my favorite? In all the world?" he asked, cocking his head as if to ponder.

"Yes."

"Fifty-five East Washington Street," he answered quickly, his eyes meeting hers and twinkling in a most disconcerting fashion. He was teasing her. He must be because fifty-five East Washington Street was surely a joke.

"Fifty-five East Washington... in Chicago?" Her voice flattened with skepticism.

He laughed, a nice rumbly sound. "Yes."

With all his wealth and connections, he must have been to a great many fabulous places, so this was indeed an odd choice, but perhaps Mr. Bostwick was an eccentric. That would explain the little dogs and his apparent penchant for walking in thunderstorms, yet she could not resist the question.

"Why?"

He shrugged, nonplussed by her apparent curiosity over his choice. "It's our company building. My office is on the top floor and the view is spectacular. I can see the lake for miles – when I remember to look up from my desk."

He was grinning now, and she found herself smiling back because it was impossible not to.

"And what do you do for work, Mr. Bostwick?" She already knew, of course. You couldn't live in Chicago and not know that Bostwick & Sons supplied investment capital to the likes of Vanderbilt, Stuyvesant, and Gould, but she wanted to see how he'd explain it. Surely, he'd boast like the industry mogul he was. With any luck, he'd talk the rest of the way to the hotel, and she wouldn't have to reveal another thing about herself while he'd reveal much, at least much about what kind of man he was.

It was an old artist's trick, a way to get the sitter relaxed during a portrait session and Jo was as good at drawing people *out* as she was at drawing them with charcoals. All she had to do was get them talking about whatever they loved the most. Apparently what Mr. Bostwick loved most was working.

"I work in finance," he said simply. "And where do you call home, Mrs. Talbot?"

His brief answer caught her off guard and she blurted out her response without thinking. "I'm from Chicago, too. Well, I used to live in Chicago, but I'll be moving to Paris in the autumn." *Or so she hoped.*

"Ah, another Chicagoan? I wonder if we might have crossed paths and never known."

"Perhaps," she said even while knowing they never had, and

while also knowing he was just being polite for certainly he'd guessed they were not of the same circles. She *had* seen his mother at the milliner's once, though. Mrs. Constance Bostwick was purchasing the kind of garishly outlandish hat that only the very wealthy could claim as fashionable, a turquoise blue felt with black trim, lots of frilly ribbon, and an entire stuffed dove perched on the brim, as if the pitiful thing had simply landed there... and died.

The carriage lurched, and Jo tightened her grip on the art box, but not before a tube of paint slipped out and fell, plunking a dog on the head then hitting the floor. Mr. Bostwick picked it up easily and handed it to her and as he did so, she took note of the paint on her glove. She tried to wipe it away with her other hand but to no avail, and a sigh escaped before she could catch it. The brief buoyancy of her mood, lifted by their conversation, crashed down as she took in her ruined gown, the mud and paint stains beginning to dry and crack looking even worse, if possible, than they had when wet.

How? How was she to make herself presentable before meeting her new employer? How was she to stroll into the lobby of the Imperial Hotel looking as if she'd *rolled* there through the muck? She pressed her lips together tightly to still their trembling. Tears welled and threatened to spill but she was not the crying sort. Crying was for children and actresses, not grown women. Not *married* women. Not women with *jobs*.

Mr. Bostwick pulled a white silk handkerchief from inside his jacket pocket and offered it to her.

It was too fine. She shook her head. "No, I'm all right. Thank you."

He waved it at her ever so slightly. "You might want to dab just a bit, right here," he said tapping at his cheek with his other hand.

"Have I something on my face, too?" She gasped.

"Just a little paint. From your glove, I think. It's quite festive but not exactly the fashion at the Imperial." It was thoughtful of him to treat the matter so lightly. He was trying to cheer her up with his teasing, it seemed, but she was suddenly despondent. Being plucky and optimistic took an immense amount of effort and she was tired from her travels.

"Oh," she sighed again, and let a tear escape although she quickly dashed it away. "It seems I am doomed to make a very poor first impression with my new employer." She reluctantly accepted the handkerchief and wiped at her cheek, but he shook his head and tapped his own cheek a little higher.

"Not quite," he said, reaching out. "Here. If you'll allow me."

She returned the handkerchief, and he opened the window of the carriage, extending his arm to let the silk dampen in the rain that still fell. Then he brought his hand back inside the carriage and leaned forward toward her.

"May I?" he asked.

She wanted to do it herself. It was beyond the boundaries of propriety for him to be so intimate with her, but he could see the mess she was, and she *(perhaps thankfully)* could not. She nodded her acquiescence like a sticky, reluctant child and found herself staring at his face as he, using just the cloth so that his fingers would not actually touch her, scrubbed gently at her cheek. He frowned after a moment and pressed a little harder.

"I'm sorry," he said as he rubbed. "It's a little stubborn."

"That's all right," she answered with another sigh. "So am I."

He smiled then, and his eyes met hers. If there was thunder or lightning or another lurch to the carriage, she wasn't certain, but something jolted her, and she moved away quickly.

three

"Perhaps you should try again yourself," he said, handing her his handkerchief.

He'd startled her somehow although he hadn't meant to. He'd taken care not to press too hard or rub too vigorously, reluctant, in fact, to apply any pressure at all against so delicate a cheek. Her skin was as smooth and pale as porcelain beneath the paint, but now her cheeks were stained with red of a different sort. She was flushed, embarrassed no doubt, by the whole situation. As would any proper woman be.

She was well and truly a mess, and she could only see half of it! If she had a mirror, she'd certainly be weeping for her dress was an unmitigated disaster, with mud from hip to hem, and how she'd gotten paint from elbow to earlobe was a real mystery. A few dark tendrils of hair had escaped the pins and lay in lanky, curling strands against her shoulders, while her hat sat askew, tilting to the left rather than forward. Given the wind, it was a wonder it had stayed in place at all. Considering the unattractive style, it was honestly a pity the thing hadn't given up and blown away.

Yet, despite the gruesome hat and crimson blush and stains of paint and mud, he found himself thinking she was rather pretty underneath it all. Big brown eyes with thick lashes, hair so dark it was nearly black, and a wide but hesitant smile. She was slight in frame yet carried herself with the aplomb of someone much hardier. A weaker woman would have succumbed to some well-deserved tears by now but this one appeared to have a fighting spirit.

He sensed a bit of false bravado too in the way she'd boldly shaken his hand and pretended not to recognize his family name. If she were truly from Chicago, she'd know of them. And if she'd truly ever been to Paris, he'd eat that ugly hat of hers for the girl was as green as the first shoots of a springtime daffodil and had clearly seen little of the world.

Even if she had, why on God's green earth was she traveling alone without so much as a maid or companion? What manner of husband would allow such a thing? A negligent one, to be sure. Or an idiot, for today was just a hint of what might have gone wrong. Good heavens, if someone as fierce as his mother needed Chase for an escort, this little bit of a girl certainly needed someone looking after her.

He, however, was not that person.

As much as chivalry might compel him to step in, he had his hands full enough with his mother and her dogs and his sister, Daisy.

Wait a moment... Daisy...

Yes, Daisy, his kind-hearted sister who was forever taking in strays. She could help this poor woman. Chase would simply escort Mrs. Talbot to Daisy's room where she might clean up a bit before meeting her employer. There'd be nothing improper in that. Perhaps even his mother would be in attendance and then certainly no one could question it. After all, along with Mrs. VonMeisterburger, Constance Bostwick was the final authority on what was deemed socially acceptable on the island. Problem solved.

"But who is she?" demanded his mother some twenty minutes later as Chase stood on the Aubusson rug in the parlor of her hotel suite, the dogs now yipping and scampering about at her feet, overjoyed at being reunited with her at long last.

Chase had left a very uncertain Mrs. Talbot in the carriage to wait while he made the arrangements. She'd refused his offer at first and was in fact quite emphatic about not needing assistance, but after much cajoling, she'd come to see the wisdom of his words. She really didn't have much choice. It was either accept his aid or march into the Imperial lobby leaving a trail of muddy debris in her wake and present herself to the desk clerk with paint stains still splashed against her cheek.

"She's an artist. A portraitist," he answered. "A Mrs. Emerson J. McKenna Talbot. Perhaps you've heard of her?" Suggesting this woman was someone his mother *should* know would go a long way in helping Mrs. Talbot become a woman his mother would *want* to know.

"Emerson J. McKenna?" Daisy said, finally looking up from the window seat where she was reading a novel. *(Something frivolous, no doubt.)* His sister favored their father, with light brown hair that softly curled, and eyes the color of sage, but her roundly curved chin betrayed the feminine version of their father's cleft. Chase and his brother had the more pronounced variety.

"Surely, you've heard of Emerson J. McKenna," Daisy continued. "He's from Chicago and has painted dozens of important people. His portrait of Mayor Harrison hangs in City Hall." Her tone held no small amount of dismissive superiority, as if such esoteric facts should be a matter of general knowledge. "But he's a man. And I think he died last year. Oh! Perhaps you've encountered a ghost!" Her expression shifted from disdainful to optimistic. Like many young girls of the day, she'd recently become infatuated with all things mystical and supernatural, a hobby their mother did not encourage so he ignored that last part.

"This Emerson J. McKenna is very much alive and very much a woman." He found himself blushing at his own words because they implied he'd noticed her curves. He had, of course, even though it was hard to see them underneath the mud.

"A woman? Oh." Daisy seemed disappointed about the lack of ghoulish potential. "Perhaps she's his daughter."

"Perhaps." Chase nodded. "She did mention something about the art box belonging to her father." It would make sense. The decrepit art box, the moving to Paris, the awkward boldness in her manners. Weren't all artists bohemians? Perhaps she'd been raised as such, which is why she'd felt entirely comfortable hollering at him and shoving him in the middle of the street.

Daisy swung her stocking-clad feet to the floor and leaned forward. "Hm. How old is she?"

He shrugged. "I didn't think it proper to ask but I'd guess around twenty or so. She's been hired by the hotel to teach art classes so she may be older than she looks."

Daisy's eyes lit up once again. "Art classes? At this hotel? How fascinating." She turned, clasping her hands together. "Oh, Mummy, I must attend. May I?"

"No one will be able to attend any of her classes if we don't provide her with some assistance," Chase replied. "As I've stated, she took a tumble in the mud and needs a place to freshen up before presenting herself to anyone else at the hotel. At minimum, we should offer her a place to wait until her trunks arrive. Loitering in the lobby is quite out of the question."

"And how is it that you got involved?" Constance eyed him suspiciously, pulling the dogs onto her lap.

"You have those two mutts to thank for that," he answered, pointing at the now benevolent looking beasts. "They all but attacked her on the street."

"Attacked her? These two?" She picked up each dog in turn staring into their slightly bulbous eyes. "Flossie? Regina? Is this true?" They gazed back at her dolefully, admitting nothing. Constance shook her head and squinted at her son. "No, I can't believe such a thing. You must have incited them."

It was a fine thing to know that, given the choice, his mother would take the dogs' side over his, but Chase was hardly surprised. It was that quarter of an hour of labor he'd put her through all over again. Just once he'd like someone to suggest that perhaps he was being the gentleman by *letting* Alex go first but so far, no one had ever considered such a thing.

"Attacked is a strong word," he conceded after a pause. "But they jumped all over her and she got tangled in the leashes. Apart from us needing to make amends for the dogs' poor behavior, this could be quite a feather in your cap, Mother. Mrs. Talbot must be an artist of some renown if Daisy's heard of her."

"Daisy has heard of her father, not her." Like her peers, Constance Bostwick was not one to welcome a newcomer without a fully vetted pedigree.

"Nonetheless," Chase said, "she's the one who's been hired by this hotel and therefore sure to be a sensation among the other guests. I cannot think what Breezy VonMeisterburger will have to say about the Imperial's artist in residence being indebted to you for your goodwill." He tossed his hands upward while shaking his head as if the enormity of the social coup was too immense to articulate.

In all honesty, he had no idea if Mrs. Talbot would be a sensation. Were people impressed with young, female artists? Or any artists for that matter? He knew Daisy was fascinated by them, but she was sixteen and hardly set the standard for what constituted importance among society's matriarchs. Still, playing upon his mother's sense of self-importance was a sure-fire way to get her participation.

"Oh, Mummy, we must come to her aid," Daisy said dramatically, rising from her seat. "She needs us, and how exotic to befriend an artist while on holiday. Pearl Mahoney will be utterly and thoroughly jealous."

His sister winked at him, and he bit back a smile, sensing she didn't really care what Pearl Mahoney thought. She was just helping him nudge their mother into doing the right thing.

Constance stroked the dogs for a moment, pursing her lips.

"Very well," she finally said. "The woman is welcome here but keep an eye on her. Don't leave her alone in the room. She may have sticky fingers and I don't want her helping herself to a piece of my jewelry."

"What a thing to say, Mother," Chase said with a scoff. "She's an artist, not some petty thief."

"That's what she wants you to believe but we don't know what kind of person she is."

"I will personally vouch for Mrs. Talbot's good character, and besides, won't you be here to observe her?"

His mother shook her head. "No, I'm late to meet some friends in the lobby to play a few rounds of Crokinole. Mrs. Helms wants to win back the thirty-five cents she lost to me yesterday."

"Mrs. Helms cheats, you know," Daisy said. "She moves her discs when no one else is looking."

"So do I," Constance said with aplomb. "But I'm more discreet. That's why I always win."

Chase gazed down at his mother. "So, stealing jewelry is wrong but cheating at silly parlor games with your close, personal friends is an acceptable kind of thievery?"

She rolled her eyes at him, not even attempting to look innocent. "Don't look so shocked, darling. It's no different than having the upper hand with a business competitor. And anyway, it's her own fault."

"It's the fault of Mrs. Helms that you cheat more proficiently than she does?"

"It's her fault that vanity prevents her from wearing spectacles. If she'd put them on, she'd see me moving the pieces when it's not my turn. All's fair, as they say." She rose from her chair, letting the dogs slide to the floor with dueling thuds and yips, and Chase finally understood why his father thought she needed looking after.

It wasn't to protect her from *other people*. It was to protect other people from *her!*

After their mother left, Chase and Daisy stepped through the doorway leading to his sister's room and she rang for their maid, Adele. The Bostwick women were staying in a suite-style accommodation with bedrooms located on either side of a small sitting area, while Chase was in a standard room down the hall although all the upper-level rooms on this side of the hotel were appointed with small balconies where you could linger to enjoy the incredible views of the Straits between Michigan's upper and lower peninsulas. Underneath the balconies, the grand front porch ran the entire length of the hotel, some six-hundred feet wide. Each afternoon, tea and cakes were served, and each evening, guests might enjoy music and cocktails.

"Have you a long cape or a cloak she might borrow to cover her dress?" Chase asked as he crossed to the window to see if the carriage was still there. For some reason, he had the uneasy sense that Mrs. Talbot might skedaddle if given the chance, although where she'd go, he didn't know. But it appeared she had waited just as he'd advised.

"All my capes are short, but I have a shawl that might fit the bill. Will this work?" Daisy asked, holding up a navy-blue wrap with fringed edges.

"As well as anything. Have you another? Or a large bonnet? She may want to cover her head."

"Cover her head? Gadzooks, is she in such a bad state as all that? You make her sound like quite the ogre."

"Not an ogre in the least, but do you remember that day years ago when we visited Kloosterman's farm and Alex and I got into a tussle while feeding the pigs?"

His sister's eyes went round at the memory.

Chase nodded. "She not as bad off as all that, but she's damn muddy."

Daisy giggled at his colorful language. "Perhaps three shawls then," she said, tucking one more over her arm.

four

D aisy Elizabeth Bostwick chattered like a magpie – nonstop and mostly inane – but Jo enjoyed their conversation immensely. Not only did it serve as a sweet distraction from her troubles, but in the forty-five minutes she'd spent with the youngest Bostwick, Jo learned more about their family than she would have had she lived with them for a year, and yet all the information was delivered in the most unpretentious manner, as if it never occurred to sixteen-year-old Daisy not everyone had a multitude of servants, their own snowy white pony named *Diamond*, or a home with so many rooms you could hide with a book for hours and never be found. The girl was indulged and yet unspoiled, and Jo could not begrudge her any of the extravagances since Daisy was also generosity personified, loaning her a plum-colored walking dress by far the nicest thing she'd ever worn.

Adele, the Bostwick's maid, had styled Jo's hair, first brushing it clean and then gathering it securely upon the crown of her head in intricate loops and twirls. Daisy even insisted upon loaning Jo a clean pair of ivory gloves, a brooch that looked like a peacock with a gemstone in the center of each feather, and a buttery-soft leather satchel in which to carry all the pieces and components of her broken art box. And all the while, there was prattle, prattle, prattle delivered without an ounce of discretion.

In the world according to Daisy, her oldest brother Alex was always cheerful and teasing and loved to play pranks. She felt he deserved a fiancée with a far sweeter disposition than Isabella Carnegie, who had no sense of humor at all. Daisy's brother, Chase, on the other hand, was funny, patient, and kind but also intense and competitive. Daisy liked him best because he *(usually)* treated her as an equal although occasionally admonished her for wasting time reading novels. She loved her parents but wished she could spend far *more* time with her father and certainly *less* time with her mother. She secretly believed that women were every bit as smart and as capable as men and should have the right to vote – although she wasn't exactly sure what she would vote *for*. She thought Chicago was a wonderful city but too full of people. She preferred the company of horses and kittens. She believed in ghosts and loved everything about art. That last bit in particular had warmed Jo's heart.

"I will take every class you offer," Daisy told her enthusiastically as they said their goodbyes in the doorway of the suite. "You are certain to be a sensation, just as my brother said."

Such an encouraging sentiment. Whether founded in reality or not, that, along with the beautiful new ensemble and artistically coiffed hair, infused Jo with just the confidence boost she needed, and her ebullience lasted right up until the very moment she confronted the sour-faced hotel manager.

"This simply won't work," said Mr. Beeks from behind the tall, mahogany check-in desk just to the left of the grand staircase in the hotel lobby. "We were expecting *Mister* Emerson J. McKenna, *the artist.*"

"I am Emerson J. McKenna, the artist," she replied, lifting her chin haughtily *(which was now blessedly free of paint)*. "I have all the credentials you require, and I have a signed contract right here." She tapped the paper she held in her other hand, thankful she'd had an opportunity to remove it from beneath her corset.

"I'm the one you've been corresponding with for the past several months," she added. "I'm the one who negotiated these terms and I'm the one you've hired."

"But you're a woman."

"Indeed."

His ruddy cheeks turned ruddier still, and his overly robust eyebrows nearly met in the middle of his forehead mimicking the look of his equally robust mustache, as if you could turn his face entirely upside down and it would look much the same. And either way, it would be frowning at her.

"We were expecting a man," he said brusquely.

"You were expecting Emerson J. McKenna, the artist, and that's who you have. I promise I am completely up to the challenge and any hotel patron who participates in one of my classes will be completely satisfied. As soon as my belongings are brought to my room, I can unpack my portfolio and you'll see the quality of my work for yourself."

"We don't have a room for you," he said dismissively.

"You don't have a room? How is that possible? You just said yourself you were expecting me."

"I said we were expecting a man and so the room for Emerson J. McKenna is near the other men." He enunciated the word *men* as if that explained everything and thus was the end of the conversation.

This was not something she'd considered when responding to the letter of inquiry and leading them to believe she was *that* Emerson J. McKenna instead of *this* Emerson J. McKenna.

And yes. Of course.

She'd realized what the hotel management thought when extending the offer. She knew they presumed to be communicating with her father – the well renown painter – but if they'd known anything about anything, they should have realized he'd passed away months before the offer was even posted. And quite frankly, when said offer found its way to her, it was a Godsend, and she wasn't sorry for misleading them. She could do this job, and the room situation was hardly an insurmountable obstacle.

"This is a hotel, is not, Mr. Beeks?" she asked. "I assume there are other rooms? Ones not filled with men? Perhaps rooms for, shall we say, women?"

"Of course, there are other rooms but that's beside the point. We entered into this agreement under the assumption that you were the artist who painted *Lady Agnew of Lochnaw* and *Carnation, Lily, Lily, Rose*. Merely being the child of that artist does not make you qualified nor reputable enough to instruct our guests."

This was undoubtedly not the time to mention that she *wasn't even* the child of that particular artist since those were paintings by John Singer Sargent, not her father, but at least it proved to her that this mean, jowly, sweaty-pated little man knew nothing at all of art.

"True, I did not paint those pieces, but I did, in fact, paint *Mrs. Endicott with a White Rose. (She didn't actually because there was no such painting, but this stuffy prig didn't know that.)* And I painted *Three Lilies on a Pond. (Also non-existent.)* And I'll be painting a portrait of Daisy Bostwick during my stay here as well."

Technically that last part was true although she'd only just that moment decided to do so, and only thought of it because she'd spotted Chase Bostwick sitting in a chair across the lobby, prompting the idea.

"You have been commissioned by the Bostwicks?" That got the manager's attention. A single bushy brow lifted but the scowl remained.

She all but glared back at him. "I was in their suite not fifteen minutes ago having a lively conversation with young Miss Bostwick, and not that this is any of your business, sir, but I journeyed from the dock to this very hotel in a carriage hired Mr. Chase Bostwick himself."

All implicitly true and not remotely an honest answer to his question.

If the hotel manager followed up on these details, she'd be sunk but she was in the boat now. She'd even used Charles Bostwick's well-known nickname for extra emphasis, as if she had an intimate acquaintance and that chatting with the family was practically routine. *Oh, Alex, you're such a prankster. Oh, Chase, you work too hard. Oh, Daisy, your maid can style my hair anytime.*

"It's also quite possible," Jo said, lowering her voice as if the secret were one of great import, "that I'll be painting the wedding portrait of Mr. Alexander Bostwick and his fiancée, Miss Isabella Carnegie. This would be a lovely setting for such a work but alas, there's no point in me inviting them to the Imperial Hotel if I'm not here because you saw fit to defy the legality of this binding contract. I'll just have to paint them at the Island House."

She was really building up some steam now and either this was going to work, or she was going to crash brilliantly against the rocks. The image of her splintered paint box popped into her head, and she wondered if that had been a sign of foreboding, not that she put much stock in that sort of thing. If she did, she'd have heeded all the warning signs surrounding Oliver.

Mr. Beeks tapped his stubby fingers on the mahogany desktop. They'd had privacy for the entirety of their conversation, but a clerk walked up, and Mr. Beeks came out from behind the desk and motioned for her to follow him to the nearby corner.

He was no taller than she and had a protuberant belly that challenged every button of his vest. Like many of the male employees, he wore a tuxedo, but unlike most men, he didn't look any better for it. His shiny patent leather shoes squeaked when he walked sounding very much like flatulence and she knew with certainty that for the duration of her stay here, be it four more minutes or four more months, she would never again see him without thinking that the noise suited his personality. Gaseous, unpleasant, and something to avoid.

Nonetheless, right now, she needed to sway him to her way of thinking. She could sense his indecision as they halted in the corner, and she allowed herself to feel a spark of optimism. Just a tiny spark. If he refused her still, she didn't have any idea what she'd do next. She certainly could not afford a room in this hotel, and she had barely enough money to make her way back to Chicago. Even if she could get home, what then? She crossed her arms and tried to look indignant rather than petrified.

"I'll need to speak to Mr. Plank," he finally said. "He's the owner of the Imperial Hotel and I shouldn't think he'll be in favor of having a young, single girl instructing our clientele, but I will ask him."

"I'm not a single girl, Mr. Beeks. I am a married woman, and my husband, Oliver Talbot, will be joining me later in the summer." Lies were rolling off her tongue like poetry now but who was to say that Oliver wouldn't actually show up? Lord knew he was good at disappearing. Maybe he'd surprise her and be just as adept at reappearing? Very unlikely (*and would be most unwelcome*) but if anything good had come from knowing him, at least she'd learned how to manipulate people with half-truths and obfuscation.

"Good afternoon, Mrs. Talbot. Mr. Beeks."

The low-timbered voice floated over her shoulder giving her heartbeat a skip as she turned to see Mr. Bostwick standing beside her. She'd not noticed him leaving his chair, but did noticed now that since their carriage ride, he'd changed into a pale brown suit with a dark brown stripe and wore no hat, allowing the chestnut waves of his hair to do their own distractable bidding. She had the presence of mind to register how unfairly handsome he was just before her stomach plummeted to the plush rug beneath her feet because with just a word, this man could ruin all she'd been working toward. Maybe she should not have been so specific – and emphatic – with her half-truths.

Mr. Beeks straightened his spine to his full five-foot, four-inch stature and tugged at the hem of his vest as if that might disguise the paunch of his belly. *(It did not.)*

"A very fine good afternoon to you as well, Mr. Bostwick, sir. I do hope you are finding your accommodations acceptable."

"My accommodations are fine, thank you, Beeks. Mrs. Talbot, I trust your accommodations are adequate as well?" He turned his gaze to Jo.

Looking at his face, *she sensed* that *he sensed* there was some issue at hand. The real question was, how involved was he about to become – and whose side would he be on? He had no reason to defend her or vouch for her. He knew nothing of her other than her clumsy misfortune from earlier in the day and had already gone above and beyond to come to her aid. If he thought she'd played him for a fool by exploiting his family's name for her own purpose, he could seal her fate. But his eyes were bright, almost mischievous, and she felt she had an ally in him. It was worth the gamble and in truth, she had little to lose.

"I've yet to see my accommodations, Mr. Bostwick," she answered smoothly. "Mr. Beeks has taken issue with the fact that I am a woman."

Mr. Bostwick's quizzical gaze swung to Mr. Beeks. "Is this a fact, Beeks? Do you not care for women?"

"I care deeply for women, sir. My mother was a woman! It's just that this woman... she's not... well... she's..." he stammered and sputtered for a moment, tripping over his words, until he finally said, "We were expecting her father, sir."

"Her father?"

"Yes, sir."

"I have a signed contract from the hotel offering me – Emerson J. McKenna – the position of artist in residence," Jo said, "but Mr. Beeks apparently thought he was communicating with a dead man. May my father rest in peace."

five

From a green velvet upholstered chair across the lobby where Chase had been attempting to read a three-day old issue of the Chicago Daily Tribune, he'd instead been observing the exchange between Mrs. Talbot and the gib-faced hotel manager. He could not hear what was being said but it did not take an astute judge of communication to sense that Beeks was being unpleasant. As usual.

For someone whose very job depended upon being a gracious host, Chase found the little man toadying with guests while portentous with his staff. It was a character flaw which Chase found contemptable, especially since his own father was quick to admit he himself had come up from nothing. A dirt-poor, Illinois pig farmer's son with an affinity for numbers who moved to the city at just twelve to work at a bank. By the age of nineteen, the original Alexander James Bostwick was a bank manager and – as Chase's father liked to tell it – he'd never looked back, but he also never forgot the deprivation he'd known, the hopelessness and the hunger. He'd warned a young Chase that fear of it made some men greedy, and other men generous. Chase was glad his father was *(for the most part)* the latter, and that he treated everyone *(for the most part)* with equal respect.

"Fortunes turn, son," A.J. had once said. "Staying on top is just as hard as getting there in the first place and you never know what might send you tumbling to the bottom again, so help others when you can."

Maybe that's why Chase felt compelled to fold up that newspaper, rise from the chair, and cross the lobby to see why old Beeks was being... himself to Mrs. Talbot, for certainly she deserved a cordial greeting. His intervention had nothing to do with how attractive she looked now free of mud and paint and wearing a stylish, dark purple dress. She'd successfully coaxed her dark hair upwards but softly curling tendrils framed her delicate features. This might have lent an ethereal air were it not for her stern expression.

"Mr. Beeks apparently thought he was communicating with a dead man. May my father rest in peace," she said while looking more annoyed than grief-stricken.

"Communicating with the dead, you say? Beeks, I didn't take you for a member of the occult," Chase said, goading the man.

Beeks pulled a dingy handkerchief from his pocket and mopped his brow. "I'm no such thing, Mr. Bostwick, I assure you. What the girl meant—"

"Mrs. Talbot," Chase interrupted.

"Begging your pardon, sir?"

"The lady's name is Mrs. Talbot. Mrs. Emerson J. McKenna Talbot."

Mop, mop, mop. "Well, yes, of course, sir, but you see, we thought we were hiring a world-class portraitist and painting instructor for our guests, but it seems there's been a misunderstanding. We wanted her father, not her."

Twin splotches of pink appeared on Mrs. Talbot's otherwise pale cheeks and Chase could all but feel the humiliation emanating from her, a far cry from the feisty scrapper she'd been after colliding with him in the street. He found he liked the original version far better and although he had a sneaking suspicion there was more to this story, and more to her, he could not abide by Beeks' disrespect.

"Then you're a fool, Beeks," he said after the briefest hesitation. He felt Mrs. Talbot's eyes turn to him, but he frowned at the manager instead. Watching this little weasel squirm might be the most fun Chase had had in days.

"Excuse me?" Beeks replied, his nasally voice going up an octave.

"Not more than an hour ago, people in the street were clamoring around this woman, trying to get close to her. I could barely reach her side for all the crowd, and you think she's not good enough for your hotel? I suspect the truth is that this hotel does not deserve her."

Beeks opened his mouth to speak but only a mousy squeak came out.

"In fact, my sister Daisy is so eager to take instruction from Mrs. Talbot that she's begged our mother for a chance to enroll in every single one of her classes. Is it your intention, Mr. Beeks, to disappoint my little sister? Is that your goal?"

"Oh, my goodness, sir! Of course not, sir! I'd never do such a thing!" His face grew redder with every word, and it was all Chase could do to not laugh out loud at the poor sop.

"And did you not say there is a signed contract stating that Emerson J. McKenna has been hired by this hotel?"

"There is. It's right here," Mrs. Talbot said, holding up a somewhat crinkled paper.

"May I see it?" Chase asked.

She handed it over and he perused, not really reading it. He didn't care what arrangements they'd made or if it was legally binding. Perhaps it wasn't since she'd said her name was McKenna *Talbot*, but she may have signed this document before saying her vows – which meant her marriage had been a very recent thing – which meant she was indeed a newlywed – which also meant her groom was well and truly an idiot. What sort of fool would let this pretty bride out of his sight before the honeymoon was officially over? Chase nearly shook his head in puzzlement, but instead nodded at the document as if to confirm its validity. Beeks would take his word for it, regardless.

"Is this your signature?" he asked the manager, tapping at a scrawled marking at the bottom of the page.

Beeks nodded.

"And Mrs. Talbot, is this your signature?" He pointed to another spot. She nodded as well, her eyes hesitant as if she was as uncertain of the outcome as the apoplectic Beeks. A moment later, Chase handed it back to her. "Everything appears to be in order. Perhaps I should take this up with Mr. Plank."

"Oh, no sir. That's not necessary, sir. It's all just a misunderstanding," Beeks said, all but bowing to him now. "We needn't involve Mr. Plank. I'm sure we can make do. Mrs. Talbot, we'd be amenable to having you instruct our guests. If you'll allow me a few moments to check our registry, I'll reassign you to a room in the women's dormitory and have your trunks sent there as soon as they arrive."

"The women's dormitory?" Chase pressed dryly, giving a slight, impatient tap of his foot. He should probably leave well enough alone now. It appeared Mrs. Talbot could claim the job as her own, but having Beeks under his thumb was too entertaining. Chase was *that* bored.

Beeks seemed to tamp down a sigh. "The women's dormitory. It's where all the female employees stay during their time here."

"I see. And was the original plan to house Mr. McKenna in the men's dormitory?"

This time the sigh was audible. "No, sir."

"Well, in that case I'd expect you to find Mrs. Talbot a room comparable to the one her father was assigned. One with a sunny exposure, undoubtedly, and view of the water since she's sure to do some painting in there during her stay."

Beeks pressed his lips into a flat line for the briefest hesitation before responding. "Only our premium guest rooms on the front side of the hotel have water views, Mr. Bostwick."

Chase said nothing. Just lifted a brow and stared... and tapped. He was being pushy and obnoxious and enjoying it a little too much, but since it wasn't for his own personal benefit, where was the harm? Beeks very nearly tried to stare him down, bold little man, but at last he folded with a huff.

"Very well, Mr. Bostwick. She shall have a room with a water view."

"Excellent, Beeks. I'm so glad we were able to work this out. I'll be sure to mention your cooperation when I next have lunch with Mr. Plank." Reminding this pretentious squish of man that Chase was well acquainted with the hotel's owner would help ensure he'd keep his word.

"Thank you, Mr. Bostwick. Mrs. Talbot, I'll be back in a moment with your room key."

Beeks scuttled away and Chase allowed himself a chuff of laughter before turning to his accomplice. The flush remained on Mrs. Talbot's cheeks and though she smiled, her eyes seemed clouded by doubt, leaving him to feel curious rather than smug.

"It seems I find myself further in your debt, Mr. Bostwick," she said quietly. "It's all too much. The carriage and the aid from your sister, and now this." She gave a tiny, seemingly reluctant sigh that he didn't understand. This was all a lark, was it not? A bit of nanty-narking? She should be laughing right alongside him. They'd bested Beeks and she was the sole beneficiary, but perhaps he'd embarrassed her.

"Think nothing of it, Mrs. Talbot. I assure you I find myself with little to do on this island, yet today has been, at the very least... interesting. I do hope the remainder of your stay is entirely free of calamity."

"As do I." She nodded in earnest agreement. "I intend to make certain of it."

"Indeed."

He thought to stay and converse with her since he'd enjoyed their time in the carriage, once she'd relaxed enough to stop looking as if she were about to open the door and jump out into the rain, but now she seemed back to that skittish girl. And no wonder. She was up to something. Of that he was entirely certain, although he possessed no notion of what it might be, or how anyone who appeared so guileless could have secrets to hide.

All things considered, it would probably be best to remove himself from her company, because, quite frankly, she looked too pretty, her dark-lashed eyes wide with sincerity. She seemingly had no idea the lovely picture she made in the dark-purple dress with her hair styled just so, and while he had few qualms about entertaining other men's wives, those wives were... seasoned. They were members of a society that understood the rules about such things, that dalliances were merely transactional in nature and rarely involved matters of the heart.

It was obvious this young woman was not cut from that cloth, and he was not the sort to toy with an innocent woman's emotions. Besides, if his earlier assessment was correct, Mrs. Talbot was a newlywed and most likely still enamored of her husband, even if the dunce had seen fit to let her travel completely and totally alone.

"Did I hear you tell Mr. Beeks that your husband would be joining you soon?" He hoped that was true, for his own sake. *She really was lovely.*

Her expression shifted once more, ever so slightly as her gaze darted away from his, toward the wide, open doors of the lobby.

Yes, secrets. Definitely.

"It's a possibility although nothing is certain. It may be difficult for Mr. Talbot to get away," she answered.

"Away from..."

"Work." She looked back at him, her face now void of emotion.

"Naturally, but what does your husband do for a living, Mrs. Talbot?"

She fidgeted with the cuff of one sleeve as she spoke. "He's... an art dealer."

"Ah. How convenient. I expect that makes the two of you a

perfect match." He was fishing. He couldn't help it. It was habit. And... he was curious.

Her pause was too long to be insignificant, until at last she gave a tiny shrug of her shoulders, and said, "As any artist will tell you, Mr. Bostwick, nothing is ever perfect. Or constant. The image shifts in the light and suddenly what you thought you saw is no longer there."

His breath caught in his throat. Goodness! Was she flirting with him? Was Mrs. Talbot telling him her marriage was imperfect? Perhaps she *was* cut from that same cloth after all. He suddenly found himself hoping that were true because uncovering the mysteries behind her dark eyes would be a delicious way to pass the time while trapped on this island.

But then she blushed again, and blinked rapidly, as if realizing what she'd said. She smiled widely and added, "But originality lies in imperfection, don't you think? Wouldn't life be dull if everything went according to plan? I much prefer adventure to predictability."

"As do I, Mrs. Talbot," he said after a pause, realizing that although she may have sounded forward, there was a naivete which clung to her like a sweet fragrance. She spoke from inexperience, not boldness, and whatever her story, she was too complicated for him. Chase was simply going to have to take up lawn tennis and golf and sailing and that silly game his mother was always playing. That Crokinole. Maybe Constance would teach him how to cheat, and he could while away his summer swindling all the matriarchs out of their coins.

And now, he'd take his leave. He needed some distance between himself and the temptation of Mrs. Talbot because he'd done a fair share of good deeds today and if he loitered any longer, he was apt to suggest something illicit that would undo them all.

He cleared his throat while trying to clear his mind. "Well, Mrs. Talbot, since your employment is secure and your room will soon be ready, I believe I'll say good day. I'm certain Beeks won't give you any more difficulty, but if he does, send me a note." He tilted his head forward in acknowledgement, adding, "It has indeed been an adventure meeting you, Mrs. Talbot."

"Thank you, Mr. Bostwick. For everything."

"Again, my pleasure." He turned to leave but after taking a single step, he stopped and looked back over his shoulder. "One more thing, though, Mrs. Talbot..."

"Yes?"

"I'm not entirely certain what you're up to, but I sure as hell hope you can paint."

six

L ike her borrowed dress, this hotel room was the finest thing Jo had ever seen.

The large window did indeed provide a breathtaking view of the water. Late afternoon rays from the sun that finally appeared after the storm cast yellow beams across the bed – a bed three times as wide as the lumpy cot she'd been sleeping on in the back room of an art studio of late. Even at home, before her father had died, her bed had been much smaller and not nearly so plush. But here, the polished brass of the frame gleamed gold against the rich scarlet wallpaper, and the pink and burgundy striped duvet was so puffy she might think she was sleeping in the clouds. On the pine floor lay a thick rug patterned in bold, swirling jewel tones. It was all so beautiful she felt like a trespasser for certainly she would not have had so superb a room were it not for Mr. Bostwick. Indeed, she might not have had a room at all. Or employment.

While she may have gotten the recalcitrant Mr. Beeks to where she needed him eventually, the deal had been all but sealed once Chase stepped into the conversation. (*Chase. Could she call him that, if only in her mind?*) But even if she had secured the job on her own, this posh, palatial room was all Mr. Bostwick's doing.

(No, she could not call him Chase. Not even in her own mind.) She twirled slowly to take it all in and marveled at the shifting fates that had finally brought her some good fortune. Everything had been so difficult for so long and at last she had a reprieve.

But worry seeped into her mind like a noxious vapor.

"I'm not entirely certain what you're up to, but I sure as hell hope you can paint."

Damnation! Less than an hour on this island and already she was arousing suspicions. But if Mr. Bostwick was wary, why insist she have such an exquisite room with a breathtaking view... and a sinfully large bed? Perhaps she should have refused, just as she'd refused the new art box. She'd accepted without pondering the cost and now, by her own admission, she was indebted to Mr. Bostwick. Times three. She *owed* him. But... surely, he was just being kind. It had cost him nothing but a few minutes of his time, and he'd seemed to enjoy taunting the hotel's manager.

She allowed herself a small chuckle. It was all rather funny even if it did leave her in a precarious situation. Because the truth was, she had no tangible way of knowing if Mr. Bostwick's intentions were generous or self-serving. Now that Oliver had robbed her of the ability to accurately judge a person's character, the only thing Jo knew for certain was that *trust* was a gossamer web, spun slowly, strand by strand, immobilizing you – until you were trapped.

She was back on the steamship as it pitched wildly. A wave, four stories tall, rushed forward, faster than any locomotive. She tried to scream, but the water rushed over her, knocking her down and muffling her breath. She thought this was the end of her, for surely, she'd drown... until a rapping startled her awake. *Thank goodness!* She pushed upwards, realizing she'd dozed off, face pressed into the satin coverlet.

The knock sounded again.

"Hello?" she called out hesitantly, wiping a hand over bleary eyes.

"It's the porter, miss. I've some trunks to deliver to room 328."

She rose on unsteady legs, her body still caught up in the fear of the dream and crossed to the door. Opening it, she found the tallest, widest, darkest-skinned man she'd ever seen. His mass filled the entire doorframe. His dark hair, sprinkled with silver, was cropped close to his head, and he wore a blue serge jacket with a gold embroidered emblem on the front pocket, the insignia of the Imperial Hotel.

"Good afternoon, miss." His voice rumbled so deep it reminded her of the thunder from earlier in the day, and she marveled at the way he held her trunk aloft as if it weighed nothing at all.

"Good afternoon. Please come in." She opened the door wider, and he stepped inside.

"Thank you, miss, and welcome to the Imperial Hotel. I hope you enjoy your stay."

"Thank you, I'm sure I will Mister...?"

He stood slowly after setting the trunk down near the foot of her bed. "Begging your pardon, miss?"

She smiled, extending her hand. "Missus. I'm Mrs. Talbot. And you are?"

He looked at her hand and kept his own close to his sides "I'm the porter, miss. Uh... ma'am."

"Yes, of course, but I'll be working here all summer and we're sure to see each other again." She wiggled her arm. "So, we should be acquainted." She needed all the friends she could get, and the hotel staff was the place to start.

"Parnell, ma'am. Beauregard Parnell." He hesitantly reached out one gloved hand and let her shake it although she could tell he put no muscle into it. He could probably fling a boulder like it was a skipping stone judging from the way he carried the trunk.

"It's a pleasure to meet you, Mr. Parnell. Do you have my

other things? There should be two more bags and a large, narrow box."

"Yes, indeed, ma'am." He went back to the hall and brought in two satchels and her portfolio, the remainder of her meager assortment of worldly goods and as he set them next to the trunk, she tried not to lament that her life had been reduced to such a tiny pile.

"Thank you. I wonder if you might tell me where the staff dining room is, and when the evening meal is served. I'm famished."

"The staff lounge is open from five in the morning until eleven in the evening. You can stop in anytime to get something to eat but hot meals are served at six, two, and six. If you've a hankering for something special, go to the kitchen and ask for Chef Culpepper. He'll try to whip it up for you, if he's not too busy. Tell him Parnell sent you."

She smiled. "Thank you, and where might I find the lounge?"

"Next to the kitchen. It's not quite supper yet, but if you'd like, I could get you a sandwich while you unpack your things."

Her mouth watered at the thought. She hadn't eaten since early that morning. "That's so kind but I couldn't ask it of you. That's surely not a porter's job."

"Not usually but we all tend to help out where it's needed. With the hotel being so new, we're all learning. I've been here for a month but several of the staff have been here less than that."

"Goodness. I thought I'd be the newest, but it sounds as if I'll be in good company."

"Yes, ma'am."

"In that case, if you would be so kind as to bring me a sandwich, I'd be most obliged." She pulled her coin purse from the pocket of her borrowed dress, but Mr. Parnell held up one wide palm.

"No need, ma'am. The food from the staff lounge is free to us and as I said, we help one another out around here. I'll be back in a jiffy."

Once Mr. Parnell departed, Jo made quick work of unpacking her few belongings. Her garments fit easily into the oversized armoire, both because of its ample size and because her attire was so limited. It hadn't always been that way – but things were different now.

She shut the door, closing her mind to haunted memories, and reached into her bag for one final item, a silver-framed photograph of her father. The picture was flat and monochromatic, the original Emerson J. McKenna staring back at her with little of the life of a portrait, showing none of the sparkle in his eyes, or capturing his unique persona, but of course, she was biased. How could anything truly embody her father's spirit? How could anything emulate his warmth or keen, ribald sense of humor? Or his love for her?

It couldn't.

Even so, she cherished this image of him. Pressing the frame against her heart, she let a tear slide. She missed him. So much.

"I've stolen your job, Papa," she whispered to the empty room. "Again."

seven

"The broiled trout is the finest I've had," Breezy VonMeisterburger announced to everyone seated around the linen-draped table inside the opulent Imperial Hotel dining room. "But you simply cannot go wrong with the tenderloin of beef. Or the tongue. Or the raspberry pie."

"Is there anything she hasn't eaten?" Chase's mother murmured under her breath. "It's a wonder her laces are holding."

Constance Bostwick believed in an excess of everything – except food and empathy but still, Chase had to muffle his laughter behind a napkin because she was not far off the mark. Louisa "Breezy" VonMeisterburger had an appetite of a lumberjack, and while she wasn't rotund, she was certainly... sturdy. And if his mother was fond of excess, it was nothing compared to the intemperance of Mrs. VonMeisterburger who was extravagant in every way.

In the glowing light of the gasoliers, Chase counted no less than six peacock feathers fluttering from her elaborately piled hair, a dozen strands of freshwater pearls draped around her fleshy neck, and a collection of gem-stone encrusted bracelets on both wrists, but despite her immoderation, Chase liked the woman. She was the only person capable of putting his mother in her place and had a propensity to say exactly what was on her mind. Some people found that off-putting, but he considered it refreshing. Perhaps because his mother had a habit of only hinting at what she was thinking as if it were a test to see who could guess correctly. *(He never guessed correctly.)*

And of course, the younger women of Chase's acquaintance had, to their detriment, been raised to believe that stating their own opinion was tantamount to blasphemy. How often had he met a pretty face and hoped for some unique personality to go with it, only to be left wanting. Young ladies were instructed to speak only of inane topics such as the weather or perhaps the beauty of their surroundings. They might inquire about his latest travels or if they were particularly daring, would ask what it was like to be an identical twin.

Most of them were well educated, but when put to the test, not one of them dared offer views on virtually anything at all. They wouldn't speculate if three-year-old *Sir Dixon* might be the fastest horse at Belmont Stakes this year or say if they preferred to ride in a Brewster Park Drag or a Kimball Town Coach. They certainly would not comment on the state of Chicago's burgeoning industries or if they thought Benjamin Harrison might unseat Grover Cleveland as the next president of the United States. Good heavens! Discuss politics with a debutante? He may as well be extolling upon the finer nuances of fornication.

Chase tamped down a sigh. It was all well and good for a woman to be demure, but he wanted more. He wanted to know what was going on inside of her brain as well as in her bodice!

It made him wonder just then... Had Isabella Carnegie displayed some personality? Some frank opinions? Some original thoughts? She must have. Surely, she must have, or he would not have found her so captivating, so compelling, so charming, for certainly she was all those things. Wasn't she? Odd that now he couldn't actually remember what she was like... so... perhaps she'd been as blank a slate as all the others and he'd just filled in the empty pauses in their conversation with thoughts of his own, while attributing them to her. No wonder he'd found her so wise and agreeable.

And then of course there was Mrs. Talbot.

Despite her rather shy demeanor, he suspected she had opinions. Strong opinions, even. Perhaps he might go so far as to assume she had convictions. Otherwise, she'd not have had the courage to journey – alone – to a place she'd never been before – to accept a job that she was only *probably* qualified for. And no timid, retiring girl would shove a man in the middle of the street as she had and call him... what was it?

Oh, yes. A nincompoop!

He smiled to himself at the memory of her misplaced indignation and the way she'd glowered at him from underneath that homely, homely hat. Gadzooks, the thing was heinous. While she'd refused his offer of a new artist's box, perhaps he should have offered her a new bonnet instead. The notion elicited a quiet ripple of laughter from his throat.

"What's funny?" Daisy asked, poking his forearm none too gently with her silver shrimp fork.

Ah, his sister – now here was a young lady full of ideas, and views, and opinions. Truthfully, from her, he found that annoying on most occasions because she pestered *him* with *all* of her thoughts, and judgments and beliefs, but deep down, he was secretly proud of her, and proud of himself for encouraging her to question things. To never take something at face value without considering the source from whence it came, and to resist being forced into a gilded cage of society's design. Daisy was bright, and tenacious, and with any luck she'd stay that way and not be cowed into submission by their mother, and the world at large. So far there seemed to be little indication of that happening, he realized, as she jabbed him again with her fork.

"Ouch. Nothing's funny. I'm just recalling something Mrs. Talbot said."

"Well, whatever she said must have been funny because you're laughing about it when she isn't even here."

Yes, Daisy was bright, and a little too insightful.

"All right, yes. It was funny, but I'm not going to share it," he said.

"You needn't share it because I had my own delicious conversation with Mrs. Talbot, and she is an unmitigated delight. She sent me a note to say her first class is tomorrow morning. I suspect she's to become my most favorite person on all the island," Daisy responded with a broad smile. "And she looked like the jammiest bits of jam in my dress. You should have seen her."

"I did see her," he said.

She raised an eyebrow. "And... didn't she look fine?"

"Fine, indeed." He took a hearty *(practically ill-mannered)* gulp of the Veuve Clicquot champagne from the Waterford crystal glass in front of him and decided to change the subject – because talking about Mrs. Talbot and her *jammiest bits* was not a conversation fit for the dinner table and most certainly not a conversation fit to be had with his little sister.

"So, what activities is Mother insisting you participate in this week?" he asked instead. "Or are you hoping she'll let you waste the entire summer reading?"

Daisy jabbed him with her fork again, less gently this time. "Reading is not a waste of time. It's a wonder, like traveling to faraway lands without ever having to leave your sofa."

"What in heaven's name is the advantage of never leaving your sofa? Girls are so peculiar," he teased as he took the fork from his sister's hand and laid it back down on the table.

"I am not peculiar. *I'm fascinating.* Mrs. Talbot said so."

And there they were. Right back to where they'd started.

"Mortimer," he called across the table to Breezy's only son, a twenty-year-old man with pale blond hair slicked back with a liberal amount of Woodsworth & Sons pomade and an Adam's apple the size of an actual crabapple protruding from his neck – which people seldom noticed because they were too busy noticing how unfortunately cross-eyed he was. "What are your plans for tomorrow?"

Mortimer looked his way. Or maybe he didn't. It was hard to tell, but regardless, his head swiveled toward Chase.

"Me?" he asked with a squeak then cleared his throat. (*Maybe that Adam's apple impaired his speech.*) Mortimer straightened the lapels of his wool dinner jacket and said importantly, "Well, Mummy and I attended today's lecture with Mr. Greiner of the Audubon Society, and he has assured me that if I dedicate myself to the task, I might be so fortunate as to find myself a hairy woodpecker. Of course, you know that the hairy woodpecker has a chiseled beak which differs from the short, dainty beak of the downy woodpecker. That's why I intend to bring along my new roof prism binoculars. And if I am indeed blessed, I might even come across a white-breasted nuthatch!"

Mortimer continued on enthusiastically for several minutes with more UN-fascinating ornithological factoids about buffleheads, and fulvous whistling ducks, and something called a Eurasian wigeon, and Chase thought about picking up that fork of Daisy's and sticking it right into his temple as she leaned over and whispered, "And that's why I stay inside to read."

"Morty, darling," his mother finally interrupted. "You must order the salmon this evening. I want to try it."

"Then why don't you order it?" he asked, swiveling his head in her direction, and getting a feather in his face for his troubles.

"Because I'm having the trout almondine."

"Well, I was going to order the trout for myself," he replied.

"Wouldn't you prefer the salmon?"

"No, I'd prefer the trout."

"But I want to taste the salmon."

"Then you order the salmon."

The exchange went on thusly while everyone else at the table observed, eyes going back and forth from mother to son as if this were an exciting round of lawn tennis – except that this was not, in fact, remotely exciting. It was excruciatingly dull, although Chase did feel a certain kinship for the poor hen-pecked Mortimer. Their mothers were birds of a feather.

At last, the young man relented so Breezy might have her way, and then she launched immediately into a dramatically divulged saga about her quest for a new gardener because her last one had no skill *(none, whatsoever!)* in cultivating a new species of rose – which she intended to name *The Beautiful Breezy.* Meanwhile, Mr. Albert VonMeisterburger, with his dark curly hair and drooping, red-hued mustache, bore the look of a hungry Airedale Terrier as he chomped on a dinner roll.

Chase glanced around the room, hoping to signal for the waiter. There was not enough French champagne in the world to make tonight enjoyable. This he knew because so far this evening was proceeding much like the four previous evenings had. With Breezy monopolizing, and Mr. VonMeisterburger chomping, and Mortimer's countenance seeming to volley between self-importance and self-doubt. The only difference tonight was the addition of a new young couple at their table, a Mr. Percival O'Keefe and his petite, auburn-haired wife, Ruth.

"Mr. and Mrs. O'Keefe," Chase finally said, interrupting Breezy because there was no other way to get a word in. "How are you finding things on the island? Are you enjoying yourself?"

"We are, although we've only just arrived," Mr. O'Keefe answered, the lilt of his accent revealing Irish heritage. He was a man of average height and average looks with the only distinguishable thing about him being his intensely bright blue eyes, so light they nearly looked like frozen lake water.

"We're looking forward to a tour of the hotel properties with Mr. Plank tomorrow, though, if my wife is feeling up to it."

"I'm quite well," she chimed in with a smile, patting Mr. O'Keefe's hand. "Just a bit fatigued... from the travel. I'm looking forward to the tour as well."

Chase was no expert of dialects, but if he could trust his ears, her accent was Scottish, but what he noticed more than that was the lovingly solicitous way her husband gazed at her as she spoke, with utter fascination and obvious devotion. It gave Chase a start, the notion that affection could be so... obvious. His own parents, and in fact, most every couple of his acquaintance were far more subtle with their emotions. Even Alex and Isabella who were *madly in love.* Or so Alex said.

"And from whence do you hale, Mr. O'Keefe?" Mortimer chimed in, dabbing at the corner of his thin-lipped mouth with a napkin yet somehow missing the droplet of wine that had found purchase on his meager mustache.

"We're from Detroit most recently, by way of Dublin and Glasgow. I'm with Barnaby Shipping. And yourself?"

"Oil," said Mr. VonMeisterburger abruptly before his son could answer.

If Breezy was about excess, Albert VonMeisterburger was about frugality with both his wallet and his words. He was a stingy businessman with few close friends. Diminutive in stature, he was the opposite of his wife in every way. Chase considered him fractious with a singular focus; to make as much money as possible while also investing the least in his workers. It was no secret that his employees disliked him immensely. Then again, not many titans in the oil business were well-loved. No one ever accused Rockefeller of being affable.

"Do you enjoy painting, Mrs. O'Keefe?" Chase heard his sister ask.

"I do," she answered pleasantly. "But I confess I've only dabbled. I'm no proficient."

"Well, that's perfect, then. You must come to an art class with me."

"An art class?"

"Yes, the Imperial Hotel has brought in the most inspiring artist to give instruction. A Mrs. Emerson J. McKenna Talbot, daughter of *the* Emerson J. McKenna. She's teaching a class tomorrow morning and I do hope you'll consider joining me."

Chase all but sighed. It seemed there was to be no avoiding reminders of Mrs. Talbot. Not with Daisy around. His sister was being far too forward, but whether from excellent social grace or perhaps genuine interest, Mrs. O'Keefe agreed to participate, and much to his relief, the conversation veered onto other topics.

As they ordered their meals and partook of an admittedly delicious dinner, they talked of the upcoming dance to be held on Saturday evening, the impending yacht race with guests from the Island House, and the breathtaking views to be found all over the island. Mostly banal subjects and Chase found his mind wandering again and again, back to Chicago and the various projects he'd been working on before being exiled, then forward into the future and his plans to solidify his reputation as a brilliant businessman, and then... *damn it...* back to Mrs. Talbot.

Was she dining somewhere in this room tonight? So far, he'd yet to see her although his search was limited to his current view. Even with all the elaborately gilded mirrors on the walls, he could hardly pivot about in his chair to get a better look without revealing his purpose, and besides, *why* was he looking for her? *That* was as much a mystery to him as the woman herself.

Perhaps it was simply that she was new. And different. And brashly outspoken. And yet what (*what, indeed!)* had she meant about things being imperfect? Those hardly seemed to be the words of a blushing bride, but perhaps the very fact that she was *here,* and her husband was *not* explained everything. Perhaps all she meant was that she *missed* her spouse, that circumstances had unavoidably separated them for a short time, and she longed to be reunited. That was likely it and Chase would do well to keep that in mind lest he create intrigue – and look for opportunity – where none existed.

Then, of course, there was the matter of the demolished artist's box. Although it *was* she who'd set off the chain of events which ruined it, he could not in good conscience leave the thing unreplaced. He had been tangentially *involved,* or at least his mother's *dogs* had been, and any gentleman worth his salt would see to it that Mrs. Talbot received another kit in spite of her protestations. He'd order it and have Daisy make a gift of it since, what was it his sister had said? *Mrs. Talbot was to become her favorite person on all the island?* Surely such a kinship warranted a new artist box, and he found himself that very evening back in his hotel room penning a note to his secretary in Chicago.

Mr. Hayden,
I am in need of an artist's kit. I know nothing of these things but make sure it's of the finest quality and is filled with whatever supplies normally come with such things, especially pots and tubes of paint. Speed is of the essence. Send it directly to me at the Imperial Hotel and bill it to my personal account.
Thank you,
C. Bostwick

Then he penned another note to his father, possibly prompted by the several glasses of champagne he'd imbibed in during dinner.

Sir,
I am mad with boredom. Send me a project to work on or I shall be forced to allow Mother to purchase land on the island and begin design work on a summer cottage which is sure to cost you a fortune. Or better yet, send Alex in my stead and let me come back to Chicago.
Cordially,
Your better son

And since he had pen and parchment at the ready – and was admittedly a little drunk – he sent a note to his brother as well.

Alex,
The air here is clear as paradise and the scenery spectacular. The fishing is so blessedly easy the trout all but jump into the boat. No baiting hooks required. In addition to that, there's lawn tennis, golf, sailing. The food is excellent. I just ate my weight in beef and spring potatoes yet cannot help but feel guilty knowing you are toiling away

in the heat of Chicago while I'm lounging about here in this oasis.
I've told Father I'd be most agreeable to trading places with you and
come back to the city. If you could find a way to bring Isabella here,
I'm certain the two of you would have a most wonderful time. Or
you could come stag and enjoy those last days of bachelorhood. I
truly wouldn't mind. I'd be happy to return to the office.
I look forward to your response.
Yours,
C.

His brother would see through this charade before he'd even read the words, but it was worth a try. And other than that part about his feeling guilty (and the fish jumping into the boat), the rest was actually true. Alex would love it here. He enjoyed milder pursuits, and he had a much more convivial relationship with their mother. It would be better for all involved if Chase went home. He needed to go home.

The doorway to his balcony was open letting in the fresh night air, and although the musicians had stopped playing for the evening, he could hear low voices wafting up from the porch along with the pleasant crash of waves against the shore. Rather than soothing him though, the sounds only served to leave him feeling forlorn – and perhaps a bit lonely, which was not an emotion he was accustomed to. He enjoyed his solitude immensely so long as he had something worthwhile with which to fill the time. A few more days of this irritating *relaxation* and he'd be forced to read a *novel* just to get through the hours.

He looked around the room as if he might spot something to relieve his sense of restlessness, but it looked the same as it had yesterday. Green papered walls, a green and gold striped coverlet on the brass-framed bed, gasoliers flickering as the breeze moved through the open balcony door, rustling a stack of papers that needed to go to Mr. Hayden – a stack he could post tomorrow morning along with the letters.

Or he could do it now. There was probably someone at the

front desk. Perhaps a short, brisk walk would shake off this case of the morbs and then he could come back and get some sleep. He sealed the letters, packaged up the papers, and soon found himself passing these along to the night clerk at the front desk.

"They'll go out with the post first thing in the morning, Mr. Bostwick," the skinny, blue-coated youth said while stifling a yawn. "Oh, begging your pardon, sir."

"Long day?" Chase asked amicably.

"Yes, sir, but glad to have the work."

"Do you like working at the hotel then?" He was that bored. Bored enough to strike up a conversation with a mop-headed, fifteen-year-old boy sitting at a desk at 10:45 in the evening.

"Sure," the clerk answered with a crooked-toothed grin. "It beats working in the stables or down at the docks. So long as you stay on the good side of management, it's a corker of a job."

"Management pretty tough around here, are they?"

The boy's cheeks flushed as he realized he was possibly sharing too much with a guest and tried to cover his tracks. "Oh, no sir. They're all first-class, it's just some are more particular than others."

"Mr. Beeks," Chase said knowingly. "Is he particular?"

The boy regarded him for a moment, as if measuring his trustworthiness. "Mr. Beeks is exacting, but that's his job, I suppose, and as long as I do mine then I won't get the boot."

Chase regarded him in return, and then tapped a knuckle on the desktop. "Good lad. Glad to hear it. I wonder if you might be able to tell me where the reading room is. I know I saw one the other day but darned if I can remember where." This conversation had neither stirred his intellect nor relieved his tension. He was going to need a book after all.

The boy gave him some vague, yet complicated directions and Chase set off down a long hallway. Some five minutes later, after wandering past a multitude of rooms, a candy shop, a barber shop, and tailor's shop – all closed due to the late hour, he realized he was lost. He'd decided to retrace his steps back to the lobby when a door opened and who should step out into his path but one Mrs. Talbot. She was wearing a different frock now. Not his sister's and not the mud and paint splattered blue one from earlier but a loose-fitting, pale green tea gown that was modestly adorned and complemented her figure in a way most becoming.

"Oh, my goodness, Mr. Bostwick," she exclaimed as they very nearly collided. Again.

He took a step backward out of an abundance of caution. "Mrs. Talbot. You do pop up most unexpectedly." *(In the street, in the hallway... in his mind.)*

Her short laugh sounded more nervous than amused.

"I could say the same of you," she answered. "What are you doing down here by the employee's lounge?"

He looked up and down the yellow-painted hallway as if seeing it for the first time. "Is that where I am? I was looking for the reading room. But what has you wandering around so late in the evening?"

She blushed prettily and smiled – also prettily. "Lemon meringue pie," she answered. "I had some with my dinner and it was so delicious I could not stop thinking about it. I had to have another piece."

He chuckled at her confession because apparently while he'd been thinking about *her*, she'd been thinking about *pie*. Clearly her priorities were less fanciful than his.

"Would you like some?" she asked. "I could go back into the lounge and get you a piece. They're just cleaning up but I'm sure there's one more slice."

"No, thank you. I had quite enough at dinner. I didn't see you in the dining room," he couldn't resist adding.

"I dined in my room. I wanted to get settled. And I'd hoped to have time to find out where I'll be teaching tomorrow, but I wasn't able. This hotel is a bit of a labyrinth, isn't it? Did you say you were looking for the reading room?"

He nodded as he peered behind him, back down the hall. "I saw it yesterday, but it seems to have disappeared."

"I know where it is," she said, her smile widening with humor. "You're nowhere near it."

"I'm not? I got directions from the night clerk, but he was so drowsy I'm not sure he was sharp enough to give advice."

"It's near the tearoom, off the far side of the lobby opposite the dining room," she said.

Oh, yes! He knew which area she meant, and her words jogged his memory. That's exactly where he'd seen it. Yesterday after dropping his mother off at the tearoom. He was also quite certain he knew how to get there from here, but she didn't know that he knew...

"Do you suppose you could show me?" he asked.

eight

Wandering around the Imperial Hotel with Mr. Chase Bostwick as the clock struck 11:00 p.m. was not how Jo expected her first day on the island to end, but of course, she hadn't expected most of anything that had happened to her today.

She'd tried to tell him how to get back to the lobby and on to the reading room but perhaps he'd had too much wine with dinner because the man simply wasn't getting it.

"Turn left at the staircase, you say?" he'd asked.

"No," she'd patiently repeated. "Right at the staircase and then left at the tearoom."

"At the tearoom?"

Finally, she'd given up and offered to escort him, and they were halfway there when she realized... she'd been duped! She halted in her tracks and turned to face him.

"Mr. Bostwick," she said in the sternest voice she could muster. "You are toying with me. You know exactly where the reading room is."

He seemed not at all chagrined to have been unmasked but merely smiled in a playful way that belied his twenty-five years. "I confess that's true. Although I was genuinely lost until you gave me directions."

"Then why have me escort you if you could find the way yourself?"

His broad shoulders gave an easy shrug. "I was bored."

She let out an unpolished bark of laughter at his equally unpolished but honest answer. "And so, you thought to lead me on a goose chase just to amuse yourself? That's not very sporting of you, is it? To play me for a fool?" *(Well, wasn't she was a pot calling the kettle black.)*

His smile turned earnest. "I would never play you for a fool, Mrs. Talbot. I just wanted some company, and you would have had to come this way to return to your room anyway, wouldn't you?"

"No, I could have taken the back stairs near the lounge which leads right to my door. Now I'm closer to the lobby and must traverse the entire length of the hallway to get back to my room." Her admonishment was delivered with a smile, but still she added, "And so now that I am on to your ruse, I will say goodnight. I teach my first class tomorrow morning and need to be rested. Goodnight, Mr. Bostwick."

"Ah," he said. "I apologize for causing you extra steps."

She gave him a nod and turned to leave just as he added, "I wonder, have you seen it?"

She reluctantly turned back. "Seen what? My room?"

"No, the reading room. It's got quite an impressive library, or so I'm told. I mean, if books are something that amuse you. Are they?"

Her notion that he'd had too much wine with dinner resurfaced. He seemed determined to elongate this exchange, but it was late and anyone who saw them together was bound to get the wrong idea.

"I love books and I did peek into the reading room not long ago when I was looking around. It is indeed impressive."

"Which authors do you favor?"

That was like asking her which color in her paint box was her favorite. An impossible question. "Many. It depends on my mood."

A tilt of his smile returned, and he leaned forward conspiratorially. "Then say, for instance, you were trapped on an island with your waspish mother and your annoying little sister and worried that boredom would turn your brain to mush. Which author would you recommend in that case?"

She found herself laughing again. "Is that how you feel? Trapped here? And bored?"

He nodded. "Just this very evening I wrote to my father asking him to send my brother in my stead. I find myself quite unable to enjoy so much leisure. I need something to keep me sharp."

"I shouldn't think a few weeks away from work will turn you into a lunkhead, Mr. Bostwick, but very well, let me think." She tapped her chin. "Were I choosing for myself, I might select something by Henry James such as *Washington Square*, or perhaps *The Woodlanders* by Thomas Hardy. For you, though, under the circumstances, I think anything by Mr. Twain might keep you amused, although I assume you've already read *The Adventures of Huckleberry Finn*. Perhaps *Treasure Island* by Robert Louis Stevenson? Or if something a bit darker and more mysterious would be to your liking. *The Strange Case of Dr. Jekyll and Mr. Hyde* is most original."

"You've read all of those?" He seemed most impressed.

"I have. Those and many more."

"How do you find the time?" His interest remained genuine, and she smiled.

"The library is free, Mr. Bostwick. For those of us whose evenings are not filled with the opera or the symphony or grand balls, there is reading."

He blushed at her answer as if he thought he'd insulted her, but she understood it was an honest error. His life was so different from hers in every single way, how could he even imagine?

How could he know that after Oliver had left her penniless, most of her friends had turned their backs, refusing aid? Or that she'd resorted to moving into the back room of an artist's studio, paying rent by cleaning brushes and sweeping the floors – until that landlord demanded something far more personal than money in payment? How could he know she'd resorted to selling her dresses just to buy food? And how could he know that during those long, lonely, desperate nights, free books from the library had been her only escape – until the job offer for her father had arrived.

"For what it's worth, I rarely go to the opera," he said. "But I do thank you most sincerely for the recommendations." His mood had sobered a bit and she was sorry for it. She liked his casual, playful manner, so different from most men of her acquaintance who were either pompous louts, priggish fops... or diabolically deceitful. Mr. Bostwick appeared to be none of those things. Instead, he was friendly without being false – *or so he seemed.*

"You are most sincerely welcome, Mr. Bostwick. I'll be interested to hear which one you chose and what you think of it. Now, I really must retire. I have a full day tomorrow so I will say goodnight."

"Goodnight, Mrs. Talbot. Best of luck to you with your first class. Daisy will be there and is sure to be a nuisance."

"Then I shall look forward to that as well."

She left him then, standing in the hallway as she made her way back down the hall and up three flights of stairs. Back in her room, she realized a maid had come in and turned down her bed for the night and for some reason *(perhaps there were several reasons)* the gesture made her sit down in a chair and cry. It was so small a thing. An anonymous thing even, for the maid didn't know her. She was just doing her job and had likely turned down the beds in every room on this floor of the hotel. But it had been so long since someone had done something kind for her, and Jo realized she wasn't crying over the covers being turned. She was crying over all of it. The cavalcade of losses and the cruel fragility of her current position. The perpetual uncertainty and the immensity of the work that lay ahead. The shame and the fear and the aloneness of it all. She had no one to turn to. No one to lean on.

And yet... she was also crying for the kindnesses that had come her way from every direction today. Mr. Bostwick, and Daisy, Mr. Parnell bringing her a sandwich, Adele taking such time with her hair, and all the friendly hotel employees who'd greeted Jo warmly in the lounge and encouraged her to join them for breakfast the next morning.

That's why she cried.

She cried because every wonderful thing that had happened to her today gave her reason to *hope*. To hope for something better, for something more, for something *good*, and Jo knew *(oh, she knew!)* that *hope* was the most deceitful force she'd ever wrestled with – because it lied with such ease. It tricked and taunted like a cat with a mouse. It made you want. It made you believe in fantasies, filling your heart and mind with joyful expectations and buoyant anticipation, only to let the vagaries of life snatch it all away. To destroy your dreams like a broken art box.

And yet... even so, Jo ached to believe in hope's divine goodness because without it, life was simply too bleak to bear. Whether a curse or a blessing, at the moment, hope was the single thin reed keeping her from the torrent of the rapids, and so tonight she'd cling to it. With all her might.

nine

"Good morning. We're early. I was excited." Daisy explained breathlessly from the doorway of the spacious room where Jo was currently standing – and staring in frustration – at some large wooden crates piled high upon more large wooden crates. It seemed the hotel had made good on its promise to provide ample art supplies, but currently the boxes, each as tall and wide as steamer trunks, were stacked three high and shoved haphazardly against the lovely, lavender-painted walls and Jo had no idea how to get them unpacked.

Although Daisy was early to arrive, she herself had been late in getting to the studio, having overslept for the first time in her life – no doubt due to the sublime softness of her bed, the sheer exhaustion of her travels, and perhaps, in part, because despite that exhaustion her evening encounter with Mr. Bostwick had kept her mind wide awake with thoughts she had no business having. *(Damn, that face.)* She'd not succumbed to slumber until well into the wee hours of the morning, and the sun had been high in the sky by the time she'd pulled herself from under the satin covers.

Breakfast had been a fast cup of blessedly strong coffee gulped in haste in the employee lounge, and she'd kept her morning ablutions succinct, tying her hair into a simple knot and donning the pale green tea dress she'd left draped over a chair last evening. Her appearance, she'd noted as she'd caught a quick glance in her hotel room mirror, was acceptable, but certainly not stylish. Once again, it seemed she was destined to make a poor first impression. She hoped her new students would find her eccentric rather than sloppy.

But there was Daisy looking as fresh... as a daisy in a bright yellow day dress that suited her name and her sunny disposition. Next to her stood a slender redhead in a lacy, cream-colored ensemble that complemented both the hue of her auburn hair and the brown-rimmed hazel of her eyes. She was quite stunning, the type of woman who would never appear disheveled in public, and Jo wished, for the one-hundredth time that morning that she'd had more time to fuss over her appearance. Fortunately, the woman was smiling as graciously as her companion.

"This is Mrs. O'Keefe," Daisy said, pulling the woman into the room by her wrist. "She's come to paint as well."

The woman chuckled as Daisy tugged her along. Jo estimated she was close to her own age, somewhere in her early twenties, perhaps, and had both flawless skin and an emerald and diamond ring on her left hand so large it must've cost more than an entire summer's worth of lodging at the hotel. It was the kind of ostentatious piece that old money abhorred and new money adored, indicating Mrs. O'Keefe must be the latter.

"Mrs. O'Keefe. How lovely to meet you. And good morning to you both. I'm thrilled you're here, however, I must apologize. I'm not quite ready. Could you come back at ten?" (Not that she'd be ready at ten, either, but at the very least she could find some paper and pencils for an easy sketching lesson. Perhaps they could draw a still life called *Too Many Crates?*)

"What's in the boxes?" Daisy asked, moving to her side, and ignoring Jo's plea.

She bit back a sigh. "I'm hoping it's my supplies. It appears the hotel has gotten everything I asked for, which is wonderful, of course, but it will be a bit time-consuming to unpack. I'm sure when you return, I'll be far more organized. I do hope you'll forgive me for the delay." It was embarrassing to not be ready for her very first students, and if they mentioned her unpreparedness to Mr. Beeks, she'd be on the next boat back to Chicago, but Mrs. O'Keefe's friendly smile never wavered.

"Or we could help you," she said. "If we won't be in your way."

The offer was a genuine surprise which must've shown on Jo's face because the other women laughed.

"Oh, no," Jo said. "I couldn't ask it of you. Go enjoy a cup of tea on the porch and I'll be ready when you come back." *(She probably wouldn't be ready.)*

"I've had three cups of tea this morning already," Mrs. O'Keefe answered. "If I have another, I shall float all the way back to Detroit. And anyhow, Mrs. VonMeisterburger is on the porch and that woman is a church bell clanging all day long. I heard quite enough about her gardener drama last evening." Then she blushed and stole a glance at Daisy. "Oh dear, I'm sorry. She and your mother are friends, aren't they? I didn't mean to offend."

But Daisy's laughter was sincere. "They're only friends because they don't dare to be enemies, and quite honestly, I'm happy to avoid them both. So, please, Mrs. Talbot, let us help you. I'd like to be useful."

"As would I," Mrs. O'Keefe concurred with an emphatic nod.

Jo ought to say no. It wasn't professional to have her blue-blooded, finely dressed, richly bejeweled students helping with such mundane tasks. It was one thing to have them clean up their own supplies, to wash their brushes and make sure all the lids of their paint pots were sufficiently sealed, but this task was going to be actual labor. There were at least a dozen boxes and, in fact, without a crowbar and a few strong men to wield it, Jo wasn't sure even the three of them could manage on their own. The task was more fit for the likes of Mr. Parnell.

But both women were smiling at her expectantly, until Jo

finally relented and said, "Truly, I'd welcome the help if you're sure you don't mind."

"Excellent," said Mrs. O'Keefe, clapping her hands together in a single clap. "Where to begin?"

"I think the first order of business is to find the hotel porter and get these crates unstacked and opened. I know just the man we need."

~

As expected, Mr. Parnell, along with a few other able-bodied men in their blue serge jackets, made short work of opening, unloading, and carting away the now-empty boxes, and as the women organized the contents, Jo's nervousness began to dissipate. She hadn't realized just how very ill at ease she'd been until the feeling lifted, but it was no wonder, really. She desperately needed these classes to be a success so the hotel guests would *(hopefully)* accept her as a talented artist, which would *(hopefully)* garner her portrait commissions which would *(hopefully)* earn her enough money to get to Paris.

There was that pesky word again – *hope*.

When the ten o'clock hour chimed, the room was ready, and so was she. There were easels and canvasses at the ready, sharpened charcoal pencils in jars along with sable brushes and cleaning cloths. Fifteen minutes later, when she realized no other aspiring artists would be joining them, she shrugged off her disappointment as best as she could and decided to give her full attention to Daisy and Mrs. O'Keefe, for they certainly had earned it, as well as her gratitude.

"Well," she said, as the three of them sat down at a long pine table near a large window framed with sheer, white, ruffly curtains. "What is your preference today, ladies? Charcoals? Watercolor? Pastels?"

"I confess I haven't drawn in years," Mrs. O'Keefe said apologetically. "You'll have to start at the very beginning for me."

"Everyone starts at the beginning," Jo assured her. "And the beautiful thing about art is that it's always developing within you. Regardless of your skill today, there's always more to learn. The important thing is to let yourself explore, enjoy the process, and don't judge the quality too harshly. It's hard not to, I'll admit. There were friends of my father's who quit painting altogether because they felt they weren't getting better, and that's the saddest thing of all. Who knows what they might have accomplished if they'd continued on?"

She wouldn't tell them that even her own father had sometimes suffered bouts of melancholy and insecurity that no amount of her encouragement could ease. It was an artist's curse. The quest for perfection in a field that was mercurial and subjective. And to the artist, even the greatest masterpiece had its flaws. The goal was to accept them. To not internalize those flaws on the canvas as flaws within yourself, or in your skill, but rather to see them for what they were. Tiny, misplaced brushstrokes that few others would even notice. And to recognize it was often those very flaws which made a painting unique.

"That's good advice. I'm glad to know you won't be looking for perfection," Mrs. O'Keefe said, smiling, and Jo was struck again by her effortless, unpretentious beauty. She'd make a wonderful subject for a portrait with her ivory skin and deep red hair. She reminded Jo of a delicate ballerina, or a fairy princess. Perhaps if she ever painted her, she'd add a glowing crown and some fanciful wings.

"And what about you, Daisy," Jo asked, turning her way. "What medium do you prefer?"

"I enjoy all of them. I'm probably the most proficient with charcoals but watercolors are what I'd like to improve upon."

"Excellent. Well, let's begin with some sketches so I can see where you're starting."

She pulled out an apple she'd brought from the lounge and set it on the table between them. It was intended to be her lunch, but she could eat it when they were finished. For now, it was their subject.

As the moments floated by, the scritch and scratch of charcoal pencils against linen paper created a welcome, familiar sound. Jo offered intermittent instructions and suggestions, showing them the best way to position their hands or how to add depth with shading, but mostly they talked of other things, their favorite flowers or birds, the remarkable speed at which a locomotive traveled (*New York City to San Francisco in just six days!*), and how very lovely the Imperial Hotel was.

Daisy told them about her friends back in Chicago, and Mrs. O'Keefe revealed she'd thought her husband Percy rather dull the first time she'd met him, but he'd won her over with his subtle humor, his kind nature, and she admitted with a rosy blush, his propensity to steal her kisses when no one else was looking.

"He still does. All the time. So, what drew you to your husband, Mrs. Talbott? Does he try to steal your kisses?" she teased, and Jo nearly scowled at the irony. Her kisses were essentially the only thing Oliver *hadn't* stolen. Those she'd given willingly.

"Mr. Talbot charmed me from the very first moment we met," Jo answered. (*That was true enough.*) "I was utterly under his spell."

"Was?" Daisy prompted.

Jo's own musings had caught her off guard. "What? Oh, I mean, I am still. Of course. It's just that the nature of men when they're wooing changes once they're wed so naturally it makes marriage quite different from courtship, wouldn't you agree, Mrs. O'Keefe?"

Jo looked to her for affirmation but at Mrs. O'Keefe's uncertain expression, she added hastily, "But then again, our honeymoon was cut short by the passing of my father so perhaps my experience has been unique." *Unique, indeed.*

"Oh, I'm sorry to hear about your father. Did he pass recently?" Mrs. O'Keefe seemed glad to change the subject, as if talking about dead parents was preferable to dissecting the state of Jo's marriage, and she wondered if she should steer the topic toward something frivolous and light to keep her students in a cheery state of mind. It wouldn't do to have them morose as they left, or they'd never come back!

But no one had asked about her father in such a long time, Jo found herself tearing up. "Last year," she said, "but it feels like yesterday. I miss him terribly."

"Oh, dear," said Daisy, reaching over and squeezing Jo's wrist. "How very sad. I should be desperately forlorn if something happened to my father. And what of your mother?"

Ah, yes, what of her mother?

"I'm afraid she died when I was quite young. I don't remember her. But Papa told me stories, and he'd painted a dozen portraits of her so at least I know what she looked like."

She tried to say that last bit brightly, as if stories and paintings made up for her having no mother. Or for having a terrible one since the stories she'd heard had only been told once, and only because her father had been ruinously drunk and was shouting at those very same portraits.

Because it seemed Jo's mother hadn't, in fact, died but had, instead, left them both soon after Jo was born. She sometimes wondered if her father's string of audacious, meaningless affairs were because his broken heart had never healed, and lately she'd also wondered if Oliver's betrayal would doom her to the same fate.

"I do know she was French," Jo added with a false smile, still hoping to bring up the mood. "She loved to drink chocolate and called me *bébé potelé* so I must've been chubby."

She laughed as she said it, glad that the harmless fabrication made the other women smile. And who knows? It *might* have been true, or it might have been simply one of the many fantasies she conjured up about a mother she'd never met and knew so little about.

"Chubby baby," Daisy said with a giggle. *"Pouvez-vous parler français?"*

Jo shook her head. "Only a little and I must improve if I'm to move to Paris in the autumn."

"You're moving to Paris? How divine," Daisy said with a dreamy sigh.

"Paris is especially lovely in the autumn," Mrs. O'Keefe agreed. "Mr. O'Keefe and I went there on our honeymoon tour last year and soon realized that neither of us is as conversant in French as we'd thought. I fear we shocked a great many Parisians by saying the wrong thing."

"Je parle Français couramment. Je peux être ton tuteur," Daisy said, then laughed at their bewildered expressions. "I said, 'I speak French fluently and I can be you your tutor.' We could practice while we paint. Two birds with one stone. *Deux oiseaux avec une pierre.* Only when it's just the three of us, of course. I'm sure the other classes will be much more crowded."

Jo was hoping perhaps (*just perhaps*) they hadn't noticed no one else had shown up.

"Apparently not everyone is as eager to study art as you are, Daisy," Jo said. "But I do hope you're right. Mr. Beeks was quite disappointed to learn he'd hired me instead of my father. I suspect he's looking for a reason to escort me to the door, or should I say *the dock?*" Her laughter was unconvincing, and Daisy's smooth brow wrinkled with concern.

"Can he do that?"

"Well, I suppose if there aren't enough students, there's no need for an instructor but I'm sure it won't come to that. I just need to make myself visible and ensure the hotel guests know I'm available. I'm hoping to entice a few guests to commission portraits. That being the case... I hope you won't think this too forward, but I wonder if I might paint a small portrait of each of you? At no charge, of course! But if I could display them in the lobby, I think it would encourage others to seek me out."

"You would paint my portrait?" All the worry left Daisy's expression to be replaced with girlish awe.

"It would be my honor," Jo answered truthfully. A portrait of Daisy Bostwick, even a small one done for free, would be a great accolade to claim and was sure to enhance her reputation. Not to mention it would show Mr. Beeks she'd meant what she said about painting the young Bostwick – even though she'd been stretching the truth at the time.

"*J'adorerais que mon portrait soit peint, et j'aimerais améliorer mon Français,*" said Mrs. O'Keefe. "Yes, to the portrait and *oui* to practicing my French. In fact, my wedding anniversary to Mr. O'Keefe is coming up. What a delightful gift it would be to surprise him with a portrait. But I insist on paying for it. And I'll whisper to everyone I meet how excessively expensive it was."

"Oh, that's too kind of you, Mrs. O'Keefe," Jo said. "But wouldn't being expensive deter others?"

Mrs. O'Keefe's smile grew mischievous, and she leaned forward as if to share a confidence. "One might think that, but I've learned over the past few years that nothing makes the wealthy feel quite so self-important as paying a ridiculous amount for something. It's rather butter upon bacon if you ask me, but neither Mr. O'Keefe nor I came from money. Now that we have an abundance, I insist upon paying you an exorbitant amount for my portrait."

"Then I shall pay an exorbitant amount for mine as well," added Daisy with a determined nod. "Or rather, my father will."

"Oh, my goodness," responded Jo. "You're both entirely too generous. You've already helped me set this room to rights. I should like to pay you both back for those kindnesses with free portraits. Mrs. O'Keefe, perhaps you could just pretend you paid for it?"

"Nonsense, I won't dicker with you. And you must call me Ruth. We are all friends now, are we not?"

Tears threatened Jo's eyes again, but they were of the joyful sort. Happy tears, for it had been a long time since she'd had a friend she could rely upon and now it seemed she had two, not to mention the lovely hotel employees she'd met in the lounge last evening. Perhaps her luck had truly taken a turn for the better. That thin reed of hope she'd been clinging to suddenly felt sturdier.

"I should be honored to have you both as my friends. Please call me Jo."

"Jo? Not Emerson?" Daisy asked.

"No, my father was Emerson James, and I am Emerson Joan, but my closest friends call me Jo, and so now must you."

ten

"It's nearly noon. Go find your sister," Chase's mother said from the dainty, white wicker rocking chair on the hotel's massive front porch. "We need to eat lunch soon so we can go on our drive this afternoon."

Chase looked up from his newspaper, which was now four days old, and cast a wayward glance at his mother. She wore a long-sleeved, high-neck peach-colored morning dress and sat fully in the shade with a fringed silk parasol nearly covering her face. Heaven forbid the sun should touch any sliver of her skin and give her a freckle. Only the working class had freckles.

"I have no idea where she is, Mother. I wouldn't begin to know where to look."

He was in no mood to go on their afternoon outing and had no interest in aiding and abetting his mother's attempted land grab. He just wanted to finish re-reading this outdated article about a March blizzard that had buried much of the east coast under forty feet of snow and count down the days until he heard something back from his father or his brother. Surely one of them would take pity and call him home because his late evening, not-so-accidental excursion with Mrs. Talbot had left him more irritable than ever.

After she'd left him standing in the hallway, he'd made his way to the reading room, searched in vain for any of the books she'd mentioned, or anything that might captivate him as thoroughly as had the gentle curve of her cheek, but found nothing. *(Nothing!)* He'd resorted to grabbing a random something from the shelf without reading the spine and only when he was back in his own room did he realize it was *poetry.* For God's sake. Poetry.

He'd then dashed off another note to Mr. Hayden asking him to send a copy of that Dr. Jekyll book and went to bed – where he tossed and turned and tossed and turned until at last drifting into a restless sleep full of dreams about Mrs. Talbot eating a piece of lemon meringue pie in the most sinfully provocative manner.

"She's taking an art class with that woman," his mother responded. "Although they should've finished long before now. Good heavens! How long does it take to draw a picture?"

Chase all but grimaced. Daisy was with Mrs. Talbot. Of course, she was. How had he managed to block that relevant piece of information from his mind? With practice, perhaps? Since he'd had a night full of trying *not to* think of her which only served to make him think about her that much more. It was ridiculous.

But with the morning came a fresh sense of things. A new resolve. He was being juvenile, letting his libido run circles around his mind. Yes, she was pretty, but not remarkably so. Lots of women were pretty. And while he'd given her credit for being bold and courageous, was she? (*Was she really?)* Or rather was she *imprudent?* And perhaps a bit *impudent,* as well. Was her plucky sense of humor a tad too cheeky? Too brash? Was she altogether just too... much?

Yes, taken as a whole, Mrs. Talbot was simply too much, and had he encountered her in Chicago, he'd have not given her a second thought. (*Would he? No. Likely not.)* This mild infatuation was simply the result of proximity and tedium and the fact that he'd been so tied up in knots over his brother's engagement to Isabella Carnegie he hadn't made the time in months to visit his lovely widow friend's bed.

Thankfully, the Imperial Hotel was hosting a dance on Saturday night in the grand ballroom. He would go to it and see all the other pretty women in their organza gowns, with their ruffles and their curves, and then these ruminations of Mrs. Talbot indulging her sweet tooth and licking meringue from a spoon would dissipate.

But in the meantime, he'd go tell his sister it was time for lunch.

Checking at the front desk, he got directions which were, fortunately, more accurate than those he'd received last night, and in minutes he found himself in the hallway near the art studio. He could hear laughter coming through an open doorway and recognized Daisy's girlish guffaw. He slowed his steps, suddenly curious to know what topic of conversation had the women in such a state of good humor.

Again, he heard his sister. "And then Alex gave him a hearty kick to the backside, and Chase fell face first right into the pig slop!"

More peals of laughter, and Chase's face burned at the realization they were laughing because of him. At him. Daisy had no business telling such stories to outsiders. He'd give her a stern talking to as soon as they were alone, but then he recognized Mrs. Talbot's voice.

"Oh, goodness, Daisy. That makes me feel ever so much better. You cannot imagine the horror of being so unkempt yesterday, and I must say, your brother was a champion for not laughing at me himself. He acted as if I had nothing more than a smudge on my skirt."

Chase straightened his shoulders. *Well... that was good to hear.* It didn't absolve Daisy, of course, but at least it had brought the accident-prone Mrs. Talbot some comfort. He stepped inside the doorframe and was mildly relieved to see the room wasn't full of women It was just his sister, Mrs. O'Keefe, and Mrs. Talbot. Still, Daisy had no business...

He gave a discreet cough to announce his arrival and they all turned at the sound.

"My sister is far too free with tales of my humiliation," he said. "And my brother came out the worse for it. I got my revenge, but I won't bore you with the details."

"My brothers are very competitive," Daisy said, adding in French, "*Et Alex gagne presque toujour,*" as if he wasn't fluent enough to know she said, "Alex always wins." His cheeks heated up another degree.

"Daisy," he scolded, his tone sharper than he'd intended because she was poking him with a fork again, if only figuratively, and the other women had laughed. He was a fine sport most of the time and not opposed to a good ribbing, but this time he was not in on the joke. He was the butt of it. "Mother is waiting on you for lunch. It's time to go."

His sister turned to her companions, unremorseful and seemingly indifferent to his agitation. "Oh, this has been such fun, ladies. Won't you both join us for lunch?"

His jaw clenched involuntarily. After a sleepless night of imagining Mrs. Talbot eating a slice of pie, actually watching her do it would be a particular exercise in frustration. That Saturday night dance could not come soon enough. Thankfully, Mrs. Talbot rejected the invitation.

"Thank you, Daisy, but I have some work I need to do before my afternoon class."

"And I have plans with my husband," Mrs. O'Keefe said, rising gracefully from her chair. "I think we're touring the hotel today. I'll see you tomorrow, though. Perhaps I can try my hand at drawing a pear since I did so well with the apple."

Chase gazed around the room as his sister took her sweet time in saying her goodbyes, as if the women were the closest of friends bidding adieu before a long voyage, but Daisy was sentimental that way. She'd inherited all of their father's gregarious generosity and none of their mother's pragmatic detachment. Today he would prefer the latter.

"Did you find a book, Mr. Bostwick?" Mrs. Talbot asked once Daisy had stepped away, forcing him to look at her. Her hair was up, but loosely so, and she wore the same pale green dress she'd had on last night. Not that he paid much attention to what women did with their hair or what they wore. Usually...

"None of the ones you suggested, unfortunately, but I found something," he said.

"Oh, good. What did you choose?" Her smile was expectant and seemed full of genuine interest.

"Uh... Tennyson," he answered after an awkward pause, and his sister let out an unladylike squawk.

"You're reading Tennyson? Gadzooks, you are bored!" Daisy exclaimed, bringing an additional flush to his already heated cheeks.

"Perhaps I'm trying to broaden my tastes," he said tersely. "I am capable, you know."

"Good for you, Mr. Bostwick. I do hope you enjoy your reading," Mrs. Talbot said. "And if I may, are you familiar with Ulysses?"

"Is he a poet?" Chase found himself teasing her. (He was not so unlettered as to not know of the epic Ulysses. He'd never *read* it, of course, but he had *heard* of it.)

She smiled back. "Very clever. But if you haven't read it recently, I think, given your present circumstances, it might resonate with you."

"How so?" Nothing about his present circumstances lent itself to poetry as far as he could see.

"*How dull it is to pause, to make an end, to rust unburnish'd, not to shine in use!*" she replied, and he was struck anew.

Damnit. She was worthy of his infatuation.

"Ah, yes," he said. "Indeed." He could think of nothing more to add for she addlepated his senses, gazing at him the way she did, without a hint of guile, and it would not do for her or anyone else to notice his attraction to her. He motioned to his sister. "Daisy, now."

Moments later he was striding down the hall, his sister bounding along at his side. She was practically bouncing with exuberance.

"You had no business sharing that story about me, Daisy," he said as soon as they were out of earshot of the others. "Think of how ridiculous that made me look."

"It made you look dotty, all right," she answered with an unrepentant snicker. "But I only shared it because Jo was recounting her experience of meeting you yesterday afternoon and lamenting upon the poor impression she'd made."

"Jo?"

"Yes, Mrs. Talbot."

So, her name was Jo? It suited her. Short, sweet, informal. "And you are on a first name acquaintance with her already? Do you really think that's proper?"

"Why wouldn't it be? We're the best of friends. And guess what else?"

Chase was trying to scold his sister for her oversharing and lack of propriety, but Daisy's mood was so effervescent she failed to notice, all but skipping next to him as they headed toward the lobby.

"What?" he asked with a resigned huff. No wonder their mother was trying so hard to bring this girl to heel. She was incorrigible.

"Jo wants to paint my portrait! One of just me, not some silly family gathering. Can you imagine? Pearl Mahoney hasn't had a portrait painted of her. I'll be the first of all the girls I know. I'll be the envy!"

"Mrs. Talbot wants to paint your portrait?" His stomach gave an odd twist, but he didn't know why. Why should it matter if Mrs. Talbot – Jo – painted his little sister's portrait? Why should it matter that Daisy so casually addressed the woman by her first name or professed them to be the best of friends? And why should it matter that Mrs. Talbot had quoted Ulysses to him with a line that succinctly encapsulated his current state of mind? As if she knew him. As if she *understood* him. He'd told her as much last night so this was not some remarkable insight into his psyche, and yet... it had seemed a personal moment, a shared exchange that only the two of them knew about, and that made it feel... special.

His stomach gave another turn. Perhaps it was just hunger. It was lunchtime, after all. Hunger was to be expected. Yes. That's what it was.

Chase was hungry.

And thirsty.

eleven

"Mrs. Talbot?"

Jo looked up from the roll of canvas in her hands to find a man so tall and narrow he could have been the mast of a schooner. His dark green and brown plaid sack suit hung loosely on a frame, and a streak of white ran through his thick black hair giving him the look of a dashing but spindly skunk.

"Yes, hello. I'm Mrs. Talbot. May I help you?"

He entered the studio and came quickly to her side, his easy smile creating deep crevices in both narrow cheeks as he reached out a twig-like arm to shake her hand.

"So good to meet you. I'm Jullian Tippett, Social Director for the Imperial Hotel. My apologies for not having sought you out sooner but I only recently learned of your arrival. Please forgive me."

His congenial demeanor put her instantly at ease. "No apology necessary, Mr. Tippett. I arrived rather late yesterday afternoon."

"Yes, yes, and I heard there was some squabble with Beeks. Please allow me to apologize on his behalf and extend my warmest greetings. I'm familiar with your father's work and if you inherited half of his artistic talents then our guests will be in good hands."

A wave of relief washed over her. "Thank you, Mr. Tippett. I'm ever so eager to be useful to the hotel."

"Wonderful. Wonderful," he said, adjusting the wire-rimmed spectacles perched on his beaklike nose and glancing around the room. "It appears you've made yourself at home. Glad to see it. Are these supplies satisfactory? I tried to obtain everything you requested but sometimes getting things to the island is a bit of gamble."

"Yes, thank you. I'm still organizing but everything seems to be here."

"Splendid. Splendid. Now, I was hoping to discuss some plans I have with regard to your duties. Are you available to meet with me now? Or perhaps later this afternoon?"

"Of course. According to Mr. Beeks, my next class isn't until 2:00 p.m. so I am entirely at your service," she answered.

He shook his head. "Mr. Beeks is misinformed. When you didn't arrive as planned, I removed you from our daily roster of activities until we knew for certain you'd be here. I hope you haven't been sitting here waiting for attendees."

Ah, hopefully that was why no one came to her first class. "Please do accept my apologies for the delay in my arrival, Mr. Tippett. We had inclement weather on the lake," she said, setting down the roll of canvas.

He nodded, unperturbed. "That's to be expected this time of year. I'm just glad you arrived safe and sound. Now, has anyone taken you on a tour of the hotel?"

"No, not yet. I did do a bit of exploring on my own, but a tour would be most welcome."

"Excellent. Excellent. In that case, might I suggest we have a quick lunch in the main dining room and discuss a few things, and then I'll take you on the tour myself. Unless you've already eaten?"

The apple she'd brought from the lounge was long gone, and

Jo's mouth watered at the thought of eating in the Imperial Hotel dining room. Judging from the leftovers she'd found in the employee lounge, the food was sure to be scrumptious.

"Lunch would be lovely. Thank you."

"The dining room is two-hundred and thirteen feet long with a ceiling height of twenty-seven feet," Mr. Tippett informed her as they lingered at a table in a back corner of the opulent room.

For such a slender man, he ate like a farmer and had been peppering her with details about the hotel since the moment they'd left her studio. She sincerely hoped she wasn't expected to remember all the minutiae about how many pine planks made up the floor. Perhaps Mr. Beeks would question her later and if she failed to recall that the dining room windows were twelve feet tall, she'd have yet another mark against her, but she could not deny that the hotel was indeed grand.

From her velvet cushioned Morris chair, she noted dozens of gilt-framed mirrors adorning the pearl-colored walls, and the lovely way sunshine poured in and bounced off the crystal chandeliers sending tiny rainbows in every direction. Above the expansive front entrance was a balcony where the musicians played in the evenings, and off to the side was a smaller dining room for patron's children.

"The residents of the island have taken to calling this the Mansion on the Hill and I'm sure you can see why," he said, adding another cherry scone to his plate. "The Island House has nothing on us, nor does the Astor Hotel, but you see, it's not merely enough to surround our guests in luxury and elegance. We must also keep them entertained throughout their stay. In fact, not only do we want our guests to remain on the property as much as possible, but we also want to draw in patrons from other locations. Therefore, starting next week, we plan to host lawn games every Wednesday, open to the public. Tennis, archery, foot races, and the like. We'll host music programs on Tuesdays, and on Saturday evenings we'll have a visiting orchestra in to play all the latest music as well as the familiar classics, of course. We've hired a dancing master from France, a Mr. VanderLinden, and there are discussions of a horse show, a field day, a casino night, and so much more! You see, my job is to make the Imperial Hotel the epicenter of activities for the entire island."

His enthusiasm was infectious, and somewhat intimidating. Energy radiated from him like one of Mr. Edison's new lightbulbs. "My goodness. That's a tall order," she said, sipping sweet, fresh, lemonade from a crystal glass.

"Yes, it is a tall order and I'm hoping you'll help me achieve it."

She choked a little at his words. Clearing her throat, she said, "Me? Of course, I'm happy to oblige in whatever way I may." She was sincere, but not naive enough to think her artistic skills were sufficient to lure people to the hotel. She wasn't even certain she could lure the current guests to one of her classes!

Mr. Tippett seemed oblivious to her discomfort and continued on. "Excellent. Excellent. I'm glad to hear that because Mr. Beeks and I are not in full agreement as to what your duties should actually be. When we created your position, well, forgive me for being insensitive, but we were thinking of your father and how our older guests might enjoy getting to know him, hearing of his travels, his life story. However, having met you, I personally think the fact that you're a young woman at the beginning of her artistic journey is entirely to our advantage."

Jo had no idea how that was an advantage, but Mr. Tippett was about to inform her.

He leaned forward and lowered his voice. "To be perfectly frank, Mrs. Talbot, we anticipate that most of our older guests will return here each summer just to see each other. They want fine food, plush accommodations, and an elite space to mingle with their peers. We can provide that in spades, but it's the younger set we'd like to turn into lifelong visitors, and to them, you'll be much more appealing. You're young, pretty, progressive, a bit of a novelty."

He took a bite of the scone and chewed thoughtfully as a prickly sensation took hold at the back of Jo's neck. She wasn't interested in being a novelty, and she was even *less* interested in creating friction between Mr. Beeks and Mr. Tippett.

"This position is quite important to me, Mr. Tippett," Jo said reluctantly. "I'm dedicated to fulfilling whatever role you see for me but must confess I'm concerned about alienating Mr. Beeks. We did not get off on the best footing yesterday." She might have kept that to herself, but it seemed Mr. Tippett had already heard, and did not care. He waved his hand as if shooing away a pesky gnat.

"You need not concern yourself with Beeks. Trust me, the man has no imagination whatsoever. He's the stodgy sort, set in his ways and determined to see the world as it was. I'm a visionary, just like Mr. Plank, if you'll forgive me for the comparison. This is his hotel, his dream, and he doesn't want our guests to go home thinking they've just had a pleasant holiday. He wants them to go home knowing they've had an *experience*."

Again, Jo wasn't sure how she was meant to fit into this *vision*. She would certainly bring her own passion for art to the guests, but she would have done that anyway. Did he want something more? Something different?

"I recall from your portfolio you're proficient with caricatures. Is that correct?" Mr. Tippett asked.

"Um... yes, quite proficient." She didn't consider caricatures to be art so much as they were doodles but in the right circumstances, she didn't mind doing them. Still, hardly the stuff of unique *experience*. Perhaps he thought to have her draw them while standing on her head?

"And how do you feel about working with an audience?"

"An audience?" Good Lord, did he mean for her to be on stage? On her head, and on stage?

"Yes, for instance, what if we were to set you up in the lobby or on the front porch where you could do caricatures or charcoal drawings for our guests? Or perhaps you could even work on someone's portrait if we found a willing participant. People could observe you while you worked. I think they might enjoy that. What do you say?"

She'd say it wasn't ideal. There were messy stages to progress through before landing on the final product and she didn't necessarily want people to pass by and judge her abilities on an unfinished piece.

"I suppose I could do caricatures or drawings in a more public place, but a portrait is an intimate thing between an artist and the sitter. It requires trust. Perhaps I could work on one in the studio and only people who were truly interested in learning could come and watch. I've plans to paint both Miss Bostwick and Mrs. O'Keefe. They might be agreeable to this. How does that sound?"

"I like that. It's a good compromise. A very good compromise." He nodded, taking a small notepad from an interior pocket of his plaid jacket along with a tiny pencil and jotting some notes. The respite from conversation gave her a moment to formulate her next thought.

"Mr. Tippett, not to beleaguer this point, but how will Mr. Beeks feel about me being in the lobby?" Perhaps she was worrying over nothing but as the general manager, it seemed Mr. Beeks was the one to keep happy about her presence.

"Oh, he's entirely opposed to it but he's also entirely wrong." Mr. Tippett's tone was light, almost dismissive but it made her heart sink and she felt compelled to add, "And might I inquire as to which of the two of you is my... supervisor?"

Is that how she should phrase it? She was contracted by the hotel – via a contract signed by Mr. Beeks – but she was not a typical *employee*. Once again, she was living her life in the grey space between two worlds, fully belonging to neither.

"I'm your supervisor. Technically Mr. Beeks is mine, but we all work for Mr. Plank, and Mr. Plank loves my ideas. I promise, you have nothing to worry about."

That did not ease her worries. At all.

In fact, it sounded very much like something Oliver would've said.

Trust me. It'll be fine.

Just finish that painting. No one will know.

Just sign these house papers. It's a formality.

Just lift those skirts, we'll soon be married.

"We could also have you available at the Saturday night dances. Would that be acceptable?" Mr. Tippett asked, moving on from the topic of Mr. Beeks without allaying her concerns.

"At the dances? For what purpose?"

Mr. Tippett shrugged although his shoulders were so dainty his jacket barely moved.

"To draw caricatures, or to dance if you're asked. Some of the older gentlemen have trouble finding partners among the young ladies and as social director, it's my job to make sure everyone feels a part of all the festivities. That's only if you feel comfortable, though. You needn't participate in anything that doesn't appeal to you. It's completely your decision."

Well, *there* was something Oliver never said. And anyway, all Mr. Tippett was really asking was for her to be sociable. Dancing with a few grabby grandfathers was hardly the worst thing. She knew how to avoid a lecherous hand, and maybe if she flirted a bit *(just a bit)* she might even convince a few of them to request a portrait. This might actually work to her advantage, and she needed every advantage she could get.

"Yes, I suppose I could attend the dances."

"Excellent! Excellent. And now that I think of it, do you play Euchre? We're having a tournament soon and we may need you to sit in for a hand or two if one of the players needs a break."

"Um...yes. although I haven't played in quite some time. I'm not sure I remember all the rules." And also not sure how that fit into her job as artist.

"That's fine. We'll have a few refresher rounds before the tournament starts."

He scribbled more notes onto his little pad of paper while she pondered over this strange turn of events. He wanted her to draw caricatures, play cards, and... dance with old men? Then he went so far as to inquire if she rode horses or bikes, swam, played croquet, enjoyed archery, or could balance an egg on a spoon. Where was he going with all this?

"I ride horses occasionally, bikes never, swim rarely, have played croquet many times, and I am quite adept with a bow and arrow. But I have not, to the best of my recollection, ever tried to balance an egg on a spoon. Is that something people typically practice?"

Mr. Tippett chuckled with good humor. "I should think not but that's half the fun. Trying something silly you've never tried before. So, are you game?"

"Game for which thing?" Her head was starting to throb from this strange interrogation, little of which seemed to have anything to do with *art* – the thing for which she had been hired.

"Any of it. All of it?" he said optimistically. "I'm hoping to assemble a core group of personable, energetic employees dedicated to representing the hotel in the best possible way. People full of vitality, eager to participate in the festivities, but more importantly, ones who'll encourage our visitors to do the same. Sometimes guests are reluctant to join in and it's our job to get them involved. We want to make them feel as if we're all one big, jovial family."

Goodness gracious. "But will I still have time to offer painting classes?"

"Oh, to be sure. We'll work out a flexible schedule of when you're teaching classes or doing other artistic things around the hotel and grounds, but when you're not teaching, I do hope you'll join us for these other activities. I'm sure the guests would enjoy getting to know you, and naturally, since none of this is part of your original contract there would be an additional stipend."

Additional stipend? She definitely liked the sound of that, and it wasn't as if she had anything to occupy her time outside of her artist-in-residence duties. Everything Mr. Tippett had mentioned sounded fine, enjoyable even, with the only drawback being the potential opposition of the hotel manager.

"If you're sure it won't cause friction with Mr. Beeks then I'd be happy to participate in any activities where I'm needed."

Mr. Tippett smiled. "Wonderful! Wonderful. I'm glad to hear of it. And don't worry about Beeks. His bark is worse than his bite. I'll handle him. Now, shall we take that tour of the hotel?"

twelve

Hugo Plank was a man to be admired, and Chase liked him very much.

He especially liked the fact that the builder and owner of the Imperial Hotel had just offered to take them all on an extensive tour of the properties directly after lunch, thereby rescuing Chase from having to take his mother on her scouting mission disguised as an aimless carriage ride. And she couldn't argue with this change in agenda because Breezy VonMeisterburger was right there next to her, and the woman would surely be suspicious if such an invitation were refused.

"We'd be delighted to take a tour with you this afternoon," Chase answered before anyone else could chime in. Daisy giggled – because she was clever and knew exactly what he was about. His mother also knew what he was about. (*She did not giggle.*)

They assembled in the lobby some fifteen minutes later, Chase with his visibly pouting mother and perpetually excitable little sister, along with the ever-smiling Mr. O'Keefe and his equally smiley wife, a dour and rather gruff Mr. Crocker whom they'd only just met, and cross-eyed Morty VonMeisterburger who informed them his mother had begged off, complaining of a bout of indigestion.

"She doesn't have indigestion. The woman can eat anything. She has the constitution of a goat," Chase's mother whispered curtly in his ear. "She's scheming, and we're about to lose the most coveted piece of property on the entire west bluff just because you want to see what the inside of a hotel kitchen looks like. Alex would have taken me on the carriage ride."

"Oh, trust me, Mother. No one wishes Alex were here in my stead more than I do," Chase responded, just as curtly. He moved away, closer to Mr. Plank. Surely his mother's grousing would cease if she thought the hotel owner could hear her. (*One would hope.*)

"I know some of you have been here for a few days," began Mr. Plank, "but please do allow me to officially welcome you to the Imperial Hotel." He turned, spreading his arms wide and grinning like a circus ringmaster. He was a tall man, barrel-chested with sand-colored hair, a rather large proboscis, and the wingspan of an eagle. "It is an honor and a privilege to be your host and earnestly hope your visit with us this summer will be just the first of many. As we walk, please feel free to ask any questions. And ladies, if you need a moment to rest, do be sure to let me know. I've been told my stride is rather difficult to keep up with."

The tour began and as they wound around the expansive, richly decorated lobby, past the pale-hued tea room, a dark-paneled cigar study, a milliner's shoppe stocked with seemingly every variety of hat, and the elusive reading room (for which Chase now felt an odd affinity), Mr. Plank provided a myriad of details ranging from the utterly mundane to the uniquely fascinating, and since Chase would rather be listening to virtually anything other than his mother, he found himself feeling satisfied and rather entertained.

"All this white pine was milled in Michigan's Upper Peninsula and brought here over the ice when the lake froze last January," Mr. Plank explained. "Then it took my 600-man construction crew just ninety-three days from start to finish to get my hotel completed. Three shifts working around the clock. They lived in tents on the front lawn. Can you imagine, just six months ago all I had in this very spot was a mile-high pile of wood in a muddy field. But now, it's a marvel!" His eyes sparkled as if he, himself, was seeing it all for the very first time. "I have merged impeccable style with thoughtful design, from the Aubusson rugs under your feet right up to the tip of the spire on the 4th floor cupola. Every element, and adornment, every knob, pull, and bell was chosen with the utmost care."

Chase nearly chuckled at the hyperbole sensing Mr. Plank was as much a salesman as he was an architect. As if he didn't realize they'd already reserved rooms for the entire summer, and even if they hadn't, fancy doorknobs were not likely the thing to make them stay. Nonetheless, the man's sense of pride in his hotel was as understandable as it was enviable. It was something Chase could relate to – a job well done. That feeling of accomplishment in knowing he'd *made* something happen. He'd made a difference somehow. That his actions had value and purpose, and therefore, so did he.

"In addition to everything we offer on the main floor," Mr. Plank was saying, "upstairs we have two hundred and eighty-six superbly appointed guest rooms. The Island House only has one hundred and fifty." This he added as an aside, as if one hundred and fifty guest rooms were so subpar as to barely warrant mentioning.

"Good afternoon, Mr. Plank!" A voice called out from the hallway behind them, and Chase turned to see a stovepipe of a man loping toward them with Mrs. Talbot trailing in his wake. Naturally. Nearly three hundred rooms in this gargantuan place and still he kept crossing paths with her. Divine intervention? Or the devil playing tricks?

"Ah, Mr. Tippett!" Mr. Plank called back. "Ladies and gentlemen, have you had the pleasure of meeting our Mr. Tippett? He's the hotel's social director extraordinaire, in charge of all our fabulous entertainment and activities. If there's anything, anything at all you'd like to do, he's the man to see.

And who have we here?" He gestured to Mr. Tippett's companion.

Chase noted the sudden flush on Mrs. Talbot's face as her hand moved to tidy her hair. To no avail. She wasn't remotely the disaster she'd been in the coach yesterday, and she'd looked entirely presentable – if somewhat casual – this morning, but a few extra pins in that mass of dark curls was certainly in order because once again, she had tendrils escaping. (*By God, when had he become such an expert in ladies' coiffures?*)

"Oh, it's Mrs. Talbot!" Daisy squeaked and waved and tugged the sleeve of Mrs. O'Keefe as if Mrs. O'Keefe might not recognize the woman from two hours ago in the art studio.

"Who?" demanded Chase's mother, squinting although her eyesight was perfectly fine.

"The artist, Mummy. Certainly, you remember." Daisy waved again, and Mrs. Talbot responded with a very tiny, almost indiscernible wave back.

More squinting from his mother. "Ah. Of course. *The artist.* That explains her dishabille. She must have been roving the streets again."

"For God's sake, Mother," Chase muttered. He thought to add more but Mr. Tippett was making introductions.

"Mr. Plank, sir. Please allow me to introduce our artist in residence, Mrs. Talbot. She just arrived yesterday and already I'm certain she'll be a wonderful addition to the Imperial Hotel family."

"How do you do, Mr. Plank?" She reached out an arm to shake his hand and Chase's mother all but flinched at the breech in protocol. A lady did not instigate contact with a gentleman. He must extend his hand first, not the other way around. And... she wasn't wearing gloves. Egad. She may as well have been standing there in nothing but her unmentionables as far as Constance Bostwick was concerned.

Chase's mother didn't say as much but he'd known the woman all his life, and she did not suffer impropriety lightly. She seemed determined to dislike Mrs. Talbot and he had no idea why. He also had no idea why that should bother – or surprise – him. His mother didn't like anyone.

"A delight to make your acquaintance, Mrs. Talbot," said Mr. Plank, shaking her hand and seeming not at all affronted by her manner. "I understand from Mr. Beeks there's been a slight misunderstanding but rest assured, it's a pleasure to have you here."

Her cheeks took on a rosier hue. "Thank you, Mr. Plank. I intend to be an asset in every way."

"Of course, you will, I have no doubt."

He turned his attention to Mr. Tippett. "We've just toured the front rooms of the main floor and I thought to take our guests to the gardens next. Where might you be headed?"

"Ah, how fortunate. We were just heading to the gardens as well. I wonder if I might hand off Mrs. Talbot to you then? I have some appointments this afternoon I'd like to prepare for."

"Certainly. Mrs. Talbot, you are most welcome to join us."

Daisy gave another squeak of delight at this turn of events while Chase tamped down a sigh of frustration. Discretion was the better part of valor and during lunch, he'd once again come to the conclusion that avoiding Mrs. Talbot was in the best interest of them both. And yet here she was, looking flushed and adorably unsophisticated – with untidy hair that conjured up an image in his mind of kisses made in haste, kisses from an ardent lover who could not keep his hands to himself. He stuffed his fists into his pockets, just to be on the safe side as Mr. Tippett took his leave.

"Mother, you must meet Mrs. Talbot," Daisy said, all but pushing Chase out of the way. "She's a delight and you're sure to adore her."

His sister was either blindly obtuse or doggedly determined to make their mother a devotee. Either way, Daisy made the introductions with as much pomp as the situation allowed. His mother, to his relief, was cool but not rudely so, and for her part, Mrs. Talbot greeted her and the other members of the tour with a smile and a nod, but thankfully, no more handshakes. She offered Chase a tentative glance in his direction since they'd already met. (*And then some.*)

Once outside, the tour commenced and as they strolled along the front porch from one end to the other Chase noted how the air was rich with the scent of recently bloomed lilacs, newly hewn lumber, and... something else. It took him a moment to realize what he smelled was an *absence* of soot, smoke, and the crush of humanity found in Chicago. Air so pure the educator and orator Horace Mann called it *Eden fresh*, alleging it was sure to increase your brain power.

Perhaps that's why Chase's imagination was running in haphazard circles, wild as a boy just out of short pants. He was getting too much fresh, clean, untainted air! Yet another reason for him to return home where the pollutants of city life would keep him focused on his work. If he'd had more sense, he'd have forgone writing a letter to his father and sent a telegram instead. It would have been faster. Except that it wouldn't because the island had no such capability. *Foiled again by this remote rock.*

"As well as being a premier resort destination," Mr. Plank was saying, blissfully unaware of Chase's regret at being here, "my Imperial Hotel is the most coveted employer on the island, almost single-handedly keeping its economy strong. In addition to my dedicated interior staff such as maids, waiters, chefs, et cetera, I employ over one hundred carriage drivers, stable hands, blacksmiths, groundskeepers, field guides, carpenters, even golf caddies."

"Caddies? Is there a golf course?" Mr. Crocker asked. It was the first thing he'd said since the start of the tour.

"Yes, there is. Wawashkamo golf course is just northwest of where we are now."

"Wawashkamo? What kind of a name is that?" His tone implied dislike, regardless of its origin.

"It means *crooked path*," Mr. Plank explained. "The first inhabitants here considered the whole island a sacred home to their Great Spirit, and many of the location names are attributed to the Ojibwe Indians or the early French fur traders. Cadillac, Lafayette, Anishinaabe."

Daisy frowned. "But... if the island is a sacred place for Indians, should you really have built a great big hotel here?"

"Hush, Daisy," her mother admonished immediately, although Chase had to acknowledge the question had merit, and wasn't surprised his sister would be the one to ask. Always thinking of others, that one. She'd make an excellent mother someday, in spite of her role model.

Fortunately, Mr. Plank, ever the salesman, took Daisy's query in stride.

"How insightful you are, Miss Bostwick, and what a provocative question. Let me assure you the French and British were here long before we were. Fort Beaumont is over one hundred years old and has changed hands many times over, but thanks to the efforts of our own Senator Ferry, who was born right here on the island, the United States government has designated nearly 900 acres of the island as a national park. American soldiers from the fort are tasked with maintaining the pristine nature of the landscape, but it's income from tourism that pays for it."

Daisy wanted to ask more, Chase was sure of it, but their mother was poised to discreetly pinch her arm if she persisted. Chase had been the recipient of his mother's pinches. They were effective silencers.

"And thanks to the support of the railroads," Mr. Plank continued, "a dozen or more trains come into Michlimac City each day. My goal is to ensure every one of those passengers makes their way to this island, stays at my hotel, and supports local businesses."

"Well, surely not *every* passenger," Mr. Crocker remarked. "Just our sort. Those who can afford it, and not the riff raff."

Chase decided right then he didn't like Mr. Crocker. The man was pompous and derogatory, embodying just the kind of closed, narrow-mindedness that strove to keep other people small so that he could feel big. If Crocker had his way, someone like Mrs. Talbot would not be welcomed as a guest at the hotel, for surely, she could not afford five dollars a night! Chase cast a glance her way to see if she might be thinking the same thing, but she was engrossed in a whispered conversation with Daisy, and for once, he was glad his sister was a distracting chatterbox.

"Yes, tourism and investors," Mr. Plank all but shouted at Chase some three hours later as just the two of them sat at an oversize mahogany desk in his wainscoted office sipping a fine Kentucky bourbon. It was smooth, warming Chase's insides and mellowing his disposition – a disposition made tetchy from having spent the entire afternoon doing a *terrible job* of avoiding Mrs. Talbot.

She'd strolled through the garden arm-in-arm with Daisy and Mrs. O'Keefe which annoyed his mother to such extent she'd gone back to the hotel just moments after leaving the front porch. Mr. O'Keefe seemed enamored of the kinship, pleased to see his wife had made new friends, even if they were a bohemian artist and a sixteen-year-old debutante. And as for Chase? Well, he'd decided to give his undivided attention to Mortimer VonMeisterburger and his vocal litany of botanical factoids rather than engaging in a long, unsatisfying study of *Mrs. Talbot's nape.* He didn't need to watch as the breeze softly stirred those curling tendrils. He didn't care about that.

Instead, he'd learned about pistils and stamens and corollas and a number of other parts of a flower which he'd already forgotten the names of. Perhaps he hadn't actually been listening that closely, but he had garnered a new appreciation for Morty. In spite of the crossed eyes and excessive pomade, the man had a vast fund of knowledge about nature. Birds and bees, flowers and trees. Unfortunately, all of that appreciation and expertise would soon go to waste because Morty was destined to join his father in the oil business, a place he most definitely did not belong. Much like Chase and this island.

"So, what do you say?" Mr. Plank asked, and Chase realized his mind had drifted away, back to the garden, and he'd not heard a word the man said.

"My apologies, Mr. Plank. The fresh air and bourbon have made me inattentive. What were you saying?"

"I was asking if you'd be interested in becoming an investor in the Imperial Hotel. I have big plans for expansion but that takes revenue."

"What of your other investors?"

"They're short-sighted and skittish. They want to make sure I'll turn a profit before increasing their funding, but they haven't even been here. You have. You can see for yourself this place is destined to be a success. And haven't I heard you're the Bostwick to go to with bold ideas?"

Chase chuckled, not sure if he was being seduced with flattery or if Mr. Plank really believed that. He took another sip from his glass and let the bourbon burn.

"Where did you hear that, Mr. Plank?"

"Oh, for God's sake, man. Let's not stand on ceremony when it's just us gents. Call me Hugo. Here, let me fill your glass."

thirteen

"Painting en plein air is different than studio painting in a number of ways," Jo said to the group of attentive women sitting in chairs around the sunny studio.

Her painting classes had been added to the daily roster and although interest was slow to build, today she was oh-so-pleased and ever-so-relieved to have nearly a dozen in attendance. Some had walked in with confidence as if they owned the place while others had been more tentative, peeking into the room to see what was what before fully committing, but now they were a group of eleven, each paying rapt attention, with Daisy and Ruth seated near the front and providing Jo with encouraging smiles.

Today's topic was one of Jo's favorite things – painting out of doors.

"First, and most obviously, it's done outside rather than inside."

This elicited polite laughter as she continued. "You want to find a spot with good lighting but make sure the sun isn't shining directly onto your canvas because that alters the appearance of your colors. If necessary, you can utilize an umbrella, both to deflect the sun from your work and also to keep yourself cool. Begin with a charcoal drawing and focus on the part of the scene that inspired you to choose that location. Sketch in the larger shapes first, and then add the details. All of this will make more sense once we've gone outside but given that it's everyone's first attempt at en plein air painting, I think arranging our easels on the front porch is a good idea. How does that sound to everyone?"

There were nods all around, and soon Jo had them collecting the items they'd need – field easels, a canvas or two, one Pochade box each, and aprons to keep smudges from their pretty dresses. She gathered up several #7 sable brushes, a few cloths, and a jug of water to clean them with, and eight Japanned tin boxes containing moist colors with hinged lids to use as palettes. The boxes were fresh and new, items supplied by the hotel at her request, and although she knew they'd soon look used and worn – the way they ought – she couldn't help but think of her father's battered artist kit. The remnants were stuffed into a satchel tucked into the wardrobe in her room. She'd clean the pieces soon, and see what was salvageable, but for now, she'd use the new supplies. Impersonal but adequate.

They made their way down the hall and through the lobby, the ladies following her in a single row like baby ducks, getting a predictable glare from Mr. Beeks, and an equally predictable smile from Mr. Parnell, on down to the furthest edge of the porch they went where views of the lake were in abundance. There was plenty of room, and once they'd donned their aprons, Jo continued on with her lesson, moving back and forth between each student and providing instruction.

Several of the women were quite good, while a few others were hopelessly inept. Art was a skill that could be learned by virtually anyone, but a little innate talent was certainly helpful.

"Are you excited about the dance?" Daisy asked Jo as the class continued.

"The dance? Oh, goodness. Today is Saturday, isn't it? I hadn't thought much of it."

Actually, she'd thought of it a great deal. Mostly about how her dress was sure to look shabby amidst the guests' elegant attire, and how she'd be left to dance with the old and the feeble, or be relegated to a stuffy corner, drawing caricatures while feeling as if she were one herself – a comical figure, similar to but not exactly like the others.

"I might not attend," Jo said hesitantly.

"But you must attend. It's the very first of the season, and you said yourself you want guests to commission portraits. What better way to encourage them do so than spending time in their company so they'll see how delightful you are?"

Daisy's loyalty was devout, and Jo wasn't sure what she'd done to deserve it, but there was some truth in her comment. At least the part about getting to know the guests. Jo being found delightful by them was another matter entirely.

She looked over at the women in her class, standing at their easels, each intently focused on their task. Thus far they'd been cordial and receptive, some seeming friendlier than others, but would they act the same toward her in a ballroom full of tuxedoed men and bejeweled women? Would they wonder why she was there? Or would they assume she was just part of the entertainment?

But then again... she *was* part of the entertainment.

Like it or not, she was an employee of the hotel, and her purpose here was to work, not socialize. Her aim was not to make friends but to find clients. The fact that Daisy and Ruth had so warmly accepted her was a bonus to be sure, but she should not, could not, would not expect the same from others.

Her hesitation, her fear, was really just pride standing in the way and undermining her confidence – because she didn't want to be seen as socially inferior – even if she was. But pride wouldn't get her to Paris. Pride wouldn't fill her stomach or put a sturdy roof over her head. Only money could do that, and Mr. Tippett had promised an additional stipend for attending the dances.

"I suppose perhaps I should attend," Jo said at last, and Daisy smiled.

"Of course, you should. You must. You're sure to regret it if you don't."

Yes, she was sure to regret it if she didn't go, and yet it was equally possible she'd regret it if she *did*.

∽

"You look lovely, Mrs. Talbot."

Betsy, one of the younger maids, had offered to help her dress and even to style her hair and Jo was as grateful for the help as for the companionship. She was as skittish as a mouse in a roomful of hawks, but Betsy's sweet disposition had a soothing effect.

"Thank you, Betsy. You've done a wonderful job with my hair. I never could have managed on my own. I hope I can repay you somehow."

Betsy blushed and dipped her blonde head, responding hesitantly. "Well, I might like to have my picture drawn."

"A picture? Of course. I'm happy to oblige," Jo answered.

"Really?" Betsy's pretty face lit up. She could not be more than sixteen and Jo couldn't help but compare her to Daisy. Both girls had the same youthful exuberance, the same joyful smile, and the same excitement over the prospect of having their image committed to paper, although Jo knew Betsy's life was sure to be more difficult. Or at least more strenuous.

"I have a sweetheart, you see," Betsy added. "I'd like it for him."

"A sweetheart? How lucky he is," Jo replied, pushing down memories of those early days with Oliver when the world had seemed so bright and full of promise. "Does he work at the hotel?"

Betsy nodded. "He works in the kitchen and sometimes he sneaks out with a fancy dessert and shares it with me." As soon as the words were out, she gasped and covered her mouth. "Oh dear. I shouldn't have told you that. He's not a thief, Mrs. Talbot. He just knows how much I like sweets."

But Jo wrapped an arm around the girl's slender shoulders, guiding her toward the door. "Your secret is safe with me, Betsy. We can do your drawing next week. Just come find me when you have some time."

Betsy departed and now Jo stood in front of the looking glass, dressed in the best she had, still uncertain about attending the dance. But sitting in her room, listening to the orchestra play, knowing that others were having a wonderful time would only make her despondent, so, after one more twist and turn before the mirror, making sure that the unremarkable ruffles of her outdated pale blue dress were properly flounced, she made her way to the grand ballroom.

It was early yet, and although a few patrons lounged in the lobby adorned in their best bibs and tuckers, Jo made her way into the room and toward the corner furthest from the entrance where Mr. Tippett had set up a small table for her, along with a chair. Earlier that afternoon, she'd left paper and pastels to use for caricatures or other drawings, should anyone ask.

But no one asked. No one seemed to notice her at all, tucked away in the corner as she was. She'd been there nearly an hour as guests strolled in, and waiters rushed past, in and out of the door just behind where she sat, their trays laden with crystal glasses of champagne and canapes.

She watched for Daisy and Ruth, hoping to see a familiar and friendly face, but as the room filled, she lost sight of the entrance, and when the dancing began, she chose to enjoy the spectacle rather than feel glum she was not a part of it. She mostly failed at this endeavor but remained determined to make the best of things. She even went so far as to decide she was actually better off far from the dance floor because her years-old gown would stand out for all the wrong reasons amid such finery. She was a thorn among roses.

"You thirsty?" one tall, energetic server finally asked her on her way back out of the ballroom. "Or hungry?"

"Both," she answered, and so he came back a few minutes

later with a glass filled to the brim and a plate piled high with delectable morsels, a veritable feast.

"My goodness," she said. "This should do it. Thank you."

"My pleasure. Clancy Callaghan at your service." He bowed formally, a shock of red hair falling over his freckled brow. He was perhaps twenty or so, long and lean with broad shoulders, the kind of frame that would eventually fill out and make him seem more man that boy. For now, though, he bore the look of a scarecrow in spite of the dashing tuxedo.

"A pleasure to make your acquaintance, Mr. Callaghan. I'm Jo Talbot."

"Nice to meet you, Miss Talbot, but why's a pretty gal like you sitting in this corner?"

"Move along, Callaghan," another server snapped, rushing past. "Or Beeks will hear about it."

"Beeks," Clancy muttered with a good-natured scowl. "That little man has eyes everywhere. Beware!" He waved his hands in mock alarm, then with a wink at Jo, followed his fellow server through the door.

She looked around at his exit, her foot tapping in rhythm under the table. She sipped the champagne and nibbled on the hors d'oeuvres, then finally picked up a pencil and began to draw. Not far from her sat a collection of young ladies of assorted shapes, sizes, and visages. The wallflowers, left to watch as the prettier, more polished girls were pursued by partner after partner. It was unfair that they should be ignored, and Jo felt a kinship, an allegiance of sorts. She knew what it was like to hover at the periphery. To observe but not participate. These young ladies deserved better.

She got up and approached the closest one, a girl of about seventeen, she'd guess, with lanky ringlets the color of a mud puddle and a mouth that was perhaps a bit too small for the rest of her features.

"Good evening. You are a vision in that dress. I wonder if I might draw your picture?"

The girl appeared startled and placed a delicate hand against her decolletage. "My picture? You want to draw my picture? Right now?"

Jo nodded. "Yes, I would like to very much. If you're not too busy."

The girl blushed and smiled, and Jo realized her mouth was not so small after all. It was only that she'd pressed her lips into a thin line, a grimace almost, as if watching the dancers caused physical discomfort.

"I'd love to have my picture drawn," she answered with a blush.

Jo pulled her own chair over, sat down in front of the young lady, and began. In moments, it seemed, she was surrounded by *all* the wallflowers who *all* wanted their picture drawn. And so, she drew them, not as caricatures, but as they were, emphasizing their best features while subtly minimizing their less desirable attributes.

They'd been a silent, reserved bunch when Jo first approached, but now were buzzing about like happy bees, commenting on how lovely each one looked. They were sweet, and funny, and vivacious, and Jo felt proud at how she'd brightened their evening. Perhaps they were not in the thick of things, nor was she, but they were enjoying themselves, nonetheless.

"I wonder, Mrs. Talbot," said a toothsome young lady, "If you might draw us as a group? Or would that take too much time?"

"I'd be delighted," she answered. "I have all evening."

Jo arranged a few chairs for some girls to sit on while others stood, and two settled on cushions in front. Satisfied with their positions, she started to sketch, her pencil moving over the paper with confidence, almost as if by magic as her eyes, and mind, and hand worked together in practiced harmony, absorbing all her thoughts, and focusing her awareness on nothing but the image emerging.

So engrossed was she, in fact, she didn't notice when the girls' chatter slowly came to a halt, or when their eyes widened and seemed singularly directed toward something behind her. She didn't realize he was there, until he spoke, and she felt the heat of his body near her left shoulder.

"Well, here you are, Mrs. Talbot."

Her hand halted, her breath held as she turned in her chair and let her gaze travel from his midsection (hmm...), up his torso (mmm...), stopping finally at his face. (*Damn, that face...*) She could pretend it was just the angle from her seat which made his shoulders seem so broad or made the edge of his jawline seem so sharp, but alas, she knew it was *not* the angle. It was just... him.

Chase Bostwick had looked fine enough in a wet, wool suit with rain dripping from that face, and more than fine in the dove grey suit he'd worn yesterday, but Chase Bostwick in a stark, formal, black tuxedo was a heart-stopping sight to behold.

Yesterday's garden tour had been a trial, what with him smiling in the sunshine, wearing no hat and being terribly kind to the awkward Mr. VonMeisterburger, asking question after question about *flowers* when it was obvious his own mind was elsewhere. On work, no doubt. He'd probably been longing for his office and his desk – while she'd been longing for him to address her directly because it seemed he had not appreciated her teasing him about Ulysses earlier that morning.

In fact, he'd left her studio rather abruptly. She hadn't meant to offend and wished above all else he'd say something friendly during the tour so she might know all was well. But he'd avoided her for the duration, not even saying goodbye when they'd all returned to the lobby. Instead, he'd merely nodded in her direction then followed Mr. Plank down the hall to discuss – she could only assume – *some business.*

But here he was now, next to her in the grand ballroom looking almost stern. She probably ought to stand to greet him, but her lap was full of paper and pencils and scooping it all up in her arms or dropping it all to the floor would seem clumsy, so she kept her seat.

"Yes, here I am, Mr. Bostwick."

"Yes, well..." he paused, and she wondered if he expected more, and then he said, "Would you like dance?"

The invitation could not have come as more of a surprise, which surely showed upon her face. Through the prism of that surprise, she contemplated the drabness of her gown and her absence of jewels – because she'd sold the few that hadn't been stolen – but most of all, she contemplated the dizzying handsomeness of Mr. Chase Bostwick. He was utterly and entirely too handsome.

She was a happily married woman – or at least portraying one – but if he pulled her into his arms and spun her around the room in an intimate waltz, if she must face him for the eternity of a song, feeling the strength of his hand in hers, and the gentleness of his other on her waist, infatuation would surely overcome her. It would splash across her cheeks, darken her eyes, and leave her breathless. It would make her tremble. And he might *notice*. It would make her want – and he might *know*.

So, even though she was loathe to do it, she gave the only sensible answer. "No, thank you, Mr. Bostwick. I am otherwise engaged."

The look of surprise on her face when he'd asked her to dance was assuredly *nothing* compared to the look of surprise on his face at her refusal. It was nearly comical and yet she found nothing funny about it.

"Ah," he said, folding his hands behind his back, his expression shifting quickly to an impassive coolness. "So, I see. Do forgive the interruption." He nodded at her once, and then gave a curt nod to the bevy of wallflowers now staring at this exchange as if they'd never seen so extraordinary a thing. A pauper refusing a prince. "Ladies, my apologies. Enjoy your evening."

He turned and strode away, and Jo wondered if she could have bungled that more spectacularly. (*Probably not.*) She'd insulted him. (*Again!*) She should have explained that his invitation was most gracious and appreciated but she'd promised these girls their drawing. That perhaps she might dance with him another time. That her refusal was nothing personal. *(It was, in fact, something entirely too personal.)*

Those explanations, though insufficient, may have at least spared him the embarrassment of being rejected outright. But he'd caught her so off guard, she hadn't had the time *(or capacity)* to think.

"You may dance with him, you know," said one of the wallflowers quietly.

Jo tore her gaze from his retreating form and turned back to look at the girls assembled before her. "Pardon me?" she asked.

"If you'd like to dance, you should dance. You needn't sit here with us."

All the girls nodded, and she recognized the same longing on their faces that she felt deep inside herself. They wanted to be *asked*. They wanted to be *seen* and held and adored. Not necessarily by Chase, but by *someone*. It was the kind of longing that had blinded Jo to all of Oliver's flaws, and yet she could not fault them for it. They wanted to be loved... and so did she.

She shook her head and smiled at them, a falsely bright smile, and said, "I may dance anytime, but how often do I have so many lovely subjects to commit to paper? I much prefer to be here with all of you."

Lies. All lies.

fourteen

Is this how a sheep felt when shorn? Exposed and half the size? Damn, but that woman confounded him!

He'd observed her half the evening, sitting alone, looking wistfully out into the crowd, until at last she'd cast her lot in with a mischief of mice so hopelessly drab they could not stir a man to lust if they'd bared their breasts and promised him a sizeable dowry.

Against all his better judgment (*spurred on by nothing more than generosity!*), he had crossed the ballroom and asked her to dance. And she'd rejected him! *She.* Had rejected. *Him.* She'd turned him down as dispassionately as a housemaid turns down the bedcovers, and with less finesse. Without a hint of apology. Or regret. She'd all but *dismissed* him!

Once again, he was reminded that his thoughts with regard to Mrs. Talbot were as fanciful as they were unrequited. In fact, hadn't his mission this very evening been to seek out *other* women? Somehow, he'd forgotten, but now his aim was clear. To purge his mind of all thoughts of her.

He found a waiter with a trayful of champagne and helped himself to a glass, or three, gulping down the contents as if it was the cheapest of ale, and then surveyed the crowd, looking for the prettiest girl he could find.

It didn't take long. The ballroom was full of them, and so he spent the next hour twirling one debutante around the dance floor, and then another. And another. So many that their faces blended together in his mind, and their names (if he'd bothered to ask) were quickly forgotten. Although he'd made sure to note who their fathers were. *That* information was useful. Marshall Field, the owner of a department store, William Ogden, president of the Galena and Chicago Railroad, and lumber merchant, Henry Getty.

Then there was Frances Pullman, who'd arrived with her father George, just that afternoon. Though perhaps not a great beauty, Chase found the twenty-year-old serviceably pretty, but more than that, she had a substance to her that appealed to him. She was rumored to be a steadfast companion to George, as well as his frequent advisor. And since Mr. Pullman was a businessman Chase very much wanted to get better acquainted with, befriending the daughter was an excellent place to start.

"I wonder, Miss Pullman," Chase said as the orchestra music quieted between songs, "if you and your family might like to join mine for lunch tomorrow?"

She seemed to hesitate, and Chase thought he was headed for another rejection, but then she smiled.

"I'm sure that would be lovely, Mr. Bostwick. I'll speak to my father and send a note in the morning if we're available."

Hm. A rather tepid answer. Not quite yes, but at least a more thoughtful response than the outright *no, thank you* he'd got from Mrs. Talbot. Still... was he losing his appeal? Women in Chicago seemed universally enamored of him and yet tonight he was having to work far too hard. Did he have something in his teeth? Was his breath offensive? Did his lack of mustache make him seem unsophisticated? (He'd grown one once, but then Alex did the same and so Chase had shaved his off.)

"Then I shall I look forward your answer," he said with a tilt of his head toward Miss Pullman. He wouldn't mind talking with her a little longer, but the music was swelling once again and if he asked her to dance twice in a row, there'd be rumors. And anyway, he'd had enough of dancing for tonight. He'd made his point. *Most* women would say yes, even if *some* might say no.

Gadzooks, his ego was fragile as a teacup these days. It must be all that damn Eden fresh air. It was time to find the cigar room full of fermented tobacco stink and soft-bellied, middle-aged, men whose conviction of their own importance was as solid as it was overt – and for no other reason than that they *chose* it to be.

He left the ballroom and immediately encountered Mr. O'Keefe. "Good evening, Percy. Are you heading up for the night?"

Mr. O'Keefe shook his head. "On the contrary. My lovely wife has retired but I find myself craving a drink. Care to join me on the porch and bend an elbow? I'm in search of something stronger than champagne."

"I'd be delighted." What a relief. Percy's company was far preferable to stodgy old men and their stodgier cigars.

They settled into chairs not far from the doors leading into the lobby and a waiter brought them crystal glasses filled with enough bourbon to keep Chase asleep until noon the next day. Percy held up the glass, eyeing the amber liquid and quirking his brow at the amount.

"One thing's for certain," he said. "Plank doesn't skimp on the amenities."

"No, indeed."

"Then again, for five dollars a night, I'd expect as much."

"Yes," Chase paused, "indeed." And then paused again.

Percy chuckled. "Must you monopolize the conversation?" Prompting Chase to chuckle as well.

"My apologies. It's been a long evening and I find myself rather chatted out."

"Ah, yes. I saw you dancing with every eligible deb. Are you in the market for a bride?"

"Good heavens, no."

Percy laughed outright. "Do they know that?"

Chase shook his head and took a sip. "I have no idea. The conversations never took that turn. What I mostly encountered was innumerable comments about the pleasantness of today's weather and if I thought the weather tomorrow might be equally pleasant."

"Well, it's hard to get much more than that in the space of a waltz. Maybe one of them will get under your skin as the summer progresses."

Under his skin? The phrase was new to Chase but a perfect way to express what *Mrs. Talbot* had done. Like an itch he could not reach.

"I don't particularly want one of them, as you say, getting under my skin. I'm rather happy with my bachelorhood. My brother is getting married soon and one new addition to the family is quite enough for now."

"Well, should you change your mind, there's a lovely assortment to choose from at the resort. Not that any of them can hold a candle to my wife. She's a treasure." He lifted his glass to toast.

"To Mrs. O'Keefe," said Chase, clinking his glass against Percy's before taking another sip. Larger than the last. In fact, it was nearly a gulp because talking about wives gave him reason to drink.

"What do you think of Mr. Plank?" Chase asked next, intent on changing the subject. Over the course of the past few days, he'd grown to enjoy Percy's company, and to appreciate his opinions and his good humor. They'd discussed a variety of topics, both important and inane, and he found the man to be thoughtful, insightful, and open to progress. All traits he admired.

"I haven't decided yet," Percy answered. "Plank's an excellent host, to be sure, but as to whether or not he's a wise businessman remains to be seen. He's asked me to invest in an expansion of the hotel."

Now it was Chase's turn to laugh out loud. "You as well? I thought I was an exception due to my superior financial skills."

"I'm sure your superior financial skills would benefit Plank immensely as would my organizational and management skills, but I suspect it's mainly our cash he's after. I spoke with George Pullman tonight and he told me Plank was pushing hard for more funds."

"Ah, I'm hoping to have lunch with George tomorrow for exactly that reason, to see what he says about this venture."

Their conversation moved on from there, heading off in various directions and circling back again. The orchestra stopped playing and guests wandered on and off the porch, men talking loudly, couples whispering quietly, until the moon was high in the sky, nearly everyone had gone back inside, and Chase's glass had been refilled twice more giving him a languid peace of mind at last.

As the bourbon dulled their senses, their talk grew ever more candid, veering decidedly toward the personal, until Percy leaned over in his chair, squinted at Chase, and seemed to be concentrating quite hard, undoubtedly because this bourbon was potent stuff, and being half Chase's size, the other man was likely feeling its effects more strongly.

Holding his drink aloft, he said, "Chase, may I ask you something?"

"Of course."

"What do you make of Mrs. Talbot?"

Oh, for God's sake, there was no escaping the woman.

Cognizant enough to mind his tongue if not his thoughts, his answer was noncommittal. "Make of her? I don't suppose I make anything of her at all."

"Balderdash." Percy's drink sloshed as he scoffed. "Surely you've noticed the way she looks at you."

"Looks at me? When does she look at me?"

"Uh... Yesterday, in the garden. Unless it was Morty VonMeisterburger she had her eye on, but I highly doubt that."

Chase shook his head. "You're mistaken. Not about Morty, perhaps, but about me. She's married, you know."

"Not happily."

"Not happily? What makes you say that?" He'd already suspected as much so why did the simple comment feel like a snowball to the center of his chest?

"Ruthie doesn't think she's happy," Percy replied. "They've spent some time together these past few days and it seems Mrs. Talbot has made remarks which make her think it's a bad match. And..." Percy looked around to make sure no one was near, "that maybe Mr. Talbot is a *bad* man."

Another snowball, cold and solid, right in the sternum because although Chase had suspected her marriage was less than ideal, hearing Percy say Jo might be bound to someone unkind, someone *bad*, suggested that whatever she was hiding was not playful in nature, but rather something more... dire.

"In what way is he bad? Other than letting her travel alone and spend the summer working here, of course." As if that wasn't bad enough.

"Mrs. Talbot hasn't said anything specific, although she did mention that her husband's nature changed significantly once they were married. Ruthie says she seems uncomfortable discussing him, as if she wants to say more but resists. And not to disparage Mrs. Talbot in the least, but my wife noticed patches on her dress yesterday. Discreet, but nonetheless, *patches.*" For the tone of his voice, he might as well have said *boils,* as if patches were contagious as well as unsightly.

"Patches?"

"Yes, but her father died last year so she must have recently come into some kind of inheritance. I'd never heard of him, of course, but Tippett said Emerson McKenna was a sought-after painter so... wouldn't she have some money? At least enough to buy new frocks for her stay here? And, oh!" Percy suddenly exclaimed, twisting toward Chase, and pointing as he recalled something else, something of great import. "And then there's the matter of Paris!"

"Paris?"

"Yes! She's saving money to move to Paris." He emphasized the *puh* in Paris so strenuously he very nearly spat, but Chase already knew about Paris. She'd told him in the carriage the day they'd met. He hadn't given it much thought at the time. He'd been too distracted by her ugly hat. (And now he felt bad for the uncharitable thoughts he'd had about a hat she could apparently not afford to replace.)

"Why is moving to Paris significant?"

Percy frowned, his lips jutting like a duck's beak, and settled back into his chair. "Perhaps it's not, but again, couldn't she just go if she wanted to? Why must she work to secure the funds for travel when her father should have left her a respectable amount? Not to mention the fact that no decent husband would expect his wife to earn her own money, the cheap bastard. I have some theories." He pointed again at nothing in particular.

A drunken man's theories rarely held up in the harsh light of day but the revelations about Mrs. Talbot were disheartening enough to allow for speculation.

"What theories?" Chase asked.

"I suspect Mrs. Talbot is on the run... from her husband."

"On the run?" A startling notion which had not occurred to Chase. Perhaps it should have?

"Yes," Percy continued. "Think about it. A young bride who leaves her newlywedded husband behind for employment at a remote hotel hoping to earn enough money to leave the country? I suspect he doesn't even know she's here. Maybe she's not even named Talbot. It's a *nom de plume*, of sorts."

Chase suddenly wished his own mind were clearer so he might contemplate this with more alacrity. She *had* fumbled over her words when giving him her name in the carriage. He'd thought it was just nervousness, but what else was it she'd said? Something about things not being perfect? Or constant? Or something to that effect. What *exactly* had she said, and more importantly, what *exactly* had she meant?

"Do you think she left him because he's malicious towards her?" Chase asked quietly, his pulse accelerating. It was a leap to go from negligent husband to abusive, but if Talbot was the latter, something would have to be done about it.

"It's not implausible," Percy said. "Ruthie suspects so. Not because of what Mrs. Talbot said but rather in the way she said it, and if she left him in haste, that might explain her state of poverty. Or perhaps her father left debts of some sort? I don't imagine an artist, even a successful one, would be astute at managing money. Who knows? But maybe that's why her husband's manner changed once they'd wed? He was angry at inheriting nothing but empty coffers?"

Percy hiccupped then, splashing bourbon onto his thigh, and Chase realized much of what the man said was the stuff of unsubstantiated conjecture embellished by too much drink. Well-intentioned, perhaps, but his theories were not facts. Patches on a dress notwithstanding, alleging that Mrs. Talbot was escaping a difficult marriage or that her father had left her penniless was merely gossip.

And yet, he'd known something was off kilter about her story from the moment she'd climbed into his carriage. A suspicion which grew as he'd helped her convince Beeks of the legitimacy of that dubious contract. And indeed, why *did* she need the job, anyway? He'd assumed her husband was lazy and negligent – and stupid – but what if the O'Keefe's were correct? What if Jo's husband was cruel? Cruel enough that she'd had to run away?

It made his gut burn, and if it were true, then Chase needed to do something about it. Any gentleman would, but first, he had to find out precisely what kind of trouble she was really in. Fortunately, there were discreet, efficient ways to accomplish that.

After escorting the soused Mr. O'Keefe to his room, Chase retired to his own and penned a scribbled, ink-blotched note to Mr. Hayden.

Mr. Hayden,

I have a matter requiring the utmost delicacy and discretion. It must remain entirely confidential between you and myself.

Please contact our man with the Pinkerton Detective Agency. Have him find out everything he can about one Mr. Oliver Talbot – an art dealer who recently wed Chicagoan Miss Emerson Joan McKenna, daughter of the artist Emerson James McKenna. It is possible that Oliver Talbot is not his real name.

Although this may not be relevant, Mrs. McKenna Talbot is now employed by the Imperial Hotel as their artist-in-residence.

Again, discretion is imperative, but please make all haste. Time is of the essence.

C.B.

fifteen

"You have a note from Mr. Plank," Mr. Beeks called out to Jo as she entered the lobby.

The hotel seemed all but empty this morning as the late evening revelers were still asleep, and the holy were all at church. Jo had gotten to bed rather early herself, having left the ballroom after finishing with the wallflowers. The picture she'd drawn of them had turned out lovely but provided her with little joy since the cloud of having insulted Mr. Bostwick hung like a fog over her mood. She thought to find him today and formally apologize. Not that she thought her refusal had weighed heavily (*or at all*) on his mind. He'd left her and gone on to dance with more beauties than she could count. As he should have. He was an eligible bachelor, after all. He *should* be dancing and flirting and cavorting. Hadn't he complained to her of his boredom? Yes, he had, but last night he'd obviously found a solution and so she *should* be glad for him.

But she was glum. The night had made her, once again, acutely aware of her loneliness. And her longings. Paris would be the thing to cure all her woes, but for now it remained an ocean – and a fortune – away, and so she'd hoped breakfast might brighten her mood.

She accepted the note from Mr. Beeks, an embossed card bearing the emblem of the hotel. The words were concise, written in a bold hand.

Mrs. Talbot,
See me in my office today at your earliest availability.
Hugo Plank

This did not seem like good news, for certainly anything having to do with her job duties would come from Mr. Tippett. Perhaps Mr. Beeks had complained? He'd said nothing when he'd handed her the card, merely extended his arm with it in his hand, hardly meeting her eyes or even acknowledging her. Good Lord, was she about to be sacked?

Shaking legs carried her to Mr. Plank's wide office door. It was early, and she hoped perhaps he wouldn't be there, but he answered her timid knock with a loud, "Come in."

She stepped inside the lion's den, and he waved her further into the room. Books and ledgers and papers were stacked high on his desk and on the shelves, along with architectural schematics of the hotel and grounds spread out and held in place with simple rocks. Everything about this resort was luxurious, and ornate, making the commonplace stones seem glaringly out of place. Like her.

"Ah, Mrs. Talbot. Come in. Take a seat." He didn't sound particularly angry or unpleasant, but neither did he sound... friendly.

She did as instructed and waited while he finished reading the document in his hands. Then her heart somersaulted inside her ribs as she realized... it was her contract. He was reading her contract. *Lord almighty!* She *was* about to get sacked.

After a moment that seemed a year, he set it down and looked up at her, still neither unkind nor friendly. She would never play poker with him. His face was as unreadable as a statue, and she thought to say something. Anything, but decided it was best to wait for him to set the tone. Plus, if she opened her mouth, whimpers might come out.

"Mrs. Talbot, I'm an incredibly successful businessman. I didn't get to where I am today by being reckless. Nor did I get here by being ignorant. I got here by thoughtfully, carefully analyzing situations and making educated decisions."

"Yes, sir."

"I have excellent instincts about people and about commerce. In fact, the hospitality business is about exactly that. Having the insight to read people and to meet their needs before they even know they have them. My goal for this hotel is to surround my guests with elegance and luxury, the very best of the very best, and to fulfill their every whim so they might never want to leave."

He paused, his gaze on her face never wavering, until she said again, "Yes, sir."

He tapped the contract on his desk. "Now, if my purpose is to provide my elite, socially superior guests with the very best of the very best, why, pray tell, would I have offered the coveted position of artist-in-residence to an untried, inexperienced young woman with no established reputation in the art world?"

The question seemed rhetorical in nature, and since her answer would not benefit her in the least, she remained silent. Plus, those whimpers were threatening to choke her. Apparently getting sacked tasted a lot like bile. Mr. Plank leaned back in his chair, assessing her, his eyes as dark and fathomless as a python measuring an unsuspecting rodent for a snack.

"I think you and I both know this contract was an offer for your father, not for you," he finally said. His voice remained neutral, giving her no hint as to how he truly felt about the matter. Certainly, he wasn't pleased, but he seemed willing to hear her side of things. Or at least give her a chance to defend herself. Maybe she could turn this around yet.

"With all due respect, Mr. Plank, my father passed away some six months before that contract arrived giving me no reason to think it was meant for him, rather than for myself."

He crooked a disbelieving brow, and she felt herself deflating. He was too astute, and the lie was exhausting as well as unconvincing. It seemed throwing herself upon his mercy was her last option. Perhaps she could escape with a modicum of dignity, such that it was. She straightened in her chair.

"Oh, very well, Mr. Plank. You are indeed insightful. I did suspect the contract was for my father, but he had no use for it, and I did. And I assure you I am a far better teacher than he ever would have been."

The first hint of interest showed in his eyes. "You think yourself a better artist than your father? He had years of experience and a fine reputation."

"Experience and reputation, yes. Patience? No. If you wanted someone who would have come here to crow about his own expertise, to boast about his elusive talent, then he would have been your man. But if you want someone who will surround your guests with instruction and encouragement, and delight in their artistic accomplishments so they might leave the hotel feeling a better version of themselves than when they'd arrived, then I am the one you want."

A smile, just the barest hint, began to emerge at the corners of his mouth. Either at her audacity, or the delight he was about to have in tearing that contract to pieces right in front of her since she'd just admitted to knowing it was fraudulent.

"Were you not on good terms with your father?"

"On the contrary. We were on the best of terms. I loved him. I still do, but I also *knew* him. He had all the traits of an egocentric artist. He was arrogant and overbearing and would have left your guests feeling humiliated rather than inspired. Trust me. He was my teacher, and I can attest he was not an easy man to learn from. But I did learn from him, and at the risk of sounding arrogant myself, by the end of his life, he declared I had surpassed his talent."

It was a moment etched on her heart, a conversation they'd had just days before her father had died when he'd held her hand in his own trembling one and lavished her with unexpected praise.

"You've outdone me, my dearest. My greatest sorrow is only that I won't be here to see all that you might accomplish. I'm so very proud of you, and so glad you now have Oliver to guide you."

He'd been utterly mistaken about that last part, but she hoped he'd been right about the former, that great accomplishments were in her future. In fact, it was her father who'd encouraged her to move to Paris with her new husband so she might develop her talent along with the likes of Cassatt and Bracquemond. And Oliver, in his deceit, had promised to take her. Instead, of course, he'd taken everything else.

Mr. Plank now seemed more intrigued than dubious, but she could barely breathe, having used up all the air in her lungs on a speech which had come from nowhere. Everything she'd said about her father was true, yet she had never acknowledged such things, not even to herself. He'd been loving, yes, but he'd also been moody and demanding, a harsh taskmaster, and stingy with his praise. And he had pushed her toward Oliver at the end, thinking, probably, that marriage would protect her once he was gone. Oh, the irony.

"I'm a fine instructor, Mr. Plank," she continued. "Give me a chance to prove it."

He repositioned in his chair, smiling at last. "You're a bold one, Mrs. Talbot."

She shook her head. "I'm really not, but circumstances have turned me in that direction."

"What circumstances?"

She'd said enough. More than enough. "I need this job, Mr. Plank. Might we leave it at that?"

He regarded her for another moment, until he said, "One month."

"Sir?"

"You have one month to prove to me that you are what we need in an art instructor."

"One month. I see. Might I ask for some clarification?"

"If you need to."

"Mr. Tippett has asked me to teach two classes per day, except for Sunday, as well as participate in a variety of other social activities around the hotel. How may I be certain I'm fulfilling the edicts of my position as you see it? Especially since Mr. Tippett and Mr. Beeks seem to be of different minds about my duties?" If she was to walk a tightrope like a circus performer, she'd best know what this audience of one hoped to see.

He paused, and then said, "Ask me again in a month."

Ask him again in a month? That was maddeningly vague. Should she persuade Mr. Tippett to add more classes to the daily roster? Somehow ingratiate herself to the odious Mr. Beeks? Encourage private lessons among the hotel's guests? Plant herself in the lobby like a carnival barker shouting "*everyone must learn to paint!*"

She had no idea and yet Mr. Plank stood indicating their meeting was adjourned. Given that it could have gone much worse, she also stood and said, "I sincerely thank you for your time, Mr. Plank, and for this opportunity. Please know that I am fully committed to this endeavor."

"I expect no less."

Then he walked her to the door, closing it shut the moment she was through the frame. The snick of the latch echoed in an otherwise empty hallway. She stood there for the space of a breath, heart pounding, pulses racing.

"Are you all right, Mrs. Talbot?"

She turned to see Mr. Parnell coming around the corner, his brow furrowed in concern at her immobility.

"Oh, yes, Mr. Parnell. I'm fine." *(She wasn't, really.)*

He nodded. "Have you had breakfast? I was just heading to the lounge. Rumor has it Chef Culpepper has made raspberry crepes."

Jo had not, in fact, had breakfast and perhaps raspberry crepes were just what she needed to stave off this sense of impending doom. Certainly, the isolation of her room would only make her fret, and so she turned toward the porter.

"I have not had breakfast, Mr. Parnell. Crepes sound delicious."

He held out an arm. "Then please allow me to escort you."

~

"Well, you hardly addressed her at all," Constance Bostwick scolded as the driver guided their rented carriage from the grounds of the Imperial Hotel and headed toward the west bluff.

Chase was finally taking his mother on that drive so she might see what the VonMeisterburgers were determined to keep her from having for herself, but at the moment she was more intent on admonishing him for his alleged neglect of Frances Pullman during lunch.

"I was talking to her father," Chase explained, "and anyway, I could hardly get a word in what with Daisy pestering her with questions. And *opinions*." (Daisy had had the temerity to ask Miss Pullman if she thought women should have the right to vote and had received a kick under the table from his mother that nearly sent the water glasses flying.)

"I thought you said it was good to have opinions," Daisy argued while stretching arms high above her head and trying to reach the overhanging tree branches as the carriage passed beneath them.

"There's a difference between a well-considered opinion and a radical notion spouted off with no context," Chase answered.

She all but scoffed, as if his age and wisdom meant nothing. "Chase, in what context would it not be better for women to have the right to vote?"

This was a bear trap he'd rather not step in, but it was either argue with Daisy or argue with his mother, and so he would indulge her.

"Suppose women were asked to vote on matters in which they

had no knowledge?" he asked. "How could they make an informed decision?"

She gave an exasperated snort. "The same way men with no knowledge should. By educating themselves to the best of their ability and then following their good conscience."

She made it sound so simple but of course it wasn't. Not every woman had his sister's inclination to indulge in such educational and civically minded pastimes.

"And you're suggesting that most women would bother to investigate and reflect upon all the aspects of an issue before casting their vote?" he asked.

"As much as men do. Even more so on issues important to them, yes. Of course."

"Daisy," he said patiently, "issues important to women are rarely on the ballot."

"And you don't see that as a problem?" Her voice rose indignantly.

"Daisy!" their mother said, equally indignant, casting a glance at the driver as if he might overhear. Her throat was sure to be raw by the end of this drive if she kept scolding both her children. "Stop that this instant. Discussing politics is simply not ladylike under any circumstances, but it was especially inappropriate in front of the Pullmans. Honestly, I'm aghast at both of you." She all but harumphed.

Daisy persisted, immune to the recrimination. "Why *especially* in front of the Pullmans?"

"Because Frances Pullman would make an excellent wife for your brother." Constance turned to Chase. "Frances Pullman would make an excellent wife for you. I assumed you knew that when you invited her to lunch but then you wasted the entire time talking to her father about *investing*." She said investing as if what she meant to say was *disgusting*. As if investing and finance were not the things allowing her to purchase an obscenely large plot of land on which to build an obscenely large cottage and fill it with an obscenely vast number of items.

But more importantly, *a wife?*

"I am not interested in Frances Pullman for a wife, mother."

She very nearly dropped her parasol. "Why ever not? She's pleasant enough and appears bright, which for some reason seems to matter to you."

"I am not currently interested in having anyone as my wife right now. Can't you focus your attention on getting Alex down the aisle first?"

"Your brother did perfectly fine finding a bride for himself. He didn't need my help, but you do."

"I don't."

"You do if you keep ignoring perfectly good prospects while they're sitting across the table from you. What if Mortimer VonMeisterburger courts her right out from under your nose? What then?"

Daisy giggled and Chase knew why. There was no way in Hades Frances Pullman was going to set her cap for Morty. Not for all the oil in Albert VonMeisterburger's reserve tanks.

"Then I would wish them both the best and be happy for them, Mother," he said.

"Happy? Happy! To let her entire fortune slip away?"

"I don't need her fortune. I have my own."

"You have your father's, not your own," she snapped.

That stung. He could *(mostly)* brush aside the disparaging remarks she made about all the ways he'd failed her as a son throughout his lifetime but to suggest he had not *earned* his money was false and unfair. *Christ,* if the only thing he'd ever done for his father was go on this damn trip, he'd have earned his money.

"That's enough, Mother."

She must have sensed she'd gone too far, or at least that he'd reached the end of his patience because she said nothing more, and neither did Daisy. They rode in silence along the bluff until coming upon some properties with the boundaries marked, indicating their availability. Numbered flags identified which parcel was which.

"There," his mother said pointing. "That's the one VonMeisterburgers want."

They got out and walked around, taking in the lovely view of sparkling waters down below, the boulder-filled shoreline, and Michigan's mainland off in the distance. Standing on the edge of a rocky cliff, feeling the warm sun and cool breeze upon his face, Chase could understand why someone would want a cottage here. Even with his fondness for the hurly-burly energy of Chicago, or maybe because of it, he could appreciate the quiet solitude and the sense that the rest of the world had simply gone away.

And then, because it had been hours since he'd thought of Mrs. Talbot, he stared out at the beautiful panorama before him and wondered how she might paint it.

sixteen

On Monday morning, Jo's heart was full of trepidation. Although she'd felt better about her situation while having breakfast in the company of lively hotel staff, she'd spent Sunday afternoon and evening penning letters to every artist friend, peer, or acquaintance her father had ever mentioned living in France hoping against hope that one might respond to offer her sponsorship. She'd omitted her secret hardships, saying only that her father had passed recently and that his dying wish had been for her to study in Paris.

She would be there in the autumn, she wrote, and hoped they might agree to (*at least!*) meet with her. If she could make her way to the City of Lights, surely one of them would offer some assistance. A meal, a night of lodging, advice, instruction... friendship. Of course, that was assuming these letters would ever make their way to the rightful recipients. She didn't have firm addresses for most of them, nor did she have her father's old address book.

"Good morning, Mrs. Talbot." A cheerful voice greeted her from behind as she stood at the front desk of the hotel lobby waiting for Mr. Beeks to acknowledge her so she might post her letters to Paris.

She turned to see one of the wallflowers, a Miss Palmer, alongside an elegantly clad couple who, though obviously husband and wife, appeared to have a good many years between them. He had thinning, snowy white hair and a trim goatee, while she had a thick mane of wheat-colored tresses bedecked with a dozen diamond studded combs.

"Why, good morning, Miss Palmer. How lovely to see you," she responded, not certain if she should go over to where they stood or to keep her place at the desk, but Miss Palmer solved that dilemma by closing the distance between them, the older couple following along.

"Mummy, Papa, this is the woman I was telling you about," Miss Palmer said, smiling brightly. "The one who drew such a beautiful picture of me at the dance. Mrs. Talbot, please allow me to introduce my parents, Mr. and Mrs. Palmer."

Mr. Palmer offered a slight bow.

"How do you do, Mrs. Talbot?" he said. "Our dear Priscilla has spoken of little else since meeting you. It seems you made quite an impression."

"As did she upon me," Jo answered. "It was an honor to commit her beauty to paper." Neither comment was entirely true. Miss Palmer had made a modest impression upon Jo, being one of the quieter girls in the group, and her beauty was, perhaps, more internal in nature, but just like the creative liberties Jo had taken with the drawing, she'd take some now as well. Especially given her recent conversation with Mr. Plank. She needed every friend she could get.

"You're quite talented," Mr. Palmer added. "My wife and I are enthusiasts of the French Impressionists."

"As am I," Jo responded.

"Are you now? My daughter tells me you offer classes. Is that so?"

"It is," Jo answered. "I teach a variety of styles and techniques and in addition to my classes, I'm available for private lessons as well." She allowed herself a slight turn of the head to see if Mr.

Beeks had heard this exchange, and his dour expression suggested that he had.

"I plan to attend your class this very morning," Miss Palmer said. "I believe Miss Getty and Miss White will be there as well."

"Oh, I'm so glad," Jo said, and that she truly meant.

"As much as I appreciate fine art, I don't imagine my skills would meet my expectations," Mrs. Palmer responded with a polite smile. "But perhaps I could make the attempt and blame my inability on poor eyesight. As for now, we're off to breakfast. I'm famished. A pleasure to make your acquaintance, Mrs. Talbot."

Jo felt slightly dismissed by Mrs. Palmer's manner, but when the ten o'clock hour arrived, much to her surprise and relief, the studio was graced with a lively collection of aspiring artists. Wallflowers, a few women from her previous classes, Daisy, and Ruth, and all three of the Palmers! Oh, that Mr. Plank might wander by and see the room full!

With so many students to give her attention to, the time went by in the blink of an eye, and although the class was meant to last an hour, she was glad to have a few stragglers, because they kept her from her next unavoidable task – apologizing to Mr. Bostwick. When Bertha Palmer invited Jo to join their family for lunch, she was glad to delay the mea culpa for another few hours.

In fact, it was nearly teatime when Jo decided she could no longer avoid the unavoidable. She was on the front porch and spotted Mr. Bostwick coming up from the lawn alongside Mr. O'Keefe. He was wearing a tennis costume and carrying a racket. His face was tan, his hair disheveled in the most attractive manner. He looked like an advertisement for masculine vitality, and she suddenly wished for eyesight as poor as Mrs. Palmer's so she might be immune to him, but even from twenty feet away, and then ten, and then five, even with a fine sheen of perspiration on his brow from his efforts on the tennis court, he spurred in her a riot of emotions. None of which were useful or appropriate, and each one laced with an edge of carnal frustration.

Maybe she didn't need to apologize. He'd probably only asked her to dance out of sense of charity anyway and was likely *relieved* when she'd said no. Although... she had sort of embarrassed him. Maybe the best course of action was just to avoid him (*for an entire summer?*) but it was too late. He'd seen her, and it was obvious she was waiting.

She glanced past him, hoping there might be someone else she could pretend to be waiting for but the only ones behind him were his stern-faced mother and the garishly dressed Mrs. VonMeisterburger. The women appeared to be arguing in hushed tones, and Jo could only imagine what topic had them so animated.

"Good afternoon, Mr. O'Keefe. Mr. Bostwick," Jo said as the men climbed the steps.

"Mrs. Talbot," they responded in unison.

"How was your game?" She nodded at the rackets in their hands.

"Excellent," said Chase.

"Abysmal," answered Mr. O'Keefe. "I have feet of lead and could not hit a watermelon with this racket."

Jo found herself laughing at his answer, along with Mr. Bostwick as the gentlemen reached the porch and came to stand beside her. She liked Mr. O'Keefe. He was respectful and engaging, and by all measures seemed to be a fine husband.

"Surely it was not as bad as all that?" she responded.

"Tennis is too swift a game for me," Mr. O'Keefe said, mopping his profusely sweating brow with an embroidered handkerchief. "But golf, now there's a game where I'm sure to be victorious. The Scots invented it, you know, so I'm practically a natural. Ever played, Bostwick?"

"I have not."

"Excellent, then I challenge you. Tomorrow afternoon."

"Tomorrow?" Mr. Bostwick said with an easy chuckle. "That gives me no time to practice, or even learn the rules but... very well. Challenge accepted."

Mr. O'Keefe's ice-blue eyes lit up. "Wonderful. And how about you, Mrs. Talbot? Have you ever golfed?"

She watched as Mrs. Bostwick and her jewel-encrusted companion reached the top of the steps and continued on past into the lobby, still clearly arguing. Jo had the distinct impression they were about to come to blows with their lacy parasols.

"Me?" Jo asked, returning her gaze to Mr. O'Keefe. "No, I've not had the opportunity to play golf."

"Then you must play with us sometime," he continued. "Not tomorrow because I intend to run Mr. Bostwick into the ground but some other time. My wife plays quite well. Perhaps the four of us could make an outing of it one of these days, yes?"

No. No, no, no. "Uh, yes, I suppose we could," Jo heard herself answering.

"Excellent," he said again. "Now, speaking of my wife, I'm off to freshen up and then take her for a carriage ride around the island. Who knows, Bostwick? Perhaps we'll end up with a piece of property right next to yours and we can be neighbors. Good day to you, Mrs. Talbot. Mr. Bostwick."

With a wink and smile he was gone, and suddenly she was alone with Mr. Bostwick. There was no avoiding that apology now.

The exertion of tennis had left Chase breathless and hot, and encountering Mrs. Talbot did nothing at all to ease that. Quite the opposite, in fact. Walking across the lawn to find her waiting on the front porch made his ability to breathe *decrease* and his temperature *increase*. None of which was aided by the way Percy had just cornered him into agreeing to a round of golf, a game which, to Chase, looked very much like a *stroll* and nothing at all like an actual *sport*. It was sure to be tedious. He was already regretting it, but he could hardly have refused the challenge. Not in front of Mrs. Talbot. That would have seemed the modern-day equivalent of walking away from a duel without firing his pistol. When the gauntlet was thrown down, even in good fun, a gentleman must pick it up.

"Property?" asked Mrs. Talbot casually, effectively reminding him of the *other* gauntlet recently thrown at his feet – by his mother.

"Ah, yes. My mother is determined to have a cottage on the west bluff. Something ostentatious to rival the Imperial Hotel in both size and luxury but don't tell Mr. Plank." He was jesting about the latter, but her forehead creased at the mention of Plank, and she looked around as if worried the man might be listening.

"I wonder, Mr. Bostwick, if I might have a word with you?" she said, not bothering with additional pleasantries. Her gaze was back on him, and he thought, for a moment, to say he was *otherwise engaged* as she'd said to him Saturday night, but that might make him seem petty, and he wasn't petty. He was, however, curious. Very, very curious.

Yesterday morning, as the sun had risen high in the sky and the hazy fog of bourbon dissipated from his mind, he'd reconsidered posting that letter instructing his secretary to contact the Pinkerton Agency about investigating Oliver Talbot – because the affairs of Mrs. Talbot were really none of Chase's business. Regardless of his own motives or intent, if she was truly on the run from her husband, what right had he to get involved? He was not the type to pry into other people's business.

But then he'd reasoned, what right had he to *not* get involved? If her situation wasn't something easily rectified with a fresh dress from his sister or a decent room from Mr. Beeks, if she was truly in some sort of peril, Chase could not, in good conscience, leave her to fend for herself. No woman deserved a despicable husband. Chase would do the same for any damsel in distress. It had nothing to do with the fact that Mrs. Talbot had big brown eyes and a lush mouth. That was just a pleasant coincidence. And so, he'd sent the letter. Once he knew the details of the situation, he'd decide if he could, should, and would get involved. In the meantime, perhaps he might learn more from the woman herself.

"A word, Mrs. Talbot? Of course." He gestured to a shady spot on the porch, away from the incessant foot traffic of hotel guests going up and down the stairs between the lobby and the games on the lawn. She walked quickly to the railing, then turned to face him. He took note of her flushed complexion and the speck of blue paint on her dainty earlobe, wondering if she was ever completely free of the stuff.

"Mr. Bostwick, I must extend my apologies for the other night," she said, her tone direct, almost forceful, sounding more of accusation than atonement.

"The other night?"

He knew what she meant, of course, but apparently, he was a *little* petty, petty enough to play ignorant and make her work for his unnecessary forgiveness. A man had his pride, after all, and Chase was blessed with enough humility to acknowledge that his was *massive*. His pride, that is.

"Yes, at the dance," she said impatiently.

He very nearly chuckled at the insincerity of her contrition. He had a brother, after all, and recognized a false apology when he heard one, so he was definitely going to make her work harder for his clemency. (*At least a little harder.*) He tapped his chin and gazed up thoughtfully at the pale blue porch ceiling as if trying to recall... *The dance... the dance... what had happened at the dance?*

"Ah!" he said at last, snapping his fingers. "At the dance. I suppose you mean to apologize for the way you spurned me without cause or hint of regret?"

"I had... cause," she responded, suddenly seeming a bit less sure of herself. "But nonetheless, I handled it badly. You surprised me, you see. I was in the middle of a drawing. I couldn't leave the girls just then. It would have... made them sad."

He crooked an eyebrow. "And so, you chose instead to make me sad?" He'd thought to indulge in a bit more mischief at her expense because she still didn't appear to be that sorry, and because she had been discourteously blunt in her rejection the other night, but at his words, that uncertainty cascaded over her features like a bucket of cold water.

"Make *you* sad? I didn't... I mean, that is to say... um... oh, my goodness."

For the first time since he'd met her it seemed Mrs. Talbot was at a loss for words. He might have enjoyed outwitting her into silence, but by God, the girl donned emotions the way most women donned hats, unambiguously, and right on top for all the world to see. He'd meant to goad, not scold. Didn't she know that?

"Oh, come now, Mrs. Talbot," he chided gently. "I am teasing you, of course. Surely you don't presume to be the first woman ever to refuse my offer of a dance?"

"I'm not?"

"No, you are not." He was pleased by her apparent surprise and leaned casually against the railing to add, "You are the second. Maisy Baxter was the first, but her rejection should not count against me."

A hint of a smile touched her lips as she regarded him for a moment before asking, "And why is that?"

"Because we were both twelve years old at the time and of disproportionate heights," he said. "My youth and lack of stature made me eye-level with – and utterly fascinated by – her very tiny bosoms. She'd have none of it."

Jo blinked at him, once, slowly, and he watched as that hint of her smile blossomed into something both comfortably familiar and yet wonderfully special. She let out a soft chuckle and shook her head.

"Mr. Bostwick, you are a rascal. I think I was right to turn you down."

Now it was his turn to shake his head. "No, you were harsh and unjustly cruel. Because of you I had to dance with every marriage-minded miss in the room. My ego demanded it. Do you know how dreadfully dull that was?"

"Dull? You appeared to be enjoying yourself well enough."

He smiled with the knowledge that she'd noticed, although why that should please him was something he didn't want to examine too closely.

"Nonetheless," Mrs. Talbot continued, "I do want you to know that I appreciated your kind gesture, and should I ever have the opportunity to refuse you again, I promise to do so with much more compassion."

"Or... you could say yes." *Was it such a far-fetched idea? That she might dance with him?*

She glanced down at her hands for a moment. Once again, she was not wearing gloves, and there were ink stains on her fingers, faint but ever-present. When she looked back at him, her smile was bright but there was a tension on her face that hadn't been there the moment before.

"I think your time and attention are far better spent on the single young ladies in their beautiful dresses, don't you?" she said quietly.

"I don't pay much attention to their dresses, Mrs. Talbot, and besides, those young ladies have a set agenda, and it would be unfair of me to distract them from their goal of matrimony when my own aim is to remain unencumbered."

"Ah," she nodded perceptively, the smirk taking hold once more. "And you think a single dance with you is all it would take make them throw over any other potential suiters for the chance to win you as a husband?"

Hm, perhaps she was not so much perceptive as she was sarcastic, and a worthy sparring partner.

He straightened his shoulders. "I am a catch, Mrs. Talbot. And a fine dancer, which you would know if you'd seen fit to take a turn about the floor with me."

"But to what ends, Mr. Bostwick? If your charm is so irresistible, am I not wise to stay far away lest I fall prey to it?" Now *she* was teasing him, mocking him in a most playful manner, but as was often the case, humor was merely the truth dressed in disguise. She *was* wise to stay away from him. And they both knew it.

"But you already have a husband," he said.

She gazed at him directly, and in that moment, something passed between them. A bond, of sorts. An unspoken agreement. An understanding. Yes, she had a husband but he, and her marriage, were egregiously flawed somehow. She was all but admitting it with that bold stare and Chase wanted to ask more. He needed to ask more but they were on a porch full of hotel guests and busybodies making this neither the time, nor the place for such a conversation.

Still, he wanted her to know he was an ally. She could trust him. He wanted her to trust him. And so, he said good-naturedly, "Anyway, I suppose I must accept your apology, such as it was, but in return have a request for you to consider."

"A request?"

"Yes, I propose that you and I agree to be friends." He hadn't anticipated making such a suggestion at the start of this conversation, but it seemed the right thing given the circumstances.

"Friends," she said. "What manner of friends?"

He knew what she was asking. Did this friendship come with requirements? Did he say friends when he meant something more? God knew he was amenable to that. He'd wanted to kiss her for days now, but Mrs. Talbot didn't need the complication of a lover. She needed a champion.

"The usual manner of friends," he said. "You know, more familiar than acquaintances, less cloying than relatives? The kind who discuss books and art and golf and... the merits of Chicago."

He was grasping at straws here, his mind suddenly devoid of all suitable topics since the only thing he ever discussed with his male friends was business and politics, but she might not be interested in that type of thing, yet suddenly he wanted to know what things she *would* be interested in discussing.

"You are friends with my sister, after all," he continued. "And since we seem to be forever crossing one another's path, sometimes to the point of impact, I think it's only logical. Perhaps even kismet." He was trying to tease again, and her smile turned indulgent.

"You think it was kismet that caused our collision on the street?"

"No," he answered with a chuckle. "I think it was my mother's ill-behaved dogs which caused our collision on the street, so perhaps it wasn't destiny but merely disobedience. Regardless, I'm bored, and I could use a friend."

He understood well enough that playing on her sympathy for him would make it easier for her to say yes. She could claim generosity instead of need. "So, will you consider it?"

"I don't..." She paused and he thought for a moment she was about to say she didn't think it wise *(and she'd probably be correct)* but much to his relief, she answered, "I don't see why we cannot claim friendship. I would be honored."

"Ah, wonderful. As am I. I'm glad we are in agreement."

An awkward pause followed, as if neither were sure how to proceed with this newly declared kinship. Should they shake hands? Exchange calling cards? Kiss? No, of course they should not kiss but damn his brain – and body – for wanting to. This platonic friendship was going to be an adjustment. Perhaps he'd made an error in suggesting it?

Uncertain, and wanting to leave well enough alone, he pushed up off the railing. "And now, Mrs. Talbot, unless there's something else you'd like to discuss, I must go find someone who can teach me to golf before tomorrow afternoon."

seventeen

"More coffee, Mr. Parnell?" Jo asked as she walked past him in the crowded lounge.

The room was full, and noisy, and boisterous, yet having breakfast here with other hotel employees had quickly become a favorite part of her morning. Not just because the food was always abundant and delicious, but because it made Jo feel like part of an exotic, raucous, and even loving family. One in which Mr. Parnell was the unofficially declared patriarch.

"Don't mind if I do, Mrs. Talbot," he answered, holding up his mug for her to fill.

"I'll have some of that, missy," Harlan Callaghan added, stretching his arm over the table to offer his own cup. "And then I'll show you a new card trick."

Harlan Callaghan was Clancy's brother and, between the two of them, Jo could not decide which was friskier, but since their constant flirtations were delivered in such a joyful and overt manner, no one seemed to mind.

Edna Fitzroy, a rather plain, brown-haired housekeeper, scoffed at him good-naturedly. "Harlan Callaghan, you couldn't perform a successful card trick if the patron saint of magicians came down here and bonked you on the noggin with his blessing."

Harlan moved over to sit down next to Edna – very close – and grinned as he set his cup on the table. "Darlin' it's not about magic. It's a skill. It's called *sleight of hand*. It's all about the razzle dazzle." He waggled his fingers near her face, and she swatted them away with an indulgent grin.

"Son," Mr. Parnell drawled. "You got no razzle, and even less dazzle. What you need to focus on is how to properly carry a serving tray. You darn near spilled a dozen water goblets on Mrs. VonMeisterburger yesterday."

"That was not my fault," Harlen responded, popping an orange segment into his mouth. "That lady's got so many feathers sticking out of her head one caught me in the nose. She's lucky I didn't sneeze all over her as well as spill the water."

"No," Mrs. Culpepper, the chef's wife interjected. "*You're* lucky you didn't sneeze all over her. Mr. Beeks would've run all the way from the lobby desk into the dining room just to sack you for that one."

They all nodded, and Jo was reminded she wasn't the only one intimidated by the hotel manager. It was yet another thing that bonded them together, along with commiserating over their long work hours, discussing their beloved social director's constant requests for more participation, and a solid appreciation for being a part of this exciting new venture. Loyalty to Mr. Plank's vision was universal, and Jo sincerely hoped she might remain a part of it.

In fact, remaining a part of it was a point she stressed later that day during an impromptu visit with Mr. Tippett. He'd come to her studio just as she was finishing up a portrait session with Mrs. O'Keefe.

"Good day to you, Mrs. O'Keefe," he said. "I do hope you're enjoying your stay at the Imperial Hotel."

"I am, Mr. Tippett. Especially the art classes. It seems Mrs.

Talbot can indeed draw blood from a turnip for she's turning me into quite the *artiste.*"

"Wonderful, wonderful," he said, then plopped down on a wooden chair, stretching his long legs out in front of him as Ruth made her exit.

"It seems you have another supporter," he said, tilting his head toward the door she'd just disappeared through.

"So, it would seem," Jo answered, wiping her brush with a cloth.

"Good. Good," Mr. Tippett nodded. "Glad to hear it. Your outdoor painting class seemed well received, too. I've been hearing positive comments about it."

"I'm so glad, and since you mentioned it, I was wondering what you might think of me holding all my morning classes out on the front porch? The light is ideal that time of day and seeing us enjoying ourselves might encourage interest among the other guests."

He nodded thoughtfully. "Indeed, Mrs. Talbot. I like the way you think. And what's your opinion on teaching a few children's classes to our younger guests?"

"I like the way *you* think, Mr. Tippett," she answered. "Children have such an innate sense of art and they're not nearly as inhibited as adults. Depending on their ages, though, I might need an assistant or two."

"That's easily remedied. And speaking of assistants, our new dancing master, Mr. VanderLinden, has arrived direct from London, and I wondered if you might be amenable to helping him with his classes?"

"Help in what way?" she asked.

"Generally speaking, whatever he might need. Making sure everyone has a partner, keeping the guests organized, ensuring the musicians are ready."

"Yes, I suppose I could do that, but Mr. Tippett, I wonder if I might confide something to you. I've had a conversation with Mr. Plank and he –"

"Yes, yes, yes," Mr. Tippett said, flicking his wrist. "I know all about your conversation with Mr. Plank. He's putting you through your paces, I'd imagine. He wasn't pleased to learn you'd manipulated that contract, but you mustn't worry."

"You know about that?" Her deceit was apparently a poorly kept secret, and that was embarrassing.

"Yes, of course. Beeks wasn't about to take the fall on his own and tried to blame the whole situation on me, but Hugo Plank is an astute businessman as well as a modern thinker. Regardless of the means in which you came to us, you're here now and the initial response from our guests is that you're a delight."

"I am? Who thinks so?"

"Well, I do, for one, and frankly my own opinion is the only one I truly care about. Well, mine and Mr. Plank's."

"And..." Jo paused. "Does Mr. Plank... think I'm a delight? He told me I had just one month to prove myself and yet I don't know precisely what he's evaluating me on." She couldn't keep the unease from her voice. Perhaps she shouldn't share so much but it didn't seem there were many secrets between the hotel owner and social director. "I want to make sure I'm spending time on activities he'll find valuable. Preferably things no one else could do."

Mr. Tippett ran a hand through his skunk-stripped hair and snickered. "My dear Mrs. Talbot, somehow you managed to lure Potter Palmer into a room full of debutantes just to paint a bowl of fruit. I don't imagine anyone else could have accomplished that. The man owns half of Chicago."

"He does? He seemed so unassuming." She wasn't about to mention it was really Mr. Palmer's daughter who had done the luring. *God bless the wallflowers.*

"Mr. Palmer is a truly gracious gentleman," Mr. Tippett said with a nod. "And a knickerbocker through and through. A single word from him to Mr. Plank is all you'd need to ensure your position for the summer. Or a word from Mr. Bostwick. I saw you two speaking on the porch the other day." His voice betrayed nothing, but she wondered if he thought their exchange involved anything untoward.

Or, more likely, her worry stemmed from a guilty conscience – because although she'd agreed to be *friends* with Mr. Bostwick, there'd been a moment when she thought he'd meant to ask for something more. A moment so brief and fragile she wondered if it was just her own desire that made her think it was something of significance. She was lonely, after all. She'd enjoyed the intimacies of her marriage, brief though it had been, and although Oliver was a scoundrel, she did miss *that* aspect of having a husband.

Perhaps she was wanton...

Maybe that's what Oliver had seen in her that made her such an easy mark, but a leopard could not change its spots and she could not deny that she'd *liked it*. Quite a bit, and now she was without.

But Chase Bostwick... he was a cosmopolitan man of the world. Might he consider a romantic dalliance with a *(mostly)* married woman? Didn't the rich live by a different set of rules about such things? Didn't they indulge in liaisons of all sorts, protected by their wealth and position? She'd worried on that first day he might have licentious intentions toward her... but now it seemed she was worried he might not.

It wasn't a notion she could seriously entertain, of course. Leopard spots or no leopard spots, morality didn't have a sliding scale based on income, and she wasn't the sort to dabble in adultery, so, alas, Jo might indulge in her fantasies, but they must remain just that. Chase Bostwick was a *friend* and could be nothing more.

She was forced to remind herself of that the very next morning when Chase strolled out onto the front porch, a book tucked under his arm, and settled himself in a cushioned chair very near to where she was teaching her class. A waiter brought him a cup of coffee which Mr. Bostwick held casually by the rim, prompting her to wonder why he didn't use the handle. And then she realized... his hands were simply too big for the dainty China. *God... damn.*

"Good plein air work requires your whole arm, not just your hand. Hold your brush loosely at the end," she said to the collection of students while her gaze traveled from their canvases over to his silhouette at least a dozen times. It was breezy today, and the clouds seemed poised to rain and so her class was small. Even Mrs. O'Keefe had opted to stay inside but of course Daisy was there, as always.

As the week progressed, and Tuesday turned to Wednesday, and Wednesday to Thursday, Daisy's attendance proved as dependable as a compass. She showed up every morning fifteen minutes before the class began so she might gather her supplies and chat with Jo, (*en français*). Sometimes she'd bring Jo a flower she'd picked from the garden that morning, or a piece of candy she'd bought from the shoppe. They were tiny gifts, but Jo cherished Daisy's thoughtfulness. They made her feel special.

And just like his sister, Mr. Bostwick became a reliable presence on the porch as well, showing up soon after Jo's class began, with a book in one *(big)* hand and a cup of coffee in the other. He would smile at her and offer a nod of greeting, and then simply... read. He never even looked over at her. She knew this because she was so frequently looking over at *him*.

On Friday morning, as the week drew to a close, and the weather turned ideal for outdoor painting, the entire collection of wallflowers showed up for class, some even dragging along their mommas. The end of the porch was full of easels and artists and giggles and chatter. They were boisterous and silly and most certainly a distraction to anyone trying to read.

"I wonder, Mr. Bostwick," Jo said after walking over to where he sat, "if you might not be more comfortable moving farther down the porch? We're a noisy bunch this morning and I fear we'll keep you from your book."

He smiled up at her and she mentally listed all the different flecks of color in his eyes. "Not at all, Mrs. Talbot. I'm quite engaged in the story. No need to move." He held the book aloft so she might see the title. "Have you read this one?"

"*Around the World in Eighty Days*? I have."

His gaze was neutral, and she wondered if he'd gotten to the part of the story where Phileas Fogg risks everything to rescue Aouda from the aftermath of her miserable marriage. *Oh, the irony.*

"It's a captivating novel, indeed," she agreed. "And yet I wonder if the other end of the porch might prove more conducive to reading?"

He glanced to the left, and then back at her (and she noticed even more distracting flecks in those dark blue eyes). "Mrs. Talbot, do you see all those men down there at the other end of the porch?" He gestured toward them, and she nodded.

"Well, every single one of those men fancies himself an authority in his field and to the last, they want nothing more than to bludgeon me with their opinions and their so-called expertise. Since I am attempting to *enjoy* my leisure, I am avoiding them."

For a man who reportedly considered his *office* his favorite place to be, this was a surprise. Perhaps work wasn't all he was interested in.

"Ah, I see," she said. "But my class is twice its typical size this morning. Won't the chatter of my students and I be a distraction?"

"Not a distraction but rather a shield," he said.

"I beg your pardon?"

"A shield, Mrs. Talbot. With you over *here*, those men will stay over *there*." He smiled now, as if his strategy was both clever and amusing. *(And damn her if it wasn't.)*

"So... you're saying... I'm repellant?" She couldn't imagine posing such a question with a smile on her face and yet here she was doing just that.

He paused, as if to contemplate. "Repellant? No, not you personally, but certainly your army of artistic maidens is enough to keep those men at bay. And since I, fortunately, have no such aversion, I consider this spot to be perfect for reading."

She laughed at the delivery of his peculiar hypothesis. "Well, then, how lucky I am that you do not find me personally repellant."

"Not in the least. In fact, I find you quite the opposite."

There it was again. That suggestive invitation in his gaze. Teasing, but not entirely. As if the door was unlocked but he was leaving it to her to push open. But surely only scandal lay on the other side. She knew better, in spite of her longings and all the late-night dreams she kept having.

And who was to say Mr. Bostwick wasn't making those sensual, bed-roomy eyes at every woman at the hotel? For all Jo knew, he could be loitering on the front porch, not to read, but to observe the young ladies perambulating on their flirtation walks.

She tilted her head, regarding him. "Sometimes, Mr. Bostwick, I'm not sure when you're teasing me and when you are in earnest. Therefore, I think the safest thing is for me is to assume you are teasing at all times."

He let his warm gaze linger a moment longer, and then picked up his book. "That would be wise, Mrs. Talbot. I am prone to teasing."

No, he wasn't. He wasn't prone to teasing. Why had he said that?

Perhaps because it was far safer to play off his attraction to her as nothing more than casual, meaningless banter. The kind of verbal flotsam and jetsam heard in every ballroom and parlor of his peers, inconsequential flirtations, soon forgotten.

But this felt different.

This *was* different. Somehow.

He stared down at the page of his book, not seeing the words and resisting the urge to watch her walk back to her students. This was a dangerous game, being *friends* with Mrs. Talbot. One in which he should have every advantage since he knew the rules, and yet, in truth, *she* had every advantage because she was the one deciding if it might become real. *When* it might become real – because husband or no husband, he wanted her. He would never take advantage, of course. The choice was entirely hers, but he hoped she was considering it.

In the days since their conversation on the porch last Monday, when they'd agreed to be friends, he'd encountered her numerous times. Sometimes by pure happenstance, such as in the lobby when he was waiting for Percy and Mortimer to go sailing and Jo had been drawing a caricature of the hotel porter, Mr. Parnell (a mountain of a man who Chase would always want on his side in a fight).

Or on the front lawn when Chase had been returning from the stables after an afternoon ride and discovered her with an easel, working on a painting of the Imperial Hotel (a gift for Mr. Plank, she'd told him). They'd had a lengthy conversation then about how one must block the shapes of a painting by contrasting light, medium and dark and how *value did all the work, but color got all the credit.* Or something to that effect. He hadn't understood most of what she'd said because he was quite hopeless when it came to art but more so because he'd been so thoroughly enchanted by the animated manner in which she discussed her craft. (*Oh, that she might direct some of that unbridled passion toward him.*)

Other times, such as this morning, their meetings were more deliberate in nature – at least on his part. Reading on the porch near her painting class (very *obvious*), escorting Daisy to her side when they'd made plans together, (*slightly less obvious,*) or stationing himself in various places he knew she'd have to pass by on her way to something else *(not at all obvious and quite clever, in his opinion).* Sometimes she would stop, and they'd exchange a few words, other times she'd merely acknowledge him with a wave and a nod. But whether words were spoken or not, a message was conveyed...

There you are...
How pleased I am to see you...
You have been on my mind...

Or... maybe that's just what *he* was trying to convey?

She, herself, was still a blank canvas. He'd learned nothing of significance about her inconvenient husband or problematic marriage, nor had he gleaned any details about what had truly prompted her journey to the Imperial Hotel or what was pushing her toward Paris. And no wonder. These were not topics easily broached or expounded upon in the hallway outside the tearoom.

What he had learned, however, was that she was painting a portrait of Mrs. O'Keefe as well as a maid named Betsy, that she greeted nearly every hotel worker by name (but would go out of her way to avoid Beeks), and that she occasionally ate dinner in the Imperial dining room, but each time sat at a different table leading him to believe she was there as someone's guest. He'd like to invite her to dinner himself but putting her within earshot of his mother – and Breezy – seemed too risky for a variety of reasons. So, he didn't. But he wanted to.

"If we delay on that property any longer, Albert and Breezy are sure to claim it," his mother admonished him at lunch later that day, making him doubly glad he'd not invited Jo to join them. "And we'll be left with nothing."

"This island is littered with desirable building locations, Mother. I think you can make do with a different lot."

"Make do? Make do? Why should I have to make do when the exact piece of property I want is right there for the taking? It's only your dilly-dallying that's keeping me from it."

"I'm not dilly-dallying, Mother. I'm waiting to hear from Father. Of course, I could have purchased the lot for you myself but as you so kindly pointed out the other day, I haven't any of my own money. Only Father's."

She harrumphed. "Now you're just being contrary. Why are you always so contrary?"

The obvious problem with being called contrary was that he

couldn't defend himself – without being contrary. Conversations with his mother were often like this – like navigating an endless hedge maze but with every avenue leading to a dead end.

"Have you heard any updates about the wedding plans?" he asked instead, hoping the topic of Alex's personal achievements might distract her from harping on about his own apparent failures. It was just the two of them dining at a small table near a huge window overlooking the lake. Daisy was off with the Mahoney girl and his mother had requested this location although he didn't know why. Perhaps she thought isolating him was the best way to press her point, but he'd not rise to her taunts today. He had other things on his mind.

Returning to his hotel room after lunch, Chase found a stack of letters and a few small boxes waiting upon his desk, obviously delivered by a hotel employee. Most of the items were from Mr. Hayden and pertained to standard business matters – files to be reviewed, documents to sign and return, newspapers to be read – which Chase would peruse more carefully later that evening.

But one letter from his secretary spoke about the art box for Mrs. Talbot. Chase shrugged off his jacket and loosened his tie as he walked to the window with the letter in hand. It felt as if he'd sent the request ages ago, but it hadn't truly been *that* long. Island time moved slower, or so it seemed.

Dear Mr. Bostwick,
Per your request, I've procured a Winsor & Newton artist kit from A. Sussmann's in New York as I've been assured it's the finest available. You may expect delivery of it to the Imperial Hotel by the middle of next week along with all the requested accoutrements. I took the liberty of requesting additional brushes and paper be included with the kit as my sources said this would likely be appropriate.
Sincerely,
C. Hayden

The realization that Chase could soon provide Mrs. Talbot with a new art kit brought a smile to his face, and surely now that they were friends (or *whatever they might ultimately be)*, she could accept it from him directly, but he'd make certain Daisy was in the know and perhaps they could present it to her together, just in case Mrs. Talbot still had any reservations. And then, alone in his room, he laughed out loud at the incongruity of his desires.

He wanted Jo Talbot in his bed, to pleasure and plunder and please her in at least a dozen different ways, while simultaneously worrying he might offend her delicate sensibilities with the gift of some *paintbrushes?* Such was the nature of seduction.

If he dwelled on this matter for too long, he'd have to fling himself into the chilly waters of Lake Huron before going to dinner, and so instead he turned his attention to the Western Union telegram, also sent by Mr. Hayden. It doused his ardor more sufficiently than a plunge into the lake.

HAVE CONTACTED PDA AT YOUR REQUEST. STOP.
MR N WILL REVIEW MATTER AND CONTACT YOU
DIRECTLY. STOP.

PDA - the Pinkerton Detective Agency. Mr. N. was likely Edgar Newhouse, a no-nonsense man Chase had worked with in the past when investigating potential investment clients. He was a blunt instrument when something with a more refined edge might be better suited, but he was efficient at his job. He'd get answers, and he'd get them quickly, which is what Chase wanted. *Wasn't it?*

Then why did he suddenly feel as if he was doing something wrong? He wasn't investigating Mrs. Talbot. He was investigating Mr. Talbot – *on her behalf!* With any luck, she'd never even know he'd taken this path. She'd tell him everything of her own accord and he could deal with the matter based on information she herself shared with none the wiser. If this was a business matter, he'd have no qualms at all.

But it wasn't a business matter. It was personal. Perhaps the most personal matter of all – the relationship between a husband and wife. Still... he'd set the ball in motion and there was nothing to be done about it now. All he could do was wait and see what Newhouse discovered.

He re-read the note about the art kit as if to remind himself he was *doing a good thing!* But to no avail. He turned to the next letter instead, which only added annoyance to the mix. It was from his brother.

Chase,
Your offer to return to the city so I might take your place is indeed a generous one. I wish I could comply, but wedding plans have taken over our lives. My fiancée and future mother-in-law have all but tethered me to a chair so I might say, "Yes, dear, that sounds perfect," to every decision being made without the benefit of my input. Married life is sure to be much of the same and yet I find myself not minding. It seems impending matrimony has made me malleable. Perhaps you should seek a bride for yourself, brother. I look forward to your return. Until then, enjoy the reprieve from those many hours spent at the office. Father and I have things well in hand and when you are home, and I leave on my honeymoon, you can step right into my place as if you'd never left.
Give my love to Mother and D.
Alex

Step into *his* place? Into *Alex's* place? What about his *own* place! The place he'd left behind when his father sent him off to play chaperone! A dull throb began at Chase's temples and traveled to his jaw. He was an essential component of Bostwick & Sons was he not? It wasn't Bostwick & *Son!* There were two of them and he did twice the work of his brother.

Surely the company felt the void of his absence. Certainly, opportunities were being missed and details overlooked. But of course, Alex wouldn't realize such things because Alex never realized such things. And it wasn't just the distraction of being engaged.

And that was another thing!

Perhaps you should seek a bride, brother.

Was the dig deliberate? Chase had never confessed his fondness for Isabella to his brother, of course. Their courtship had led to an engagement so fast he'd never had the chance, but the letter was smug. *Wasn't it?*

Chase hardly dared to open the letter from his father, sure to find more of the same. More dismissal and indifference. He poured himself a glass of whiskey and downed it in one gulp. It burned as he read.

Son,

There are no urgent matters requiring your attention in Chicago, but I am not at all surprised to hear of your mother's interest in having a cottage built on the island. I suspect this was her scheme from the start and I commend you for your interest in designing and overseeing the construction. You have my permission to proceed. Please keep me abreast of the plans and maintain a reasonable budget. Just because Vanderbilt spent $450,000 for that place in Newport, don't let your mother talk you into going above $75,000. You know she'll try.

He went on to mention a few other things – how Thomas Hoyne of the Astronomical Society had recently donated an eighteen-and-a-half-inch refracting lens to the Dearborn Observatory, how the Republican National Convention occurring downtown created snarls in traffic, and how he'd recently dined with the Fairchilds and met a strange and wonderful British actress by the name of Ellen Terry. None of this was of any consequence to Chase, of course. He was fixated on that first paragraph.

I commend you for your interest in designing and overseeing the construction.

His interest? He had no interest in doing such a thing! He hadn't been making an offer. He'd been making a threat! Damnation! Had the wording in his own letter been unclear? Had he misrepresented his intentions? Or was his father being deliberately obtuse? That seemed more likely.

Regardless, it seemed he was stuck here for the duration of the summer. Their apparent lack of need for him in Chicago stung, more than a little, and yet...

There *was* Mrs. Talbot...

eighteen

"You press the button. We do the rest. That's their motto." Mortimer VonMeisterburger was holding court in the lobby as Chase descended the stairs on his way to breakfast Saturday morning and although hungry and in desperate need of coffee, he made his way over to the small cluster of onlookers to see what object of fascination Morty had on display. It appeared to be a small, unremarkable, brown leather box.

"What have you there, Morty?" Chase asked, remaining on the periphery. He'd learned through trial that, due to the young man's encyclopedic knowledge of esoteric facts, it was wise to have an exit strategy before engaging in conversation with him. Chase didn't want to get too close and be pulled into the vortex. Not on an empty stomach.

"It's a camera," Morty said enthusiastically, holding it up for Chase's inspection.

"That little thing is a camera? How is that possible?"

"Science and innovation, Mr. Bostwick. Come and see for yourself."

Was it a trap? It must be a trap. Against his better judgment, Chase moved forward and accepted the thing from Morty's hand.

It was light, weighing less than a pound or two, significantly smaller than a hat box, and certainly nothing like any camera he'd ever seen.

"What you hold there in your hands," Morty continued, clasping his own lapels like an orator, "is a Kodak, number one, fixed-focus, single shutter speed camera. Thanks to my good friend, Mr. George Eastman, and his dry-plate coating machine, this tiny feat of engineering has the ability to take one hundred photographs. One hundred, I say. Can you imagine?"

"I cannot imagine. Where are the plates?" Chase asked, still unconvinced and feeling rather bad for poor Mr. VonMeisterburger who had surely been duped by some conniving huckster. This thing was nothing but a box.

"That's the beauty of it, sir. There are no plates," Morty answered with glee. "It comes pre-loaded with flexible paper film. All I do is just press this little button and the camera captures the image." He showed Chase the button and continued. "Then I crank this little key, and voila! It's ready for the next photograph."

"But... where are they? Where are the photographs?" Frances Pullman asked, giving Chase a start. He hadn't realized she was among the group of gawkers, but there she was looking serviceably attractive in a pale-yellow morning dress and peering intently at the so-called *camera* in his hands.

"Once I've used up all one hundred exposures, I ship this unit off to Rochester where they'll develop the film, then send me the printed images along with a new, fully loaded camera that's ready for one hundred more photographs. A modern marvel, is it not?"

"Ingenious," muttered someone.

"Remarkable," murmured another.

"I don't like it," groused the man on Chase's left. "Before you know it those pesky boxes will be in the hands of every man, woman, and child and people will be taking pictures willy-nilly. All the time. Of everything. It's not the natural order of things."

"Certainly not every man, woman, and child," said Mr.

Crocker, ever the monitor of what the lesser classes should not have access to. "It must cost a small fortune."

Mortimer leaned toward the fellow and lowered his voice, although they all could hear.

"Mr. Eastman means to charge twenty-five dollars for the first unit," he said. "And another ten dollars for the development of the film, but that's a small price to pay for such advanced technology, wouldn't you say?"

Chase passed the camera to Miss Pullman who seemed quite intrigued. "And where might one purchase such an item?" he asked. He still had his doubts but if it worked the way Morty said, he couldn't deny he wanted one. Not that photography was of particular interest to him, but a new gadget might help Chase pass the time in between monotonous meals with his mother and those uncomfortable bouts of sexual longing for Mrs. Talbot.

"This was shipped to me by Mr. Eastman himself, as a gift. There are currently only four hundred available, but at some point in the future they'll be available from average merchants," Morty answered.

Chase nodded and made a discreet exit as a few new bystanders wandered up to see what the fuss was about. Just outside the dining room entrance he encountered Mr. Plank.

"Ah, Hugo. Just the man I was looking for. Will you join me for breakfast? I have some business to discuss."

Mr. Plank's brows rose with apparent optimism. "Ah, excellent. I like the sound of that. Let's find a private spot." He led them to a corner table not far from where Mrs. Talbot had rejected him, and Chase hoped that wasn't a bad omen. Fortunately, he wasn't superstitious.

"I assume you've made the wise choice to invest," Hugo said the moment Chase's backside made contact with the chair, and he chuckled at the man's tenacity (and impatience).

"No time for pleasantries, eh, Hugo?"

"Not when there's business to discuss." He smiled at Chase and signaled for a waiter. Within minutes they had fresh coffee and plates piled high with enough food to feed ten men. It was impressive but wasteful, a thing Chase might mention if he actually did invest.

"Well, as you assumed," Chase said as they dug into their breakfast, "I would like to invest, but I have a few caveats and things I want clarification on first."

"Naturally," Hugo said.

"And I have a favor to ask."

"A favor?"

"Yes, my mother has her sights set on some property on the west bluff. She wants a cottage, and I'm hoping you can help me make that happen."

"I'd rather you just stayed here at the hotel." He was being facetious, but Chase thought to reassure him, nonetheless.

"Of course, but just imagine how many friends and relatives we'll encourage to stay here over the years if we have a summer place of our own. And to be perfectly frank, I'm planning to invest my own personal funds in the hotel, not my family's, and not funds from Bostwick & Sons, so I'll be particularly motivated to ensure my investment sees a return."

Hugo paused, regarding Chase carefully. "Your own personal funds? Not company money? Why is that?"

Chase expected the question. "Because, as you said yourself, I'm the Bostwick willing to take bold risks. I'll be the one putting the time and energy into this, so I want to be the one to reap the rewards."

Hugo leaned back in his chair and paused before saying, "It's not easy being second fiddle, is it?"

"I'm not sure I know what you mean." *(Yes, he did. He knew exactly what Hugo meant but his ego wouldn't let him admit it.)*

"I'm the fifth of six brothers," Hugo said. "Born right here on this island. I was fifth in line for bathwater and didn't own a brand-new pair of my own pants until I was seventeen years old and could pay for them myself. We all worked, of course, but every penny went right back into the family. I didn't resent it, but

I did spend my childhood vowing that one day I'd be my own boss. That my money would be my own, and here I am. Now, obviously, you've had a different time of it. I doubt you've ever had to share much of anything, but let me tell you, son, there is no satisfaction equal to standing on your own two feet and being your own man. I know of your father. He is smart and savvy. Bostwick & Sons has a solid reputation and I'd be happy to do business with them, but I'd be downright honored doing business with just you."

Damn, but Hugo Plank could charm the stripe off a skunk. The man was such an inveterate salesman he wasn't just accepting the investment from Chase, he was making him feel *proud* to hand his money over for the righteous cause of expanding the Imperial Hotel. And damned if it wasn't working. He wasn't off the mark, either. He was right in suggesting Chase's own goal was to get out from under his father's (and his brother's) shadow, but the man had purposefully turned this investment into a matter of personal growth. Chase would seem all but weak and cowardly to change his mind now.

Never mind that his father would lambaste him for this, for not doing enough research, for not having their lawyers look it over, for not seeking A.J. Bostwick's paternal advice and council, but Plank was right. It did feel good to stand on his own two feet. And the next time his mother pointed out it was A.J. who was rich, and not Chase, hopefully he'd be able to contradict her.

nineteen

"It's not as if cultivating a new rose is some impossible feat of botany," Mrs. VonMeisterburger complained, "and yet every single gardener I've interviewed has been too lazy to even attempt it. One would think I was demanding Frederick Olmsted to suddenly appear on my front step with an entirely new species of flower!"

It was the afternoon of the *Imperial Hotel Euchre Tournament*, and Jo was fast coming to the conclusion that Breezy VonMeisterburger was the most exasperating woman she'd ever met, although Constance Bostwick ran a close second. Actually, between the two of them, it might be a tie.

They were sitting at a small, square table in the midst of the crowded ballroom along with Jo's randomly assigned partner, Miss Eliza Spilsbury, a wispy, nearly translucent spinster whose grandfather had made his fortune inventing the jigsaw puzzle.

"Am I supposed to know who Frederick Olmsted is?" Mrs. Bostwick asked – in possibly the most disinterested tone Jo had ever heard – while deftly shuffling the playing cards.

"*Who* is Frederick Olmsted? Oh, my goodness, Constance," Mrs. VonMeisterburger sniggered behind a satin-gloved hand. "How inexplicably ignorant you are. He's only the most renown landscaping architect in these United States. He designed New York's Central Park. How could you possibly not know who he is?"

Jo pressed her lips tight to keep from laughing at the venomous glare Mrs. Bostwick directed toward Breezy. She could practically feel its heat, and surely the overblown Mrs. VonMeisterburger was the only person (*in these United States*) brave enough, or perhaps foolish enough, to call Constance Bostwick ignorant. To her face! At any moment this acerbic verbal catfight might devolve into actual fisticuffs, and the mental image of that forced Jo to faux-cough into her handkerchief just to disguise her amusement. She did not want that poison-spewing stare of Mrs. Bostwick's to swing in her direction.

Mrs. Bostwick continued shuffling the cards. *Shuffle, shuffle, shuffle,* finally asking, "And why, pray tell, should I care a whit about some landscaping architect? I already have a rose named after me."

"Pssshhhh and poppycock. That rose is not named after you, and you know it," Mrs. VonMeisterburger volleyed back. "Stop telling people that it is."

And so, it went. On... and on... and on... until Jo's sense of humor faded away and her head began to ache from the bickering. Between that and Miss Spilsbury's questionable mental acuity, Jo seriously contemplated playing poorly – on purpose – just to get this round over with. However, try as she might, she could not manage to play worse than Breezy, nor could she hope to compete with the blatant cheating executed by Mrs. Bostwick. The woman had no shame. If they were west of the Mississippi she'd have been shot by now. But they were not west of the Mississippi. They were in northern Michigan at a luxury resort which catered to the kind of people who thought nothing of bilking a little old spinster and a penniless artist out of their winnings.

"I think that's game, isn't it?" Mrs. Bostwick said, *surreptitiously* sliding the score cards around with the ruffly cuff of her sleeve, giving herself and Breezy two more points than they'd earned.

But Jo was fine with that. It wasn't actually game, of course, but she needed some fresh air – and some fresh players.

"Your mother cheats at cards," Jo informed Mr. Bostwick as they encountered each other in the lobby just outside the ballroom doors. Her comment elicited his unexpected laughter, and he nodded in obvious good humor as they moved toward a more secluded spot.

"Yes, she does. I'm sorry you had to witness it for yourself."

"She wasn't even subtle about it," Jo added emphatically.

"No, she rarely is but seldom gets called out. Did you say anything to her?"

"Oh, good heavens, no. I'm not likely to challenge your mother. And anyway, Mrs. VonMeisterburger plays so poorly it was a mercy to end the game and let us all move on. That woman never stops talking and cannot keep her bowers straight. At one point she even laid her cards down on the table, face up, because she was *tired of holding them!*"

He laughed again, so loudly that heads turned, and Jo wondered if she'd ever grow tired of the deep, rumbly sound. Or the thrill of prompting it. She wished she might collect the melody of it in a bottle, the way one does sand or stones from a particularly lovely beach, but of course, she couldn't. Instead, she silently vowed to hear it as often as possible over the next few weeks – before he went home to Chicago, and she moved on to Paris.

Daisy joined them soon after. "What's funny?" she asked, poking her brother with an index finger. He batted her hand away but hardly seemed to mind.

"Mother's bad behavior," he said.

"Ah, I suppose she's cheating again?" Daisy stated knowingly, then asked, "Why must she always win? Why is it that the people who have everything always want more?"

That wasn't a question Jo felt equipped or qualified to

answer. Not while standing there in her three-year-old dress and well-worn shoes surrounded by the excessively privileged as they indulged in their excessive privileges. She mostly counted herself lucky to be here and was not about to draw attention to anyone's misdeeds. She'd done worse than cheat at cards.

"Maybe that's why she cheats?" Chase responded, more in contemplation than opinion. "She's never had to work for anything so perhaps cheating feels like an accomplishment of sorts?"

Daisy stared up at her brother thoughtfully. "That's generous of you, Chase. Personally, I think she cheats because she can't tolerate the thought of anyone else having something she might claim as her own. Even something as inconsequential as a round of Euchre. Or a piece of land that doesn't suit her purpose."

He frowned. "You think that land doesn't suit her purpose?"

Daisy shook her head and Jo wondered if perhaps she should step away. The conversation had turned very Bostwick-specific, and she didn't want to intrude, but there was no way to discreetly excuse herself.

Daisy continued. "No, I don't. She only wants that particular spot because VonMeisterburgers want it. If she'd paid any attention at all when we took our drive, she would have realized that the spot closer to the water is far superior."

"Superior? How so?"

It was Daisy's turn to frown, as if the answer was obvious, and Jo noticed how much alike they looked, at least when they were scowling.

"The view of the lake was more impressive, it wasn't nearly as rocky, and the grade was more gradual and thus better for building on. Maybe God can move mountains, but that lot the VonMeisterburgers want will surely require dynamite to blast into the hillside if they want a cottage of any respectable size."

The pause was significant as Chase's gaze turned from skeptical to bemused to appreciative. "Good heavens, Daisy. Where did you learn so much about civil engineering?"

She smiled, satisfied that she'd impressed him. She'd impressed Jo, too, but that was nothing new.

"I suppose if you can read poetry, I can read about construction," she said smugly. "I am capable, you know."

Daisy had confided in Jo during one of their pre-class, French-speaking conversations that there was a young man with whom she'd struck up a friendship. The son of a stone mason who lived on the island and who'd participated in the building of the hotel. Apparently, he'd made quite an impact on Daisy but that was not Jo's information to share.

"You are entirely capable," Chase agreed. "And just between us, Father has said to move forward with the cottage plans." He lowered his voice. "I haven't told Mother yet but have asked Mr. Plank to view the properties and offer his opinion."

"Good," said Daisy. "I suspect he'll say I'm right. And now, I'm off to play some Euchre. Oh, and speaking of Mother, she wants me to remind you to partner up with Frances Pullman. Something about her making an excellent wife." She winked at him and with a flounce of ruffles, was gone, and the joy Jo always felt at her presence took a tumble.

Mother wants you to partner up with Frances Pullman.

Oh, that's right. Because Chase was a catch. He'd said so himself, and even though he'd also said he was determined to remain unencumbered, the sunshine of the day dimmed.

Jo had no right to feel this way, of course. He wasn't hers and he never could be. Still... she felt the words deep in her chest, and the ache of longing that had been building for days and days turned to a vise, squeezing her lungs.

"I've no interest in Frances Pullman," he said quietly, but Jo smiled as brightly as she was able – because it would not do for him to see her distress.

"Well, you should have interest in her," she said. "I hear she'd make an excellent wife."

～

Damnation. Why would Daisy say such a thing in front of Mrs. Talbot?

Why? Because she was sixteen years old and oblivious to the undercurrents all around her. She thought marriage was romantic and love sublime. She thought husbands were good and true and wives were faithful and happy. But Chase knew better.

And Jo knew better.

She'd left his side so quickly after Daisy's words he'd nearly felt a whoosh of wind in her wake. She was jealous. Jo Talbot was jealous of Frances Pullman, but for no reason at all because Chase had no designs on that woman. None whatsoever. And Jo was the one with the husband, after all. If anyone should be jealous it was Chase. But he had no right. There was nothing between them, *technically.* No tacit agreement, no unspoken understanding. Just a bit of unsettling flirtation and a handful of enigmatic glances.

And yet...

Things *were* getting complicated, just as he'd suspected they would on that very first day when he'd tried to wipe paint from her luminous cheek in the carriage, and tricked Beeks into giving her a better room. And truthfully, during every encounter they'd had since then. Every word spoken was a complication. Every smile, a snare. He was caught, and he had no idea what to do about it. Not because he was conflicted about a liaison. He wasn't.

But she was.

He left the tournament deciding to go for a ride instead. He needed time to think, time away from the busybodied matrons and their obsession with marriage, away from the garrulous barons and their grandiose self-importance, away from the doe-eyed debutants and their optimistic expectations. But most of all, he needed time away from Jo Talbot.

From the fifty fine horses in the Imperial stable, he requested the most spirited mount and ended up with a high-stepping paint named Doxy *(suitable for just such an occasion).* Leaving the hotel grounds, he rode aimlessly through the town of Trillium Bay, past the Island House and Saint Bartholomew's church, past Fort Beaumont sitting high on the hill overlooking the Straits, past a few shacks along the shoreline that looked sure to fall over at the next stiff breeze, and on up a steep hill leading to... he didn't know. It didn't matter. He just wanted to ride and to think.

Or to *not think*. That was the better option. To not think at all because thinking led to *feelings*... and uncertainty. He wasn't accustomed to that – to uncertainty. He was Chase Bostwick, after all! A man who knew what he wanted. *(Didn't everyone say so?)*

Perhaps he was more like his mother than he cared to admit, wanting what he wanted just because he wanted it, but this was more than that. It had to be more than that. There was something *(something!)* between him and Mrs. Talbot. Something certain yet confusing, leaving him to feel untethered and, dare he even acknowledge it... *vulnerable?*

He rode on, even as the weather turned foul and wet, eventually finding himself on the west bluff where he discovered Daisy was right. He didn't need Hugo Plank to tell him which was the superior lot. Chase would buy the flat one with the better view and his mother would just have to accept it, just as she'd have to accept that he wasn't going to marry Frances Pullman, or anyone else for that matter. At least not right now. He had other things on his mind. He had another woman on his mind. Marriage would simply have to wait.

Eventually he made his way back to the hotel, with his suit and his horse now dripping with cold rain. His shoes squished and squeaked and squelched as he walked up the drive from the stables making him seem a rather ridiculous figure. Then again, he *was* a ridiculous figure, so why not announce it to the world with a comical noise? Why not announce he was a fool, falling for an inaccessible woman whose past was shrouded in mystery and whose future would certainly take her far away from him.

In the lobby, he heard the orchestra warming up, the pluck of strings and a melancholy oboe running through the scales sounding discordant and inharmonious, reminding Chase that it was Saturday. There'd be a dance tonight, but he was in no mood to dress up and play sociable. Plus, he'd been gone far longer than he'd realized and had missed dinner. His stomach rumbled in protest.

Beeks was at the front desk – because the rodent of a man was always at the front desk. Perhaps he lived there, in a tiny little cabinet under the counter. Beeks' eyes widened (as much as they were able) as he spotted Chase in his very soggy, probably muddy, certainly wrinkled suit.

"Good evening, Mr. Bostwick. Did you get caught in the rain?"

"No, I was swimming in the lake."

"I... oh."

"I'm kidding, Beeks." Gadzooks, did no one on this island understand the concept of *teasing?* "Yes, I got caught in the rain. I wonder if you might have a dinner tray sent to my room."

"Of course, sir. Very good, sir. What would you like on your dinner tray?"

"I don't care. Anything is fine." He turned to walk toward the stairs but hesitated, looking back at the little man. "But... if there is any lemon meringue pie, I'd very much like a piece of that."

twenty

Daisy Bostwick had so many elegant frocks strewn across the end of her hotel room bed that the House of Worth would surely be envious. There were ballgowns of shimmering silk brocade, lace covered satin, and miles upon miles of frothy tule, not to mention ribbons and buttons and ruffles and fringe. Jo had never seen such an abundance of finery in her lifetime and was unlikely to ever again.

She, herself, was dressed in a casual, cream-colored tea gown which boasted few embellishments which she'd donned only because she hadn't expected to see anyone today. She'd planned to spend Sunday in her room reading or loitering in the lounge to visit with the other employees fortunate enough to have a Sunday afternoon away from their duties, or perhaps she'd write letters to the few remaining artists her father had once claimed friendship with who might offer her assistance. That was a fool's errand. She knew that, but it was worth a try. It made her feel as if she was at least attempting to improve her situation.

But a light knock had sounded on her door at half-past eleven and there was Daisy, bright-eyed and pink-cheeked, asking if Jo would come to her room to help choose the dress she was to wear in her portrait – a portrait of which Mrs. Bostwick had only begrudgingly approved because who exactly was this Jo Talbot anyway? And Jo soon found herself sitting cross-legged at the head of Daisy's bed with a growing mountain of fabrics in front of her and, somehow, a little dog on each side. With Daisy's mother not present *(thank goodness)*, Flossie and Regina apparently felt free to dole out their affection elsewhere.

"I could wear this pink one," Daisy said, holding up a gown and then tossing it aside to grab another. "But I think I prefer something blue. What do you think?"

"They're all lovely," Jo said sincerely as she stroked a snoozing pooch with each hand. "But I think we need to decide what kind of mood we hope to evoke."

"Mood?"

"Yes. Do we want something formal or perhaps something a bit more intimate? I was thinking I'd love to paint you reading on a window seat, or perhaps sitting in the garden or the gazebo?"

Daisy pondered this for a moment. "I hadn't considered that. I thought you'd want to do something stiff and conventional, but I rather like the idea of the gazebo."

"I do, too, but if that's the case, you may want to choose something less formal. Unless, of course, we want the painting to seem as if you've stepped away from a ball for some fresh air."

Daisy offered up a coy smile. "Perhaps I've stepped away from the ball for an assignation, you mean?"

"I mean no such thing," Jo responded primly, but smiled, nonetheless. She'd never had a garden tryst herself, but what young woman didn't dream of one? Oliver had pushed her behind a tree once, but then he'd kissed her so aggressively her head knocked hard against the trunk and rough bark snagged her hair. It wasn't so much romantic as it was inconvenient and uncomfortable.

"Well, anyway, perhaps we should go out to the gazebo and see if there's a good spot?" Daisy suggested.

Jo involuntarily glanced down at her own plain dress. "I'd need to go back to my own room to change first."

"You look fine. Everyone is casual here while on holiday."

Jo didn't even attempt to hide her skepticism. "My finest dress is still more casual than most of what I've seen here at the hotel, Daisy. I don't mind changing. I can't go downstairs in this." She plucked at the thin cotton fabric of her skirt. She hadn't intended to sound sorry for herself. She'd *(mostly)* made peace with the inferiority of her wardrobe, but a twinge of insecurity escaped.

"Perhaps not," Daisy nodded in solidarity but not judgment, a fact which Jo appreciated. There was no point in pretending they were social equals and nowhere was that more obvious than in their clothing.

"But," Daisy continued, "since you mentioned it, as you can see, I've brought far more dresses than I need, and I'm happy to share with you."

Jo flushed all over with a mixture of gratitude and embarrassment. "Oh, no. That's not necessary. I appreciate the offer, but I couldn't accept." *(She couldn't. Could she?)*

Daisy waved her hand dismissively. "Of course, you can. You've already borrowed one dress. Why not a few more?"

"That was different. That was practically an emergency but now I have my own clothes and don't need yours."

Daisy came over and sat down on the plush mattress, facing Jo, gazing at her with a gentle look that said, *"I'm about to give you some bad news."*

"You do need mine. If you're to convince anyone to hire you for a portrait, you must look as if you don't need their business. You must look so well-to-do that they assume you're doing them a favor by agreeing to paint them."

Probably true.

"But everyone has already seen me in my... lesser gowns," Jo said, that twinge of inferiority in her voice again.

Daisy shook her head. "No one has paid much attention yet, but once you start working on my portrait word will get out. My father and brothers discuss business in front of me all the time and I listen. You should trust me on this." She stood back up and gestured to the pile of silk and satin, saying with a broad smile, "And anyway, even if I'm wrong, wouldn't you enjoy wearing some of these fabulous dresses and helping me feel less guilty about my life of extravagance?"

Jo laughed at the ploy and could not deny that the offer was tempting. And Daisy was probably right. *Looking* successful was as important as *being* successful. Perhaps Jo could justify borrowing these dresses for the same reason she'd, in essence, *borrowed* that contract from her father. It was all a mirage but where was the harm? Except to her pride?

"May I think about it?"

"Of course, but in the meantime –" A knock on the door of the suite interrupted Daisy, and as Adele the maid went to open it, the dogs, who had surreptitiously worked their way onto Jo's lap, lifted their heads sleepily with indolent *woofs* of interest. Guard dogs, they were not.

"Is my mother here?" Jo heard Chase's voice and her silly, irrational heart missed a beat.

"I'm afraid Mrs. Bostwick is downstairs at the moment, Mr. Bostwick," Adele responded.

"Good," he said, stepping inside the suite and stopping short as he caught sight of Jo through the open door of Daisy's room. And no wonder. What a rumpled picture she must make, sitting there on the bed like a farm girl with her skirts all scrunched up around her bent legs and the dogs draped across her lap as if she were a chaise lounge. There was no way to reposition into a more ladylike posture without being obvious. Perhaps he'd be distracted by the enormous mound of clothes and not notice her. Although... he was staring right at her.

He came to the door of the bedroom and leaned casually against the frame, his smile curious.

"Has there been an explosion?" he asked, nodding at the pile. "A textile mill, perhaps?"

"You're only funny when you're not trying to be," Daisy

responded cheekily while Jo tried to discreetly unfold her legs. To no avail. Somehow the dogs had doubled in weight.

"Where were you last night?" Daisy continued, directing the question to her brother. "We nearly sent out a search party."

Jo noted the subtle roll of his shoulders, as if he was working a knot from his muscles.

"I went for a ride," he said.

"All night?"

"I lost track of time."

"But you missed the dance."

"I was there. I just arrived late."

He had been there, briefly. Jo had seen him *(because she'd been waiting)*. He'd come in well past eleven o'clock, spoke to few, danced with no one (not *even Frances Pullman)*, and then left with Mr. O'Keefe soon after. He hadn't come to say hello to Jo, either, which she might have taken more personally if he hadn't seemed so indifferent and almost annoyed by the whole affair. She thought perhaps he'd received some kind of unpleasant news, but today he seemed personable once more. Whatever had been on his mind last night, he must be free of it now.

His mind was full of her, like a fever that would not break.

After dinner in his room last night, he'd thought a hot bath might ease the chill lingering in his bones from the long, wet, uninspiring trek around the island, and then perhaps some light reading to occupy his thoughts until he fell into a blissfully unaware slumber.

Oh, not so.

Mr. Hayden had supplied him with a copy of *The Mysterious Case of Dr. Jekyll and Mr. Hyde* which he'd read from cover to cover, and which only served to agitate him further with thoughts of murder and mayhem and madness, not to mention all but forcing him to contemplate every aspect of good and evil – existing within himself...

That was not relaxing!

Captivating? Original? Thought-provoking? Certainly, but not relaxing. So, more awake than he'd been all evening, he'd donned his tuxedo and headed downstairs thinking to discuss the story with Mrs. Talbot *(always Mrs. Talbot)*, but Morty had waylaid him outside the ballroom to share that he'd requested another camera from his close personal friend, Mr. Eastman and would generously give it to Chase once it arrived. Then Mr. Albert VonMeisterburger had come by and then Mr. Somebody Else along with That Other Man and suddenly Chase was neck deep in discussing the current price of kerosene and how Rockefeller was pushing the boundaries of morality with questionable business practices – but a dollar was a dollar, after all, and so it must be all right in the eyes of God, and Chase realized then that none of these men would understand the message of Dr. Jekyll's story because they lived and died by the philosophy that *might* was *right. They* were always right, in every circumstance – because they were *rich,* and therefore they must be *good*.

He'd been so put off (although not shocked) by the notion that he'd gone in search of Percy O'Keefe so they might go sit on the front porch and get drunk. At least in that endeavor he'd been successful and his head this morning still throbbed a bit for his victory.

And since he already had a dull head, he'd thought to come by his mother's room and tell her she could have her cottage after all. She would accept this news as a matter of fact. *Of course,* she was getting her cottage – because she *wanted* it. Then he'd have to tell her he was buying the piece of property he thought was the best choice and that they must let the VonMeisterburgers have the other. For his troubles, he expected a fight. He expected some pouting and some criticisms of how he always fell short of her expectations while the sainted Alex never failed her. And he expected to feel bad about this even though *(this time, at least)* he knew he was right, and she was wrong.

What he had not expected was to find Mrs. Talbot sitting in a ruffly nest of her own skirts on top of Daisy's bed with Flossie and Regina lounging across her lap. The image was so... wholesome and adorable it had stopped him in his tracks.

"So, what exactly is happening here?" he asked, gesturing to the pile of dresses.

"I'm choosing an outfit for my portrait," Daisy answered, as if saying, *I'm choosing an outfit for my coronation.*

"Ah," he answered, then smiled at Jo. "I see you've made peace with your assailants. I hope they've apologized for all the trouble they caused on Main Street."

"On the contrary," she answered. "They seem to think it's me who owes them, and no amount of ear scratching will even the score."

"We're going to the gazebo," Daisy remarked. "We could take the dogs outside so they get a little exercise. Chase, you should come with us. That way if they get too rambunctious, you can bring them back to the room."

His jaw clenched involuntarily. *Very important* men with *very important* jobs were reluctant to tell Chase he *should* do anything, and yet his sister suffered from no such hesitation. She was ever poised to give him directions and he *should* probably point that out to her, and yet... a walk to the gazebo with Mrs. Talbot didn't sound so bad. His jaw relaxed.

"I should change first," Jo said, nudging the dogs.

"Why? You look lovely."

He'd said it without thinking. And he said it with sincerity – because it was true – she was lovely and natural in a simple dress of soft material unburdened by endless ruffles and tassels and fringe that served no purpose other than to detract from the woman, but he may as well have clashed cymbals over his head for the reaction he got. Both women stared at him like he'd shouted an obscenity, and then Daisy cleared her throat.

"Yes, you do look lovely, Jo, and anyway, we're only going to the garden."

He felt subdued as they left the hotel and went down the stairs toward the front lawn, but at least he wasn't carrying the damn dogs. Daisy had one and Jo had the other, leaving him happily empty-handed. Once on the grass, Flossie and Regina scampered to and fro, zigging and zagging as if this was their first experience with running, and their last chance to enjoy it, and soon even Chase was laughing at their antics. Maybe they weren't such bad little dogs after all...

It was sometime later, after his sister had gone on to explore the gazebo, and he was walking along the garden path with Mrs. Talbot by his side and the dogs were now calm and on their leashes that she said quietly, "Thank you for saying I look lovely."

Chase glanced down at her as she gazed up at him, and in that moment, something new and exquisite blossomed. Something tangible yet untouchable, and all his concerns from yesterday fell away because he knew, as certain as the sun rose and fell, that she'd be his. Not because he hungered for her (*although he did*) but rather because he *cared* for her. He wanted to possess her, yes, but more importantly, he wanted to protect her. He'd never felt this way about a woman before, and while he might have once thought such a sensation would cause him distress, instead, it gave him a new sense of purpose.

"You always look lovely," he said. They stopped walking, pausing in the fragmented shade of a birch tree.

Her smile was wistful. "Even covered with paint and mud?"

"Even then."

She regarded him thoughtfully. "Are you teasing me, Mr. Bostwick?"

He shook his head. "No, I'm not teasing you. And I wish you'd call me Chase. Mr. Bostwick is a name I share but Chase is all mine." He'd never minded sharing the name, but suddenly it mattered. He wasn't just part of a set. He was... himself.

"I share a name, too, but... I'm mostly Jo."

"Jo," he said, and she blushed, and looked away.

"I suppose we should go find Daisy," she said after a pause. "She'll be wondering where we've gotten to."

He didn't want to go find his sister. He wanted to stay here in the dappled sunlight with Mrs. Tal... with Jo, saying nothing – and everything – but people were about, and Daisy was waiting, and the dogs were pulling on their leashes. It seemed he had no choice. There'd be other moments. He'd make sure of it.

But first...

"Would you say it? Before we go?"

Damn, he was being fanciful. Why did it matter if she said his name or not? He wanted to pull the words back as soon as they were out, but she smiled, and he knew she understood why it mattered, even if he didn't.

"Let's go find your sister... Chase."

twenty-one

"My goodness, Mr. Parnell, what have you there?"

He was standing outside Jo's hotel room door with a round top Saratoga trunk but as usual, it seemed the thing weighed next to nothing as he carried it inside and set it on the floor next to her bed.

"Couldn't rightly say," he answered. "I guess you'll just have to open it. I've been asked to bring the trunk back whenever you no longer have need of it."

"Return it to whom?" Jo asked.

"To the person who sent it." His smile was wide and mischievous.

"And, who sent it?"

"Couldn't rightly say," he said again.

She frowned at him but felt her own smile tugging at her lips. "I hope this isn't some sort of prank, sir. I'm not going to open this and be attacked by a wild animal, am I?"

He shrugged his bulky shoulders. "I don't think so." And then he chuckled. "No, ma'am. I'm sure there's no wild animal in there, but I'll leave you to it to find out for yourself."

She looked over the trunk as Mr. Parnell made his exit. There were no tags or markers or any kind of identifier other than the brand – Haskell Brothers. It seemed to be in fine condition, not new, but nearly, and although there was no wild animal, the contents surprised her just the same. Inside she found no less than a dozen beautiful dresses along with a note from both Daisy *and* Ruth. It was written in French, and said:

Dearest Jo,
Our trunks and bureaus are bursting with too many items. Please help us in this hour of need and store these in your armoire. And to make sure they don't get too dusty or wrinkled, please be sure to wear each dress as often as possible. We've included a few matching accoutrements for your convenience.
Your friends,
Daisy & Ruth

She read the note half a dozen times, and each time the words seemed blurrier for the tears in her eyes, but then she turned to the bounty inside. It was Christmas morning and every birthday rolled into one as Jo pulled out one fine gown after another.

Gowns for morning and walking and teatime and dinner. And even for dancing. Gowns of pale silk, jewel-toned satin, printed poplin, and creamy lace. There were satin ribbons, silk garters and cashmere stockings, kid gloves, embroidered shoes, and even a few sheer linen unmentionables that were obviously brand new, wrapped in paper, and tied with string. It was the finest finery she'd ever touched.

Pride flickered in her chest, and she thought for the briefest moment she should refuse their charity, but her sense of friendship prevailed, promising her that this gesture was pure generosity. Daisy and Ruth didn't pity her. They *liked* her. She would have done the same if the situations were reversed, and so she carefully and gratefully hung the beautiful gowns in the armoire as instructed, except for one - a morning dress with tiny rosebuds woven into the fabric that reminded her of being in the garden with Mr. Bos... with Chase, and she blushed at the thought.

Yesterday, they'd loitered in the gazebo until teatime, letting the dogs scamper about, with Daisy lounging in different poses as they discussed her painting (*and then discussed her painting some more*). There was hearty laughter and playful taunts between the siblings, and Jo marveled at watching Chase, a man of such wealth and importance, climb a tree to the highest branch just because his little sister had dared him to. The fact that he'd removed his jacket and rolled up his shirtsleeves to do so made the memory that much more delicious.

Everything about the afternoon had been light and frivolous on the surface, but there'd been moments, too, when she caught Chase gazing at her with the most peculiar expression. As if trying to discern something about her that was invisible to the eye. Then he'd smile and turn away. Perhaps it should have made her feel self-conscious, but instead it made her feel... pretty, and she'd hadn't felt pretty in a very long time.

She felt pretty in this new dress, though!

Surely Caroline Astor could not have felt more regal than Jo McKenna Talbot did as she descended the staircase to the lobby and made her way to the ballroom to assist Mr. VanderLinden, the newly arrived dancing master. The gown even made her feel taller, although perhaps that was from the slight heel of the shoes. Somehow, Jo didn't think that was it.

"How pretty you are, Mrs. Talbot," said Priscilla Palmer at her entrance.

"I must return the compliment," Jo replied with a smile, managing to be both honest and polite at the same time. "And I'm so glad you're here. This is sure to be great fun."

"Yes, I hope so," Priscilla responded. "If a man finally asks me to dance this summer, I'd like to ready."

Jo felt a twinge of sorrow for the girl. Miss Palmer had so very much, but not what she wanted – and needed – the most. The affection of a decent man. Perhaps there was something Jo could do about that. Crossing the room a few moments later, she found a suitable target.

"Mr. VonMeisterburger," Jo murmured, as if her message was for him alone. "I wonder if you might be in need of a partner? Miss Palmer is in some demand, but I suppose I could put in a good word for you, if you'd like."

"Miss Palmer?"

"Yes, let me introduce you. She's a delight," Jo said, taking the bold liberty of clasping him by the elbow and steering him in the right direction. Given his visual acuity, it seemed necessary. "Miss Palmer, please allow me to introduce to you Mr. Mortimer VonMeisterburger. He was just telling me about his fascinating new camera."

"I was?" Mortimer squeaked, and Jo squeezed his elbow. "Oh, I was. Indeed. Do the photographic arts interest you, Miss Palmer?" He smoothed his hands over his lapels.

Priscilla looked at Jo who gave a subtle nod.

"Why, yes, Mr. VonMeisterburger," Priscilla answered. "I find the photographic arts most interesting but would surely like to learn more."

"Well, then," replied Mortimer, taking a rather large breath before launching into what was sure to be a detail-oriented monologue. Jo stepped away quickly, hoping she'd made the correct assumption. Based on what she knew of Priscilla Palmer – who was, as it turned out – slightly hard of hearing, and what she'd learned about Mr. VonMeisterburger from Chase yesterday, she suspected they may be a good match.

As luck *(and some skill)* would have it, she found matches for the other wallflowers, too, and by the time Mr. VanderLinden was ready to begin, everyone had a partner, although a few of the ladies had paired up with friends since the women outnumbered the men, and she found herself happily partnered with Ruth O'Keefe.

"Where is Mr. O'Keefe?" Jo asked Ruth as the pianist struck

the first chord and they began to move. "Is he so fine a dancer he doesn't need instruction?"

Ruth laughed out loud, her head tipping back. "I wish that were the case but it's quite the opposite. He's so heavy on his feet, and my toes, that no amount of practice will help. He's with Mr. Bostwick and Mr. Plank this afternoon. They're working on cottage designs."

Jo nodded. "Ah, yes. I'd heard something about that. Do you and your husband plan to build here as well?"

"That's who I was talking about. Who are you talking about?"

"Uh... Oh, I was under the impression that the Bostwicks planned to build here as well but perhaps that's a secret still."

"A Bostwick family secret that you're privy to? How interesting." Ruth's smile was enigmatic. "Something tells me it wasn't Daisy you learned that from."

Jo nearly stumbled over her dance steps. "Daisy and I were in the garden yesterday and Mr. Bostwick was there as well. They were discussing it."

"Mm, hmm."

Ruth's manner seemed without ill-intent, yet Jo couldn't help but wonder at her meaning. As Mr. VanderLinden led them through various three-quarter time polkas, gallops, a five-step waltz, the Mazurka, and even a graceful Varsovienne, Jo fretted and mused. And later that afternoon, as the two women met in the studio so Jo could work on Ruth's portrait, she contemplated asking for an explanation.

However, she didn't need to.

"I'm sorry to have teased you about Mr. Bostwick," Ruth said almost as soon as she'd entered the room. "It was insensitive of me."

Her frankness momentarily stole Jo's breath, until at last she responded, "I appreciate you saying so, and yet... I can't help but wonder what you meant by it." (Although, in truth, she knew exactly what Ruth meant.)

Ruth moved gracefully, sitting down in a chair by the window and gesturing for Jo to come and sit in the other, which she did, but almost reluctantly.

"It's just that, well, the two of you seem... close," Ruth said cautiously once Jo was seated across from her. "And as your friend, I feel compelled to say he seems rather enthralled by you."

"He does?" Jo said that with as much optimism as surprise. *So much for discretion.*

Ruth's smile was patient, almost sympathetic. "Yes, he does, and I hope you don't mind me being extraordinarily blunt, but you don't seem to object to his interest."

She didn't object to it. She craved it. But how could she admit such a thing out loud? What kind of a woman would that make her? She was – in the eyes of the God and the law – and in the eyes of all the people at the Imperial Hotel – a married woman. She glanced at Ruth and found her expression curious but not judgmental.

"I don't suppose I do object to his interest... but everyone thinks I have a husband."

"Don't you?" Ruth's voice rose in surprise.

"Yes," Jo answered quickly. "I do. In a manner of speaking."

"In a manner of speaking?"

Oh, Lord. If Jo were wise, she'd say something non-committal and change the subject. If she were wise, she'd say her infatuation with Chase was nothing of import. A passing fancy and that her beloved husband, Oliver, would soon arrive at the Imperial Hotel and all would be right with the world. If she were wise, she'd keep all her secrets to herself, but she was longing for a confidante. A faithful friend who she might share this burden with because it had grown so very, very heavy to carry alone.

"What I mean to say, Ruth, is that my husband has left me."

"He left you? Oh, my darling. How dreadful!" She pressed a palm against her decolletage. "That's appalling. Why would he do such a thing?"

Why, indeed. How many nights had Jo lain awake and asked

herself the very same question. But all the answers came back to the same thing.

"Greed, I suppose. The truth is I'm not sure he ever loved me at all. Soon after my father died, he left and took everything with him."

Ruth gasped. "Everything? What do you mean by everything?"

"I mean quite literally everything. All my father's art, my own art, all the money – what little of it there actually was – even my house."

"Your house?"

Jo nodded slowly. "Yes, he sold it right out from under me. He left me penniless and with no place to live."

Ruth's display of astonishment was oddly comforting given that Jo had numbed herself to the shock of it all, forced to set aside her own despair to focus on survival. But like a tea kettle, every now and again, the steam needed release.

"That is diabolical," Ruth said. "I'm so very sorry. I can't even fathom it. You mean to say that he really took *everything*?"

"Truly everything. All my father's journals and sketches, his clothes and shoes, even his hairbrush."

"His hairbrush? How on earth did he manage all that?"

Yet another question Jo had asked herself. Just how much advance planning had Oliver put into this despicable endeavor? Had he known before he married her that this was his plan? Or had the scheme unfolded as her father lay dying? Not that it mattered much now. She'd end up in bedlam if she tried too hard to comprehend the incomprehensible, and so she'd chosen instead to make plans for her future rather than trying to fix the past. Though heaven knew, there were things she herself had done that she wished she could change.

"He encouraged me to visit a friend for a few days – *to ease my grief* – since my father's funeral had been just a few weeks earlier. When I came home, the place was bare, except for a note saying the new homeowners would be arriving in a week."

Ruth shook her head slowly, side to side to side, staring at Jo, finally whispering, "What a diabolical miscreant. I'm so very sorry. Have the authorities been of any help? Any help at all?"

"The authorities have been... unable to do much."

"That's shameful!"

Jo nodded even while knowing the truth of the matter was she'd never contacted the authorities – because she still had some secrets of her own to keep, and because Oliver's note had been full of threats, warning her that if she tried in any way to find him, she'd be sorry. And she believed him.

She wasn't prepared to tell Ruth that part of her story, though. Not yet. Perhaps not ever. Because how could she confess to her beloved new friend that Jo could not go to the police to report *that crime* because Oliver had coerced her into committing a *different one*?

twenty-two

Lawn games were not really his forte, but of late, Chase had been indulging in all sorts of things he'd never before found interesting. Reading fiction, learning about photography, even golf and watching people paint. Why, last Sunday, he'd actually climbed a tree, for heaven's sake. Maybe there was something to this idea of *taking of a holiday.*

Of course, he was making time for work as well. He'd gone through all the papers Mr. Hayden had sent with the last batch of mail, then requested more files. He and Percy had met with Hugo Plank to start drawing up plans for cottages along the west bluff, and Percy, bless his heart, had purchased the lot between the Bostwicks and the VonMeisterburgers so Chase's mother couldn't stand on her future front porch and lob stones at her close *(but not dear)* friend, Breezy.

And, perhaps most importantly, not only had Chase begun the process of providing venture capital to Mr. Plank, he'd also been discussing potential investment opportunities with George Pullman and several other gentleman guests of the Imperial Hotel. There was money to be made on this island. All it needed was some salesmanship and the cash to prime the industrial pump.

Which is how he now found himself playing a one-dollar-a-point game of horseshoes with Philip Armour, Marshall Field, and the president of the First National Bank of Chicago, Samuel Nickerson. Naturally, they were all fiercely competitive, loose with the rules when it came to their own turns, and not above ganging up on whomever was winning. By the end of five games, Chase had lost $15 but gained agreements from all three men to participate in the development of a new marina on the east side of Trillium Bay. Not bad for two hours of work in the beautiful sunshine while drinking surprisingly cold lemonade which was (not surprisingly) spiked with exceptionally good gin.

Other games were going on all over the expansive lawn, although not likely for such high stakes. To one side, a raucous group including Frances Pullman was playing a rigorous round of badminton, their laughter, and their joyful squabbling wafting through the air like birdsong, while on the other side of the lawn, an equally boisterous game of croquet had no less than seven players vying for victory, including Morty VonMeisterburger and a rather drab young lady who appeared to be hanging on his every word.

Ladies in white linen dresses strolled across the grass under lacy fringed parasols, and children (*Heaven help him! So many children!*) scampered all about running every which way like rambunctious puppies, bumping into one another, and tumbling to the ground with giggles and shouts.

The scene was practically bucolic, and hardly one that Chase would have considered appealing a month ago, before coming to this remote oasis. He still missed Chicago, of course. He was still eager to return to his real life and his real job and his real *purpose*, but in the meantime, this wasn't nearly as mind-numbing a way to pass the time as he'd once suspected. It was almost... enjoyable.

Of course, he wasn't so lacking in self-awareness to not realize much of his change in attitude was thanks to Mrs. Emerson Joan McKenna Talbot. The lady in question was, at this moment, sitting on a pastel-hued, quilted blanket on the grass surrounded by a mellower group of youngsters engaged in some kind of art project that looked very much like... rock painting, although why anyone would paint a rock, he could not imagine. Regardless, they seemed to be enjoying it. And she seemed to be enjoying it.

Every time he looked her way *(which was often)* she appeared to be smiling. She had neither hat nor parasol, seemingly indifferent to the rays of the sun, and he noted *(yet again)* how her lack of artifice and pretention made her that much *more* attractive. At least to him, and once his game of horseshoes ended, he wandered her way.

"Good afternoon, Mrs. Talbot," he said. First names were for private, and he'd not have people speculating about the nature of their... friendship by addressing her too informally in public.

"Good afternoon, Mr. Bostwick. Would you like to try your hand at rock painting?"

Why? "I would not but thank you for asking."

He sat down on a log that served as a makeshift bench not far from her, close enough that he might reach out and touch her skirt, but not so close it would be obvious. And anyway, they hadn't reached that stage yet. There'd been no touching, other than the occasional brush of their arms against each other as they'd walked down the garden path the other day. The anticipation was a delicious agony. Perhaps she'd never give him permission, and his hunger would go unsatisfied, but he allowed himself the indulgence of imagining. A lot. He imagined it *a lot.*

And suddenly, into his imagination popped an unexpected scene. One which he had not considered until this exact moment, but which was brilliant in its simplicity.

"Mrs. Talbot, I've something to ask you."

She looked at him expectantly. "Yes?"

"I realize this may not be something you're interested in, and if it's not, I completely understand. I won't be offended as it may be somewhat beneath you and not serve your reputation."

Her eyes rounded with wariness, and she glanced at the children all around them before quickly looking back at him, and he suddenly realized it sounded very much as if he was about to proposition her for an unseemly act. *A delicious but unseemly act.*

He felt his smile go wide. "Oh. No, Mrs. Talbot, not that." And then he burst out laughing at his own clumsiness. She let out a tiny chuff of sound, and then her laughter joined with his. They laughed so heartily that the children on the quilt all stopped painting their rocks and instead watched the two adults being ridiculously silly.

"I'm very sorry," he said, trying to regain his composure. "I worded that poorly."

"I should hope so, Mr. Bostwick." She dabbed a tiny tear of good humor from the corner of her eye, naturally getting a little splotch of bright turquoise paint on her cheek in the process. "What, pray tell, are you trying to ask me. Right here in front of all these big ears?" She glanced over at the children.

"Well, you see, my mother's birthday is coming up and I was thinking, hoping actually, that you might be amenable to painting a picture for her?"

"For your mother?" She sounded dubious.

"Yes, but I have something special in mind. A portrait of sorts."

"Of... you?"

"No." He glanced around as if anyone might hear besides the collection of vastly interested children sitting on the blanket with her. "I'd like you to paint... Flossie and Regina."

"The... dogs?"

"I know it's a strange request but she's far more fond of them than she is of me so perhaps I could finally get into her good graces if I made a gift of their portrait. I realize you probably don't paint pets. I hope I haven't offended you."

"You have not, Mr. Bostwick," she said with no hesitation. "In fact, I think your idea is rather marvelous. Not quite the caliber of painting a thoroughbred racehorse such as Tremont, but certainly more attainable. I should be delighted."

"You would?"

Well! He had pulled this off rather remarkably given that he'd only just thought of it as he'd sat down and had fumbled the question abysmally. Not only would he be able to present his mother with a birthday gift she was sure to appreciate, but he'd also found a way to spend more time with Mrs. Talbot – because, of course, he'd have to *hold* the dogs. He would not be included in the portrait, but he'd have to keep them still while she did her work. *Damn, he was clever.*

It was late that afternoon as Jo made her way to Mr. Plank's office with a canvas stretched over a wooden frame and she felt no small amount of relief when he received her with a warm smile.

"Good afternoon, Mrs. Talbot. What have you there?"

"It's a gift, Mr. Plank. A small token. I'd like to thank you for the opportunity of spending time at the Imperial Hotel. I sincerely appreciate you giving me a chance." She turned the canvas around to reveal the painting she'd created of the hotel with golden sunbeams streaming down from a pinkish-blue sky and the garden blooming with a profusion of colorful flowers in the foreground.

She was pleased with how the painting had turned out. She'd done a fine job and was proud to sign her name to it. Her own name – Jo McKenna. (*She'd never sign any painting with the name Talbot. Oliver be damned.*)

Mr. Plank took the painting and held it aloft, perusing it carefully as his smile grew.

"This is wonderful, Mrs. Talbot. I'm so pleased," he said.

"In that case, so am I." *Ah, what a relief! Such a relief.*

He nodded. "I know just the spot for this. Come with me." He escorted her out the door of his office and strode quickly to the lobby where Mr. Beeks was jotting notes into a ledger. (A list of employee infractions, no doubt.)

"Beeks, look what Mrs. Talbot has done. I think this might look fine right behind the desk. Go fetch a hammer."

The hotel manager looked up from his scribbles, conflicted over whether to grin ingratiatingly at Mr. Plank or to glower menacingly at Jo. Over the past few weeks, she'd annoyed Beeks repeatedly with her presence in the lobby while drawing caricatures. (If he had any idea how many she'd done of him without his consent, he'd be even more displeased.)

"A hammer, sir?" Beeks asked.

"Yes, and few nails so you can hang this up right there." Mr. Plank pointed to the wall right between the board of room keys and the mail slots, directly behind the desk. A place where every single person who entered the hotel was sure to see it.

"That's quite a place of honor, sir," Jo murmured, flattered but embarrassed. "I was thinking you might want this in one of the guest rooms or perhaps a hallway."

"Yes." Mr. Beeks nodded. "A hallway."

Ah, at last. Something upon which they agreed.

But Mr. Plank would hear none of it. "Nonsense. This is the first painting of my Imperial Hotel, and it deserves a visible spot. A hammer, Beeks, or I'll be forced to pound in the nails with one of your shoes."

With a subtle grunt and squinty frown in her direction, Beeks ventured off on his mission. Mr. Plank walked around the desk and held the painting up against the wall. It really was an ideal place if Jo did say so herself, and she took this as a good sign. Mr. Plank must not be ready to sack her if he was willing to hang the painting. At least, not yet.

Mr. Plank lowered his arm, still gazing at the picture. "I suppose this needs a frame first, come to think of it." He came out from behind the desk. "I'll have Parnell deal with it tomorrow," he said, turning back toward his office. After taking a few steps in that direction, he gestured for her to follow and Jo bit back a satisfied chuckle, realizing the dour Mr. Beeks was about to return to his post with the hammer and the nails only to find no picture to hang. She could not have planned a better amusement.

"Has it been a month yet?" Mr. Plank asked as he moved down the hall and she hurried to keep up.

"Uh, do you mean a month since our last discussion? Not quite, sir, but I do hope you've been pleased with what I've done so far."

He halted in his tracks, and she nearly plowed into him. He turned and regarded her for a long moment, a smirk on his face that she could not quite interpret.

"To be perfectly frank, Mrs. Talbot, I haven't been paying a lick of attention. I'm far too busy with more important matters, but Tippett assures me you're doing a good job and if this painting is any indication, I'd say you are indeed a fine artist."

"Thank you, sir. So..." she let that linger, "Does that mean I should I plan to be here until the end of summer?"

"Ask me again in a month," he said, then laughed at her expression. "Yes, Mrs. Talbot. Please plan to stay for the remainder of your contract. And if you don't already have plans, would you join me at my table for dinner this evening?"

Goodness. Her life had become a surreal kaleidoscope of beauty and disaster and all Jo could do was try not to lose focus. "Yes, Mr. Plank. I'd be honored."

She entered the dining room a few hours later wearing an emerald green, cap sleeved gown on loan from Daisy and as she made her way toward Mr. Plank's usual table, she noted several appreciative glances indicating she'd made a good choice. Still, she felt a bit like a child playing in a costume and hoped the evening would pass without mishap or insult.

"Ah, Mrs. Talbot!" Mr. Plank said, rising as he saw her, as did the three other gentlemen at the table. There was George Pullman and his daughter Frances (whom Jo had met in person briefly during Mr. VanderLinden's dancing class and did not particularly care for) along with Dalhia and Iris Mahoney, two plump, middle-aged sisters who had giggled nervously through an entire art class and then never returned again, a swarthy, thick-browed gentleman introduced as Thomas Weatherby, and... Chase Bostwick.

"Please, sit here," Mr. Plank said, pulling out a chair that landed her smack-dab between himself and Chase. It was the only empty seat left, and protocol dictated they alternate the men and women around the table, yet... did Mr. Plank somehow know she and Chase were... friends? If so, he hid it well. Then again, he hid everything well.

Better than Chase, at any rate because the smile that man cast her way was far too bright to be discreet. No wonder Ruth was on to them. Who else was?

"Ah, I see you two know each other," Mr. Plank said. "Splendid."

"We were on the hotel tour together," Jo said smoothly. "How are you this evening, Mr. Bostwick?"

"Very well, thank you. And you?"

"Very well."

"Mrs. Talbot presented me with the most wonderful surprise this afternoon," Mr. Plank informed the table once the gentlemen were again seated. "A gorgeous painting of my Imperial Hotel. I'm having it framed and soon you'll see it hanging right behind the front desk."

There were appreciative nods in her direction, and mild murmurs of interest, and then the Mahoney sisters started to giggle, and the evening went on from there.

"So, you finished it then?" Chase asked Jo quietly a few moments later as red-haired Clancy filled her glass with fizzy pink champagne – and then winked at her! The rascal! She'd known he was impetuous, but he should have a care! She also happened to know he was a clumsy foozler and hoped he didn't accidentally spill any of that champagne on her borrowed dress. She spread her napkin more carefully across her lap.

"I did finish it," she nodded, not looking at Chase. "Although I didn't expect it to be hung in such a prominent location. Now poor Mr. Beeks will be reminded of my existence all day long."

She heard Chase's quiet chuckle and had the distinct impression that the pressure of his leg against her own was not entirely *(or remotely)* accidental. It sent a tingle up her spine and almost helped her to not mind that Frances Pullman sat on the other side of him.

"I didn't realize you were the painter, Mrs. Talbot," Frances said, leaning around Chase. "I haven't made it to any of your classes."

"Well, if you develop an interest there's always room."

"I should imagine."

The barb was subtle, and Jo wondered at the cause of it. Perhaps Mrs. Bostwick wasn't the only one who thought Frances Pullman would make an excellent wife for Chase, but he pressed his leg against Jo's again and she could all but hear the words he'd spoken the other day at the euchre tournament.

I've no interest in Frances Pullman.

Yes, well, that was all fine and good, but perhaps someone should mention it to Frances Pullman.

twenty-three

Chase had no idea if this was a superior art box or not, but he trusted Mr. Hayden to have done the proper research and it seemed nice enough to him. Examining it in his room, he lifted the satin-lined lid to find cakes of paint in a multitude of hues, each embossed with the emblem of Winsor & Newton, along with a dozen or more silver tubes of colors with names such as Payne's grey, Prussian blue, and chrome yellow. He paused momentarily to wonder if Venetian red and scarlet vermillion were not actually the same color but set the thoughts aside because he was no artist. Jo would know the difference and that's all that mattered. She'd know what to do with the assorted charcoal pencils and pastel crayons, along with the Indian ink, the sable brushes, the oval-shaped palette, and the two diminutive glass cups each tucked into their own little cubby.

Next to the box, wrapped in humble brown paper, was a stack of sheets bearing the watermark of J. Whatman, which, according to some previous correspondence with his secretary, Chase now knew was the finest watercolor paper available. He'd requested these items from Mr. Hayden a few weeks ago, but upon reflection was glad it had taken some time to get to the hotel. Giving it to Jo sooner would have seemed a polite but impersonal gesture. Now it was a gift, imbued with meaning and sentimental value.

At least... he hoped that would be the case, given the intriguing time they'd had at dinner last night. He'd pressed his thigh against hers a dozen times, and she, in turn, had skimmed her fingers along his under the guise of passing the butter dish. He'd delighted in hearing her thoughts on a variety of topics, and it was no surprise to him that Jo Talbot was as well *informed* as she was well *formed*. She'd looked sublimely beautiful in that dark green dress. And he'd wanted to kiss her. Badly. Thoroughly. And repeatedly.

In fact, he'd nearly invited her for a secret midnight stroll around the shadowy gardens with the intention of pursuing that mission, but Mr. Plank had asked Chase to join him on the front porch for a cigar and a nightcap and he could think of no way to refuse.

But today... perhaps today he would get that kiss.

He sifted through the letters which had been delivered to his room that morning, along with the crated artist's box. There were a handful of items from Mr. Hayden, but none included any update on the Pinkerton situation, nor was there anything from Mr. Newhouse himself.

Chase was getting impatient but acknowledged there was a simpler, more expedient solution to that problem. He was just going to have to ask Jo himself. Surely, they were to a point where he could press for information.

Daisy rapped on his door a few minutes later with Flossie and Regina in her charge. They came inside his room and sniffed around disdainfully. (The dogs, not his sister.)

"Mummy doesn't suspect a thing," she said as Chase slid his arms into a jacket. "She thinks I'm taking the dogs outside."

"Thank you for your help. She never would have believed I wanted to take them for a walk."

"Not likely, although she may have thought you were trying

to make amends." Daisy sorted through a few books stacked on his desk next to the art kit and picked one up.

"Amends? For what?" Chase asked, although asking *for which thing* might have been a better question.

"Oh, you know." Daisy shrugged. "For not purchasing the correct property. For not courting Frances Pullman."

Chase grunted. "I don't suppose you defended my honor by admitting it was you who discovered the better property?" He sat down in a chair to put on his shoes.

Daisy shook her head while absently leafing through the pages of *Treasure Island*. "Even if I had told her, she wouldn't have listened. It's not ladylike to discuss topography. Or architecture. Or the tenets of what constitutes being a good person."

Chase chuckled. "I don't imagine you'd get far with that conversation, but is she really still annoyed with me about not courting Frances Pullman? Why her?"

"Because she's rich. And because she's not Jo Talbot."

She clapped the book back down on the desk with a well-timed thunk and Chase paused in his motions, staring down at his feet for a moment. His little sister would make a good witch, always stirring, stirring, stirring up a cauldron of trouble.

At last, he looked up. "Because she's not Jo Talbot? What's that supposed to mean?"

Daisy's innocent look was not convincing. "You have been spending a fair amount of time with her. People are starting to notice."

"Notice what? There's nothing to notice. We're friends. I spend time with all sorts of people."

"Mm, hm. Well, be that as it may, I was with you two in the garden the other day, remember? I hope I have a friend someday who looks at me the way you look at her."

Another thunk, but this one wasn't a book hitting a desk, it was Chase's stomach hitting the floor. "Daisy, that's a very dangerous thing to say. Such an allegation could damage Jo's reputation. Don't you care for her?"

"I do," she said emphatically, all pretense of casualness evaporating. "I care for her a great deal, and that's why I'm telling you, people are starting to notice. You should be more careful. More... discreet."

"Discreet? Why? We have nothing to hide. We've done nothing to be ashamed of."

Yet.

Unless one was judged by one's licentious thoughts and vivid imagination. If that were the case, Chase was in immense trouble.

Daisy crossed her arms and regarded him as if he was a recalcitrant child. "So, hypothetically, if I were to leave you two alone in her studio with the dogs and went to spend my afternoon with Pearl Mahoney instead, are you saying nothing untoward would happen?"

"Of course not."

"Of course not, nothing would happen? Or of course not, you're not *saying* that?"

"Damn it, Daisy." He got up and paced around the room which suddenly felt exceedingly small and cramped. His sister wasn't a child, she wasn't obtuse, and apparently, she wasn't one to mince words.

He dragged a hand through his hair. "What exactly are people saying?" he asked.

"Different things. A few people seem to think she has designs on you and is after our money, but most people think you have designs on her and that she's not in a position to turn you down."

His stomach lifted from the floor and flung itself down again, splat against the wood. "That's vulgar, and it's not true in either case."

"If you say so, but then tell me, what exactly is going on between the two of you? I know she's not happy in her marriage, but I also hope you're not using her to assuage your ego just because Alex is marrying Isabella Carnegie."

"Jesus, Daisy! I care not a whit that Alex is marrying Isabella, and I am not taking advantage of Mrs. Talbot!" *(Was he?)*

Honestly! All this time he'd thought Daisy was oblivious and naive when in reality, she'd been on to him and taking notes the entire time. Somewhere along the line, while Chase wasn't paying attention, his little sister had grown up into a diabolically astute witness. He took a deep breath to calm himself. It wouldn't do if Daisy thought he doth protest too much.

"Listen, I am fond of Mrs. Tal... of Jo. I'm fond of Jo, and I suspect she is fond of me as well, but beyond that, there is simply nothing to tell. Nothing has occurred between us." *(Technically.)* "She has a husband and is moving to Paris, and I have a life in Chicago. As you get older, Daisy, you'll come to learn that some people walk in and out of our lives for a very brief time. Sometimes it's impactful, and other times it amounts to nothing but regardless, it's no one else's business. And it's temporary."

Temporary.

He didn't like the way it felt to say that, even if it was true. *Especially* since it was true. Time might hang suspended during the lazy, idyllic days of a summer holiday, but it marched on in the real world. Someday not far beyond this moment, he'd have to say goodbye to Jo and that was going to hurt. And while any sensible person would change direction now to avoid that pain later, he knew, even as he denied it to his sister, this only made him want to rush forward, faster, into Jo Talbot's arms... and into her bed.

"As for what people are saying," he admonished, "Shame on them. You must rise above the noise and disregard it."

"And if one of those noisy people is our mother?"

Chase grimaced. That woman was a thorn in his side just as assuredly as Alex was his twin brother. *It was fourteen damn minutes, Mother. Perhaps you could have pushed me out faster.*

"I'll talk to mother myself, Daisy, but in the meantime, please make sure you're not contributing to the gossip. Mrs. Talbot and I are merely friends, nothing more, and we must protect her reputation."

"What about yours?"

"I'm not worried about mine."

He spotted the art box on the desk, now annoyed that this conversation had dulled his excitement in giving it to Jo. Perhaps he should let Daisy present it alone. In fact, maybe he should let Daisy hold the damn dogs for the portrait and he'd excuse himself from the whole process. People couldn't spew hogwash if no one ever saw him and Jo together.

In fact, maybe he should go out on the lawn today and play loud, silly games so everyone would notice him *not being with her*. Perhaps he should make a great to-do of walking about in his tennis clothes looking for a game or loiter on the porch with the moguls discussing their mogul-ness. Or better yet... perhaps he should court *all* of their daughters since nothing would drown out the whispered roar of scandalous gossip quite so efficiently as *different* scandalous gossip. He could take the blows to his reputation. Jo could not.

It was the most luxurious art box Jo had ever seen, so fresh and pristine she hardly dared touch it. It even *smelled* good, but Chase seemed almost awkward in presenting it to her. As if worried she might not like it, or accept it, but goodness knew she was long past refusing it now.

"It's as much from Daisy as it is from me," he said as she slowly ran her fingertips over the row of embossed paints. "From our family to you. I ordered it the first day we met – uh, that is to say, the day you first arrived, as a replacement for the one that broke."

"It's... I don't know what to say," Jo said, feeling her heart soften and expand as she stared at the beautiful tubes and brushes, opening the small drawer at the bottom of the box to peer at its contents. She'd never had new art supplies all to herself. She'd used the new items provided by the hotel, of course, but those were to share. This glorious box was all for her alone, along with all the paper and the brushes and the ink. Even the case itself was a thing of beauty, with its gleaming varnished wood and shiny brass hinges. She breathed a sigh of pure indulgence and felt, for the first time, as if she were a *real* artist.

"Chase, I know I told you not to order me a new one that day in the carriage, but oh, my goodness, I'm so glad you did," she said, her voice solemn with joy. She looked up to find his face enigmatic, wistful almost, although she could not imagine why.

"And to think," Daisy said abruptly, her voice uncharacteristically loud, "the first thing you're going to paint with it is our dogs." She hoisted Flossie up between Jo and Chase and jiggled her long, doggie body in front of their faces. "She can hardly wait. She's so excited. See?" She jiggled the pooch again, and Chase stepped back.

"I wonder," he said, "do you need me here for this? Daisy can hold both dogs, don't you think?"

"I can't," Daisy responded immediately, grinning at her brother. "I've made plans with Pearl Mahoney. You'll have to hold them both."

Jo heard the quietest huff of annoyance from Chase as he glared at his sister. She'd spent enough time with the two siblings to know this was not unusual, but today the provocation seemed different. Real rather than playful.

"We should be able to manage," Jo said, hoping to ease that tension.

"*Bonne chance, Jo. Il est plutot grincheus aujourd'hui.*" *Good luck, Jo. He's rather grumpy today.*

"I am not grumpy," Chase said tersely after his sister had left and he'd settled into a chair with the dogs. Fortunately, Flossie and Regina were compliant and relaxed, ready to be immortalized on canvas.

"Daisy likes to tease," Jo said. "Just like you."

His gaze flickered across her face and then he looked away.

"Although... you don't seem quite yourself," she added hesitantly, feeling the stirrings of unease.

Jo had pulled up a chair to sit right in front of him so she

might make a preliminary sketch of the dogs before moving to
the easel. Her knees were close *(very close)* to his, and though it
was the dogs she was drawing, it was difficult not to notice they
were laying in relaxed abandon across his thighs, and behind them
was his chest. A chest she very much wanted to press her body
against.

She should have made Daisy stay and hold the dogs. Definitely.

"Not quite myself?" he said. "No, I suppose I'm not. I have
some things on my mind."

So did she and none of them were mentionable. "Would you
like to talk about it?"

He gave a rueful chuckle, and his voice was strange as he said.
"I suppose we should."

She looked up from Flossie's furry face to meet his intense,
blue-eyed gaze, and her heart tumbled like a boulder over a cliff.
Had he heard something about her? Something from Ruth? Or
someone else? Something that might cause the end of them before
they'd even had a chance to begin?

"All right," she said calmly, feeling anything but. She sat up
straighter and set the pad and pencil down on the small table next
to her chair while trying to rein in her mind from jumping to a
dozen different yet equally unpleasant conclusions.

"There's been... talk," he said. "And although I hate to dignify
it with any sort of acknowledgement, I think you need to know.
People are apparently... speculating," he said.

"Speculating?" *Breathe, Jo. Just breathe.*

"Yes. About you and me. And our... friendship."

A wave of relief passed over her. *Oh, thank goodness.* It seemed
this conversation wasn't about Jo's *past* scandals. It was about her
new scandals – which should not be a source of relief. She did
recognize that, but at least this time she knew in advance.

"I see. And what is the nature of this speculation?" she asked.

"On the whole it seems to be... uncharitable," he answered.
"The scuttlebutt is that I'm trying to take advantage of you."

A chuff of laughter escaped her. "And they assume I'm so

naive as to fall prey to that?" She had been naive once, with Oliver, but she was naive no longer.

"I'm not sure they consider it a matter of naivete but rather a situation of you being a beautiful, young woman who, married or not, is alone and unchaperoned. At a hotel. Some men might use that to their advantage."

"Would you?"

"No, of course not. You know I wouldn't, but such is the nature of society to be concerned for a woman... such as yourself."

She laughed again, not so much in humor but in dismissal. "Concerned? You know they're not concerned for me, Chase. They're passing judgment on that which they know nothing about." *Of course, if they did know, they'd judge her even more harshly.*

Chase set the dogs down on the floor and moved forward in his chair, leaning toward her. She wanted nothing more than to do the same, to move forward and bring them even closer, but she stayed in place.

"You're right," he said. "They are passing judgment. I want you to know that I'll defend you with all my breath, but... there are things about you that I don't know, either. Maybe things I'm not entitled to know but, I'm going to ask you anyway. Jo... what is the truth about your husband?"

So, it seemed Ruth hadn't said anything to him. Good.

And yet, while Jo had been expecting the question from Chase, it still left her without words. Without an explanation she could live with. Because how could she admit to *him*, to handsome, cultured, desirable Chase, that she'd been duped like a stupid, foolish girl by the first man who'd called her pretty. That she'd been... *used*. She had been Oliver's wife in *every sense*, but he'd taken her to his bed, whispered lies of love, then discarded her like yesterday's rubbish. She'd meant nothing to him. Less than nothing. So how could she admit all that to Chase without feeling... *soiled. Stained. Unworthy.*

Because, deep down, she *was* those things. She was soiled, and stained, and unworthy, and if she told Chase the whole truth, he'd see her that way too. He'd see her as dirty and inferior. Then he'd turn his adoring gaze elsewhere and she'd be lost.

"He's no longer a part of my life," she said at last. "Can we leave it at that?"

Her answer didn't satisfy him. She could see that on his face, the way his brow furrowed in consternation.

"Why isn't he a part of your life?"

"He just isn't."

She heard his huff of frustration. Felt the tension emanating from him, and she understood it. He deserved better from her, and still she hesitated.

"Do you love him?" he asked next. The question was a challenge, as if he was daring her to say yes. At least in this, she could give him satisfaction.

"No," she said, without pause, without emotion, as if she were revealing someone else's story because claiming it as her own was simply too painful.

He regarded for another moment, and she could feel her every heartbeat thudding in her chest. *Thud. Thud. Thud.*

"Did you ever?" This he asked quietly, earnestly, and she realized he wasn't asking her this because of the gossip. He was asking because *he* needed to know. Because he *cared* for her, at least a little, and she owed him some of the truth. (*At least a little.*)

"I thought I loved him. Once. But it wasn't real. He… he had a duplicitous nature and wasn't who he pretended to be."

Chase reached over and clasped both her hands. "And so, you ran away from him."

Oh… he had it backwards.

She hadn't run. Oliver had. But that was simply a detail, wasn't it? Did it really matter which of them had left the other? Did it matter who had abandoned who? Other than his name, Jo had no real link to Oliver Talbot anymore. He was nothing more than a bogeyman, a dark, shadowy figure best left ignored and undisturbed – and in the past.

All Jo wanted now was some semblance of a future. A tiny taste of happiness and the promise of a few glorious weeks with Chase before fate forced them to say goodbye forever.

What, then, would be the harm of this one small untruth? This minor fabrication to protect her from the shame of being sullied and abandoned. One little lie whispered now... so she might keep the bigger lies to herself.

"Yes," she said. "I ran away from him."

twenty-four

"Yes," she said at last. "I ran away from him."

Her answer gave him some miniscule sense of relief and yet he knew there was more she wasn't telling him. The gritty, painful details. The ones that would surely make his blood boil and long for retribution on her behalf, but she wasn't ready to tell him. Perhaps in time she'd share more, but for now, he'd ask the easy questions.

"And so, you ended up here? At the Imperial Hotel?"

"In a roundabout way," she answered. "Through necessity I've learned to be... resourceful. Such as taking a job that wasn't mine."

"The contract," he said, suddenly understanding, and it actually made him chuckle. "By God, you *are* resourceful."

"Resourceful. Desperate. The lines are blurred. I knew the offer was for my father when I signed it, but it appears Mr. Plank has forgiven me. He doesn't know the whole of my situation, of course, but he's allowing me to stay through until the end of summer."

Chase held her hands more tightly, twining his fingers with hers.

"And... Paris? Do you really hope to go there?"

She nodded. "I do."

"Because it's a good place to hide?"

She shrugged. "As good a place as any, and I do want to study there. My father wanted me to go. And my mother was French."

"Ah, so, you have family there?" He was glad for that. She'd have someone to rely on, but she quickly dashed that comfort from his mind.

"I'm not sure who I'll be staying with yet. My plans are... uncertain." Her smile was wistful, and it broke him a little.

She was so beautiful, and so vulnerable. She was the kind of woman a man wanted to make promises to. Lifelong promises, but Chase wasn't duplicitous like her husband. He wouldn't offer her something he couldn't provide, and they both knew their lives were fated to take them in different directions. Still, he leaned forward in the chair and whispered, "For whatever it's worth, I'm real."

Her smile remained sad, even as she reached up to gently touch his jaw with her fingertips. "Yes, you are, but the rest of this isn't."

He knew what she meant. She meant that all the exquisite emotions burgeoning between them were too raw and uncertain to be sure of, and yet, somehow, he'd never felt anything so deeply and assuredly in his life.

"Just because it's destined to be brief, doesn't mean it isn't real. And worth pursuing."

She pressed her palm fully against his cheek, and he felt the gentle caress to his core. "I'd like to believe that." she whispered.

"Then believe it. It's real if we say it is, regardless of the duration. Is a shooting star any less a star?" It was a dreamy, romantic, schoolboy thing to say, and he found himself smiling as he said it, and she chuckled at his whimsy.

"Why, Mr. Bostwick," she murmured. "I do believe all that poetry you've read is making you quixotic."

He shook his head and moved closer still, until their faces were mere inches apart. "It's not the poetry, Jo. It's you. You're driving me to madness. The more I struggle to free my mind of you the more ensnared I become, but... there is gossip. We can't ignore it. I have no wish to make your situation even more complicated than it already is, so if all you want from me is friendship, I'll respect that."

"It's not," she said before he'd even finished saying the words.

"It isn't?" *Thank God.*

"No. I want more."

"You do?" *Hallelujah.*

"Yes, I want... everything. All of it. I want... all of you. For what ever time we have."

No other declaration could have struck him with such force or filled him with such a potent combination of desire, fascination, and purpose. She would be his. (*Not now, of course. Not this moment in her studio, but soon.*) And at least he could finally kiss her. *Finally!*

His heart sped up even as time stood still, and he realized he was nervous, worried he might disappoint her in some way. Worried she'd find his kiss too timid or too bold or too much or not enough. He'd kissed a score of women in his lifetime, and all had seemed satisfied with the exchange, but this was different. This kiss... this kiss needed to be perfect.

"For what ever time we have," he whispered, reaching over to cup her delicate face in his hands. He marveled at the contact, at the velvety softness of her skin, and the warmth that traveled from her to him. It filled his chest and stole his breath. Her eyes were tidepools pulling him in, threatening to drown him, but he knew he'd willingly dive in just for the chance to be surrounded by her, to surrender to this vortex of longing.

He ran a thumb over her lips, and they parted at his touch. She arched closer, offering a tremulous sigh of anticipation and need, and he marveled at the knowledge that she wanted him, as much as he wanted her. And then he kissed her, and all his worries flew away. Because this kiss was perfection. She was perfection, and he knew then, beyond the shadow of a doubt, that what ever time they had together, it would never be enough.

She should probably tell him the truth. If she didn't, she was no better than a hypocrite, calling Oliver duplicitous when she was no better. But, oh... his gaze was so endearing, so compassionate, his hands in hers so warm and strong and comforting, she could not find the words. Or the courage.

And then he kissed her, and she realized in that singular, sublime moment that everything she thought she knew of passion was pale and false because...

This was desire.

This was need.

This was... *Chase.*

And he was hers. For now, at least.

At any moment, the dominoes of her life might tumble over, and everything would turn dreadful again. And she'd have nothing. Jo wasn't greedy, or selfish. She didn't want her happiness to be at the expense of anyone else's – but she wanted... more. More than she had. She wanted her most basic needs accounted for. She wanted love and the chance to prove her worth. She wanted absolution from her sins, and a chance to begin again. Perhaps that's what Paris was for. New beginnings.

But right now, what she wanted most of all, was Chase. She wanted to gather up as much of his ardor and affection as she could – until they had to say goodbye. Like shoring up supplies for a long, harsh winter, the memories she could make with him this summer would keep her warm – for the rest of her life – because his kisses were turning her world upside down, leaving her breathless and longing for more.

She pulled at his jacket lapels, and he wrapped his arms around her, gathering her as close as the chairs would allow.

Everything faded and nothing else mattered, nothing except Chase and this moment. Chase and the pressure of his mouth, the warmth of his caress, the sound of his breath as it mingled with hers. She was blissful in the heaven of his kiss.

Until voices in the hallway outside of the studio reminded them of where they were.

"This is not the way to avoid gossip," he'd murmured huskily, moving away from her, but his smile showed no regret. Only the promise of more. Later. When they had more time and more privacy.

"No, I suppose not," she answered reluctantly, already missing his touch. "But how do we avoid it? By avoiding each other? At least in public spaces?"

"We can hardly avoid each other, and quite frankly, that would make me miserable, but perhaps with impeccable manners, and some thoughtful planning we can deflect any damage. I'll think on it."

He didn't say more about the subject, and instead stood and gathered up Flossie and Regina, saying, "I suppose you ought to draw these mutts, or the next suspicious person will be my sister."

And so, she smoothed her skirts and picked up her pad and pencil once more, laughing as the dogs made themselves comfortable on Chase's lap. Then laughed again as he took Flossie's head in his hands and turned it every which way.

"Is this her best side?" he asked playfully, then pivoted her face in the other direction. "Or is this? Or this?" He held her ears aloft. "I certainly want the best rendition possible. My mother's hard to please."

"So, I've gathered," Jo answered. "I wonder, was she always?"

"Certainly, for as long as I can remember," he said. "I have a hard time imagining her as a young, carefree girl. I think she escaped the womb wearing a stiff corset and a contemptuous frown. Although... Alex can make her laugh. He seems to be the only one."

She noted the tone in his voice, the one that seemed to creep in whenever he mentioned his brother. It wasn't derision or even jealousy. It was... vulnerability. Alex was his Achilles heel, the favored son – at least in Chase's eyes.

"What's your father like?" she asked, pencil scratching across the paper.

"Formidable. Decisive. Entertaining. Merciless to his adversaries. Generous with his colleagues. And opera singers."

"Opera singers?" She paused and looked at him.

He crooked an eyebrow as he scratched Flossie absently behind the ears. "My father has a penchant for opera singers."

"Does your mother know that?"

"I've never asked her. It hardly seems a thing she'd want to discuss, especially with me."

"But perhaps that's why she's so cross all the time."

Chase chuckled. "I hardly think that's it. I'm sure she's glad he takes his... affection elsewhere."

Jo frowned. She was no admirer of Constance Bostwick, but his answer seemed too flippant. Surely buried beneath all that shiny satin and expensive jewelry was a woman with a beating heart. A woman who at one time in her life had thought love would be the grandest adventure, only to be disappointed. Then again, perhaps Mrs. Bostwick had always been cold while the opera singers were warm.

Either way, Jo said, "She may *prefer* he take his affection elsewhere but I'm certain it doesn't make her *glad*. Wives must bear the burden of their husband's indiscretions, while husbands get to go out... and have all the fun."

"Is that..." Chase paused, and she knew what question he meant to ask. *Is that what happened to you?*

She shook her head. "No, that was not my personal experience, but my father painted a great many society women who were disillusioned by their husband's extramarital antics. And I won't deny he frequently enjoyed helping them to *even the score*, as it were."

Actually, she couldn't think of a single woman her

father had painted that he hadn't also bedded. Or sometimes he painted the husband but bedded the wife! None of it was proper, of course, but such was the world she grew up in.

"And how did your mother feel about that?" Chase asked.

"My mother..." Jo very nearly said her mother had died when Jo was young, because that's what she always said. It was the lie her father had told her at his knee, and by the time she'd discovered the truth, the story was so ingrained she told it without thinking.

But she didn't want to tell Chase another lie. The last one was still tugging at her conscience and causing her regret. This, at least, was something she could confess.

"My mother... was one of those women."

His eyes rounded in surprise. "How so?"

"My father was studying in Paris. She was French. They met, fell in love, and then came me." (*On second thought, maybe she shouldn't be telling him this, but she was halfway in it now.*) "After I was born, my mother went back to her husband and left me with my father. It's why he named me after himself. So no one would ever question my paternity."

There. She'd said it, although the honesty didn't feel good and righteous. It felt scary, like indigestion about to take a very violent turn.

Chase scratched at the dog's head more vigorously. "So... are you saying your parents were never married?"

"No. I mean yes. I mean, yes, I'm saying that no, they were never married. Which, of course, makes me illegitimate, although my father came back to Chicago and told everyone he'd wed in France, and that his wife had died in childbirth." She was flustered now and could not seem to stem her rambling. "No one knows the truth of that. In fact, I was twelve when I learned it for myself."

(*Goodness. Come to think of it, Jo came from a lengthy line of seasoned liars. Why, then, did she struggle with it so?*)

She took a deep breath and stared over at Chase, unable to decipher his expression.

"Is there nothing about you that's typical?" he asked at last.

"I promise there's a great deal about me that's average and dull. Just not this. Do you mind?"

After a pause, he shook his head. "No. I can hardly fault you for things over which you had no control. It must have been a blow to learn she'd left you that way."

That was her opening. She'd tell him now. Admit that it was she who'd been abandoned by a feckless spouse and not the other way around. Chase would understand, and perhaps if that went well, she'd even tell him the rest of her history with Oliver.

"Chase, There's somethi—"

"Ah, there you are Mrs. Talbot!"

Jo's gaze swung to the studio door as Mr. Tippett pushed it open and loped inside while Flossie and Regina, startled by his entrance, sprang from Chase's lap, barking with such ferocity one would think the hotel's social director was covered in cats.

"Yes, here I am," she said, stealing a glance at Chase. "Mr. Bostwick has asked me to draw his mother's dogs."

Mr. Tippett tilted his head. "How unique. Good afternoon, Mr. Bostwick."

Chase stood. "Good afternoon, Mr. Tippett."

The social director turned back to her. "I wonder, Mrs. Talbot, how much longer you might be? There's a gaggle of children wreaking havoc in one of the flower beds and I wondered if you might come to engage them with some kind of art project."

She wasn't a nurse or a nanny or a guardian and as much as she enjoyed the company of children, she much preferred the company of Chase, especially given that they had things to discuss, but Mr. Tippett must have sensed her hesitation.

"Mr. Plank sent me to find you," he said. *Clever, clever Mr. Tippett.* He knew she could not refuse *that* request.

Jo looked up at Chase. "I suppose we could continue this at another time. Is that agreeable to you, Mr. Bostwick?"

"Of course, Mrs. Talbot. Another time." He gave a small nod. "Just let me get these hounds on their leashes and... Oh... no... Tippett, you left the door open."

Jo turned her head just in time to see the fluffy back ends of Flossie and Regina as they bolted from the room in search of their own adventure.

twenty-five

D inner this evening was, for Chase, a unique kind of hell, due in no small measure to his capricious little sister and her undisciplined machinations. For a girl who professed wanting nothing more than to spend the summer reading on the sofa, Daisy had most certainly found other ways to pass the time and he seemed to be the one to suffer for it.

Thanks to her, Chase was, at this very uncomfortable moment, sitting at a table in the Imperial Hotel dining room wedged between his mother and Breezy VonMeisterburger while across from him sat (*the admittedly handsome*) twenty-eight-year-old silver mining heir Courtland Zuiderduin and his (*admittedly even more handsome*) younger brother, Fabian – and between them – sat Jo Talbot.

Someday (*God willing*) Daisy was going to have beaus pursuing her and when that time came, Chase would take great delight in creating trouble for her in every imaginable way. In the meantime, his sister was clearly enjoying herself by annoying the snot out of Albert VonMeisterburger with all her *thoughts* on how the oil industry might better serve humanity and watching Chase squirm every time one of the Zuiderduin brothers murmured something into Jo's ear.

It was Daisy, *of course,* who had invited Jo to join them for dinner, telling Chase she thought the best way to prove nothing untoward was occurring between them was to show everyone how Jo was just *one of the family.* Yes, they were just one big happy family. Except, *of course,* Jo wasn't one of their family, and it didn't matter how many portraits of Flossie and Regina she might paint, his mother would never accept her as a social equal. Chase's best hope for the evening was that his mother was *too ladylike* to sling any barbs at her across the table.

"I still don't understand," his mother said, "how Flossie ended up all the way down by the tearoom while Regina was on the front porch. Where on earth were you taking them? And why weren't they wearing their leashes?"

Because those dogs were she-devils bent on ruining his life?

Chase had spent the better part of an hour this afternoon chasing those curs around the hotel. Every time he'd get close, they'd dash off in a new direction. That is until they'd realized going in *opposite* directions from each other would be *twice* the fun. He'd finally enlisted the help of Mr. Parnell and a few of the hotel staff to help him trap the beasts, which they gladly did, but word of the shenanigans reached his mother before Chase did. By the time he'd returned them to her room, she was thoroughly informed.

"I told you, Mother," he said. "I'd removed their leashes to let them run around on the lawn."

"But how did they get from the lawn back into the hotel when they're too diminutive to climb the stairs?"

"Because I carried them," he answered impatiently. "Then I set them down on the front porch to attach their leashes and off they dashed." That seemed likely enough.

"It's true, Mummy," Daisy added. "I saw the whole thing. That's exactly what happened."

"If you saw the whole thing then why didn't you help your brother try to catch them?" Constance asked.

"I... uh... he seemed to have it well in hand," Daisy said, casting an apologetic glance his way.

"I was on the porch all afternoon," Mrs. VonMeisterburger interjected. "I never saw any such thing."

"It all happened very quickly," Chase said. "By the way, Mrs. VonMeisterburger, did you know that Mrs. Talbot is painting my sister's portrait?" Maybe if he enticed Breezy to embrace Jo his mother would have no choice but to follow suit.

"Yes, I'd heard." *And was clearly unimpressed.*

"And did you know," he continued, "that it was Mrs. Talbot's father, Emerson J. McKenna, a renown portraitist in his own right, who painted the portrait of... um..." *(Blast it all! Who was it that Daisy had said he'd painted? Someone from... city hall?)*

"The mayor," Chase finally said a little too loud and a little too late. "He painted the mayor. *Of Chicago.*"

"How charming," Mrs. VonMeisterburger responded dismissively between slurps of mushroom soup. *Slurp. Slurp. Slurp.* "We only have our portraits done by Mr. John Singer Sargent himself. I'm sure you're familiar with his work?"

"No, not really." Chase refused to give her the satisfaction of sounding impressed. "Is he any good?"

Breezy paused with the soup spoon halfway to her mouth. "I assure you, Mr. Bostwick, he's the best there is."

"Huh. Oh, wait. Yes, I do believe I have heard of him." *(Thank you, Daisy.)* "Isn't he the fellow who created such a stir in Paris for painting that woman with her dress half removed?"

"Chase!" his mother scolded. "Must you be so boorish? Have some decorum."

Breezy's spoon clanked loudly against the rim of her soup bowl. "Madam X's dress was not half-removed, Mr. Bostwick, I assure you," she whispered hotly. "It was merely a strap which had fallen from the lady's shoulder, but Mr. Sargent quickly realized the error in his judgment and rectified the situation by repainting it in the correct position."

"Ah, I see," he said, deciding to return to his meal before he made matters worse. He'd thought to elevate Jo in their eyes but that was a lost cause. Unless she could trace her lineage back to the Mayflower, there was no point in trying. Especially since he'd recently learned her lineage was so dubious.

Illegitimate?

He'd not anticipated that, but it didn't change his feelings. It's not as if they were planning to marry...

"Will you be participating in the Field Day events, Mr. Zuiderduin?" Jo asked one of the Handsome Brothers a few minutes later. *(Courtland? Fabian? Chase had no idea which one was which. Did it matter? They appeared to be a set.)*

"Yah, of course," the man nodded vigorously, responding with a thick, Dutch accent. "I am, how to say? Superior runner. I vil show de udder gentleman how vast a Dutchman can be on his veet, yah?"

"Yah," Chase said. "Or... you could show us now. Let's see how *vast* you can run to the center of the lake."

The man looked over at Chase, his thick, blond brows furrowed, and then rose high on his magnificent forehead as he laughed a great booming laugh. "Ah, a yoke. I see!" he said, slapping his hand against the tabletop.

Of course, it wasn't really a *yoke,* and it wasn't very clever, but Jo met Chase's eyes, and for the space of a heartbeat it was just the two of them in the room, and that was all that mattered. Because her eyes said, *I understand you.*

"I think that went hunky dory," Daisy whispered to Chase some three hours as they were *finally* leaving the dining room. Jo had left a few minutes earlier, having been summoned by Mr. Tippett, and now Chase and his sister were lingering behind the others. He had no wish to get caught in conversation with either of the Zuiderduins and he hoped they were never seated at his family's table again. Not only had they gawped at Jo all night and monopolized her in conversation, they'd also done something else Chase found equally distasteful. And somewhat shocking. They had made him long for Morty VonMeisterburger's droning evening commentary, but tonight, Morty was dining with Priscilla Palmer and her parents.

"You think that went hunky dory?" Chase responded hotly to his sister. He could not keep the sarcasm from his voice, even in a whisper, but Daisy, ever immune – or perhaps thriving upon – his frustration, rolled her eyes.

"Yes, I do think it went hunky dory, you dolt. Both the Mr. Zuiderduins were utterly smitten with Jo."

"And that is helpful, how?" *How?*

"Now people will be watching her interact with them instead of with you."

His sister had clearly lost her sense of reason. Not that she'd ever had any sense of reason. "That only protects me, Daisy. It doesn't protect her."

She pulled him to the side, away from the servers who were clearing the table.

"Yes, it does help her. It's a matter of ratios," Daisy said.

"Ratios?"

"Yes, the more admirers Jo has, the more divided the attention on her will be."

Chase held up his hands, still not grasping her meaning.

Daisy huffed. "Ratios, I tell you. Consider this. If Jo is constantly having conversations with just one man – hypothetically, let's say you – then people will find that significant and make assumptions. But if she's having conversations all over the place with a dozen different men, the likelihood of any one of them making an impression upon the gossipmongers is decreased by a ratio of twelve to one."

His head was beginning to throb. He'd either had too much wine at dinner or not nearly enough.

"So, let me see if I understand this," he said. (*Actually, he did understand it. He just didn't like it.*) "Your plan... is to surround Jo with a dozen different men at all times... so that no one will notice that she's also talking to me? Doesn't that seem a little convoluted? And complicated?"

Not to mention exhausting for Jo and aggravating for him.

Daisy crossed her arms. "It's the best I could come up with on short notice," she said. "But I suppose if you really wanted to throw people off the scent of you and Jo, the easier solution would be for you to propose to Frances Pullman."

twenty-six

To anyone observing, the morning surely seemed like any other.

At one end of the Imperial Hotel's grand front porch, mustachioed patriarchs clustered around small bistro tables where they drank tiny cups of rich, dark coffee and boasted of their plans for world domination, while at the other end of the porch, Jo and her en plein air painters had gathered, loaded up with field easels and Pochade boxes, and were about to go further afield. She planned to have them work around the gazebo today since the garden had looked especially lovely yesterday when she was working on Daisy's portrait.

Then again, everything looked especially lovely to Jo these days. Because Chase Bostwick had kissed her. And because her classes were routinely well attended and Mr. Plank and Mr. Tippett seemed pleased. And because she was building friendships among the hotel staff as well as with the hotel guests. But mostly everything seemed lovely because Chase Bostwick had kissed her.

Last evening at dinner he'd all but glowered at the Zuiderduin brothers every time they'd so much as blinked in her direction, and while his jealousy was as unnecessary as it was indiscreet, her heart fluttered at the memory. It felt good to be wanted, although she'd have to speak to him about his lack of subtlety. They were supposed to be displaying an indifference to each other as well as impeccable manners but suggesting Courtland Zuiderduin should run – *as vast as he vas able* – straight into the center of the lake was not the stuff of polite discourse!

"Is everyone ready?" Jo asked the group of lady painters. At the nods and answers in the affirmative, she continued. "Wonderful. Let's make our way through the garden and on to the gazebo. If you see a spot between here and there that captures your fancy, feel free to set up your easel and begin."

She was halfway down the staircase when she heard his call.

"Mrs. Talbot?"

She turned to see Chase on the top step holding a book aloft.

"Begging your pardon, Mrs. Talbot, but I have a query about this story you recommended. Do you have a moment? It won't take long." He started down the steps toward her.

"Carry on, ladies," she said to the class. "I'll be right along."

And so, the ladies did move forward, but at a snail's pace, as if surreptitiously lingering to hear his question, until Daisy scampered down the step past them all in a rather unladylike fashion, all but shouting, "Pick up those hooves, ladies. We're losing the light."

"Your sister is a hoyden," Jo said to Chase as he reached her side, and the steps were finally free of all the others.

"You don't know the half of it," he replied, then held out a copy of *Treasure Island,* a book which she knew he'd finished more than a week prior. She took it from his hand.

"You have a question about *this* story?" she asked.

"I do. It's on page fifteen."

She glanced at him and noted the smirk. And the smolder.

"Ah, subterfuge," she murmured, and opened the book to page fifteen where she found a slip of paper. It was a note, written in what must be his own handwriting. She'd never seen his handwriting before and for some odd reason, it seemed especially intimate to be reading it now. Especially given the words he'd chosen.

Will you meet me in the reading room? I must kiss you soon or surely die from longing.

The request sent tingles through her body in every direction for she felt very much the same. Kissing was needed. Lots of kissing. It seemed her expression showed as much, since all she'd had to do was meet his eyes and watch a sensual smile ease slowly across his face. She slipped the paper from his book and discreetly tucked it into her sketch pad, wanting to keep this as a memento. Someday when they were miles – and years – apart, she could read those words again and remember this moment.

"Eleven-thirty," she said, handing him the book.

"Eleven-fifteen?" he asked optimistically, and she laughed.

"I'll see what I can do. Daisy is the one likely to delay me."

"Such a hoyden," he said.

But Daisy, Saints be praised, did not delay her, and at exactly seventeen minutes after the hour of eleven, Jo walked into the book-scented, dark paneled reading room, heart thumping in delightful anticipation. Chase rose from the brown leather chair when he saw her, and she halted her steps a few feet from him.

"Is anyone else here?" she whispered.

"No," he whispered back, then pulled her by the hand into the dimmest corner, behind a sturdy bookshelf that would hide them should anyone else enter. She laughed as she willingly followed, and when he stopped and turned to face her, she pressed herself against him without hesitation, wrapping her arms around his shoulders. He ran his hands up her back, bringing her closer still, and exhaled, long and slow, as if he'd been holding his breath in anticipation of her arrival ever since she'd read the note.

"By God, Jo. I never knew time could pass so slowly." He pressed his cheek against her temple.

"I'm here now, but I can't stay long. I have to meet Mr. Tippett."

"I'm beginning to dislike that man. He took you away yesterday afternoon and again from dinner last night and now this?" She sensed he was teasing. Mostly.

"Speaking of dinner last night, you were being ridiculous, you know." She tilted her head back to smile up at him and he gave an affronted albeit unconvincing frown.

"Those Dutchmen were pawing at you like privateers just home from sea." (Still *mostly* teasing.) "Although Daisy seems to think the more men you have flitting around you the safer you'll be from gossip."

"Daisy? What has she to do with anything?" A twinge of unease passed through Jo.

"I've admitted nothing," Chase said, "but she's an astute observer and claims that when she's with us, my feelings for you are rather transparent."

That unease faded to be replaced by a lovely flutter inside Jo's ribcage, along with a warmth that felt both physical and metaphysical.

"And which feelings are those, exactly?" she asked.

The warmth magnified tenfold at his blush. *Chase Bostwick was blushing. For her.* It turned her pulse into a drumbeat as he dipped his head and pressed his cheek lightly against hers so he might whisper in her ear.

"I am... enamored. Besotted. Beguiled." His arms tightened around her waist, and she could not resist running a hand through the thick hair just above his collar, prompting a low, lusty sound to rise from his throat. He lifted his head and gazed down at her, and she thought it might be the perfect moment to die because surely nothing in her life could ever be better than this, this buzzy anticipation, this dreamy, irresistible attraction that pulled her into him like the moon pulled the tides, but then he kissed her, slowly, softly at first and then deeper, and she realized she was wrong... the best was yet to be.

"I should very much like to dance with you," Chase murmured into Jo's ear as he paused next to her at the Saturday evening dance. She was wearing a satin, garnet-colored gown and he thought she'd never looked more beautiful, but then again, he thought that nearly every time he saw her. Apparently, he was not an objective judge when it came to Jo Talbot.

They'd snuck away a dozen times over the past few days, a handful of stolen moments here and there, but the time was always too fleeting, the location always too risky, and the kisses always too few. He wanted more. He wanted an entire night with her. A dozen nights, or more, with her warm, pliant body beneath him. Or above him. Or beside him. Or in front of him. It didn't matter. He wanted her in any way. And in every way.

But this evening they'd agreed to keep their distance from one another. It was to be a night where Chase would flirt and dance with all the other women, and Jo would dance with other men. *Too improve the ratios,* as Daisy might say. Thus far, Jo had taken a spin with Percy, Mortimer, and Mr. Palmer which had not phased Chase in the least, but when Courtland Zuiderduin bent low and kissed her hand, then pulled her to the parquet floor and held her far closer than was necessary, or appropriate, for a five-step waltz, Chase knew the night was sure to be a torment.

As the hours passed, watching Jo dance elegantly, gracefully with one partner after another, seeing her smile and laugh, he reminded himself to be glad. At least for her. The attention was a good thing, an indication of just how immeasurably her social standing had improved since that first Saturday when she'd sat in a dark, dismal corner of the room with a sketch book on her lap looking so sad and forlorn. Since that night, slowly, incrementally, she'd eased into the fold.

Oh, she still wasn't a member of society. They didn't consider her *one of them.* This crowd wasn't gracious enough for that, and if they knew her parents had never been married, they'd drop her like a hot potato. But they didn't know, and thanks to her natural charm, she'd been accepted as a suitable dinner guest, a teatime companion, someone who might teach their daughter to paint, and even someone who might dance with a gentleman and not cause (*too much*) scandal.

The underground rumblings of something illicit going on between she and Chase were still there, beneath the surface, but damn it all to hell if Daisy hadn't been right with her theory of *more* men being a helpful distraction. Chase didn't like it, but if it protected Jo and her reputation, well, he supposed it was worth it.

"I cannot dance with you," Jo whispered back to him. "We agreed to keep our distance. Remember. Why do you keep asking me?"

"You know why." He couldn't keep the low growl of need from his voice.

She smiled behind her fan. "Yes. I do. Which is precisely why I must say no. Now skedaddle. Go dance with some girls who have yet to be asked."

"Wouldn't that be unfair to them?" he teased.

"Because you are determined to remain unencumbered?"

"No," he whispered. "Because I have eyes only for you."

She blushed. "Mr. Bostwick, in spite of *my* feelings, I promise the other young ladies will survive a single dance with you and escape with their hearts intact. And once you've shown an interest in them," she continued, "the other gentlemen might be prompted to ask them as well."

"Do you think so?"

"I do. Nothing attracts a man more than a woman they deem unavailable."

He saw the look pass over her face, as if she'd said the words without considering them, and only just realized.

"That's not why, you know," he said quietly.

"What's not why?" Her response was unconvincing.

"I'm not infatuated with you just because you have a husband. It's so much more than that. In fact, it's completely independent of that. To be honest, I find the fact that you have a husband quite aggravating."

"As do I. Now please go dance with someone and leave me alone."

He sighed dramatically. "Very well, but I'm doing this entirely for your benefit, you know," he whispered. "Miss Getty spits when she talks, and the girl I danced with before her trod on my feet at least a dozen times."

"Perhaps your feet were in the wrong place."

"My feet were right where they were supposed to be – at the end of my legs – and yet somehow, so were hers."

Jo laughed and shushed him. "You're not even supposed to be talking to me. We have no interest in each other, remember?"

"Yes, but how am I to remember that when you're dressed as you are?"

"Didn't you once tell me you don't pay attention to the dresses?" she asked.

"I don't, unless they're being worn by the most beautiful woman in the room."

"Go away from me," she demanded, brows furrowed in mock ire. "Or I shall scream."

"Very well," he said. "But... I wonder..."

She crooked an eyebrow, refusing to ask and yet obviously wanting to know.

He lowered his voice to a husky whisper and leaned dangerously close. "I wonder, were I to knock on your door at midnight, would you let me in?"

She flipped open her fan and fluttered it furiously as crimson stole up her throat and over cheeks, and Chase wondered if his candor was too rash. Too presumptuous. Too audacious. Perhaps he should not have asked such a brazen thing especially in a crowded room, although they were well out of earshot of anyone else. He wasn't *that* reckless, but he was *that* desperate. Not just to know her intimately, but to *know* her. *Intimately.*

He wanted to hear her voice and know her thoughts, to coax

her into laughter as well as release. He wanted to take his time, to meander over and memorize all the luscious curves of her body, to sample and delight in the sweet-salty nectar of her skin, and to, at last, delve into the warmest, deepest parts of her.

But Jo stared straight ahead, fluttering the fan and refusing to look at him, and he worried he'd misread the boundaries of her desire. Then the fan slowed, and his heart sped up.

"Not midnight," she whispered. "Eleven forty-five."

twenty-seven

It was fifteen minutes *past* midnight when a quiet tapping sounded at her door.

If Chase had thought to keep her waiting just to heighten her arousal, the ploy was unnecessary. Desire had been building inside her of its own accord since the very moment he'd asked if he could knock on her door. Longer than that, truthfully. Her passion for him had been growing since the first time he'd kissed her, since that afternoon on the porch when he'd asked if they might be friends, and, honestly, since that very first day when she'd landed in the mud and looked up to see his handsome face. She had wanted Chase Bostwick from the moment they'd met, and now, she would have him.

She'd changed into a sheer linen nightgown and robe after leaving the dance and returning to her room. Then worried that doing so might make her seem too, too shameless, but Chase's meaning had been clear, and she could hardly claim innocence now. Not after the past few days and the abundance of clandestine kisses and progressively bolder caresses they'd exchanged.

Still... now that the moment seemed inevitable, she was nervous, and anxious, and thrilled, and uncertain. Not about what she wanted but rather in how it might all unfold. Her past experiences, although pleasant, had been rather... brief and... basic. She wasn't so innocent she didn't suspect there could be *more* to the experience. And yet, as to what that *more* might be, she felt rather ignorant. As she was a married woman, might Chase expect her to... know things?

She opened the door, and he stepped in quickly, closing it quietly behind him. He was in his tuxedo, which was to be expected, and yet she suddenly felt exposed. Perhaps she should not have changed out of her dress, but his eyes roved over her, and she noted his appreciation.

"You're late," she said, as if to explain her current state of undress.

"I know. I'm sorry. Someone was loitering in the hall, and I thought it best if they not see me."

"True. Next time use the back staircase. It's right outside my door."

A sensual smile eased across his face. "Next time?"

"Assuming I invite you back," she said, hoping sass might disguise her nervousness, but he reached over and grasped the lapels of her dressing gown, pulling her toward him, gentle but urgent.

"Oh, you'll invite me back. I'll make sure of it."

It wasn't a boast. It was a promise.

And she believed him.

Her pulse quickened as they turned and he pressed her against the door, stealing her breath and trapping her in the welcome vise of his arms. His torso against hers was warm and solid as she wrapped her arms around his shoulders, her knees giving way as she melted into his embrace. *This* is what she'd been waiting for and dreaming of. *This* is what her body needed, and her heart ached to absorb. Chase and his touch and his heat and his affection.

He gazed down at her, the desire in his eyes matching her own.

"You are sure, aren't you, Jo?" he whispered. "Sure you want me here?"

She might have laughed if she had any breath in her lungs because she'd never been more sure of anything in her life. She wanted to tell him so. She wanted to describe all the wicked, delicious, riotous cravings storming through her body right now. To confess he made her crazy with longing and ache with desire, but words were shallow, and actions spoke louder, so all she said was, "I'm sure," and then she tangled her hands in his hair, and pulled him closer, whispering against his lips, "I'm very sure."

He groaned low in his throat, and kissed her, hard, and she reveled in it. There was no caution, no hesitation, no question. Just certainty and promise.

The pressure of his body shifted as he twisted to remove his jacket and she pushed it from his shoulders, moving her hands quickly to his tie and then his waistcoat, tugging impatiently at the buttons as he untucked his shirt. It was frustrating work, all the layers and the pieces, like a wooden puzzle with a prize inside, and Chase was the prize.

Such a prize she nearly swooned as his shirt, at last, fell to the growing pile of garments on the floor and she was free to explore his bare torso, running her hands over his chest, noting well-defined musculature that she might like to draw. But touching it was so much better, and kissing it was better still. She pressed her lips against his collarbone, and he made a strangled noise of passion before lifting her abruptly from the floor and hauling her to bed.

Chase Bostwick was in trouble. Real trouble.

Everything about this woman captivated him. The simplest things. The hungry way she kissed and clung to him. The eager way she yanked at his shirt but laughed at his frustration when his cufflinks refused to cooperate. The way she shivered under his caress, sighed in pleasure at his kiss, and murmured her need into his ear. The way her body rose to meet his until at last she forfeit all control and waves of gratification overtook her. His own release arrived soon after hers and he could not recall another that had so rocked him to the core.

He always strove to please his lovers. It was the gentlemanly thing to do, after all, but with Jo, he'd wanted her to feel everything he'd felt, all the sensations and the ripples and the waves of satisfaction. He'd wanted her to feel his heart beating, feel the blood rushing through his veins. And he wanted her to feel the intangible depths of his emotions.

Even now, as they lay naked and spent, tangled up in the sheets and in each other's arms, all he could think about was taking her again because, quite simply, he'd never felt this way before. He didn't quite understand it because it wasn't just that he'd had *her*. She'd had *him*. He'd given himself over in a way he never had before... and it left him mystified. Somehow, he felt vulnerable... and yet invincible. As if the world was his for the taking, but only if Jo was by his side.

And there lay the challenge.

Because this was a temporary arrangement. An affair of the heart, to be sure, but still temporary. And he already missed her. She was there, right there, next to him in the bed, and he was already dreading the day they'd have to say goodbye.

He kissed her shoulder some hours later and she stirred with a sigh and opened her eyes, blinking up at him.

"I should go," he whispered. "I don't want to, but the housekeeping staff will be milling about soon, and I'd best not be caught roaming the halls still in my tuxedo."

She smiled. "Maybe you could tell them you got lost looking for the reading room."

He chuckled. "It's a good ploy. It worked on you."

"Yes, it did," she answered. "I found your lack of navigational skills quite endearing. Thank goodness you managed to find your way here."

"Thank goodness, indeed." He leaned down and kissed her softly, wanting nothing more than to follow that one with a dozen more, but the sun was soon to rise, and he'd not destroy her reputation by being seen leaving her room at this hour. "Get some more sleep. I'll see you later today."

She pulled him closer and kissed him back. "Yes, later today."

"And... tonight?" he asked optimistically.

She smiled and blushed. "Yes, tonight."

"Good, because I already miss you." *Lord, he sounded like a lovesick buffoon. What was wrong with him?* But she reached up and pushed his hair back from his temple and said, "I already miss you, too."

He left her then and encountered no less than five hotel employees on the journey back to his room. All but one greeted him with a simple, "Good morning, sir," and a discreet bob of the head. The other, a tall, red-haired lad with freckles gave him a cheeky, knowing grin. "Up early or out late, sir?" he asked.

"Both," Chase answered curtly, glad he was nearly to his own room and nowhere near Jo's at the time.

Once inside, after stripping off his tuxedo, he considered falling into his own bed for a few hours. He hadn't gotten much sleep last night what with giving in to the temptation of Jo for a lengthy – and vigorous – second round. He'd even pressed for a third but for her sake, relented. She'd matched him stroke for stroke, but had, at last, laughingly pushed him aside for the sake of rest.

He smiled at the memory, and at the way his depleted body sought to respond. Thank goodness he'd be back in her arms tonight, but for now, he must focus on something else, so he turned his attention to the mail waiting on his desk.

There were the usual items from Mr. Hayden. Reports, newspapers, invitations to events occurring in Chicago in September. The latter made him glum. He didn't want to think about autumn in the city, and the notion gave him a start. He normally loved Chicago in the fall when the breezes turned cooler

and the trees in the parks flamed with red and orange, but now...
now he understood why people took holidays. He understood
why couples whispered to each other as if no one else was in the
room. And he understood now how a man could commit his
heart to just one woman for the rest of life.

Yes, he was in trouble.

He sighed and shuffled through the rest of the mail. At the
bottom of the stack was one last letter from his secretary.

Dear Mr. Bostwick,
Mr. Newhouse is making some progress in the investigation of
Oliver Talbot; however, he states the information he's obtained thus
far is conflicting in nature and he is therefore pursuing avenues to
ensure its validity. It does appear Mr. Talbot has had some
altercations involving law enforcement but the exact nature of those
alleged incidents are yet to be determined.
Mr. Newhouse is currently en route to Boston as that appears to be
Mr. Talbot's last known location. He will be in contact with you as
soon as possible.
Sincerely,
C. Hayden

Chase read the letter a dozen times, knowing he could read it a
dozen more and still question its meaning. Altercations with law
enforcement? *Is that why she ran?*

Sleep was out of the question now. He had too many
questions and yet Jo was the only person who could answer them.
He was simply going to have to ask her.

twenty-eight

"Oh, my goodness, darling! You've made me look so pretty," Ruth exclaimed holding up the portrait in her outstretched arms.

Jo had finished the painting this morning, after Chase had left and she'd been too full of joy to sleep. Once the final touches were complete, she'd sent a note, inviting Ruth to come to her room so she might present it.

"You are pretty. Prettier, even. I just tried to do you justice," Jo answered.

"And so you have. Mr. O'Keefe is sure to love it. And he can gaze upon it in the coming months to be reminded of how I look when I'm slim."

"When you're slim?" Jo asked.

Ruth's cheeks turned pink, and her eyes sparkled. "Yes, my darling, because it seems I'm to have a baby."

"A baby?" There were squeals of delight and hugs aplenty and some patting of Ruth's still trim belly, and all the while, as Jo rejoiced at her friend's good fortune, she wondered if she ever might know that happiness for herself. She couldn't imagine it.

In fact, having children wasn't something she particularly

longed for and since she'd never be able to remarry – what with already having a husband – she didn't know if she'd ever be a mother herself. Perhaps that was for the best since she'd had no role model. Still... for the first time in her life, she felt a twinge of maternal longing. A little Chase to call her very own...

But she kicked the nonsensical thought from her mind. It was one thing to pretend that what they'd shared was real. That it would endure, but it was simply a moment. A glorious, beautiful moment that's she'd cherish for a lifetime, but that didn't mean it was fated to last a lifetime.

"I was thinking to give this to Mr. O'Keefe for our anniversary, but it occurs to me, if you wanted to display it in the lobby so the other guests might see it, I must show it to him today," Ruth said a bit later, after they'd discussed various baby-related things, and art things, and giggled over the fact that Mrs. VonMeisterburger's hair pieces never seemed to stay in place and how she'd very nearly lost one into her soup the other evening at dinner.

"Oh, that's all right," Jo said. "I don't want to spoil your anniversary surprise."

"I don't mind giving it to him today, and besides, telling him he's to become a father was surprise enough. I'm not sure he can handle another," Ruth said, starting to rise from her chair by the window, but she paused in her movement, lowering back down and tilting her head to the side to stare at something. Her lips quirked into an odd smile, and she rose again, walked to the side of Jo's bed, and then knelt down to pluck something from the floor. Something just under the edge of the bed.

She stared at it a moment and then turned to face Jo with both brows raised, and the smirk now solidly in place.

"Jo," she said, her voice edged with humor. "Why do you have a gentleman's cufflink under your bed?"

Oh, good heavens. Chase's cufflink?

"I... I can't imagine," she said, but Ruth held it out for her inspection.

"A monogramed cufflink, no less," Ruth added.

"What are the initials?" Jo asked hoping to sound baffled *(However did that get there?)* but mostly she sounded guilty.

Ruth crossed her arms and laughed out loud. "Have you had so many men in here you need to ask?"

"Oh, my goodness. No. Of course not!" Jo sputtered. "Just Chase."

Ruth smiled and sat back down. "And so, you must tell me everything."

"I will, but first, please be honest. Do you think me terribly wicked?" Jo asked.

"I think you're brave," Ruth said confidently.

"Brave?"

"Yes, for taking charge of your own happiness. That despicable husband of yours could have ruined your life but you're not letting him. I'm proud of you."

"Proud of me for committing adultery?"

"Well, naturally I don't condone adultery, but he didn't leave you much choice, did he? I suppose you could live as a nun for the rest of your days, but I hardly think that's necessary. And anyway, you were bound to take a lover once you arrived in Paris."

Jo burst out laughing. "Do you think so?"

"I'm certain of it, but may I ask, how much does Chase know about your situation? Did you tell him what a monster you're married to?"

Jo sank down into the chair near Ruth. "Honestly, I got flustered when he asked about my marriage. I'm afraid I've let him believe I was the one who left Oliver and not the other way around. It's too humiliating to admit how I'd been deceived and abandoned."

Ruth nodded slowly, adding, "But if you tell him the truth, maybe he can help you get your things back. Surely a Bostwick would have significant sway with the Chicago police."

"I suppose," Jo responded, realizing Ruth had just provided a particularly good reason to *not* tell Chase the truth. The last thing she needed was him going to the authorities because if they found Oliver, her troubles would only magnify.

"You just push the button, like so," Morty VonMeisterburger said, holding the box camera out to show Chase. Again. The process was not complicated and despite his impatience, Chase could hardly complain. It was a gift, after all.

"Thank you, Morty. This is exceedingly generous of you."

"No thanks are necessary, my friend. When I shared with Mr. Eastman how greatly you coveted my camera, he did not hesitate to send me another to pass along. I also suggested that the boutique of the Imperial Hotel would be an ideal place to sell such an item and I would not be surprised if next year you found them in the hands of many of the guests. Of course, we're the first."

"And how fortunate we are," Chase agreed, reaching over and taking the camera from Morty's seemingly reluctant grasp.

"And by next year," Morty continued, "perhaps we'll be neighbors on the west bluff. What a festive time that would be."

"Indeed," Chase said, looking over his new contraption. *Could he just take it and leave?* But Morty continued talking so it seemed not.

"Have you finalized your plans?" Morty asked.

"For the cottage?"

"Yes."

"Not as of yet. We've purchased the property and Mr. Plank has been helping with the design. How about you?" he asked, not because he was particularly interested but Morty seemed in need of conversation.

"Mummy insists on having Richard Hunt draw up the designs but he's not responding to her inquiries, and Father says it makes no sense to build when we can just stay at the hotel."

"I suppose, but what do you think?"

"Me?" Morty seemed surprised to be asked *his* opinion and Chase felt a twinge of sorrow for the man. Yes, he was awkward and overly verbose and seemed not to notice when people were losing interest in his favorite topics, but he was a decent fellow. He certainly deserved better than what he got from his parents.

"Yes," Chase said. "Would you prefer to stay at the hotel or in your own cottage?"

"Well, since you've asked," Morty said, then looked around as if to ensure no one might overhear, "I suspect that by next summer I'll have a standing invitation at the cottage being built by the Palmers."

"Really," Chase said. "That's very interesting. Am I to understand that you and Miss Palmer have come to an understanding?" This island truly did have some magical qualities to it if cross-eyed Morty and the shy Miss Palmer could find their way to each other.

"We have!" Morty's voice rose an octave and his cheeks turned cherry red. "But I've not asked her father yet so mum's the word. In fact, I haven't mentioned it to my own family yet either so mum's the word on that score as well."

Chase nodded. "Understood. Mortimer, your delightful news is safe with me, and my heartiest congratulations to you both." He meant that sincerely. He truly did because they seemed a sensible, well-suited couple and Morty appeared to be quite enchanted. One might even say it was an endearing turn of events if one was the sort of person who found things *endearing*.

However, when Chase's mother learned that Morty VonMeisterburger was about to lay claim to the Palmer fortune, she was going to double (*nay triple!*) her efforts to push Frances Pullman into Chase's path. *Damnation!*

Thank goodness Jo had finished her painting of Flossie and Regina. It was currently in his room, wrapped in plain brown paper and tied with string. He'd meant to make it a birthday gift to his mother a few weeks from today, but maybe if he gave it to her sooner, it would earn him a brief reprieve from her constant nagging.

Unlikely... but... maybe?

twenty-nine

It was only 8:00 p.m. when Chase arrived at Jo's room that evening. She'd left the door unlatched so he didn't have to loiter in the hallway, and they'd agreed to meet right after dinner – a dinner which had been *interminable* – if only because he knew she was waiting. Now, at last, he was here.

Stepping through the doorway, he found her sitting near the open balcony door with her knees drawn up and her feet pressed against the edge of another chair, casual and homey and unpretentious, and wearing the same unfussy dress she'd had on that day in the garden. In truth, he'd hoped to find her in her robe again *(because that had been a delightful surprise!)* but he wasn't there *just* to bed her. He hoped that's where the night might take them, of course, but he was also there so they could simply *be* without the fear of onlookers and eavesdroppers and busybodies and gossipmongers. Just to have some time alone with her was a wonderful thing.

And he'd ask her about Oliver Talbot, as soon as the moment was right.

Jo turned to look Chase's way as he moved toward her, and he wished he'd brought his camera so he might forever capture that image. As it was, he'd have to pocket it in his memory, the dreamy, almost sleepy but sublime look of contentment on her face.

"God, you're beautiful," he said and only when she laughed did he realize he'd spoken out loud. She had that effect on him. She made him oblivious to his surroundings, warped his sense of time – and left him feeling as if nothing would ever be good again once they were apart. That part of this situation he tried not to dwell on.

He moved to the chair opposite her, scooping up her stocking-clad feet and putting them in his lap once he sat. Music from the string quartet playing on the front porch wafted in through the open doors along with the faint sound of waves crashing and the cool breeze over the lake. So peaceful and serene. Trillium Bay was nothing like Chicago, and sitting here with her was nothing like anything he'd experienced anyplace else. *God bless that Eden fresh air.*

"Hello," he said, smiling.

"Hello, yourself," she answered. "How was dinner?"

"Dreadful. Breezy has a stye."

Jo tipped forward with laughter and he wondered if he could have mentioned anything *less* romantic, but her delight made up for it.

"It's all we heard about," he added. "Through five courses."

"That does sound dreadful," she said.

"It was. How was your dinner?"

"Pleasant. Certainly more pleasant than yours."

"Who did you dine with? I didn't see you."

"I ate in the lounge. It's quite good fun, in fact. We get the same food as in the dining room without all the rules of decorum. We can use whichever fork pleases us, fill our plates a second time if we so choose, and the gentlemen seem to appreciate the freedom to burp at will."

He smiled. "It sounds rustic."

"Yes, it is rather loud and rowdy, as you can imagine, but as someone who grew up with no siblings, I find I quite enjoy the fellowship. They're like the family I never knew I was missing."

His siblings annoyed Chase to no end but he could not imagine life without them.

"An only child. Were you lonely?" he asked.

She shook her head. "No, not really. I didn't know any different and besides, I consider myself quite fascinating company," she teased.

"You are fascinating company," he agreed. "And although I did grow up with siblings, laughter during meals was highly frowned upon. We were told it interfered with digestion."

"Perhaps if you'd been allowed to burp..."

Chase laughed at the thought. "I'll suggest that to my mother at the very next meal. It's surely something she'll get on board with."

The sky turned from grey to onyx while they sipped wine that Jo had pilfered from the lounge for *just such an occasion*. And as hotel guests made their way to the porch to enjoy music from the string quartet, Chase was supremely content to sit in Jo's room and talk of inconsequential things. Books and hobbies and the upcoming field day. She mentioned how she enjoyed picnics, and he admitted to a fondness for taffy. She asked astute questions about his job and how Bostwick & Sons was influencing some of the amazing things happening in Chicago, and he asked about the art world, one vastly different than that of finance.

The talk was easy, so easy it was nearly eleven, after the musicians on the porch had stopped playing, when Chase decided he would not, in fact, ask anything about Oliver Talbot tonight. This time had been too pleasant, and he didn't want to ruin it with disturbing questions that were sure to upset her. Instead, he casually rubbed his hands up and down her calves as she slowly removed the pins from her hair.

"I've wondered what that hair of yours might look like when you let it down," he said, already wishing his hands were buried in the mass of her dark curls.

"And now you know," she said. "It looks messy."

"It looks inviting," he answered, making her blush.

She glanced over at the bed and then her gaze came back to him.

"These chairs are getting rather uncomfortable, don't you think?" she said quietly. "A gracious hostess might suggest we move to somewhere more... comfortable."

"As your honored guest, I'll go wherever you want me to go."

Truer words were rarely spoken. Chase would follow her anywhere.

Maybe even to Paris...

thirty

"This field day event is sure to be bang up to the elephant, don't you think?" Percy O'Keefe spoke loudly into Chase's ear trying to be heard over the melodious moans and harmonious hums of the ten-man brass band currently playing on the lawn next to a makeshift stage.

"Indeed," Chase agreed. "What have you signed up for?"

"Well, I'm not doing the footrace, I can tell you that much," Percy responded.

"Because you run like a duck?" Chase asked.

Percy laughed and nodded. "Yes, and because unlike a duck, I don't like having water thrown in my face."

"Water?" Chase said.

"Yes, it's a cigar race. You have to run with a lit cigar in your mouth while bystanders throw cups of water at you trying to douse the flame."

Chase's smile was broad – because he'd not signed up for that race either, but the handsome Zuiderduin brothers had. He might enjoy tossing a few gallons of cold lake water at their sculpted cheekbones.

"How about the greased pole contest?" he asked Percy. "I heard Tippett say there's twenty-five dollars at the end of it."

"I might give that one a go, although again, don't care for the water."

"Do you mean to say people throw water at you during that event, too?"

Percy shook his head. "No, you ignoramus. This greased pole is horizontal and hanging out over Lake Huron. You fall off the pole, you end up neck deep in frigid temperatures. Good God, man. Didn't you read the activity board?"

Chase shrugged, nonplussed by Percy's harmless insults. He'd heard far worse from Alex. And from his mother.

"No, I didn't read the activity board. I've been busy."

"Hm, so Ruthie tells me."

Oh, that remark was slightly less harmless.

Chase looked over to find a perceptive expression upon his friend's face, with an eyebrow crooked *just so* and a smirk so devilish it made Chase wonder if the man had been peeping through the keyhole. Obviously, there was no playing ignorant, no professing innocence. Percy was on to him.

"Where are you getting your information?" Chase asked.

"My wife found your cufflink in Mrs. Talbot's room."

Chase pressed the butt of his hand against his own forehead. At least it had been Ruth and not his sister!

"Who else knows?" He lowered his voice, although only a little since the trumpets and trombones were loud enough to drown out cannon fire.

"No one will hear of it from us," Percy promised. "But you'd best be more discreet from now on. There was already talk, you know, and although this hotel is big, it isn't that big."

Percy's advice was well intentioned and well received. Chase had left Jo's room this morning as the first rays of the sun were stretching up from the horizon and he'd encountered three of the same housekeepers on the way back to his room as he'd passed by the day before. One time he could explain away, but twice? They were suspicious for certain although they had no way of knowing whose room he'd come from. *Did they?*

He should have left earlier, before there was any light in the sky. Before any staff were up and starting their day. But, damn, leaving Jo had been too difficult, especially when he'd kissed her goodbye and, in her sleep-softened voice she'd whispered, "I miss you already."

But next time he'd leave sooner. Definitely. And take his damn cufflinks with him!

"Welcome, one and all to the First Imperial Hotel Field Day Challenge!" Mr. Plank called out from the stage a few minutes later, looking every inch the dandy in a tuxedo and top hat. He even carried a shiny black walking stick with which he gesticulated wildly. He was going to put someone's eye out if he wasn't careful.

"A day of friendly competition," Plank continued. "Fine food, cold beverages, music, prizes, and entertainment of all kinds. Mr. Tippett here has the sign-up sheets so come and register for your events!"

"The pie eating contest," Percy said as they walked toward Tippett whose tuxedo nicely complemented the skunk stripe in his otherwise black hair. "I'm sure to be victorious in a pie eating contest. Ruthie says I always eat like it's a challenge to see who can finish first."

Mr. Tippett had asked Jo to sit near the beverage tent with her charcoals and pastels in case anyone wanted a caricature drawn. She'd only been there for half an hour but was already feeling cantankerous and bored. No one wanted to sit still for a picture today, even one she could sketch in a few minutes.

Everywhere around her people were laughing and shouting and having fun and she wanted to be a part of it. Surely the *social* director wouldn't mind if she decided to be *sociable*.

She stashed her art supplies in the beverage tent and went to find whomever she might find. She spotted Priscilla Palmer walking arm in arm with Mortimer VonMeisterburger and allowed herself a smug moment of victory. She'd made that connection happen and they seemed quite pleased about it.

"Good morning, Miss Palmer, Mr. VonMeisterburger," she said, stopping to chat with them before waving to Chef Culpepper and his wife.

"Good morning," she said to the two of them as they walked past. "It's nice to see you outside of the kitchen, Chef Culpeper."

"It's nice to be outside of the kitchen," the chef responded. "I had no idea the hotel had a front lawn."

Jo laughed and continued walking through the throngs of revelers and workers. Although a number of hotel staff were flush-faced and diligently attending to their tasks, everyone seemed armed with a smile. The Callaghan brothers, each cranking the lever of an ice cream maker, were surrounded by young ladies of every social standing – ladies whose interest in ice cream was likely secondary to their interest in the two flirtatious Irishmen.

"Oh, Mrs. Talbot! Excuse me! Mrs. Talbot!"

Jo heard a shrill, feminine voice and turned to see Dahlia and Iris Mahoney bearing down on her, each wearing a hat adorned with such a collection of blue jays and chickadees that their approach felt very much like being attacked by a flock of violent birds.

"Hello, Miss Mahoney. And Miss Mahoney," Jo said. "May I help you?"

"Yes!" said Iris emphatically. "You must come at once!"

"We've been sent by Miss Bostwick to fetch you!" Dalhia added excitedly.

"Miss Bostwick? Is everything all right?" Jo asked, alarm quickening her pulse.

"Yes!" said Iris again. "But it's the dogs. You must come and see the dogs."

Each sister grabbed her by an arm and began to pull, surprising Jo with their strength.

"What's wrong with the dogs?" she asked.

Dalhia giggled. "Why, nothing is wrong with the dogs, Mrs. Talbot. They're to race."

"Race?"

"Yes!" said Iris. Again. "Mrs. Bostwick has entered Flossie and Regina in the Doggie Paddle race and it's about to begin. Miss Bostwick was sure you'd want to see it."

"Oh, good heavens. I thought something was terribly amiss," Jo said, frowning at the excitable women, but she let them pull her along until they reached the shoreline where forty people or more had gathered.

"There you are!" Daisy said, running up to Jo's side. "I was afraid you'd miss it! Mummy's over here."

Oh, wonderful.

Constance Bostwick gave Jo a casual onceover but said nothing, instead raising a pair of binoculars to her eyes and looking out over the water. Following her gaze, Jo spotted a handful of men, all guests of the hotel, standing elbows deep in the lake some fifteen feet from the shore, and each holding a pitiful looking dog that clearly had no interest in participating in this race.

Jo recognized most of them – the dogs and the men. There was Mr. Grant holding Peaches, and Mr. Getty with Buster. Next to them stood Mr. Waddington with Biscuit, as well as Mr. Rutger holding Dashiel, and then there was...

Jo let out a gasp, and covered her mouth, but the laughter could not be contained – because there, in the water, looking every bit as wretched and reluctant as Flossie and Regina, was Chase.

"Oh, my goodness," she said, laughing even harder. "How on earth did she ever get him to agree to this?" She said it thinking only to speak to Daisy, but her voice carried, and Mrs. Bostwick lowered the binoculars to peer over at Jo once more. It wasn't quite the glare she'd given Mrs. VonMeisterburger at the Euchre Tournament, but it wasn't friendly, either.

"Uh... well done?" Jo said to her, swallowing her mirth and

knowing with certainty that if ever she'd had a hope of winning over Constance Bostwick, it had just sunk to the bottom of the lake. Just as assuredly as Flossie and Regina were about to.

"Ready!" shouted Mr. Plank from the shoreline. "Set! And go!" He fired a starter pistol and the men let go of the dogs, each with a little shove forward.

"Go call to my girls," Mrs. Bostwick said, pushing Daisy toward the shore, and Daisy obeyed, for all the good it did. A few of the dogs paddled forward in the right direction but with no apparent haste while several, including Flossie and Regina, just bobbed around in circles looking bewildered. After ten or so unremarkable minutes, the bystanders started to wander away and only the dog's families remained.

Jo was still standing next to Mrs. Bostwick who had lowered the binoculars but continued to stare at her pooches as if trying to urge them forward with the sheer power of her will, and quite frankly, Jo was surprised that didn't do the trick. The woman had a gaze that could melt glass.

"Well," Jo said hesitantly after another moment. "They did their best and at least it looks like they're having fun." *(They did not, in fact, appear to be having fun, but Jo was at a loss.)*

"Yes, fun," said Mrs. Bostwick dryly. "I suppose you think that's what summer holidays are for." Then she turned to Jo and the temperature dropped twenty degrees as she added, "But you'd do well to remember that even fun has its consequences, *Mrs.* Talbot."

She turned and walked away after that, leaving Daisy by the shore, leaving Chase and her dogs in the lake, and leaving Jo feeling very much as if she'd just been warned.

thirty-one

It was Ruth who discreetly handed Jo the note at the end of today's painting lesson on the front porch, but it was Chase's signature scrawl on the envelope that Jo recognized. She tucked it in between the pages of her sketch pad and waited until all her students had departed before walking to the furthest corner of the porch and opening it. The curiosity had been hard to battle but Daisy was there, as she always was, and Jo could hardly read the note in front of her. She might recognize her brother's handwriting, and after the admonition from Mrs. Bostwick the other day, Jo wasn't taking any chances.

Once alone, she pulled an ivory card from the envelope. The note was concise yet vague in its simplicity.

Room 212. Noon. Come hungry.

Come hungry? She smiled as she read it but hardly had time to wonder at its meaning. Her class had run over, as it often did, and she had just enough time to go to her own room to freshen up before making her way to room 212.

What did one wear to a clandestine meeting in a hotel room? One where hunger was allegedly a requirement. A tea gown? A bib? She opted for the former, choosing a shell pink dress of Ruth's that had come with all the others. She brushed and braided her hair, twining it around the crown of head, and headed toward the back staircase.

Now standing outside room 212, she was suddenly anxious. She wasn't fond of surprises, having had too many unpleasant ones over the past several months. What if Mrs. Bostwick had tricked her and lay in wait on the other side of the door to warn her again? But that was silly. Surely this surprise would be *nice.*

She tapped on the door lightly and to her relief, Chase opened it to pull her inside. On the floor she saw a plaid blanket, a wicker basket full of bundles wrapped in tea towels, and a bottle of wine covered in condensation telling Jo it had recently been chilled.

She let out a chortle of laughter. "Chase, what is this?"

He pulled her toward the blanket. "What does it look like? It's a picnic."

"A picnic?"

"Yes, you said the other day that you enjoyed picnics and I realized we could never go on one here. Not outside at any rate because someone might see us, so I have secured the next best thing. We have a view of the lake," he gestured toward the window. "A nice flat surface on which to sit," he continued, "and best of all, privacy."

"Privacy," she said, "and no ants."

"I thought of bringing some in just for authenticity but decided against it. Plank would have my hide if he found out I deliberately brought insects into his hotel."

"Does Mr. Plank know about this?" she asked, suddenly worried.

But Chase shook his head. "No, not at all. I told Beeks I needed an extra room to use as an office while I'm planning the construction of my mother's cottage."

"So, Beeks knows?"

Chase frowned. "Beeks knows I need an extra room to use as an office, Jo. Nothing more. You needn't worry."

His mother's voice was like a buzz in Jo's ear, warning her that fun had consequences. Or maybe this unease was just due to the time of day. It was one thing to have Chase sneaking in and out of her room in the dark of night when few people were about, but it was different thing altogether to be meeting like this in broad daylight.

"I'm sorry," she said. "Anything to do with Mr. Beeks makes me skittish. The man hates me."

Chase pulled her into his arms and hugged her close. "Beeks is on his way out, according to Plank. Have no fear. Instead," he said, gesturing to the basket, "have some lunch."

"Your joke is inferior," she said after a pause, then stepping back and taking in the overstuffed basket and wine bottle, decided to embrace the adventure. "However, your picnic planning skills are clearly superior. I'm entirely impressed. You may feed me grapes now."

"That would be my pleasure," he said.

They took off their shoes and sat down on the floor and Jo laughed as Chase unwrapped item after item. There was enough bounty to feed a half dozen people.

"You weren't exaggerating when you told me to come hungry," she said, taking a bite of brown bread. "How did you manage this? Please don't tell me you asked Mr. Beeks."

"I asked Mrs. O'Keefe to arrange it. I knew if I asked the hotel cook for myself there'd be eyebrows raised, but no one would think anything of her doing it. See?" he said, tapping at his temple. "You have nothing to worry about."

As they ate the food, and drank the wine, and teased one another, Jo tried not to lament that every day couldn't be just like this, but out in the open. She wanted picnics outside where anyone could see them, and no one would care, but that just wasn't possible. *This* had to be enough.

Her time with Chase was like painting a panoramic vista. If you tried to include everything in your view, it would all muddle together, and nothing would seem special, but if instead, you focused on just one single exquisite element, the spot that had caught your eye and inspired you, then your painting would have meaning, and purpose, and value.

So maybe this was for the best. If Jo had a thousand days with Chase, maybe they'd all blend together and no one day would be remarkable. But if all she had were these small but divine moments, the memories would keep their value forever.

"Have you ever been to Boston?" he asked casually, handing her a linen napkin which she tucked into the basket.

"Boston? No, why do you ask?"

He shook his head. "No reason, really. I have a friend who's traveling there, and he happened to mention to me it in a letter. Do you have any acquaintances who live there?"

"In Boston? None that I can think of. Have you ever been there?" she asked.

"I have. A handful of times." It seemed he had more to add but hesitated, and then said, "Oh, my camera. I almost forgot." He pulled a small brown box from the floor near the bed. It was nearly hidden by the dust ruffle.

"I wonder, may I take a photograph of you?" he asked. "Morty just made a gift of this camera and I've yet to try it."

"That's a camera?" she asked.

"According to Morty it is." He explained to her the process and after some cajoling and bargaining and threats of tickling, she relented, posing near the window, and sitting on the blanket, and then because the wine had made her feel a little bold, she agreed to let him take one of her sitting on the bed, although her hands were folded primly in her lap and her feet were solidly on the floor.

And when it was time for Jo to go teach her afternoon class, Chase pulled her close and kissed her temple, then her cheeks, and her earlobes, and her nose, and her throat, until at last she grasped his face and kissed him on the mouth.

"I already miss you," he murmured against her lips.

"I know. I already miss you, too."

thirty-two

Jo watched as Mr. Plank galloped down the front porch steps and strode across the lawn toward her. She was sitting at a long wooden table in the shade of a maple tree teaching a boisterous group of youngsters how to create simple pictures with watercolors but thus far they'd produced nothing but wet blobs. Still, they seemed to be enjoying themselves and she was glad Mr. Plank would witness her doing such a fine job of keeping them entertained, if not actually teaching them how to paint.

"Good afternoon to you, Mrs. Talbot," he called out.

"Good afternoon to you, Mr. Plank," she answered as he reached her side and sat down. He was smiling and appeared relaxed, or rather, appeared to be as relaxed as he ever was. The man was in perpetual motion.

"What have we here, young man?" Mr. Plank asked the towheaded seven-year-old perched next to him, pointing at the boy's picture. "Is that... a mountain?"

The boy shook his blond head.

"An elephant?" Mr. Plank asked.

The boy squinted and shook his head again.

"A... bear?" Mr. Plank's voice got more hesitant with each guess.

"What have you painted, Malcom?" Jo asked. She knew it was best to let the artist do the explaining.

"It's a bunny rabbit," he said with pride.

Jo and Mr. Plank tilted their heads simultaneously, as if taking in the picture from a different angle might help. *It did not.*

"Well done, lad," Mr. Plank said, clapping the boy on the shoulder, then casting a quizzical glance at Jo as if to say *in what world is that a bunny rabbit?*

She smiled at the hotel owner, hoping the boy's lack of artistic acumen would not reflect poorly upon her teaching skills.

"Mrs. Talbot," Mr. Plank said next, "there's something of importance I'd like to discuss with you. Are you available soon?"

"I'm available as soon as the nannies come to collect these children. Say, half an hour?"

"Yes, excellent. Come to my office in half an hour."

"Yes, sir."

"Excellent. I look forward to it." He sprang up and headed off the way he came leaving Jo to watch his departure and wonder – and worry about – what he had in store for her now.

Half an hour gave her just enough time to clean up the table from her very messy art class but not enough time to freshen up herself. She hoped she wasn't wearing any paint but given her history, she probably was.

"Come in, come in!" called Mr. Plank as soon as she reached his open office door. He waved her in and gestured for her to sit. Then he stood and closed that door, giving her a moment of trepidation. Closed doors meant private conversations and private conversations meant the topic was significant, but his manner was so congenial she felt fairly certain this would not be bad news. *Would it?*

"I've had inquiries about your painting, Mrs. Talbot," he said without preamble.

"Inquiries?"

"Yes, some of my guests are interested in obtaining a similar painting for themselves."

"They are?" Certainly *not* bad news!

"Yes, and that has given me an idea. A rather masterful idea, if I do say so myself. Mrs. Talbot, how would you feel about staying here through the winter?"

"Through the winter? Will there be guests here during the winter?"

"Not this first year, although we hope to eventually offer cold weather activities. Nonetheless, my reason for asking is because I'm hoping you'll consider residing here throughout the winter and painting more pictures such as the one you've done of my hotel, as well as other landmarks and vistas around the island. My hotel needs artwork, you see, and I've realized the more specific they are to Trillium Bay, the more appealing they will be to my guests. And, if you were of a mind to paint some extras that we might sell in our boutique, all the better."

Jo sat back in her chair. This was not an offer she'd seen on the horizon, and she didn't know what to make of it, but he was smiling at her expectantly, waiting for some response.

"I'm hoping to move to Paris at the end of the summer, Mr. Plank," she said.

"Yes, yes, so I've heard." He frowned skeptically. "You do realize that Paris is full of French people, don't you?"

She couldn't tell if he was joking or not.

"I am aware, but I'm going to study painting," she said. "My father has friends there." *Kind of.* None of them had responded to her letters and she was losing hope any of them would.

Mr. Plank leaned back in his chair and steepled his fingers under this chin.

"I see. You're going to Paris to study painting, and I can only assume that the purpose of that study is to become proficient enough to become a sought-after artist, correct?"

"Yes, I suppose that's part of it, but improving upon my skill is another reason."

"Hm," he said, "I suppose art for the sake of art is a lofty ambition, Mrs. Talbot but I'm a businessman. A capitalist. Given how you recently informed me that circumstances had prompted you to seek employment, I wonder if you aren't missing the forest for the trees."

"Sir?"

"You said you needed a job, and I'm offering you one for the duration of the winter painting pictures for my hotel. Paris will still be there in the spring. Can't you go then?"

In the spring? Well... maybe?

"I'd provide room and board," he continued, "along with the same wage I'm paying you now, but instead teaching classes you'd spend your time creating artwork for my hotel. I suppose I could be persuaded to include a small bonus for each painting completed. What do you say, Mrs. Talbot? Fancy spending the winter on the island?"

"I... I'd have to think about it, Mr. Plank. It's a generous offer and I appreciate it but it's not what I had planned."

It definitely wasn't what she'd planned. Winter on the island?

She knew several of the employees intended to stay and some were already year-round residents, so she'd have good company. Still...

"It *is* a generous offer," Mr. Plank interjected. "And not the type to come along very often for a young artist. You'd be wise to say yes. A secure, reliable position versus... whatever your other situation is."

There he went, being astute again. She could hear the assumption in his voice.

"My other situation is... unique," she said quietly.

Mr. Plank came forward, resting his elbows on the desk.

"Mrs. Talbot, may I speak plainly?"

She couldn't help smiling at that. "Don't you always, Mr. Plank?"

He smiled back and nodded. "I do indeed, so I'll say this with the understanding that it stays between you and I. Mr. Beeks is a nosy meddler. I never would have given him the job but he's my wife's second cousin and I had no choice. However, I'll be sacking him at the end of season."

She wondered what that had to do with her, but Mr. Plank continued.

"One of the reasons he has to go is that he filters through people's mail."

Now she really wondered what this had to do with her.

"He does?" she asked.

"Yes, he does, and he's brought it to my attention, even though I'm the first to admit it's none of my business, that you have neither sent nor received a single letter from any Mr. Talbot."

Ohh... "That is true, Mr. Plank."

"So, that being the case," he said, "I can't help but wonder if a steady job, a fine roof over your head, and three meals a day might not be a better choice for you than wandering around a foreign city surrounded by Frenchmen. And, if you remaining here means I get a hotel full of beautiful paintings, even better."

This was all very unexpected, and she wondered just how much she should admit.

"I do have a husband, Mr. Plank, but we are... estranged."

"I'm sorry to hear that." He took a brief pause then added, "I have four daughters of my own, Mrs. Talbot. Each bright and spirited in their own way and yet, if circumstances put them in a vulnerable spot, I'd hope an opportunity like this presented itself to ease their hardship."

"That is kind of you, Mr. Plank, but I don't need charity." *(Actually, she kind of did.)*

He frowned again. "This isn't charity in the least. I've told you before, I'm a businessman who recognizes a good thing when I see it. Decorating my hotel is going to cost hundreds of dollars and quite frankly, you're a bargain. Stay the winter, Mrs. Talbot. It's the right decision."

⁓

It was another sunny day with birds chirping, music playing, and the sound of laughter ever-present over the rhythm of waves crashing on the shore as Jo and Daisy walked toward the gazebo to work on her portrait. They passed the usual assortment of guests reclining in lawn chairs and children frolicking as patient nannies looked on, yet Jo hardly noticed any of it because the job offer from Mr. Plank was first and foremost on her mind.

It *was* a good offer. A helpful offer yet she hadn't given him a definitive answer, saying only that she promised to think about it. And think about it she had. In fact, her mind had been spinning like a top since she'd left his office.

Winter on the island could be harsh, but growing up in Chicago she was no stranger to that. She knew that come December snow drifts would obliterate this garden. The wind would howl and bite at the skin, but it wasn't the weather that gave her pause. It wasn't even that she'd spent the past several months promising herself she'd go to Paris in the autumn because Mr. Plank was right. Paris would still be there in the spring, and if she postponed her travel, she'd arrive there with far more money in her pocket. Accepting his offer made sense, and yet... she knew once Chase was gone from the hotel, the reminders of him would overwhelm her and she wasn't sure her heart could take that.

"Oh, my goodness!" Daisy squeaked a moment later as they neared the gazebo. She yanked Jo from the walking path, and they halted behind an oversized shrubbery. "Look!" she said, pointing.

Jo peeked around the dense foliage to see what had Daisy in such a state, and lo and behold! There was Mortimer VonMeisterburger and Priscilla Palmer locked in an amorous embrace! A very amorous embrace!

"Oh, my!" whispered Jo.

"Indeed," said Daisy, moving a branch to get a better look.

After just a few seconds, Jo tugged at her sleeve. "We mustn't peep, Daisy. Let's give them some privacy."

"The hell you say." Daisy giggled and shrugged off Jo's hand. "Morty's going to want witnesses. No one will believe this."

Jo knew she should insist. They should leave and give the lovebirds time alone, but she didn't. Instead, she moved the branch even lower, keeping silent as she and Daisy observed a clumsy, awkward kiss which seemed to render both Mr. VonMeisterburger and Miss Palmer utterly breathless.

Then Daisy whisper-blurted in rapid succession, "Oh, my gosh! Oh, my gosh! Oh, my gosh!" as Mortimer clasped both of Priscilla's hands and dropped down to one knee in front of her.

"I'll be damned," Jo whisper-blurted back. "That sly devil is about to propose!"

Almost immediately, Priscilla squawked a happy sound of agreement, nodding her head emphatically, and Mortimer jumped back to his feet so they might engage in more clumsy, awkward, overjoyed kissing.

"I think I've seen enough," Daisy said with a giggle, as Morty's hands began to travel with the eagerness of an impending bridegroom. "I'm happy for them but my lunch is starting to churn."

With a final glance, they turned to go back the way they'd come, and as they walked away, Jo felt a curious mixture of emotions. Joy for the happy couple, pride that she'd nudged them together at the dance class, and... a little envy. Their love was so pure and good and new. She'd never had that. Her proposal from Oliver had been uninspired, nothing more than a tool of seduction and deceit. And what she had with Chase, while it was potent and intoxicating, was also full of complications and obstacles and doomed to end in heartbreak rather than matrimony, as much a burden as a blessing.

Still... she wouldn't give up these days with Chase for anything in the world. It wasn't perfect, but it was theirs.

"I wish my brother could marry you," Daisy said minutes later, as if she'd read Jo's thoughts, and the comment nearly tripped her to the ground.

"Daisy, what a thing to say! You know I'm already married."

"To the wrong man," she said. "I'm not moron, Jo. You never

mention your husband. You never say you miss him or talk about how you met. And besides, my brother is in love with you."

Jo tripped again and stopped walking. "Daisy, hush. You mustn't say such things."

"Even if it's true?"

"It's not true," Jo admonished, but at Daisy's skeptical scowl she relented. "Hypothetically, even if it were true, it's not something that should be casually talked about on a garden path."

Daisy looked around but no one was nearby. She turned her green eyes back to Jo. "I've always wanted a sister but thanks to Alex, I'm getting stuck with Isabella Carnegie who's as much fun as an itchy rash, and if my mother has her way, Chase will end up with Frances Pullman who always looks as if she has a toothache. I want you to be my sister."

Her tone was pouty and petulant, and Jo couldn't help but smile and be reminded that, for all her bold talk, Daisy was sixteen and sheltered, and maybe just a little spoiled.

"Then sisters we shall be," Jo said, reaching out and clasping hands with her. "When you're back in Chicago, and I move to Paris we'll write letters every week, and share secrets, and maybe you can even come to visit me." *(That would likely never happen.)* "But Daisy, you mustn't talk about me and your brother being together. It's just not possible."

Daisy frowned. "Even if he loves you?"

"He doesn't love me." It hurt to say, and she hoped she was wrong, but even if it was true, even if Chase loved her with all his heart, what good would it do?

Daisy turned and started walking again. "I'm pretty sure he loves you," she said. "I'm pretty sure my mother thinks so, too."

thirty-three

Chase arrived at Jo's door at half past nine, having lingered after dinner to chat amicably with several other guests in the hopes of *being seen* so he might slip out later without arousing scandal. He'd even stood in the hotel lobby and loudly challenged Percy to join him in the reading room for a game of chess which his friend had accepted with a wink and a nod, knowing full well that Chase would *not*, in fact, be meeting him in the reading room, because Chase was on his way to Jo's room to play chess with *her*.

"You have me at a disadvantage," Chase said, looking over at her across the board sometime later.

"Because I am the better player," she said with an agreeable nod.

"On the contrary. I am clearly the superior player," he responded. "But *you* are not getting distracted by how pretty you are."

"No, but I am distracted by how handsome you are, and yet I still seem to be winning. And one other thing..."

"Yes?" he prompted at her pause.

"Checkmate."

He looked down at the pieces in surprise, then huffed in mocked frustration. She truly did have him distracted.

They were sitting in chairs near her balcony as had become their habit over the past few nights. Although he longed to escort her through the garden for a leisurely stroll or take her on a carriage ride around the island, or maybe even try riding those peculiar bicycles the hotel had available, this was safer. At least in the privacy of her room they could speak freely, and touch. And kiss. And more. He especially enjoyed the *more*.

"I let you win," he said, picking up the bottle of wine on the table and refilling their glasses.

"I don't believe that for one moment. Letting me win would go against your very nature," she said.

"I suppose," he agreed, setting the bottle down, and leaning back in his chair. "I do rather enjoy winning. Do you know what else I enjoy?"

"Taffy?" she teased.

"Being with you," he said, opting to move past humor and go straight for her heart. Judging from her expression, it worked.

A full week had passed since he'd received the cryptic note from his secretary about the investigation into Oliver Talbot and yet in all that time, he had not managed to elicit any useful information from Jo. Every time he tried to ask her about the past or anything having to do with her husband, she deftly steered the conversation elsewhere.

He understood her past probably hurt to talk about. Whatever she'd been through had been bad enough to make her run away – all the way to Paris – but his need for some answers was growing exponentially. As was his inconvenient attachment to her. Perhaps he'd thought somehow that spending time together would satisfy his longings and quench his desire, but it seemed the opposite was true. Every moment he spent in her company only made his affection deepen, and the notion of parting ways with her in just a few more weeks left him heartsore.

He'd decided it was time to tell her so.

"I enjoy being with you, too," she responded. "I should think that's rather obvious."

He stared over at her for a moment, his pulse quickening. "Then... let's not stop."

She peered at him over the rim of her glass. "I'm not sure I understand your meaning."

"We don't have to stop seeing each other, Jo. Not if we don't want to."

A frown marred her forehead. "Are you planning to move to Paris? Because I am."

"I know that's your plan, but truly, does it have to be Paris?"

"Yes." Her tone hinted at defensiveness.

"Because that's what your father wanted? Do you think he meant for you to go across the ocean all on your own? With no husband or contacts or support once you get there?"

Her cheeks, already flushed from the wine, turned a deeper crimson. "Chase, you have known since the first day we met I was moving to Paris. Why are you bringing this up now?"

He sensed her annoyance and agitating her was not his intent, but he'd speak his mind tonight or go mad from circling around the topic. He needed some answers, about her husband, about her past, and about her true feelings for him.

"Because moving there isn't practical, and it isn't necessary. Didn't we sit in this very spot the other night discussing how Chicago is exploding with growth and culture? It's a city on the edge of greatness. Things are happening there, and although I haven't met the man myself, my father is well acquainted with Charles Hutchinson, the president of the Art Institute of Chicago. I'm certain we could gain you an invitation to study there. Paris isn't the only place where you can hone your talents." It made good sense to him, but she clearly disagreed.

She rose from her chair and began to pace. After a moment she said, rather sternly, "It sounds very much as if you're calling me impractical and foolish."

He wasn't. Didn't she hear the part about an invitation to the Art Institute?

"I'm not, Jo. I swear to you, I'm not. I don't doubt with your intellect and resourcefulness, you can do whatever you want to do, wherever you want to do it. I just... I just don't see why you can't come back to Chicago to study art. If you did, we'd have more time together. I'm not ready to give you up."

"And so, you think to... what? Set me up in a little apartment? Placate me with art school? Offer me a ringside seat at your eventual wedding to an heiress? But, of course, you'll still come visit me in the evenings after everyone else has gone to bed."

Now she was definitely angry. There was no doubt about it, but he hadn't meant to insult her. How was he bungling this?

"That's not fair, Jo, and it's not what I'm suggesting," he said feeling his own defenses rising.

"Then exactly what are you *suggesting?*"

He stood and walked over to her, hoping to take her hands but she held them away.

"What I'm *stating*," he said, "is that I care for you too much to say goodbye. And what I'm *asking* is that you please consider some alternatives."

The frown persisted but her anger seemed to abate. A bit.

"The alternatives aren't very good for me, Chase. Either I go to Paris where I might live freely and independently, or I go back to Chicago and try to survive on your crumbs. Don't you realize how unfair it is of you to even ask? Oliver took everything from me. Paris is all I have left, and I won't give that up just to live a half-life in the shadow of society as your mistress. Not even for you."

Well... when she put it like that it did smack of insult.

"I'm sorry, Jo. I'm not explaining myself very well, but you make it sound as if I'm asking you to *sacrifice* everything when what I'm really trying to do is *give* you everything. I'd make sure you never wanted for anything."

She arched a single brow. "I'd never want for anything? How

about respectability? Integrity? Independence? A family that welcomes me into their home? Your mother *hates* me, you know."

"My mother hates *everyone*. But my sister loves you."

"Your sister loves *everyone*."

He reached out again, and she let him take her hands this time.

"I just... I already miss you."

"I know," she said with a sigh, twining her fingers around his. "But this is the time we have, Chase. A few idyllic weeks on this island, and then... and then we move along. What we have here would never work in Chicago. You know it wouldn't, and I don't want to tarnish the memories we've made here by trying to make this last where it can't survive. We're just a shooting star, remember?"

He nodded reluctantly, disappointed that his mind agreed while his heart still wanted to argue. "Are you very sure we couldn't make it last?"

"I am sure. You've been on a holiday here, but since the first day we met, you've talked about wanting to go back to work. Once you're in your office again, you'll fall right back into your old ways. You won't be bored, and you won't need me anymore."

"Yes, I will. I'm doomed to need you forevermore. You're inside me, Jo. You're under my skin."

"Like a tick?" she asked.

He scowled and dropped her hands from his grasp. "Like something decidedly more romantic than a tick," he answered tersely. "How are you so cavalier about this?"

"Cavalier... about us? I'm not cavalier about us, Chase. Not in here." She placed a hand over her heart. "But I'm the one who's already married, remember? I have a husband out there and as much as I try not to think about him, his very existence impacts my decisions and limits my freedoms."

"People do get divorced, you know," he said quietly.

"Yes, they do," she whispered. "But let's not pretend that my getting a divorce would somehow fix anything for you and me. It wouldn't. In fact, it would likely work to my disadvantage. At least right now I can play the dutiful wife of an absentee husband. That's better than being a divorcee. An illegitimate divorcee."

He shook his head sadly. "Ah, yes. Illegitimate. I'd forgotten that part."

"It's no wonder what with all my other colorful attributes. And anyway, I couldn't get a divorce even if I wanted to. I have no idea where my husband currently is."

"He's in Boston," Chase answered automatically, distracted by his own rioting emotions. Not thinking. Not considering the repercussions.

Everything about her stiffened, and she frowned. "How do you know he's in Boston?"

He hadn't meant to say it, but there was no going back now, and maybe it was for the best. He'd wanted honesty between them. It seemed he was about to go first.

"I know he's in Boston because I hired a detective to investigate him."

thirty-four

I f the gale force winds of a January blizzard ripped open the balcony doors and whipped through Jo's hotel room, she could not have been more frozen in place. His words chilled her to the bone and stopped her heart mid-beat.

"You hired a detective? What are you talking about?"

Chase took a few steps away as if contemplating his next words more carefully. Then he turned to look at her, his expression cautious.

"This detective is someone I've worked with before. He's efficient and very discreet. I trust him implicitly."

Anger, fear, and disbelief blended with a sense of betrayal. "So, you thought to send him after Oliver without asking me? How dare you!"

"I should have told you sooner." He had the decency to appear chagrined, but not *that* chagrined, and her agitation doubled.

"Why did you do that?" she choked out.

"Because I was worried for your safety, Jo, and frankly, I still am. You've never told me why you ran away from him in the first place. All I know is that it was bad enough to make you want to hide in Paris. I've been worried he might be malicious or violent toward you. Is he?"

She didn't want to talk about this. She. Did. Not. But it seemed now she had little choice.

"He wasn't violent," she snapped, "but he may become violent now! If he finds out I'm the reason there's a detective looking into his affairs!"

"Jo," Chase said, his voice deepening with concern, "whatever he's done to you in the past, he can't hurt you anymore."

"Yes, he can! And he will if your detective confronts him or if he gets picked up by the police. Chase, you have no idea what you've done. You... damn it. You have no idea what *I've* done."

She walked woodenly over to the chair and sank down as if her limbs were disintegrating. Oliver was the villain here, but Jo wasn't blameless. If she hadn't done what she'd done, he'd have no power over her. But she had done something, and Oliver had the proof.

Chase picked up a glass of wine from the table and drained the contents with one gulp. Then he sat down across from her.

"How about you start at the beginning," he said. "I think I've earned the whole truth, don't you?"

Her laugh was bitter. "And if you haven't earned it, you'll just hire a detective to go find it for you."

He ran a hand through his hair and gripped it for a minute before dropping his arm back to his side. "If it makes any difference, I didn't know you when I first hired him. All I knew was that you were traveling alone, something wasn't right about your contract with the hotel and... and you seemed ill at ease with your marriage."

"And that warranted a detective?" she exclaimed.

"As I said, I was worried for your safety."

She snorted in disbelief. "You must obtain the services of a great many detectives if that's all it takes for you to hire one."

"Are you going to tell me about your husband or not?" He had the afront to sound impatient and she thought about ordering him out of her room without the satisfaction of any answers, but unfortunately, she needed to know what he'd discovered so far, if anything. She took breath so big and deep it made her light-headed. Or maybe that was the fear and adrenaline coursing through her. Either way, she was dizzy, and reluctant to share, but it seemed she had no choice.

"Fine. You want to know about Oliver? I'll tell you. To begin with, I didn't leave him. He left me. Although, more accurately, he tricked, manipulated, seduced, swindled, and *then* left me."

Chase refilled his glass, his jaw set hard. "Can you be more specific?"

"That was the punchline. Now you want the joke?"

"I'd rather hear the story from you than from my detective."

Again, with the irritation and impatience in his voice? *The arrogance of the man!* Jo's veins filled with frustration and dread and the regrettable realization that if she'd been more honest with Chase in the beginning she might not be making this particular confession now. But here she was. She took a swig from her own glass of wine and held it out for him to refill it. Telling this tale required sustenance of the liquid variety, so once her glass was replenished, she took a sip and leaned back in the chair. Not because she was relaxed, but because nerves were making her quake.

"I met Oliver almost a year ago," she finally said. "He said he was an art curator working with a gallery interested in featuring pieces by my father. Looking back, I suspect when he realized my father was dying, he set his sights on me instead."

"How so?"

"As an only child, I was due to inherit everything. Oliver knew that as my husband, what became mine would also be his. So, he convinced me of his deep and abiding love and asked me to marry him. I was... naive. And he was very convincing."

Chase took another hearty gulp of wine, gripping the stem so tightly Jo could see his knuckles whiten.

"The ink had barely dried on the marriage certificate when my father died and not long after that, Oliver cleaned me out. I came home from visiting a friend and my house was empty, right down to the salt box and the toasting fork."

"You're joking," he said, although he obviously knew she was *not* joking. "Jesus. Why?"

"Because he didn't want me. He only wanted my father's art."

He stared at her as if she were speaking a foreign language, a language that made him inexplicably angry.

"He left you and took everything? He didn't leave you anything?"

"He left our wedding photo," she said dryly.

Her sarcasm appeared to be too much for him. Chase burst from his chair and began to pace the room like a zoo animal kept too long in captivity. Jo knew that feeling. He was trying to make sense of the nonsensical. He was trying to answer the same question she'd been asking herself. *How could a person do that to another person?*

Then he paused in his steps and turned toward her.

"I'm so sorry, Jo. That's... horrible. Despicable." He began to pace once more. "You must have some recourse. He can't just leave you with nothing. You could sue him for abandonment."

"To what end?" Jo replied. "My possessions are long gone. My father's paintings have surely been sold, and my home is inhabited by some other family because Oliver sold it. Adding insult to my injury, if news of this became public, I'd be the one to bear the shame. His egregious behavior would become my humiliation. That's why I let you believe I'd run away. It was preferable to admitting I'd been... used and abandoned."

He turned to her once more, compassion for her battling with his ire at the situation. "I wouldn't have judged you for that, Jo."

"Perhaps not, but there's another reason I've been... evasive. Another reason I've not pursued any legal recourse. There is the matter of my own... transgressions."

That muscle in his jaw twitched again, and Chase sat back

down with a heavy sigh, almost as if he'd been expecting more. "Your own transgressions?"

Lord above, she did not want to tell him this part. This secret she'd hoped to take to her grave. The secret which left her feeling like the lowliest, rubbishy piece of rubbish. She was the grimy sludge in which rubbish decomposed. How many hours over the past months had she spent wishing she could go back and change things? But she couldn't. And now she had to tell him.

"Oliver was disappointed at the number of paintings my father had available, so... he convinced me to forge my father's signature onto pieces of my own work so he could sell them at five times the price. An Emerson *James* McKenna painting is significantly more valuable than one by Emerson *Joan* McKenna."

Chase stared at her for a moment, his expression enigmatic, unmoving, and her breath went shallow waiting for his response. She could say more, explain her reasons *why*, but they were irrelevant. They were excuses.

"You forged your father's signature on your own work?" he said at last, sounding more contemplative than judgmental, but she could see a frown forming on his brow. She could feel his disillusionment solidifying.

She nodded once. "Yes, and Oliver sold them as previously uncatalogued paintings done by my father. It was art fraud, plain and simple."

"Did your father know?"

"Absolutely not. I'm sure he's cursing me at this very moment." She tried not to think about how disappointed he must be. She believed in heaven, and if he was there, she hoped he couldn't see her and know what she'd done.

"And no one suspected?" Chase asked quietly.

"Apparently not. I'd studied my father's style my entire life. I can duplicate it in my sleep, so my work is very similar, but there's no ambiguity in what I did. I'm an art forger, and if I do anything to catch Oliver, or report Oliver, or try to reclaim any of my belongings, he's threatened to tell the world what I've done, and no art school or gallery or collector will ever accept me again. Especially if I'm in jail."

Chase stood up and moved around the room again, but not at the same frantic pace.

"So, now you know everything," Jo said flatly. "Really and truly everything. I don't have a single secret left, and if you decide to turn me over to the police yourself, I wouldn't blame you."

She sat there, feeling strangely hollow, wondering why there were no tears from her or recriminations from him. Maybe they were yet to come. Both the tears *and* the recriminations.

He turned to look at her, but she could hardly meet his gaze.

"Why would you do that, Jo? Why would you agree to forge your father's name onto own work?"

"Money. We needed it. My father's health was failing fast, and he hadn't finished a commissioned work in almost a year. And he was so pleased about having pieces in a gallery again, even though he was too weak to see for himself. But since I'm telling you everything, I may as well admit, I think my pride got into the mix, too. For the first time ever, *my* work was being seen. It was being taken seriously. People wanted it. Yes, they thought the paintings were done by my father, but the accolades were for me. Maybe that makes me a truly bad person, but it was... validating. It's what gave me the courage to come here and teach art classes – because I knew I could do it."

She let him ponder that before saying, "So... do you think I'm a terrible person?"

"I think... I'm not sure what I think." He leaned against her bureau. "This isn't at all what I thought you were going to tell me. I mean, I'm not sure what I thought you'd tell me but... it wasn't this." He sounded more bewildered than angry.

"And in your curiosity, you thought hiring an investigator was the best course of action?" She was upset about that and yet all her emotions were spent, and her words came out dull. "You couldn't just ask me?"

"I've tried asking you, but you've been evasive." His tone hinted at accusation, and her own ire rose.

"Because it was none of your business," she said tersely.

He stared at her, his gaze a challenge. "Perhaps not at first but, all things considered, I thought it had become my business."

"You overstepped," she snapped, the potential consequences of his interference setting in.

"You committed forgery," he responded defensively, stepping away from the bureau. She glared back, noting the tension in every line of his face, until at last he said, "I'm sorry, Jo. I need some air. Unless there's something else you want to tell me, I think... I think I'll say goodnight."

"There's nothing else," she said – because nothing she might add would fix this.

He gave a small nod in her direction, and then... left.

She sat in the chair for a while. She may have been there five minutes; it may have been an hour. She didn't know. She wasn't sure. All she knew for certain was that the tears had finally come, but Chase had gone.

thirty-five

A light tapping sent Jo to her door with a pounding heart. It was early, so early only the birds and the housekeepers were up and about, and so this must be Chase.

But it wasn't. It was Ruth.

Jo knew she looked a fright having spent too much time last night crying and not enough time sleeping.

"I'm sorry, Ruth. I'm not feeling very well. Might we talk later?"

But Ruth pushed open the door and strode inside, looking Jo over as if expecting to *see* her ailment.

"I imagine you do feel a little peevish this morning," Ruth said, walking over and flinging herself down into one of the chairs. "How could not tell me?"

This did not bode well. Jo was fresh out of confessions, and she didn't have the emotional stamina to explain anything about anything to Ruth. Not this morning. Not without the benefit of coffee. In fact, she didn't even know for certain which incident Ruth was referring to. It was *probably* the forgery thing, but maybe it was something else. Who knew?

Jo shuffled back over to her bed as if she was dragging the weight of fifty Mr. Parnells and crept under the meager safety of the covers, pulling the striped duvet all the way over her face. Suffocation might not be such a bad way to end things.

"Go away, please, Ruth," she mumbled.

"No, I won't go away, you silly girl, because I've come to tell you I understand."

Jo peeked out from her bedding cocoon. "You understand what?"

Ruth rose from the chair and came to sit on the bed, facing her and tugging the blankets down to Jo's shoulders.

"Chase ended up with my husband last night," Ruth said, her voice edged with dry humor. "My poor, dear husband who simply cannot handle his liquor. Although let me assure you, both of those buffoons were well into their cups by the time Mr. Parnell brought them back to my suite. I should have had him take Chase to his own room, but the man was blathering on and on about the most cockamamie bosh I simply had to know more."

Jo tried to pull the covers over her face again, but Ruth halted her. She was fast and strong for one who appeared so delicate.

"Art fraud, Jo? Really? I thought for certain Chase must be hallucinating, or deranged, but then I considered all the things you've told me about that unscrupulous hornswoggler you're married to, and I realized it must be true. I also realized the odious man must have coerced you into doing something so unethical. You wouldn't have done it without his prompting, would you?"

Jo scowled because... well, because guilt made her grumpy. "I would not have thought of it on my own, but I have no excuse for going along with it," she said.

"But it sounds as if you were concerned for the health and well-being of your father and Oliver took advantage," Ruth stated. It didn't seem a question and yet called for an answer.

"I should have known better. I could have refused."

Ruth tossed her hands up, exasperated. "Jo, I'm trying to absolve you. Must you argue with me?"

Jo pushed down the covers and struggled to sit up. "Why are you trying to absolve me? I've done a terrible thing."

"I'm absolving you because anyone can make a mistake. Anyone can make a poor decision, but as women, we're held to a higher standard. The world puts us on pedestals, and we're meant to behave like perfect, porcelain dolls so when we do fail, we fall far, and we often break. When a man makes a mistake, it's seen a *bold choice that didn't quite pan out.* Not so, for us, so we women need to look out for one another, yes?"

"I suppose," Jo replied haltingly. "But... you do realize I committed actual crimes, yes? I did more than make a simple mistake."

"Are you very sorry?" Ruth spoke as if she were admonishing a naughty child who'd stolen a piece of penny candy.

"Very," Jo replied, sounding rather like that naughty child who'd stolen a piece of penny candy.

"Do you swear you'll never do anything so underhanded or unscrupulous or felonious ever again?"

"I swear, absolutely." Jo nodded.

"Then you're forgiven." Ruth plumped the pillow next to Jo and turned around to lean against the headboard.

The whole exchange left Jo dizzy with gratitude. It didn't really absolve her of anything, of course, but knowing she might retain Ruth's friendship was a welcome relief. "Ruth, how can you be so understanding? It boggles the mind."

Ruth smoothed her pale green silk skirts. "May I confide something to you, Jo?"

"Of course."

"Do you recall me mentioning once that I didn't come from money?"

"Yes."

She plucked at a tassel on her dress. "Well, I didn't, and while that's nothing to be ashamed of, I can't deny I made some questionable choices when I was poor. Choices I'm not proud of. Now I pass myself off as sophisticated and elegant and above reproach but that's not how my life began. You see, Jo, we're all con artists in one way or another. I'd bet my bottom dollar that every person at this hotel has some secret they're hiding."

"But I broke the law."

"So have half the men here!" Ruth's eyes flashed and her cheeks pinkened. "They twist rules to make it seem as if they're just clever businessmen, but do you think they're not cheating each other every chance they get? Or worse, they're cheating the defenseless! I don't know any industry that isn't cutthroat and brutal, and people's lives hang in the balance. It sounds like all you did was sell some paintings to people who could well afford to buy them. Hardly diabolical."

Jo had never considered this, and her guilt eased – but only slightly. What she'd done still wasn't acceptable. It was still a crime, but she had done it *mainly* to make her father's last days a bit more comfortable.

She looked over at Ruth. Ruth with her ivory skin and elaborate hairstyle and couldn't picture her ever being anything less than she was at this moment – the embodiment of a stunning, tasteful, high society woman.

"Did you ever break the law?" Jo asked.

Ruth nodded casually and continued plucking at that tassel. "Minor ones, but laws, nonetheless."

"You did?"

Ruth looked her straight in the eye. "A hungry girl has got to eat, Jo."

Jo's surprise and curiosity was evident, so Ruth continued.

"I worked in a boarding house in Detroit. A busy one. It was easy to nick things because people were coming and going all the time, but one day I tried to steal a man's watch and he caught me."

Jo gasped. "Oh, my goodness. What happened next?"

"He married me."

Jo sat up straighter. "No, you can't be serious."

"Serious as a judge, no pun intended. Percy could have had

me arrested or he could have made unseemly demands for his silence, but do you know what he did instead?"

Jo shook her head.

"He gave me twenty dollars and asked me not to steal anymore. Then the next time he stayed at the boarding house he asked if I'd walk with him in the park, and so it began. He courted me for months, as if I were a proper young lady and not a scamp who stole pocket change from drunkards at a boarding house."

"That is terribly romantic."

Ruth smiled and sighed. "Yes, it is rather, isn't it? He saw me for who I was deep down inside and not just as the wayward girl I'd been forced to become because of difficult circumstances. Chase will come around," she said, patting Jo's leg. "You'll see. Although don't expect much from him today because I'd imagine his head is feeling rather like Thor's hammer is pounding at it."

"Good. Do you know he hired a detective to investigate my husband?" Jo said.

Ruth nodded. "He said so last night and let me tell you, I read him the riot act for that."

"You did?"

"Yes, but I'm not sure much of it stuck. He was drunk as a sailor. You'll have to scold him yourself when you get the next chance."

Chase woke up feeling as if he'd slept with a wool stocking stuffed in his mouth. He hadn't intended to get drunk with Percy, but they'd taken a full bottle of Mr. Plank's reserve whiskey and walked down to the lakeshore because he'd told Jo he wanted fresh air and where better to find that than *outside*? They'd sat on the rocky beach, bent an elbow – repeatedly – and before he knew it, Chase was telling his dear old friend Percy all the gritty details.

He shouldn't have. Jo's secrets were not his to share, and it was quite likely that the current pitch and roil in his gut was due as much to regret at his indiscretion as it was due to his overindulgence of liquor, but he'd found her tale so preposterous, he couldn't contain it. Now he faced the morning with a throbbing head, his stomach was currently on a sea voyage without his consent, and he had no idea what to do about Jo.

As he stared out at the midmorning sun, he contemplated all the things she'd told him – things about her rat of a husband and his trickery and his abandonment – and then Chase thought about Jo's admission of her own bad behavior – if one could call it simply bad behavior.

Perhaps he should call it what it was.

A criminal offense.

Jo Talbot had committed art fraud and broken the law, and yet… in the scheme of illegal acts, wasn't what she'd done rather low on the list? He was not an art aficionado by any means so perhaps he wasn't a good judge of such things, but technically she had signed *her own name*, after all. She *was* Emerson J. McKenna. If her lowlife reprobate of a husband chose to pass off those paintings as someone else's, was she at fault?

To the art world, probably yes.

But to the world at large?

Perhaps less so. Because the *kind* of people who spent money on paintings… were the kind of people who *could* spend money on paintings. It wasn't as if she'd stolen from an orphanage or physically harmed anyone. She hadn't copied the *Mona Lisa* and tried to pass it off as her own. She'd mimicked her father's signature – to sign her own name.

Of course, there was still the question of personal integrity. It was hard for him to accept she'd willingly deceived people. He hadn't sensed a capacity for that in her nature and it made him look at all their time together in a different light. All along he'd credited her with such innocence and guilelessness, yet she *had* tricked her way into the hotel job, and she *had* danced around the facts letting others believe things that weren't true.

But… she'd done that *badly!* So very badly!

She might be a self-professed conniver, but the *real* truth of the matter was that Jo Talbot was a *terrible liar.* Maybe trickery didn't come naturally to her. Hadn't he noticed on the first day they'd met she was hiding something? Hadn't she told him right from the start that things were not always as they seemed? He just didn't understand what she'd meant at the time. She was all but confessing, he just didn't know it.

On top of all that, of course, Chase had to acknowledge another inconvenient fact – if he wanted to judge her integrity, he'd have to judge his own, as well. He'd kept secrets, too. He'd hired a detective to look into her affairs without asking her. He'd convinced himself he had the best of intentions, that he'd done it for her benefit, for her own good, but he'd played fast and loose with the concept of honesty. His own actions, while maybe not criminal, had perhaps been... unethical. And self-serving. And potentially harmful.

His actions had put Jo into more danger instead of less.

And he needed to fix that.

thirty-six

"Mrs. Talbot, a word, if you please."

Jo heard the flinty hardness of her voice just about the same time she felt the temperature drop like an October evening. It was nearly teatime and Constance Bostwick wore a severe brown dress overlaid with black lace and was striding toward Jo on the front porch like a death omen.

As if the day could get more challenging.

That morning in the lounge, Clancy Callaghan had asked if her puffy, red-rimmed eyes were due to an allergic reaction to something noxious to which young Betsy had responded, "Nah, that's no allergy. My eyes looked just like that after I found out my sweetheart was feeding his desserts to another gal."

After that, Mr. Tippett had asked Jo if she might help with Mr. VanderLinden's dance class, so she'd spent the next two hours of the day being subtly jabbed with barbs by Frances Pullman. As the day continued, Jo still hadn't seen nor spoken with Chase. He hadn't sent a note, and her worry at his absence grew with each passing hour, so the appearance of his mother – *who wanted to talk to her* – was not a good sign.

"Of course, Mrs. Bostwick."

"Somewhere private," she said.

"How about right over there?" Jo asked, indicating two vacant rocking chairs at the very end of the porch.

"The dining room," Mrs. Bostwick said turning around. So, Jo followed obediently, wondering if she was supposed to make some attempt at idle chit-chat but she decided against it since this woman made her teeth chatter.

The dining room was virtually empty at this time of day, with all the ladies in the tearoom and the gentlemen off at their games. Only a handful of servers sat in a far corner polishing silver, but Mrs. Bostwick chose a small table in the most remote, secluded corner and sat down.

Clancy noticed their arrival and started walking forward as if to offer refreshments, but Mrs. Bostwick waved him away with a gloved hand before he was halfway across the room. He made a face and winked at Jo but not in his usual flirty manner. It was more the *wave if you need rescue* kind of wink.

"What can I do for you, Mrs. Bostwick?" Jo asked as soon as she was seated.

"It's not what you can do for me. I've decided to do something for you."

Why did that sound more like an accusation than an offer?

"Something for me?"

"Yes. My daughter Daisy speaks highly of you. I'm pleased with how her portrait is coming along, and yesterday my son presented me with the painting you completed of my dogs."

Chase had given her the painting? He'd said he was saving it for her birthday, and Jo wondered at his change in plans.

"Your dogs are such delights, Mrs. Bostwick," Jo said. "It was a pleasure to paint them, and of course, it's an honor to paint Daisy as well."

"Indeed. Mrs. Talbot, as I'm sure you are aware, the Bostwick family is philanthropic in a multitude of ways, particularly in its support of the arts. We are avid patrons of the theater, the symphony, the... visual arts."

This was probably not the time for Jo to mention she'd heard Mr. Bostwick was particularly fond of the opera...

Mrs. Bostwick continued, all the while never casting more than a passing glance at Jo's face, instead choosing to stare out the window, eyes unblinking. "Recently it has come to my attention that you seek to improve yourself with some study abroad. In Paris, I believe?"

"That's correct, Mrs. Bostwick. I plan to move there in the autumn."

Mrs. Bostwick finally turned to look Jo directly in the eyes. It was like staring down a hawk and waiting for the strike.

"I want to ensure that trip to Paris happens, Mrs. Talbot, so I'm prepared to offer you an endowment, of sorts. A single monetary gift of $500 that you may use to fund your travel, secure lodging, purchase whatever sort of fripperies one needs to be an artist in Paris."

An endowment? Or a bribe.

"That's very generous of you, Mrs. Bostwick," Jo said carefully.

"It should be enough to support you for some time if you're not frivolous with your spending. I have only one stipulation."

Let me guess...

"And that is?" Jo asked.

"I'd like you to begin your studies as soon as possible."

Ah, there it was.

"As soon as possible, Mrs. Bostwick? I have a contract with Mr. Plank that keeps me at the hotel until the end of August. I wouldn't be able to leave until then."

Mrs. Bostwick's lips twitched and pursed. "I'm sure if you were agreeable to accepting my endowment, I could speak to Mr. Plank and help him understand."

"Understand what, exactly?"

"Understand that you've realized your dream of studying in Paris exceeds your interest in remaining at this hotel and you'd prefer to leave sooner rather than later. By the end of this week, in fact. This is a sizeable offer, Mrs. Talbot and one I won't likely make again." Her civil tone, if Jo could call it that, was tilting toward menacing.

"Why the urgency, Mrs. Bostwick?"

If the woman was going to offer her a bribe to leave Chase alone, Jo was going to make her articulate it in no uncertain terms.

"I think you know why."

"I'm sure I don't."

Jo could see her struggle. Mrs. Bostwick wanted to scowl and yell, and maybe stomp her feet, but society frowned on displays of such base emotions. Anger was for the unwashed. Not the rich and polished. Somehow her face remained stoic, but her voice did reveal her frustration.

"Do you care nothing at all for Daisy?" she hissed.

Those words were a surprise...

"I beg your pardon?" Jo asked.

"Daisy. Do you care nothing at all for the welfare of my daughter or for her reputation?"

"Of course, I do, Mrs. Bostwick. I'm not sure I understand your meaning." This time she meant it. What had Jo ever done to tarnish Daisy's reputation? She adored the girl.

Mrs. Bostwick's icy-hot glare was now targeted directly at Jo and all the woman's pretenses dropped.

"If you continue to carry on with my son in such a bold and egregious manner, our family will surely suffer for the scandal. My sons will recover. Men never bear the brunt of these things for long, but Daisy's reputation will forever be sullied by her association with you. She'll fall from grace, her marriage prospects will dwindle, and all because she is too pure and kindhearted to see you for the opportunist that you are."

Jo had never been punched in the stomach but surely this must be how it felt. A broad, dense, all-encompassing blow to her abdomen, stealing her breath. Meanwhile, Mrs. Bostwick had the temerity to look satisfied that her words had landed just the way she'd hoped. She tugged her gloves on more securely.

"At last, I see I've made my point. I will leave an envelope for you at the front desk, Mrs. Talbot. If you're gone by the end of the week, it will be there waiting for you. After that, you'll get nothing."

Mrs. Bostwick rose regally and glided away as if the exchange had been nothing but pleasant, while Jo sat there, dazed, until Clancy finally came over and tapped her on the shoulder.

"You OK there, Mrs. Talbot. You look like you've seen a ghost."

Not a ghost, but perhaps a ghoul.

"What? Oh, Clancy. I'm fine. Thank you." *(She was not, in fact, fine.)*

Jo got up and walked toward the lobby, legs trembling, her mind a whirling dervish, yet one thought took hold with crystal clarity. She'd never take that money. Even if she walked out of those wide hotel doors right this very minute and boarded the first boat she saw, Jo would never accept a single dime from Constance Bostwick. Not a single dime.

The woman had just dangled a carrot from one hand and a noose in the other, while using Daisy as the bait.

thirty-seven

Betsy brought the note to Jo's room at half-past seven that evening.

"I'm so sorry, Mrs. Talbot," she said, eyes wide with apprehension. "Mrs. O'Keefe gave me this note to bring you earlier today, but I couldn't find you and then... and then I forgot about it." She made a great shuddering sound and seemed on the verge of remorseful tears, but Jo was done with anyone crying today, herself included.

"It's all right, Betsy. It was just a mistake." She patted the maid's shoulder and accepted the envelope. It seemed mistakes were being made all over the place all the time, so this one hardly registered. A note from Ruth wasn't likely urgent.

"Please tell Mrs. O'Keefe I'm sorry," Betsy said and then scurried away as if Jo might retract her forgiveness. After opening the envelope, she considered it, because the note inside wasn't from Ruth. It was from Chase. Jo had been on pins and needles all day waiting to hear from him, and now it seemed he had tried to contact her.

She scanned the note, and her heart sank.

Room 212. 3pm.

She'd missed it. She'd missed the chance to talk to him and he may have thought her absence was deliberate. Now he'd be at dinner, and it would be hours before they could meet, but there was nothing to be done about that now. She'd waited all day. She could wait a little longer.

She dashed off a note of her own.

C –
I did not receive your note until this evening, but we should talk.
My door is unlocked.

She didn't sign it. Surely, he'd know it was from her. She folded the paper, made her way to his room, and after making sure no one was in the hall to witness it, she slipped it under his door. As she turned to leave, the door opened, and there he stood.

"Hello," he said. He looked... tired.

"Hello. I didn't get your note until just now."

She saw the relief pass over his face. He *had* thought she'd chosen not to come.

"May we talk now or are you on your way to dinner?" she asked.

He opened his door and stepped back so she might enter, but not before taking his own peek out into the hall. The coast was clear, and Jo went inside. His room was much like hers, only slightly larger and decorated in dark green and sage, and his balcony was twice the size. It felt strangely familiar and yet oddly unique.

"I'm sorry we didn't get a chance to talk earlier," she said. "I would have come if I'd known."

"I'm glad you're here now."

"So am I."

They looked at each other and suddenly Jo felt much as she had that very first day in the carriage, awkward and apprehensive, with every nuance of his posture and his expression fraught with meaning that she didn't understand.

"Tell me what you're thinking," she finally said. "I'm losing my mind with not knowing. Do you despise me?"

"No," he said definitively. "I could never despise you, Jo. Everything you told me was, well, it was all rather unexpected, but I had some time to think today, once the pounding in my head ceased." He gave her a small smile and gestured for her to sit as he moved to the other chair.

"And what thoughts have you come up with?" she asked.

"I think you made a poor choice by forging your father's signature onto your own paintings, and I made an equally poor choice by hiring a detective to investigate your husband without your consent."

"I'm not sure the offenses are equal."

He shrugged. "They were very different decisions made in very different circumstances, that's true, but my point is we've both done things that seemed acceptable to us at the time, whatever our reasons. You chose to break the law, which I still can't quite comprehend, but I did something which I now realize was unethical. Something that puts you in greater danger than you were in before. I should have asked what you needed instead of rashly taking matters into my own hands. I never considered the possible ramifications. God knows I never meant to put you in harm's way, Jo, but it seems I may have."

"You may have," she acknowledged. "Can you call off your detective?"

"I can." He hesitated, then said, "And I will if that's what you truly want, but you should be aware I've learned that Oliver Talbot has had run-ins with the law. Of what nature, I'm uncertain, but don't you want to know what else he's been up to? Don't you want justice?"

"Justice could put me jail, Chase."

"I would never let it come to that. I promise you. Jo, please let me help you."

"How?"

"By finding out everything I can and using it against him. By making certain he can't come after you in any way. I know to you he's an unconquerable beast, but trust me, he's not as clever as he thinks he is. He can be exposed, and he can be broken."

Jo shivered at the cold intensity in Chase's eyes, and yet it warmed her, too. She'd been so alone in her fear of Oliver with no one rising to her aid – until now. It might be nice to finally share that burden. And possibly rid herself of it.

Chase regarded her for a moment and then continued. "You told me yesterday you didn't want to live a half-life in the shadows of society. I understand that. I do, but letting a contemptable degenerate like him roam freely while you bear the burden of being legally bound to him is a kind of half-life, too. Isn't it?"

She hadn't really thought of it that way. She'd just wanted to be safe at any cost.

"I suppose," she admitted quietly.

Chase nodded slowly. "So, even if you decide to move to Paris and the two of us go our separate ways, will you first let me help you get free of Oliver Talbot? Please?"

Chase was right. Oliver would always be an albatross around her neck, the anchor threatening to pull her under. All this time she'd thought she was running toward the freedom of Paris when what she'd really been doing was trying to outrun the yoke of her past. But there was no outrunning it, not as long as her husband had the power to destroy her. For months, inaction had been her shield, but now it seemed it was time to take up a sword.

"All right," she said at last. "You have my permission to investigate Oliver, but if I end up in jail, I will never forgive you." She meant to make light of it because the moment was crushing her.

Chase's relief was evident, and it eased over Jo, as well.

"I swear, Jo, I will never let you end up in jail. In fact, to that end, let me ask you a question. Did you say all the paintings you did with your father's signature were sold from a single gallery?"

"I believe so. Why?"

"Which gallery?"

"O'Brien's Art Emporium on State Street. Why?" she asked again.

"Because I suddenly find myself with the strongest urge to become an art collector."

"I don't understand."

"It's quite simple, really. If any of your forged paintings are still there, I'll buy them. If they've already been purchased, the gallery will have the bills of sale. I'll contact the buyer and make an offer so attractive they'll be compelled to sell the piece to me. I'm very persuasive. Once all the fraudulent paintings are in my possession, there'll be no one to question their authenticity."

He couldn't be serious.

"Oh, my goodness, Chase. You can't do that. It's almost a dozen paintings," she said.

His smile widened instantaneously. "Only a dozen? Good heavens, I thought I'd be on the hook for twice that many."

She shook her head, adamant. "I can't let you do it. It's too much."

He leaned toward her. "Jo, I'd considered doing this without telling you, then I realized that would be another bit of dishonesty between us. So, I'm asking you now. Although, perhaps I'm not really asking so much as I am telling you – this is what I'm going to do."

He was unbelievable – in both the best and the worst ways. Heavy-handed yet big-hearted. Tenacious and stubborn and yet completely generous. That he would purchase all those paintings just to protect her was more than anyone could have ever asked for. What other man would do as much?

"You're impossible," she said, but her smile could not be contained.

"And you're irresistible," he responded. "Now, we can keep arguing if that's your preference but quite frankly I'd much rather be kissing. I missed you today." His voice had turned to velvet and touched her like a caress.

"I missed you, too. And I would also rather be kissing."

She got up from her chair and walked over to his, easing down on his lap. He wrapped his arms around her hips, shifting her a little and she lamented that her bustle and skirts kept her from enjoying the full contact of his legs underneath her. There'd be time for that, though. They had all night and she intended to make the most of it.

"We are quite a pair, aren't we?" she murmured, running a fingertip over the curve of his ear. "What's to become of us?"

His gaze was tender. "You could come back to Chicago, but I understand why you won't."

"You could move to Paris with me," she teased, tugging at his necktie.

"I'd have to brush up on my French." His voice grew husky as he reached for her buttons.

"I could help you. I'd say *s'il vous plait, emmenez-moi au lit.*"

Chase's laughter rumbled in his chest. "Please take you to bed?"

"*Oui.*"

"*Je serais tres heureux.* It would be my pleasure,"he said.

Chase stretched in bed, feeling the warmth of the sun on his skin, and smiled before he even opened his eyes because the night before had been categorically and marvelously gratifying. He and Jo had kissed, and teased, explored, and pleased. She was sassy and bold, adventurous in a way that left him breathless and blissful. Somehow it seemed that all the truths they'd told and all the secrets they'd revealed had eliminated any lingering inhibitions. The encounter had been glorious – as fun as it was pleasurable.

No other woman made Chase laugh the way Jo did. No other woman challenged him or opened his mind to new ideas. And certainly, no other woman ever made him wonder if all the finely tuned plans he had for his life might need to be reexamined because falling asleep with her in his arms had blessed Chase with a sense of contentment that nearly overwhelmed him.

He loved her.

It was as simple and as complicated as that.

But what was he to do about it?

He opened his eyes and saw her sitting near the window in her sheer chemise. Her knees were drawn up with her feet resting against the sill, and her hand moved across a sheet of loose-leaf paper pressed against her thighs. She was drawing, her face relaxed, and her hair unbound and wild, just the way he liked it. She looked like an angel who'd danced with the devil – and liked it.

"Am I dreaming?" he asked, his voice still husky from sleep – and emotion.

She turned and smiled. "No, it's morning, you sluggard. Get out of bed."

"No, I'd rather you came back to bed. I'm not finished with you."

She shook her head. "You're a lazy man, to sleep so late."

"Come over here, woman. I'll prove I'm neither lazy nor a sluggard."

She smiled and shook her head again, until he said, "Please?"

It seemed to be the *please* that did it.

She set the paper and pencil aside and came over to the bed, easing down onto the mattress on her hands and knees, facing him. He reached up and pushed the hair back from her face.

"I love you, Jo."

She sat back on her knees.

"Please don't say that," she whispered.

"Why?" Although he knew why.

"Because it's already going to be impossible to say goodbye. If you say that it will just make it harder."

He ran his hand along her thigh until it rested on her hip. "You know the solution to that."

She shook her head. "I won't have this argument with you again, Chase. As much as I care for you, I'm too proud to be your mistress." She didn't sound angry or even sad, just... certain.

"I know you are. That's why I love you."

"Please, stop."

"Come here. Kiss me."

He reached his arms up and she moved toward him again, leaning over. He ran his hands down her back and over her rump, squeezing, and pulling her forward, catching her behind one knee until she straddled him.

He sat up then, so their torsos were pressed together, and through the linen he could feel the warmest bits of her pressed against his eager body. He kissed her, breathing in the scent of her skin and twisting his hands in her hair, pulling just enough to bring her closer and thrilling at the feminine sounds it elicited from her throat.

He reached between them and teased her until she finally pulled her chemise up and off her body, letting it float to the floor like a whisper. He pushed the sheets aside and at last they were skin to skin, and he was deep inside her, reveling at the mystery and the magic of her. She was earthbound but heaven-sent.

"God, Jo," he breathed against her smooth neck as they swayed together. "I love you. I can't help it."

She uttered a soft hum of pleasure as she rocked against him, her arms around his shoulders, her thighs squeezing tight against his hips.

"I know," she whispered on a plaintive sigh. "I love you, too."

Her words hit him like a solemn, reverent promise and his heart filled with hope.

"Marry me," he said.

She opened her eyes, still moving with him, clutching him. "You're breaking my heart," she murmured.

He gazed back, whispering his entreaties in cadence with their rhythm.

"I'll mend it. I love you. I'll move to Paris. Marry me."

She gasped when said *Paris*, but he wasn't sure if that was for the words he'd spoken or the pleasure pulsing between them.

And seconds later, as her body reached its peak, she pressed her lips to his shoulder and murmured, "Yes, yes, yes."

But he wasn't sure if that was passion speaking, or if Jo had just agreed to be his wife.

thirty-eight

"I suppose you might create a diversion at one end of the hall, and I could sneak out and go in the other direction," Jo said, trying to pin her hair up into some semblance of order. If she hurried, she'd have just enough time to freshen up in her own room before heading to the front porch for her morning painting class.

Chase came up behind her, wrapping his arms loosely around her waist. "Or we send a note to Mr. Tippett telling him you need a morning free of duties."

Jo jabbed another pin into her hair. "And what reason would you suggest I give him."

"Tell him you've taken on a private student. One who's not very devoted to painting but is entirely devoted to his painting instructor." He nuzzled her neck and she laughed but stepped away.

"I really have to go."

Jo wasn't sorry she'd spent the night in Chase's bed but in the bright light of day, she was realizing just how difficult it would be to make a discreet exit. His room was in a far more populated area of the hotel, and it was after 9:00 a.m. People were milling about everywhere, and all she needed was for Constance Bostwick to see her leaving Chase's room.

She hadn't said anything to him about his mother's *offer*, such as it was, and had no intention of doing so. There was already enough friction between the two of them, and soon enough Chase, Daisy and Constance would be back safely ensconced within their society bubble in Chicago and Jo would be... somewhere else. She hadn't yet decided if she'd leave for Paris in the autumn or the spring, but either way, she wouldn't be in Illinois. And either way, she wouldn't be with Chase.

Yes, she had *accidentally* agreed to marry him...

But she had no intention of making good on that promise. It was uttered in the passion of the moment, and she was no more serious with her answer than he'd been with the question. Because he obviously wasn't serious. *Was he?* Minutes later, when she sat down in a chair to button her shoes and he knelt down beside her to lend a hand, the moment seemed right for making the clarification.

"Is there anything we need to discuss?" she asked quietly as he took the button hook from her hand.

His smile came easy. "I don't think so."

She nodded in relief, and then he said, "Unless you'd like to talk about our impending nuptials."

She gave a quick, short sigh. "I assumed you were speaking in jest, as I was."

"I wasn't. I'm not. Marry me." He took hold of her hand as she pressed the other to her temple.

"Chase, that's a ridiculous waste of breath. You know I can't marry you."

"Why?" He said it sternly, as if determined to prove her wrong.

"Have you lost your capacity for rational discourse? Must I list all the reasons?" She began to count the items with her fingers. "I'm already married. I'm illegitimate. Your family would never accept me. Society would never accept me as your wife. Oh, and then there's the little matter of my felonious habit of committing art fraud. Have I missed anything?"

"No, I think that's everything," he said amicably.

"So, we are in agreement that marriage is quite out of the question?"

"No, we are not in agreement."

"Chase, I have to go teach my art class. Do you suppose we could postpone – indefinitely – this ridiculous merry-go-round?"

He began counting on his own fingers.

"We're going to find Oliver Talbot and obtain your divorce. I'm going to purchase all your forged paintings so none will be the wiser. No one will discover that your parents were never married because no one would ever think to look. And as for my family accepting you, Daisy already has, and my father and brother are sure to adore you. My mother? She doesn't even like me so the fact that she might not like you is, forgive me, rather inconsequential. And, although you didn't include this on your list, I'm rather looking forward to spending time in Paris."

"Are you suggesting you would actually move to Paris?" He *had* lost his capacity for rational discourse.

Chase gave a little bob of the head. "For a year or two, yes. Would that be long enough for you? Then after being absent from society for a bit, we'd come back to Chicago as a dull, old married couple, and by then everyone would have forgotten you ever had a previous husband. I'm sure Bostwick & Sons could benefit from some overseas investments, and if not, I've been toying with some independent ventures of my own. I am capable, you know."

She smiled. Chase in Paris. Was it possible? *Could* she marry him? Could the fates have finally turned in her favor? Dared she *hope*?

Of course, this might be the time to mention how his mother had offered her bribe money to just leave him alone, but a sharp rap sounded on the door, making Jo jump like a startled cat. They exchanged concerned looks and Chase pulled her from the chair, motioning for her to go stand on the other side of the armoire. As long as no one came inside the room, she'd be hidden from view.

"Who is it," Chase asked, reaching out for the handle.

"It's Mr. Parnell, sir. I have an urgent telegram for you."

Chase opened the door and Jo realized too late that her reflection appeared in the mirror. If Mr. Parnell looked in that direction, he'd see her. She pressed back against the wall.

"Thank you, Mr. Parnell," she heard Chase say.

"Of course, sir, but just so you're aware, your mother received a telegram this morning, too."

"She did? All right. Thank you."

Jo let out a shuddering breath, stepping back into the room, as Chase closed the door. He was looking down at the telegram, a frown marring his face.

"Do you think it's something serious?" Jo asked.

He shook his head. "I doubt it, but let's find out." He tore it open, and Jo watched as his face paled, and he turned slowly to sink down onto the bench at the end of the bed.

"My father's had a heart attack."

"Oh, Chase. I'm so sorry. What can I do?" Her own heart sank.

He looked up at her blankly. "I don't know."

"Is your father... still with us?" *What was the proper way to ask?*

He glanced back down at the telegram, and then handed it to her.

"Read it. I can't focus."

It felt invasive to read such a personal note, but he wanted her to.

CB –

AJ HAD HEART ATTACK LAST PM WHILE ENJOYING

OPERA WITH CAMILLE. ALIVE BUT BARELY. PRESS IS
AWARE. COME HOME. URGENT.
ALEX

"Camille?" she asked.

"His opera singer."

Jo's heart sank even lower. "And the press knows he was with her when it happened? Is that what this means?"

His jaw clenched. "It means he was in bed with her when it happened. I have to go see my mother." He dropped his head into his hands and Jo sat down next to him, wrapping an arm around his drooping shoulders.

"Chase, I'm so sorry." She knew the unique pain of witnessing a parent's illness, a particular agony she wouldn't wish on anyone. She understood the feelings of helplessness it stirred, the ever-present worry it created, and how it forced even the strongest to face their own mortality.

She also understood the more practical ramifications of this situation. The scandal of A.J. Bostwick having a heart attack while with his mistress was going to reverberate around Chicago like a gong. The press would have a field day, and his family's misfortune would become blather for every chinwagger, blabbermouth, and gossipmonger in every drawing room, men's club, and dinner party around the city. The Bostwicks were too big and too visible for this to go away quietly.

It wasn't fair, and Constance's words from yesterday came back to haunt Jo's memories.

Our family will suffer the scandal. My sons will recover. Men never bear the brunt of these things for long, but Daisy's reputation will forever be sullied.

∼

Chase arrived at his mother's room some ten minutes later after hastily aiding Jo in her exit, and all the while, he fretted for his father. The details of the telegram were so sparse, and he longed for more information. He hoped she'd have some.

"There you are. Finally," his mother snapped as soon as he entered their suite. He'd forgive her tone, all things considered.

She was sitting on the settee, wearing a dark blue satin robe over her nightdress with her hair in a single braid and he could not think of another time when he'd seen her thus, a time he'd seen her anything less than perfectly, strategically, implacably assembled. Somehow, she looked younger – and prettier – in spite of the pinched expression on her face.

Daisy was sitting in a red upholstered chair and jumped up as Chase entered, running forward and wrapping her arms around his waist. Her eyes were pink and puffy from tears, and he hugged her to him.

"It will be all right," he said to her, patting her back.

"No, it won't," his mother said. "He's humiliated us."

Chase frowned. "He's had a heart attack, mother. Perhaps your recriminations can wait for another day?"

"Of course, you'd say that. You're no better, lollygagging around this hotel with that opportunistic hedonist," she muttered.

Chase breathed in deeply and exhaled slowly. This wasn't how he'd intended to tell her, but his nerves were raw, and the words were out before he could consider them because he could not, would not, abide by his mother disrespecting Jo, regardless of the circumstances.

"Mrs. Talbot and I have come to an understanding, Mother. Once she's obtained a divorce from her estranged husband, she and I are to be married."

"Oh!" Daisy gasped and squeezed his waist again. "I knew it. I'm so glad for you."

His mother's expression froze in place, and she turned toward the window without saying a word.

"I'll make arrangements for the three of us to travel back

immediately," he continued. "I assume that's what you want to do?"

She paused, then shuddered with a long, woebegone sigh. "Yes, I suppose we must."

His mother *was* sad, and he *did* feel sorry for her because this was a miserable situation for them all, but the woman made it damn near impossible for him to feel any compassion. She'd taunted and judged and harangued him his entire life and he'd neverunderstood why. What had broken in her that made her so damn mean? Still, she was his mother and she had just learned her husband suffered a heart attack while in another woman's bed. Chase would be a monster not to show some kindness.

"I am sorry, Mother. I know this is painful and difficult for a variety of reasons. I am here for you if you need me."

She looked at him once more, as if wondering why he was still speaking, then said, "Tell Mr. Beeks we'll need some maids to help us pack our trunks. Adele can't do it all herself."

"George Pullman could probably arrange a sleeper car for you, but the ship will be nearly as fast and far more comfortable. Just don't tell him I said so," Hugo remarked as Chase sat in his office along with Percy O'Keefe. "I can have Tippett make all the travel arrangements if you'd like. I'm sure your mind is elsewhere."

"Thank you, Hugo. I'd appreciate that," Chase answered.

"Not at all. It's a messy business. I'm sorry you have to cut your holiday short, especially with this being the reason."

"Have you any more news on how your father's fairing?" Percy asked.

"None, and I'd rather not find out the details from the newspaper," Chase replied. "But I'm bound to."

"Maybe out of respect they'll omit the fact that it happened in the presence of his lady friend?" Percy suggested optimistically, but then added, "Although I suppose that's about as likely as Breezy VonMeisterburger sitting quietly through a meal."

"Just as likely," Chase said. "You know, my father has done a great many important, useful things. He a benefactor helping shape Chicago, and I just hope his entire life of productive enterprise isn't reduced to a singular anecdote about him dying with his pants down."

"People love scandal," Hugo said sadly. "The richer and mightier you are, the more they love to see you crumble."

"That they do," Chase said, rising from the chair. "Thank you for your help, Hugo. I'll be in my room for a while if Tippett has any questions regarding our transportation. Percy, will you walk with me?"

"Of course."

They left Mr. Plank's office and headed toward the lobby, but before they reached it, Chase halted saying, "I wonder if I might ask a favor of you, Percy."

"Whatever you need," Percy responded.

"Would you look out for Jo for me? I know people are curious, and I'm concerned that once I'm gone, they'll be less generous toward her."

"Ruthie and I will keep her under our wing and make sure she gets off to Paris without mishap."

Paris. Yes, Paris. "I'd appreciate that. You've become a good friend."

"Glad to be of service. Is there something more?"

"Just that... I've asked her to be my wife."

Percy coughed in surprise. "Uh, I hate to be a nitpicker but isn't she already someone's wife?"

"I'm working on that." Chase started walking again and Percy hesitated before suddenly trotting to catch up.

"Chase, let me say again I hate to be a nitpicker but are you sure that's the wisest course of action? She's a delight, to be sure, but if you're worried about a man's life being reduced to a lewd anecdote you might choose more wisely. No disrespect to her at all but she has a rather checkered past."

Chase stopped and turned again, staring at Percy. "Do you love your wife?"

"Yes. Of course, I do."

"Could anything prevent you from being with her?"

Percy stared at him, eyes filling with comprehension – and sympathy, and answered, "No. Nothing at all."

thirty-nine

I t seemed Mrs. Bostwick wasn't through with her yet.

Jo returned to her room late that afternoon to find a note slipped under her door written in a tight script.

Mrs. Talbot –

As you are aware, my family is now facing yet another scandal. While I am not prone to supplication, I must implore you to consider your actions and think of Daisy's future. She should not have to suffer the dire consequences brought on by other people's selfish, reckless behavior. If you have a shred of decency, or any regard for my daughter, do not persist in your pursuit of my son. While you may have preoccupied him temporarily with your lewd conduct, whatever understanding you think you've come to is patently false. He will never marry you and your continued relationship with him will only drag this family further into the muck.

Mrs. Talbot. Do the sensible, responsible, righteous thing and terminate all contact with both Daisy and Chase. End this undue influence you have over my children and pray that God, in His Goodness, will forgive you for your trespasses.

CB

The words stole Jo's breath away. They were cruel and harsh...
and yet not *entirely* without merit.

She hadn't set out to seduce Chase, but she had encouraged
him. She welcomed him into her room and into her bed. She'd
indulged in wanton behavior knowing full-well it was self-
indulgent – and indiscreet. Despite the gossip, she'd persisted.
Even after Mrs. Bostwick's first warning about Daisy's welfare, Jo
had spent the night with Chase, whispering promises in his ear
that she knew she could not keep.

She'd never marry him.

She couldn't. She'd known that all along, but Mrs.
Bostwick's note reminded her. Even if Jo could divorce Oliver
Talbot and be free from his name, she'd never be clean of the
stains he'd left on her. Her past would never stay a secret – not
with the press fascinated by the Bostwick family's every
escapade. She could never be certain her crimes wouldn't be
revealed, even for all of Chase's plans to keep her safe and
untarnished.

He'd done so much to rescue her. He'd restored her sense of
hope and faith and taught her what love really felt like. But love –
even true love – was a fragile thing and theirs would not bear up
under the pressures of society's scrutiny and other people's
expectations. They'd both known that from the start, known that
this affair was just that – an affair. Yet somewhere along the line,
they'd forgotten. This morning they'd been play-acting,
pretending the world was kind and understanding, pretending it
would accept them when they both knew, deep down – it wasn't
– and it wouldn't.

And Jo could not let Daisy pay the price.

She tore up the note and threw it in the trash basket, but the
words were seared into her memory.

Chase came to her room hours later, when most of the other
guests were making their way to dinner. She let him in and held
him close, saying nothing, letting him draw strength from her,
even though she needed it for herself.

"Are you hungry?" she asked him. "I have some food. I wasn't sure of your plans."

He pulled away and ran a hand through his hair. "I could eat," he said.

She made them plates from her lounge food contraband. Bread, cheese, apples, lemon meringue pie because she knew it was his favorite. They sat on her bed to eat instead of at the table, saying little because the topics were too large, but when the food was gone, and they lay side by side on top of the covers, still fully clothed, he leaned over and kissed her with reverence.

"I don't know how to leave you," he whispered against her ear. "But promise me you'll come back to Chicago at the end of the summer."

He lifted his face and peered down at her as if he wanted to memorize her. "I meant what I said this morning, Jo. I want you to marry me, but I have to find out what the situation is with my father, first."

"Of course, you do," she said. "You need to be there for your family."

He gave a small nod. "And the company. Alex can't run it on his own and if we let things fall apart just because my father had a heart attack, he'll never forgive us." His wan smile made her ache with empathy.

"He'll be all right, Chase." *There she went, making false promises again.*

"My father is a force of nature. If any man can fight his way back, it's him. I just wish I knew more." He rested his head on her shoulder, and she ran a hand through his hair. After a minute, he added, "So you return to Chicago, and once my father's back on his feet, you and I will solve the Oliver problem, and then we'll go to Paris together. I promise."

"Of course," she whispered even while knowing it was a lie. She wouldn't go back to Chicago at the end of the summer. She'd likely never go back to Chicago again, but she couldn't tell him that. Not tonight. Tonight, she'd tell him anything he needed to hear.

It seemed Jo Talbot was back to keeping secrets.

He left her sometime during the night, and Jo was glad he hadn't woken her up. He'd spared them both the messiness of saying words that couldn't ease the pain or change the outcome. Instead, he left a note on her pillow that simply said, "I miss you already."

Jo tucked it into the rim of the framed photograph she had of her father and got ready to face her day – feeling much the same way a person must feel when getting ready for a painful yet necessary surgery. She just had to get on with it, get through it, and get over it.

"Good morning, Mrs. Talbot," Mr. Parnell said giving her a curious glance as she entered the lounge. He pulled out a chair and poured her a cup of coffee.

"Gadzooks but that Mrs. Bostwick makes my blood run cold," Betsy exclaimed a moment later as she burst in and crossed to the buffet to fill her plate. "She never blinks. I swear the woman never blinks. Have any of you noticed that?" She looked around the room for affirmation as she continued. "It's like staring at a porcelain doll's face except for it's the doll you always make your little sister play with on account of it being so creepy to look at."

"Betsy!" Mr. Parnell said loudly. "We don't talk about our guests that way."

The maid turned around again and gave him a quizzical stare. "Since when?"

"Since today," he said giving the slightest tilt of his head in Jo's direction. Betsy looked at her and blushed furiously, and Jo realized then that not only had Mr. Parnell seen her in Chase's mirror, but apparently everyone else knew she'd been there, too.

"I didn't say anything to anyone," he whispered to Jo a minute later. "Your business is your business, and none of mine but seems the Callaghan boys keep running into your friend in the hallways at all hours of the early morning."

"Well, he's leaving today so that won't happen again," Jo said, trying to keep the crack from her voice.

Mr. Parnell gave her a discreet, paternal pat on the leg, and she wondered if she'd get through this day without some very *indiscreet* tears.

"Oh, my heavens, thank goodness!" Daisy exclaimed as Jo entered the art studio some thirty minutes later. "I was afraid I'd miss you completely and how dreadful that would have been!"

Daisy was wearing a stylish traveling dress of periwinkle wool and a dainty matching hat with absolutely no birds on it. Jo wasn't so despondent as to not notice – and appreciate – that, but as she got closer, Daisy launched herself forward with such fervor they nearly toppled over.

"I'm so sad to be leaving the hotel. You haven't finished my portrait yet," Daisy all but wailed.

Jo stepped back and smiled. "We've done enough sittings. I can finish the rest on my own and I'll ship it to you as soon as I can."

Daisy nodded with a sniffle. "Or you could just bring it to Chicago. Chase told me you'd be coming home and I'm so glad." She lowered her voice, "And it seems I was right! He does love you. Oh, Jo, it's so wonderful. Once you're married, we'll be sisters, really and truly!"

She flung her arms around Jo again and the words struck her right in the heart – because they wouldn't be sisters. Not ever. He should not have told Daisy they'd be getting married – because they would not be getting married.

"Meeting you is one the best things that's ever happened to me," Jo said truthfully. "You'll always be dear to me, even if we're far apart. Oh!" she exclaimed suddenly. "I have your dresses! Oh, no! I'll hurry and pack them right now and have Mr. Parnell rush them to the boat."

"Nonsense, you silly," Daisy chided. "Keep them. They're yours."

"Oh, Daisy, I couldn't possibly keep them. I'll have them shipped to you."

"I don't need them, and anyway, you can just bring those in a few weeks too. It won't be all that long until you're back in Chicago and then we can see each other all the time, and it'll be so fabulous and wonderful! We can paint and talk about your wedding, and I can introduce you to all my friends. They're sure to find you an utter delight, just as I do."

Jo wanted to stop her right there, to tell her the truth. To say a real goodbye because it was entirely possible they'd never see each other again. But she smiled brightly just as she'd learned to do and gave Daisy's shoulder a squeeze.

"All of that sounds heavenly, Daisy. And you're right. The time will go by in a blink," Jo said. "Until then, you must take good care of your brother for me and know I'm praying for your father's speedy recovery every day. I'm so sorry he's taken ill. Sorry for all of you."

Daisy's eyes puddled with tears, and she blinked them away.

"Thank you, Jo. You're so kind. I don't want to go but I'm already late. Mother doesn't know I'm here. She thinks I'm stopping at the candy shoppe before we get on the boat but if I dally any longer, she'll come looking."

Jo did *not* want Constance Bostwick to come looking. She didn't want Chase to come looking either because if she saw him, she'd likely fling herself at him with the same uninhibited abandon which Daisy had displayed – except that Jo would be weeping and quite possibly wailing. There was a good chance she'd also be blubbering and perhaps even howling. She'd be all manner of hysterical... and that was simply not how she wanted him to remember her.

forty

"A dreadful business," Mrs. VonMeisterburger said to her son as they relaxed in wicker rocking chairs on the front porch a few days after the Bostwick's had left. "Simply dreadful. Taken down in his prime by something as gauche as a heart attack. Imagine." She stole a glance over at Jo who was painting just a few feet away.

"I don't think he's dead yet, Mummy," Mortimer responded, not looking up from his newspaper. "This article says he's expected to survive."

"He won't if Constance Bostick is his nurse," she whispered snidely but not so quietly that Jo couldn't hear, causing her to wonder if the indiscretion wasn't deliberate. Then again, Breezy had the subtlety of a locomotive.

She wasn't alone in that, however. In fact, it seemed as if everyone wanted to discuss the Bostwicks and their misfortune and their abrupt departure from the island just to see how Jo might react. There'd been no mention of the opera singer, and thus far no one had been blatantly mean-spirited *(well, except for Breezy)* and yet Jo couldn't help but note the sensation of sand shifting beneath her feet, as if she were standing in an hourglass and time was running out.

"Did I mention I made a gift of a camera to Mr. Bostwick?" Mortimer continued. "He was most appreciative, and even asked me to send it in with my own to have the pictures developed. I shipped them off this very morning and soon, Mummy, you'll be able to witness my superior photographic art skills for yourself."

Jo clutched the brush a little more tightly in her hand. Mortimer was perhaps the only person who seemed oblivious to any of the whispers, but the fact that he had Chase's camera gave her pause since it was full of photographs – of her.

In addition to the day of their indoor picnic, Chase had taken pictures in the gazebo and the garden and a few surreptitiously on the front lawn. There'd even been one day when he'd had the camera with him in Jo's studio. He'd come there – ostensibly to fetch Daisy – and then let his sister play photographer by taking some images of him and Jo side by side. There'd been nothing provocative about their poses but just the fact that it was the two of them together might raise some eyebrows.

Assuming anyone other than Chase ever saw the photos, of course. She wouldn't get a chance to because she wasn't going back to Chicago. He just didn't know that yet. She planned to send him a letter to let him know of her decision but every time she tried to write the words, she ended up doodling pictures of his face alongside hearts shattered into a dozen jagged little shards and after several such attempts that ended in some rather disturbing drawings, she decided that perhaps her emotions might still be a bit too raw to put things into words. And anyway, there was no real rush.

"Do you think I've made the right decision?" Jo whispered to Ruth as they looked out over the swirl of pastel-adorned women and tuxedo-clad men twirling around the dance floor on Saturday evening.

Jo had considered not attending the weekly event, but the

curiosity about her had only grown over the past few days so she felt it was essential – *imperative even* – that she prove to everyone how Chase's departure had not impacted her in the least.

Nothing had been going on between them. Nothing at all.

"The right decision to spend the winter painting for Mr. Plank?" Ruth responded. "Probably. I do think winter here might be harsh but if it's too unpleasant you can come down to Detroit and stay with me and Mr. O'Keefe. There will always be room for you at our house, and who knows? Maybe you'll enjoy the area so much you'll decide to stay. Would that be so awful? To remain in the United States instead of sailing across the ocean?"

"I'm still going to Paris in the springtime." Though she tried to say it patiently, in truth, Jo was feeling rather *impatient* over Ruth's continued attempts to make her change her mind. "This is just a temporary delay so I might earn a bit more money and solidify my plans before departure," she added.

Solidify her plans, indeed. As of right now, she still had no sponsor, no place to stay, and she'd not received a single reply to any query she'd sent out. In fact, there'd been such a flagrant lack of response, she'd begun to question if Mr. Beeks had actually posted her letters. She knew he rifled through people's mail but was he malicious enough to prevent delivery too?

"I just hope you're going to Paris for the right reasons, my darling," Ruth continued, fluttering her ivory fan slowly.

Jo huffed, finally displaying her true exasperation. "Why doesn't anyone want me to move to Paris? Is my French truly so inadequate?

Ruth smiled over at her. "No, darling. It's not that at all. It's just that, well, for a time it seemed as if you wanted to go to Paris to avoid Oliver. Now I hope you aren't going just to avoid Chase."

"That's not what I'm doing at all." She frowned but strove to wipe the emotion from her face as Fabian and Courtland Zuiderduin approached. Smiling was an effort. She hoped she wasn't grimacing.

"Goot evening, ladies. Vil you dance, Mrs. Talbot?" Courtland asked, apparently not put off by whatever showed in her expression.

"I'd be delighted," she said rather too brightly – because she was not, *in fact,* delighted but it seemed Jo was back to playing a part. The plucky little artist from Chicago with an art dealer husband who simply couldn't leave his very important job to come be with his wife at the Imperial Hotel.

She was not pining away for Chase Bostwick.

She was not.

And her heart was not breaking.

It was not.

And so, she must dance.

First with Courtland, and then Fabian, and then Mortimer and Percy and Mr. Getty and Mr. Chadwick (*who had only recently arrived at the hotel*) and a dozen others. She spun around the floor and laughed at their flimsy attempts at humor and ignored their even flimsier grasps on her hand. She giggled with Iris and Dahlia Mahoney near the punchbowl and congratulated Priscilla Palmer on her engagement and introduced Miss Getty to that very same Mr. Chadwick who had only just arrived at the hotel – because hadn't he remarked that he enjoyed the piano, and didn't Miss Getty also enjoy the piano? Jo was the quintessential social butterfly flitting from one joyful interaction to the next until Mr. Tippett said, "Mrs. Talbot, I think you're after my job."

"I assure you, I am not, Mr. Tippett," she answered gaily twirling away.

And all the while, as she danced and laughed and made ever so merry, all she wanted to do was go up to her room, hide under her covers, and dream about Chase. Where was he just now? At his house? With his family? Was he thinking of her at this very moment? Was he longing for her as much as she was longing for him? Was she a fool for giving him up? Could they somehow be together?

Standing in the ballroom, preoccupied with those thoughts,

she must have let her carefree façade slip for a moment, and Frances Pullman sidled up beside her.

"Oh, my poor dear, Mrs. Talbot," Frances murmured, her voice syrupy with insincerity. "With the Bostwicks gone, you must surely be missing your playmate. Are you ever so sad?"

"I beg your pardon, Miss Pullman?"

"Oh!" Frances laughed and tapped her fan against Jo's arm. "Why, I meant Daisy, of course. Goodness, me! Who did you think I meant?"

She wandered away tittering and chortling, confident her taunt had made Jo feel worse.

But the truth was, nothing could make Jo feel worse.

forty-one

Chicago in the middle of August was always hot, but today's heat made the stench of the city particularly pungent as Chase walked home from his office. How quickly he'd been spoiled by the sweet, fresh air of Trillium Bay – and how he ached to go back. Had it only been a week? It felt much longer. He missed Jo.

He'd written her a letter each evening, and though brief, they were full of words like *love* and *adore* and *cherish*. He wondered what she was doing, and how she was feeling. He worried over her welfare as much as he missed the sound of her voice and touch of her hands, but there was little he could do about it at the moment. His family needed him here.

He made his way into the house and went directly up the carpeted stairs to see his father. A.J. Bostwick was on the mend. Slowly but surely. He retained a certain pallor and didn't move at his typical brisk pace, but as Chase entered the bedroom suite, he found his father sitting up in bed, newspapers strewn all over the covers, eating a steak so raw Chase wondered if there was a cow roaming around somewhere with a piece missing.

He took off his linen jacket and vest, tossing them on a nearby bench, and sat down in the gold brocade chair next to A.J.'s oversized bed. All the windows were open with the red damask curtains drawn to the side so despite the dark paneled walls, the room was full of light.

Glancing at his father's plate, he said, "Would you like me to have cook give that steak a bit more color, Father? I'm not sure raw beef is the best thing for your gut right now."

His father frowned. "Poppycock! A good, thick steak is exactly what I need to get my strength back up. That charlatan doctor had me eating broth, as if broth will get me out of this bed. I need to get back to work and show this town my *incident* was nothing more than a hiccup."

"You had a heart attack," Chase said dryly, picking up one of the newspapers to peruse its contents.

"So say the physicians but what do they know?"

"Um, Medicine. Anatomy. Surgery. Proper nutrition."

"Oh, aren't you the clever one," A.J. said, shoving another chunk of meat into his mouth.

"Not so clever as Alex, it seems," he said, turning a page. "How on earth has he managed to keep the details of your *hiccup* from the scandal sheets?"

"I believe we have Miss Carnegie's connections to thank for that," his father answered. "It seems her family has a kinship with Joseph Medill of the Daily Tribune, and since she's about to marry Alex that discretion now extends to us."

"That's a relief," Chase responded. "Can we assume then that Camille's involvement will be kept from the general public?"

His father nodded. "It appears so, and let me tell you, Camille's involvement was intimate, but what a way to go, aye?" He laughed and took another bite as Chase shook his head to erase the image of his father collapsing in the throes of passion on top of the poor unsuspecting opera singer.

His father continued. "You know, you've been home a week already, but it seems we haven't discussed anything other than work and my health. Tell me about the Imperial Hotel. Is it as grand as Plank says? The man is prone to hyperbole although your sister seemed to enjoy it. Your mother still isn't speaking to me, so I have no idea what she thought of the place."

"Mother is quite angry with you," Chase agreed.

"Mm, hm," A.J. said, chewing thoughtfully. "According to Daisy your mother's quite angry at you, too. What did you do, exactly?"

Chase regarded him for a moment before saying, "I fell in love."

His father's silver brow arched. "Hm, that's the same reason she's mad at me."

Chase couldn't help but chuckle, and yet, his father was being rather unfair.

"You know, Mother does have a compelling reason to be angry with you, Father. I gathered from what she told me on our journey home she's been well aware of your liaisons over the years. She's humiliated and I think it's possible you may have broken her heart."

"Broken her heart? Did she say I broke her heart?" He sounded far more dubious than repentant.

"Not in so many words. I just surmised."

The boat ride back to Chicago had been excruciating with Chase's mother drinking too much sherry and providing a litany of his father's offenses (out of earshot of Daisy, thank goodness) and yet providing Chase with a new insight into the woman's psyche. While she considered her own actions to be above reproach – which they certainly were not – she *had* been dealt a rather weak hand. It seemed that, although she'd suspected A.J. had married her for money, there'd been a time when she'd thought they might grow into something more. They never did, and it wounded her.

Of course, by the time the boat from Trillium Bay docked in Chicago his mother was back to her badger-like countenance and was so chilly toward Chase he wondered if he'd been the one sipping too much sherry and had imagined the whole encounter.

"You surmised incorrectly, son," his father stated. "If any heart breaking occurred, it was mine. A man can only be rejected so many times before he starts to take it personally."

"Mother rejected you? How so?"

A.J. squinted at him as if the answer were obvious and Chase couldn't help but recognize Daisy in his father's expression.

"Yes, she rejected me. Repeatedly, and of course, I don't blame you for this, but having two babies at one time took a lot out of her. Why do you think there's a nine-year gap between you and your sister? It took me that long to get back into your mother's bed."

That was not information Chase wanted to know, and yet... wait a minute.

"Is that why she's always disliked me so? Because having me at the same time as Alex was... traumatic?"

Come to think of it, that made perfect sense. As he quickly scanned through the memories of his life, hadn't she been telling him so all along? How that fourteen extra minutes of pregnancy had been too miserable to bear? He'd always assumed her resentment toward him was based on something larger and deeper and more nuanced. Not something as ridiculous and illogical as that, not to mention it being something he'd had no control over whatsoever. The realization he could never, ever truly appease her for this was oddly freeing. It meant he could stop trying.

"I don't think she really dislikes you, although she certainly favors Alex, but I do know that's when she began to dislike me. It's all water under the bridge, though. I'll let her build the most ostentatious cottage on the island and she'll consider us even – for a while." A.J. set his now empty plate on the nightstand and said, "Now, let's hear about this woman you've fallen in love with."

Chase's father had always been larger than life. Bold and gregarious, sometimes uncouth but seemingly welcomed by a society that usually rejected those who started with less, regardless of how much wealth they might have amassed with hard work and clever thinking. Perhaps it was his father's humble beginnings that made Chase feel he could trust him with *most of* the truth about Jo.

So, he told him about her marriage and how her husband had swindled and abandoned her – conveniently skipping over the part about the art fraud – and the part about Chase moving to Paris. He'd wait until his father's heart was stronger before getting into that. And he told him about Jo's talent and her smile and *tried* to explain how she made him feel, but that was hard to put into words. It was like trying to explain the beauty of a rainbow to someone who'd never seen such a thing.

"I've asked her to marry me, Father. As soon as we can get her divorce granted." That should make clear just how much Chase loved her, but his father's reaction was not quite what he'd hoped.

"Have you now? She must be quite a gal," A.J. said mildly when Chase had finally finished.

"She is. You'll see for yourself when you meet her."

Maybe his father was just fatigued, or maybe that steak was giving him indigestion because a frown marred his forehead and Chase felt the first stirring of unease as his father shifted on the bed, plumping the pillow behind him and readjusting his bed jacket. For each second that passed, Chase's tension grew. It was not like A.J. to hesitate with an opinion.

"I'm sure she'd lovely, son, but that's a lot to overcome," A.J. finally said. "A love match is all well and good, but it seems, based on what you've said, her concerns are valid. The truth is, she won't fit in. She will be judged, and she likely won't be welcomed."

A sharp upper cut of annoyance made Chase flinch. "I disagree, Father. She's charming and smart and engaging. She won over every single person at the Imperial Hotel, except for Mother, of course, and Jo can do the same thing in Chicago. Especially with us to support her. You will support her, won't you?"

He'd assumed that was a given. Perhaps it was not.

"I support *you*, son. If you carefully consider things and decide to continue on with this relationship, I won't fault you or undermine you in any way but consider this... Imagine, say, a horserace."

"A horserace?" Frustration edged his tone. His father was prone to analogies that often took strange turns.

"Yes. Imagine there's a long line of sleek, thoroughbred fillies." A.J. extended his arm as if to point to all those imaginary fillies.

"Show ponies, son. Proud and beautiful with a superior lineage. They've trained for this event their entire lives. They're bred to win. Now imagine, running alongside them, is a mule."

"Oh, for God's sake, Father, surely you're not comparing the woman I love to a mule!" His feet, which had been resting on the frame of the bed, thumped to the floor as he gripped the armrests in aggravation. His father's reaction was very disappointing!

"It's a crass analogy and I'm sorry, but it's apt," A.J. said. "You're asking this girl to spend the rest of her life running a race she can't possibly win. She'll stand out for all the wrong reasons, and it will exhaust her. It will break her."

"I don't believe this. I thought you, of all people, would understand." He never should have told him anything, but he'd thought his father would be an ally. Perhaps even convince his mother to be more amenable to the idea of bringing Jo into the family.

"I do understand," his father said. "Because I'm still running that race every day myself. Why do you think I work so hard? Nothing has ever been handed to me and don't fool yourself for a second into thinking we haven't missed out on opportunities because I wasn't born with a silver spoon in my mouth. Why do you think Alex is marrying a Carnegie?"

The hits just kept coming and Chase felt the surprise of that question all the way to his toes.

"I assumed it's because he loves her." Alex had certainly indicated as much, but A.J. shrugged indifferently.

"I think he is growing fond of her, and he might have proposed eventually, but he also knew the association with her family would open a lot of doors for us and quite frankly, we need the business."

"Our company is doing fine, Father. Surely, he doesn't have to marry Isabella for her connections alone."

Chase still didn't believe that was the case. His father must be wrong about the depth of his brother's feelings for Isabella, yet A.J. looked suddenly uncomfortable and Chase's suspicions grew.

"Father? What aren't you telling me?"

A.J. paused and his frown increased. "If I tell you, you must promise that this stays between us, agreed?"

Chase nodded and leaned forward with captivated interest.

"I assume you remember that investment your brother bungled last year?" his father said quietly.

"Yes?"

"Well, that error of his cost our company tens of thousands of dollars and the Carnegie girl's dowry nicely covers it."

Chase sat back abruptly, flummoxed. Thank God *his* heart was strong. "You can't be serious. Are you telling me that Alex is marrying Isabella Carnegie *for the money*? I see the accounting ledgers, Father. We're doing fine. Alex's error was not that significant."

Chase had never seen his father looking sheepish before. It was like seeing a draft horse on roller skates. It was just... *wrong*.

"There's a reason I sent you away for a few months, son," A.J. said. "To be honest, I didn't want you to see the amount of damage your brother caused, and he was determined to rectify the situation before you came home from Trillium Bay, but thanks to me forgetting I'm not twenty-five years old anymore, you're back early."

"I don't believe this. Why wouldn't you have just told me the truth in the first place? I could've helped."

"Alex asked me to keep it private. He'd never admit as much to you, Chase, but he's intimidated by you."

"Alex? Is intimidated by me?"

"Yes. You have a natural aptitude for numbers and finance

that eludes him, and quite frankly, he was embarrassed by his mistake."

The shock of A.J.'s heart attack paled in comparison to this admission. Chase had long known he was better than Alex at certain things, but it never once occurred to him that anyone else noticed, or that Alex particularly cared. His brother compensated for his lack of mathematical acumen in other ways, with his affability, his unique perspective, and his talent for taking any negative situation and crafting it into something positive – such as marrying a rich, beautiful woman just to save the family business...

"I don't know what to say to this, Father. You both should have trusted me, and Alex should have known I'd never think less of him because of an honest mistake."

"*Tens of thousands of dollars,*" A.J. said again.

Chase shook his head in bewilderment, finally saying, "Be that as it may, could we please get back to discussing the mule I'd like to marry?"

forty-two

"Here's your mail, sir," Mr. Hayden said, carrying in a package wrapped in brown paper along with several envelopes.

Chase's secretary was efficient, unflappable, and economical with his words, all traits he admired. In the two weeks since Chase had returned to Chicago, Hayden had been instrumental in getting him back up to speed, although he had to admit, staying focused was proving to be a challenge. It seemed part of his mind was still on holiday. Or at the very least, still with Jo. She'd yet to send him any kind of communication and it distracted him as much as it worried him.

"Thank you, Hayden. Set it over there, please."

Chase pointed to a cluttered table near the large window of his father's study and returned to the mountain of papers he and Alex were attempting to sift through. The brothers had agreed to divide and conquer the business tasks which continued to pile up during their father's convalescence. Typically, they handled projects independently. In fact, the last thing they'd worked on together was a fort made of blankets and quilts and sofa cushions – which they'd kept Daisy from entering because she was *a girl*, and theirs was a fort *for boys*.

"There's also something from the Eastman-Kodak company," Mr. Hayden added.

Chase paused and stood up from his spot behind the desk. "There is?" His heart skipped a beat because it must be his photographs and although looking at images of Jo would be far less satisfying than seeing her in person, at least he'd have her image. It might ease his mind, especially since he hadn't heard from her.

Alex cast an inquisitive glance from his seat on the opposite side of their father's massive oak desk. "What's the Eastman-Kodak company?"

"They make cameras," Chase responded. "Morty VonMeisterburger gave one to me and those must be the printed photographs."

"Cross-eyed Morty VonMeisterburger?"

"Do you know another Morty VonMeisterburger?" Chase asked dryly, and Alex chuckled.

"I do not," Alex said, then added. "Let's see them."

"The photographs?"

"Yes."

This was an unforeseen twist. Chase hadn't said anything to his brother about Jo, in part because telling his father the details had prompted the man to call her a *mule*. He also hadn't mentioned Jo to Alex because *that* conversation was likely to lead to a conversation about Isabella Carnegie and exactly why Alex was marrying her.

Chase had no feelings for Isabella now, of course. That was silly and long past and had been a minor fiction in Chase's mind to begin with, but to marry the woman just for her money seemed calculating and cold. It's what their father had done to their mother, and Constance had suffered for it. And it's what Oliver Talbot had done to Jo although in a much more malicious manner.

In truth, it was likely Isabella knew the score, but perhaps she didn't? And loving Jo the way he did had made Chase – well, apparently it had made him a little judgmental about people who married for business instead of affection. He understood that was the way of his world, but... it shouldn't be.

"I'll take the one from Eastman-Kodak, Hayden," he said, accepting the thick envelope and wondering if he should excuse himself to view the pictures in private, but he realized suddenly, he wanted to share them with Alex. He wanted to show off his beautiful sweetheart – even if she wasn't responding to his letters.

"Have I mentioned meeting a woman while at the hotel?" Chase asked casually as he worked to open the envelope and Mr. Hayden made his exit.

Alex smirked. "No, you haven't, but for what it's worth, Daisy filled me in on all the *jammiest bits.*"

Chase paused. "That girl should work for the newspapers," he said, then couldn't resist smiling as he pulled the stack of photos from the envelope. The very first image of Jo struck him like Cupid's arrow in the heart and made him sit back down with a sigh so lovelorn Alex doubled over with laughter.

"Well, perhaps Daisy didn't fill me in on *all* the jammiest bits," his brother said.

The photos were imperfect, with rays of sunshine washing out some areas, or his unsteady hand creating a blurry image, but it didn't matter, because there she was. Jo on the blanket during their hotel room picnic. Jo by the window and sitting primly on the bed. There were images from the gazebo, and best of all, the ones taken by Daisy of him and Jo in her art studio. Every photo took him back to the moment it captured, and he let the achy, delicious, heartwarming, heartbreaking memories wash over him. Damn, how he missed her.

Alex was quiet as Chase took his time looking through the stack, and when Chase finally handed them over, he asked, "Are you sure?"

"I'm sure."

Alex accepted them carefully. "She's pretty," he said after a moment. "Very pretty."

"Yes. She is," Chase responded with gravity because she wasn't just pretty. She was... Jo.

"Daisy said you asked her to marry you." Alex looked over at him and Chase appreciated that, for once, his brother seemed to have no sense of teasing about him.

"Yes. And did Daisy tell you she's already married?"

"She did." Alex lifted a curious brow. "So how is that supposed to work?"

"I'm not sure yet. I'm waiting to hear back from the Pinkerton Detective I hired to investigate her husband. I've been expecting a report for days now."

Alex let out a low whistle. "That's... extreme."

"Not compared to what he's done," Chase replied.

Alex stared at him for a moment, then stood. "Let me get us some drinks."

Nodding, Chase stood too, walking over to the stack of mail to see what else was there, discovering that among the standard fare was a letter from Ruth O'Keefe – which seemed odd, and potentially worrisome. His heart gave a skip and a tumble at seeing it.

"I wonder, Alex," he said as his brother handed him a glass, "if you might give me a moment. There's a letter here I need to read."

"Something worrisome?"

"I'm not sure yet."

Alex nodded. "All right. I'll be with Father if you need anything. I hope it's something minor."

"Thanks. As do I."

Chase sat down with the drink and the letter from Ruth, wondering if his life was about to take an abrupt turn. He didn't feel good about it.

Her note was short.

Dear Chase,
I hope you are well and that your father is on the mend.
Please accept this letter on behalf of Jo. She has some concerns about

*the reliability of her mail getting through to you and so she asked
me to post it for her.*
Yours sincerely,
Ruth

Reliability about the mail? Had she not gotten his letters? Had she sent some to him that he'd never received? That was something he'd look into, but first, he held Jo's folded letter in his hands and sent a wish to the Universe that all her news would be good.

It was not.

My darling Chase.
*The moments we spent together have been the best of my life. I will
cherish every memory we made until my final breath, and beyond.
You will be in my heart forevermore.*
*But I cannot marry you. I think you know that. There are too many
reasons – reasons that even the strength of my love for you cannot
overcome, and too many obstacles that even your efforts and the
strength of your love for me cannot defeat.*
*Let us say goodbye now while everything we had is still beautiful in
our minds and not turn it bitter by trying to force this rare, fragile
thing to exist in a place where it cannot survive.*
*Your willingness to come to Paris means more to me than you will
ever know, but eventually Chicago would beckon, and we'd be right
back where we started. Staying together now would only serve to
postpone the inevitable and make it even more difficult to finally say
goodbye.*
And say goodbye we must.
*Please believe I love you with all my heart. I will pray every day
that you are happy and content, because if you are, then so shall
I be.*
I love you, and will miss you, always.
Goodbye, my dearest.
Jo

No.

He couldn't accept this. His breath halted in his lungs. She couldn't say she loved him and then say goodbye. Didn't she realize there was nothing they couldn't overcome as long as they were together? No obstacle was so great it couldn't be crushed, no person or perception so powerful it couldn't be swayed or vanquished? She was giving up on everything they had, choosing a half-life of being married with no husband, and dooming Chase to a half-life of his own, knowing he was nothing but an empty shell while his heart and soul existed somewhere on the other side of the ocean.

No.

He wasn't giving up.

"Hayden!" he shouted at the closed study door. It opened almost immediately because his secretary was *that* good.

"Find me Edgar Newhouse! I want to know everything he's learned about Oliver Talbot, and I want to know it now."

forty-three

Of all the rooms where Jo and Chase had kissed, she liked the reading room the best. Well, she liked *her bedroom*, and *his bedroom* – *and then* she liked the reading room best.

Maybe it was the comforting smell of books since they'd been her only friends during other lonely times of her life, and seemed to be her friends again, now that Chase was gone. Or maybe she liked this room because it reminded her of the conversation they'd had that first night when he'd pretended to be lost. Or maybe she liked this room because books he'd touched during his stay on the island were here on the shelves. But the most obvious reason she liked this room was because of all the kisses they'd shared in its darkened corners.

Jo was right to have thought staying at the hotel after he was gone would only serve to remind her of Chase, but she was wrong to have worried it would bother her. It didn't. It had been almost a month since he'd left, and the visual mementos were a comfort because she missed him every minute of every hour of every day. She would no matter where she was. At least here, she could sense the essence of him, as if his ghost roamed the halls and watched over her.

He'd sent her letters, of course. Letters full of promise and optimism and hope. She wanted nothing more than to believe he was right, and to respond in kind, but one of them had to be sensible. One of them had to be pragmatic and realistic. One of them had to acknowledge that saying goodbye was as necessary as it was inevitable. She'd done the right thing by ending it now before their emotions grew deeper and more tangled. Even Ruth had reluctantly agreed the odds were stacked against them, although admitted she held out hope that one day, they might find each other again.

But Jo knew they wouldn't.

How could they? The whole world would have to change in order for them to be together.

The clock in the hallway stuck 3:00 p.m. and although she'd been in the reading room for a while, Jo decided to read just one more chapter. She was settled in her favorite chair, her legs drawn up, her skirts gathered around her knees. It wasn't ladylike but who was there to see? No one ever came in here, but as she flipped another page the door opened. She let out a frustrated sigh at the sound of footsteps approaching.

How annoying. Didn't they realize she was reading?

Perhaps if she ignored them, they'd go away and leave her be, so she kept her eyes firmly on the page.

"Read any good books lately?"

She blinked. *Once. Twice. Three times.* It couldn't be. It wasn't possible. But she turned toward the sound – and there was Chase. Her heartbeat tripled its rhythm, her lungs failed to fill, and the only thing that came from her mouth was an accusatory, "What are you doing here?"

He smiled and leaned casually against a bookcase, and she noted the unfortunate reality that he was still every bit as handsome as she remembered. *(Unfortunate for her, at least.)*

"I'm here because you're here," he said as if that explained everything, but it explained nothing.

At her obvious confusion, he added, "I received the letter where you threw me over, but I don't accept."

"You... don't accept?"

"No," he said amicably. "You said you'd marry me, and it's rude to go back on your word."

She must be hallucinating. That was it. *She'd broken with reality from reading too much fiction.* She was only *imagining* him there, looking so irresistibly desirable, because she missed him so much. She clutched the book in her hand and blinked again, waiting for him to evaporate. He didn't.

Lord Almighty. He was real. And he was there.

Which was wonderful – and awful – because nothing had changed for them. All the obstacles were still obstacles and now she'd have to say goodbye all over again. And *in person!*

She shook her head slowly. "I never agreed to marry you, Chase."

His face was all light-hearted skepticism as he tapped a finger against his temple. "I remember it distinctly. We were naked in my bed and—"

She held up a hand to stop him right there. "That *yes* doesn't count. I was... caught up in a moment."

"A technicality," he said, walking to the chair across from her, scooping up her feet just as he'd done a dozen times before, and sitting down. His eyes roved over her body and came back to her face.

"God, I've missed you, Jo, and we have a lot to talk about."

Did they?

"I was clear in my letter, Chase. I don't know what you could possibly say that would change the outcome."

She was proud of herself for holding fast and sounding so strong because on the inside of her head she was begging him to kiss her. She wondered if her heart could beat any faster, or if she could survive another moment without air to breathe.

"You were clear," he said with a tilt of his head. "But you didn't have all the information. Would you mind if I told you what I've recently learned? Then you can decide if you want me to stay or if you want me to leave. Either way, there are things you need to know."

Well, he had her full attention now.

"Go on," she said hesitantly.

He regarded her for a moment, and after a deep breath said, "To begin with, you are not Oliver Talbot's first wife."

She wasn't? "I'm not?"

"No, in fact, you're not his second wife, either. You're his third."

"His third?" she exclaimed. "How is that possible? What happened to the first two?" Her hand flew over her mouth as she gasped. "Oh, my goodness! He didn't... hurt them, did he?" She didn't think Oliver was the murdering kind, but she hadn't thought he was the swindling kind, either.

To her great relief, Chase quickly shook his head. "No, for all his many disreputable qualities, he didn't murder his wives, if that's what you meant. However... he also didn't divorce them."

"He didn't? I don't understand."

"Jo, Oliver Talbot was a bigamist. He charmed women, married them, and absconded with their belongings, just as he did to you."

She knew the words Chase was saying, and recognized that they were in the proper order, and yet she could not comprehend his meaning.

"I don't... I don't understand," she said again. She was numb and confused, and grateful for Chase's presence, although perhaps she was hallucinating after all?

"I was shocked myself when I found out, my love, so I can't even imagine how this feels to you," Chase continued. "He was so much more calculating and wicked than we'd realized and I'm so very sorry you got tangled up with him."

"He's a bigamist?" she finally said.

"He was," Chase said solemnly.

Those words penetrated even more slowly. Jo felt as if her

mind was made of rusted wheels and gears and sprockets and none of them were in alignment. They were grinding. Painfully.

"Was?" she whispered.

Chase leaned forward, his brow furrowed, his voice low. "It seems wife number four had a protective brother who took matters into his own hands. Oliver Talbot is dead."

"I'm... Chase this is overwhelming." All the air she'd been struggling to pull into her lungs seemed to force its way in all at once and now she truly could not breathe. She gasped for air, and Chase took hold of her hands.

"You're all right, Jo. You're all right." He pulled her up from the chair and walked her around the room until at last she was steady again. Or at least until she could breathe. She was still shaking and clammy and confused. She leaned into Chase, pressing her ear to his heart, letting its calm, soothing rhythm bring her own erratic pulse back to normal.

"How did he die?" she asked. Perhaps the question was gruesome, but she wanted to know.

Chase hesitated and then said simply, "Violently."

Should she be glad? Sorry? Relieved? Mournful? He *had* been her husband, after all. *Sort of.*

She leaned back and looked up at Chase. "If he didn't divorce those other wives, was my marriage even legal?"

"No. Technically you've never been married, but even if you had been, now you'd be a widow."

She pressed a hand to her forehead. This was all just a little too much. "I think I should sit back down now."

She was grateful to return to the chair.

"Do you want me to get you some water?" Chase asked, solicitous and gentle.

"No, I'll be all right. It's just a lot to learn all at once."

"I know. I'm sorry. I couldn't think of an easy way to tell you. If it brings you any comfort, I do have a few boxes of your belongings at my house."

"You do?" she asked, surprised there were still more surprises.

She wasn't sure she could take many more but at least this one was pleasant. Although... actually... while the other surprises were not pleasant in nature, they were beneficial to her, and she began to feel lighter. She was free of Oliver Talbot. *At last.*

Chase continued speaking. "My detective trailed Talbot to an old barn and found all sorts of treasures, yours, and other people's. There were even a few paintings."

Her heart swelled. "Really?"

"Yes," he said, smiling. "I think they'll go nicely with the ones I've already purchased for my collection."

Her smile turned tremulous because she felt bad about that. "I'm sorry you had to waste money on paintings of mine, Chase."

He laughed softly and squeezed her hands. "My love, it was a pittance."

"It was incredibly generous," she said, and he laughed again.

"It wasn't that much. I'm not entirely certain you realize how wealthy I am."

She suddenly found herself chuckling in response, buoyancy replacing sadness. She leaned back in the chair, pulling her hands from his and looking him over.

"Chase Bostwick, are you saying you're rich just so I'll marry you?"

He crooked an eyebrow. "Would that work?"

"No." *(Yes, it would.)*

He leaned back in his chair and looked *her* over. "What if I told you I loved you beyond reason and that every day we were apart I was utterly and completely miserable? Would that make a difference?"

"Hm. Maybe," she said. *(Yes. It would. It most certainly would.)*

His brow furrowed as if he was concentrating quite hard. "What if I told you I've convinced my father to open an office in Paris and to put me in charge of it?"

Breathing became difficult once more. So many surprises. Too many, and too much to comprehend. Too much to hope for. Too much to believe in.

"You'd still go to Paris?" she whispered.

He leaned forward again, the teasing gone from his face. He was earnest, intense, but a smile hinted at his lips. "Jo, I'll take you anywhere you want to go, and we can stay as long as you like. This life is ours to make, in whatever way suits us. We don't need to meet anyone else's expectations. Just our own. I love you. This is real, and I'm real so marry me and let me prove it."

It was all too wonderful to believe. And yet she did believe. It wasn't going to be easy. Jo knew that. His family (*his mother!*) and society would try to tear them up and tear them apart, but she'd rather live a full life with him, for all the obstacles and challenges, than any other kind of life without him. She loved him. And he loved her. *And Daisy would be so happy.*

She leaned forward and ran her hands along the lapels of his jacket. "You'll take me anywhere I want to go?"

"Anywhere." His voice was deep, his blue eyes full of longing.

At last, she smiled, and said, "Would you take me upstairs?"

"I'm a mule? How is that a compliment?" Jo asked Chase as they lounged with Ruth and Percy O'Keefe on the front porch of the Imperial Hotel overlooking the vast front lawn. The sun was setting, and the mid-September breeze was cool, but Jo felt warm all over, basking in the glow of being thoroughly, miraculously, and blissfully in love.

To the world, she was a lovely widow thanks to a carefully worded article placed in Chicago's Daily Tribune detailing the oh-so-unfortunate, and oh-so-accidental demise of her devoted, art dealing husband. The few remaining guests at the hotel seemed to embrace this story, remarking only that she was fortunate to have the full support of the Bostwick family to ease her grief during this challenging time. Even Breezy VonMeisterburger supported this theory and Jo suspected she had Mortimer to thank for that.

"You led me to my beloved fiancée," Morty had whispered to Jo one afternoon soon after Chase's return to Trillium Bay. "Priscilla and I are forever in your debt and honored to claim you as our friend."

His words had brought a tear to Jo's eye, and a smile to her face, and then he'd launched into a fact heavy dissertation on the merits of conservationism which lasted far longer than her interest had. Still, she was forever in *his* debt, too.

"The mule is my father's analogy," Chase continued from the porch, "so don't judge me for it, but he says society women are like racehorses. Carefully bred, well groomed. If they manage to win a race or two that adds to their value but either way, they're considered to be prized possessions. Something to covet."

He looked over at Jo and she frowned back, wondering how he might turn this around in his favor. Even the O'Keefes appeared doubtful that Chase was heading in a safe direction. Jo could already hear Percy chuckling softly.

"Go on," she said wryly.

Chase cleared his throat. "Well, I explained to my father that racehorses were skittish, and fragile, and expensive to maintain. After just a few short races, they're turned out to pasture, all but ignored and admired for nothing more than their breeding capabilities. But a *mule*?"

Chase lifted Jo's hand and kissed her knuckles, a mischievous twinkle in his eyes.

"A mule never gives up," he continued. "A mule can handle any type of adversity and keep moving forward. The weather, terrain, distance. It doesn't matter. Mules are strong and determined. If you're in it for the long haul and want a creature who won't ever let you down, a mule is the way to go."

He was teasing her, of course, because only Chase Bostwick would try to woo a woman by comparing her to a mule. Percy's laughter grew louder, and Ruth rolled her eyes.

"Mules are also stubborn and obstinate," Jo replied.

"I'd say they're determined and confident," he said decisively.

"They have big teeth and make awful, ridiculous noises," she added.

Chase gave a short sigh but was not giving up. "The analogy is not without its flaws, my love, but the point is, I know you worry you may not have the perfect pedigree, and you may not win every race you encounter while moving through the steeple chase that is society, but I will place my bet on you every single time. You're tenacious and smart and resourceful and I'm so proud of you."

He kissed her palm. Once, twice, three times, then smiled at her, a charming, comfortable smile and she couldn't help but smile back because he was always so sincere. And because he had irresistible dimples and tiny creases at the corners of his beautiful blue eyes – and she loved him.

"And let me state for the record," he added emphatically, "you are also stunningly beautiful with perfectly proportioned teeth and musical laughter that sounds nothing like the bray of a mule."

Ruth's laughter joined Percy's as Jo blinked at Chase a dozen times. "That is a truly terrible analogy. Nothing about that is endearing."

"I know." He chuckled now. "Take it up with your future father-in-law."

Jo bit back a smile and turned her gaze back out over the lawn. "You still seem to be under the misguided impression that I've agreed to marry you, and I haven't. I've never agreed to any such thing."

She could tease, too, and he was going to have to make amends for calling her a mule even if he did mean it as a term of affection.

"Haven't you agreed?" he murmured. "I could have sworn you'd said yes. But very well..."

He moved from his chair to perch on one knee before her. "Let's make this official, in front of witnesses this time. Emerson Joan McKenna, will you marry me?"

Ruth gave a tiny, happy gasp and Percy ceased his snickering as the golden rays of the setting sun cast a glow all around Chase. The light was so radiant, Jo might have thought he was an angel – if she didn't know for certain he was anything *but* an angel. He was real. Very real. And he was all hers.

She smiled back at him and wondered how her life had become so unbelievably *good*. She didn't deserve it, but she would never, ever take it for granted.

She leaned forward, certain in her answer, and whispered, "Yes." Then she kissed him and said it again. "Yes, yes, yes."

epilogue

"So, my love, is Paris everything you'd hoped it would be?" Chase asked his adorable wife as they strolled along the *Boulevard de la Madeline* on their way to dinner at *La Tour D'Argent*.

Jo was dressed in the latest Parisian fashion – or so he'd been told because he really didn't pay that much attention to what women wore. All he knew was that his beautiful bride of just over two months wore a silky mink stole around her shoulders to ward off the December chill and that sparkly snowflakes adorned her dark lashes as she gazed back up at him, somehow making her even *more* precious. *Although how that was possible, he could not imagine. Somehow he seemed to love her more each and every day.*

"No, Paris is even better than I'd imagined it would be," she answered on a blissful sigh. "And when I've finished my work at the Imperial Hotel and we come back here in the spring, all the flowers will be blooming. It'll be so beautiful."

"And my office will be set up and open for business," he added. "I've already got some pokers in the fire. I think moving here will prove very lucrative, but more importantly, our new house will have a studio where you can paint. When you're not with Madam Bracquemond that is."

"She's an amazing artist. I'm so very fortunate she's agreed to mentor me. Please tell your father once again how much I appreciate the introduction."

"He was glad to do. He's rather fond of you, it seems."

"I'm fond of him, too. Now if only I can get your mother to like me."

Chase chuckled. "Marrying you has taught me to believe in miracles, my love, but I fear my mother is a lost cause. Save your energy for other pursuits."

"Perhaps I can work my way into her heart through Flossie and Regina."

"Best of luck to you."

"Or... perhaps I can win her affection through a grandchild. Say, six or seven months from now?"

Chase stopped walking, and Jo laughed, turning to him, her face radiant with happiness.

"You aren't," he whispered, hardly daring to believe.

"I am," she said simply. "Are you glad?"

A feeling of joy and contentment filled his veins. He was thrilled to the core, surprised again that he could possibly love her *even more*.

"I am over the moon," he answered, reaching up to touch her delicate face that – for once – seemed free of paint.

"Me, too," she answered, a tear adding to the sparkle of her eyes. "And have I mentioned yet today how much I love you?"

His heart was so full it ached. "You may have told me but please tell me again," he whispered, drawing her close. "And when we get back to the hotel after the symphony, perhaps you could show me."

"That would be my pleasure," she answered, leaning in for a kiss.

"Mm," he said, his lips nearly touching hers. "I'll make sure of it."

THE END

other titles by tracy brogan

THE BOSTWICKS OF TRILLIUM BAY

ART OF THE CHASE

COMING SOON

MAGIC OF MOONLIGHT

A DAISY IN BLOOM

THE TRILLIUM BAY SERIES

(CONTEMPORARY)

MY KIND OF YOU

MY KIND OF FOREVER

MY KIND OF PERFECT

THE BELL HARBOR SERIES

(CONTEMPORARY)

CRAZY LITTLE THING

THE BEST MEDICINE

LOVE ME SWEET

JINGLE BELL HARBOR (A novella)

STAND ALONE TITLES

HOLD ON MY HEART (Contemporary)

THE NEW NORMAL (Contemporary)

WEATHER OR KNOT (Contemporary novella)

HIGHLAND SURRENDER (Historical romance)

afterword

A question readers frequently ask is, "Why do you use fictional location and landmark names when this is obviously based on Michigan's Mackinac Island?"

My purpose in doing so was to ensure I had creative liberty to change things about the island that didn't fit into the parameters of the story. The actual Grand Hotel opened its doors for the first time in the summer of 1887 (not 1888) and although it was considered "luxurious" at the time, it was not quite the opulent resort as described.

That being said, virtually all the architectural details I've included were based on research and are accurate to the best of my ability. The hotel was built in 93 days by a team of 600 men working round the clock, and rooms were just $5.00 a night (as opposed to the $300-$1000/night room rate today!) All the entertainments, the field day events, the dining room menu, and many other aspects of the story are based on fact – even the Doggie Paddle and Cigar Races.

Several of the characters are based on real people and when appropriate, I used their real names although I cannot guarantee they stayed at the hotel that first summer. In addition to that, I chose to leave out the personal attendants that the guests would have brought. Many of the wealthy patrons who spent their summers at the hotel brought along a variety of maids, valets, grooms, and even their own horses but to include them would've made this story very crowded!

My aim was to paint a picture (no pun intended) of the charm and ambiance of the island in those early days of tourism. I do hope you enjoy your visit and that you'll come back again for MAGIC OF MOONLIGHT to find out what happens to Alex Bostwick when he comes to Trillium Bay!

Until then, happy reading and big smooches!
Tracy

about the author

USA Today, Wall Street Journal, and Amazon Publishing bestselling author Tracy Brogan writes happily ever after stories full laughter and love. A three-time recipient of the Amazon Publishing Diamond award for sales exceeding three-million copies, a three-time finalist of the RWA® RITA award for excellence in romantic fiction, and a three-time finalist of the Booksellers Best award, Brogan's books feature re-imagined versions of her favorite Michigan locations – including famed Mackinac Island - and have been translated into more than a dozen languages worldwide. Her debut novel, CRAZY LITTLE THING, hit #5 on Amazon Publishing's bestselling titles across all genres.

Brogan is currently at work on several projects including a gilded age series set in Trillium Bay, the long-awaited sequel to HIGHLAND SURRENDER, and a dual-timeline rom-com that just *may* include ghosts. (Psst... it totally has ghosts.)

Brogan loves to hear from readers so contact her at tracybrogan.com or tracybrogan1225@gmail.com.

Tracy Brogan Books. Witty. Whimsical. Wonderful.